They know more than we do

No one is certain who was the first Ghoster. Or how they became aware of each other.

Ghosters are a small, loosely-connected group of individuals who travel the highways of America, curing people of their hauntings. For as much money as they can get from each client.

Ghosters have a gift the rest of us don't. But they are not kind. Perhaps because of what they do.

Here are the known Ghosters:

Stan Costello. Works with Bud Hardy. Their specialty is buying and selling bottled ghosts. For the right money, they'll bottle a fresh ghost.

Clay (last name unknown). Homely. Cold. All the food he eats tastes like mud. The apparent leader of the Ghosters. Handles the more frightening cases.

Tilda Clem. Six foot seven. Never fit in anywhere. Somewhat sympathetic to the people she takes on. But not much.

Patrick Kelly. Tall Irishman with an onion-shaped head. Will never say a bad word about anyone. But a lot of blood on his big hands.

Matt (last name unknown). Young African-American traveling with Patrick as an apprentice, to see if he'll fit in with the group. He has the talent. But does he have the stomach?

The ten stories comprising this novel are ten known cases in which Ghosters were involved.

D0291284

Critical Praise for Ralph Robert Moore

Father Figure

"It is easy to see why Father Figure has become an underground classic over the years. It is a dark, extremely disturbing but completely gripping suspense thriller with a strongly erotic subtext...Moore is an extremely talented writer with a gift for pushing the reader's emotional buttons...certainly liable to become a cult classic, and deservedly so."
— Editorial Review

Remove the Eyes

"Tired of the usual suspects? Bored with the same old genre clichés? Then follow my advice and read Ralph Robert Moore, a hell of a writer whose work is provocative and refreshing, never ordinary, always imaginative and graced by a compelling narrative style… Try him, you won't regret it." — Mario Guslandi

"…[Moore's] work is not quite like that of anybody else. He is a true original…and if you are looking for something different, then I can't recommend this collection highly enough." — Peter Tennant

"Unusual, erotic, frightening and stunningly good…This collection showcases the wide and versatile range of [Moore's] work." — Trevor Denyer

I Smell Blood

"With eight stories and the short novel "Kid", the new collection…[is] one of the best collections I've read this year, delivering exactly the kind of uncompromising thrills and spills I've come to expect from this writer." — Peter Tennant

"Ralph Robert Moore's second collection confirms the excellent qualities displayed in his previous book Remove the Eyes, namely a powerful imagination, an extraordinary degree of originality and a great storytelling ability… A highly recommended book." — Mario Guslandi

"One thing that is very evident from the moment you start reading [I Smell Blood]: these stories are far from predictable…Moore's work is consistently fascinating, original and devastating. His characters speak to you from whatever hell they inhabit, with clear, unambiguous voices…[I Smell Blood] is a worthy successor to Remove the Eyes." — Trevor Denyer

"Disturbing. Nightmarish. Terrifying. And above all original… reinforces his reputation, amongst those in the know, that here we have a genre-storytelling giant in our midst." — AJ Kirby

As Dead As Me

"Relentless, unsentimental, and with a plot that moves like a freight train. You want bleak? Read this…an excellent novel from an excellent writer." — Gary McMahon

"This book has depth. It is not only a visceral tour de force, but has the advantage of Moore's extraordinary imagination being brought to bear, introducing characters and situations that you care passionately about. Without giving too much away, the climax to the story astounds the reader by its spectacular, heartrending audacity. A brilliant achievement." —Trevor Denyer

"By making his characters so fully rounded, Moore gives us a reason to care about them, and this in turn makes the book's resolution all the more poignant and painful… These are just ordinary human beings, acting with common decency in the face of the unacceptable…He takes the familiar and makes it heartrendingly sad." — Peter Tennant

Also by Ralph Robert Moore

Father Figure (novel)
Remove the Eyes (short story collection)
I Smell Blood (short story collection)
As Dead As Me (novel)

Ghosters

A Novel in Ten Stories by

Ralph Robert Moore

SENTENCE Publishing
www.ralphrobertmoore.com

Cover design by Ralph Robert Moore. Cover image by Fahrner78/Dreamstime.com

The following stories first appeared, in slightly different form, in these publications: "Tiny Doorways" in *Cover of Darkness*; "A Woman Made of Milk" in a separate Kindle edition; "We Don't Keep in Touch Anymore" in *Shadows & Tall Trees*.

To Mary

FIRST EDITION

ISBN-13: 978-1502897572
ISBN-10: 1502897571

Patrick said nothing for a long time. When he spoke, his voice was quiet. "Life is a comedy. Not a drama. That's what God intended. Everything that happened to you in life, that you see as so tragic—You just have to see the humor in each situation. Which you clearly can't."

Naughton's face twisted. "So when an innocent child dies from leukemia at age twelve, that's supposed to be funny?"

"Exactly."

x

TABLE OF CONTENTS

xi

HALF-HAUNTED HOUSE

"Ever think how we buy most of our ghosts from farms and ranches way out in the country somewhere? Not from city folk?"

Stan, both hands on the steering wheel, kept his eyes on the wet lanes of Central Expressway, cars whizzing by on either side of their white van. Squinted up through the rain at the green overhead signs. "No, Bud, really haven't. Country folk are bigger collectors of everything, though. Got the room. All those attics and barns. You sure we didn't pass Lover's Lane yet?"

Bud looked down at his lap. "Not according to this map. Did you know that when they first dug far down into the earth to lay the foundation for what would become Central Expressway the engineers hired by Dallas found nest after nest of live gaseous worms?"

"What kind of worms?"

"Gaseous. Even though they're worms, they're longer than most snakes."

"Really. What a lovely thought."

"They're like, twenty feet long. They go back to prehistoric times."

"Good for them."

"Although they're not the longest worm. The tapeworm that settles itself into the intestines of humans after someone eats raw or undercooked fish? Thirty feet long."

Stan kept checking the rearview and side view windows to see where speeding cars were located around their white van. "That's good news. Hey Bud, love the random facts, as always, but how about a fact about where the fuck the Lover's Lane exit is?"

Bud popped another orange, barbequed potato chip in his mouth. "Should just be a couple more miles. According to Toots' directions."

Finally, one of the green overhead signs showed the Lover's Lane exit coming up.

Stan turned on the blinker, moving the van across wet lanes into the rightmost lane.

They parked their white van against the curb on a tree-lined street, in front of a large, red-bricked house set back from its emerald St. Augustine lawn.

3

Got out of the van on either side, stretching their legs.

Stan, tall and skinny, well-worn face, ran a hand over his hair to see how wet it was getting. "Call Toots. Let her know we're here, about to go in for the interview."

Bud, shorter, heavier, bent over into the opened passenger door of the van, so the phone didn't get wet.

Stan circled around to the back of the van. Found the right key on his key chain. Unlocked the rear white double doors of the van. Looked inside, to make sure all the jars filled with ghosts were intact.

Bud waddled around to the rear of the van. "She found a job for us after this in Arizona. Just outside Flagstaff. Roaring twenties and World War Two ghosts. His daddy was a collector. He's anxious to sell. Mounting medical bills."

Stan relocked the double doors. "Too bad his father's gone. Love talking to those old-time collectors."

They trotted from under the dripping trees across the lawn to the front door. Stan banged the doorbell. Could hear it sound on the other side of the tall walnut.

Stan put his hand on Bud's beefy shoulder. "I'll handle the pricing. Agreed?"

The front door swung inwards.

Always interesting to first meet the people with whom you'll be sharing something so personal.

Three of them, in this case.

A woman who looked to be in her mid-forties. Not beautiful, but definitely attractive. Root beer colored hair. Wearing short-shorts. Looked like she had a lot of fire in her. Those eyes.

A slight man standing next to her, graying black hair. Husband? He was shorter than her.

A younger man, in his twenties, shoulder-length dark hair, glasses. Probably the son she mentioned? Forehead, eyes, nose, chin similar to the woman. Didn't look anything like the short man.

The woman stepped back, big grin on her face. Spread her hands apart, which Stan took as an invitation not only to enter her home, but to admire how good she looked.

They passed over the threshold.

Stan and Bud took turns reaching their arms down, shaking hands with the son.

Stan shook the older man's hand. "Mr. Doone?"

The woman shook her head, root beer hair swinging from her shoulders. Amused grin on her face. Her fingers pointed, curled, swooped across her breasts, face.

The man spoke for her. "He is Colin, my interpreter. I am deaf."

A bit disorienting to hear Colin talk about himself in the third person, channeling the woman's words, but Stan adjusted. He'd had to adjust to much more, meeting ghosting clients for the first time. "And this younger man is your son? And your name is Sylvia?"

Sylvia, the mother, nodded enthusiastically. More hand gestures.

Colin looked at Stan and Bud. "The love of my life."

Sylvia went back to signing. Stan looked to Colin.

"You look like a country western singer. Your face."

Stan bobbed his head. "Well, thank you."

Awkward silence.

"I hope I did not offend you by saying that."

Stan raised both palms. "No offense taken."

They all made their way through the living room and library to the back of the home, into the large breakfast nook.

Everyone except Brandon sat in black chairs around the shiny black breakfast nook table. Sylvia, smiling, lifted her hands, gesturing. Stan and Bud both looked at Colin.

"While we discuss the objectives of what Brandon and I want to accomplish, with your help, I thought we'd enjoy a cold seafood salad." Colin raised his jaw, looking behind them, into the kitchen. "Bettina? Would you serve the salads now? Colin is a vegan, so he will have a cold vegetable plate instead."

Bud unfolded the white linen napkin by his place setting. "Is that a deluxe wheelchair?"

Colin, after looking at Sylvia, answered. "Absolutely. Only the best for my darling boy."

"What makes it deluxe?"

Brandon, who seemed shy, cleared his throat. His eyeglasses looked around the table. "Some of the motorized maneuvers it can make, but primarily how the seat is customized. Because someone who's paraplegic like me has to sit in a wheelchair all day, it's really important the seat be as comfortable as possible. A normal person, if they're tired of sitting in a regular chair, can stand up at any point they want to, to stretch their legs. I can't do that anymore. So the chair part of my wheelchair has to be fitted to be exactly the right seat depth, for example, so I don't feel any discomfort in my back."

Sylvia raised her hand to get back into the conversation, fingers drawing words in mid-air as Bettina brought over the seafood salads, setting them down in front of each person seated around the breakfast nook table.

Colin addressed Stan and Bud. "Nothing but the best for my baby's butt! He must be absolutely comfortable!"

The salads looked delicious. On each blue-rimmed bone china plate a large mound of chilled seafood lightly bound with mayonnaise, flecked with fresh green parsley and yellow zest grated from lemons, the mound itself plump with the orange of shrimp, the red and white of lobster, the old world beige of clams.

Bud bit into the forkful of salad he had placed in his mouth, eyes rolling. "This is…"

Colin looked at Sylvia, looked at Bud. "Thank you!"

Stan patted his lips with the white linen napkin. "So Sylvia, tell us a little bit about yourself."

Colin, watching Sylvia while he finished a chilled spear of white asparagus, sat up in his chair. "From the time of my birth, I have been deaf. I'm proud to be deaf! I stole my ex-husband, who has passed-on, from a woman who could hear. I have had to fight my entire life because of my deafness. Even the simplest social encounters are impossibly difficult for me. But I will never stop fighting. Not ever!"

Bud had worked his way through half his mound of seafood salad at this point. Probably starting to regret he ever ate that bag of barbequed potato chips on the way to this luncheon. "When did you realize you were different from other children?"

Colin shook his head. "I was not different from other children! Children played, and I played. Children love their parents, and I loved my parents. Children explored the world around them, and I did too! All that was different was that I could not speak, and I could not hear the outside world. But otherwise, I was a child like any other child."

Stan swallowed an incredibly tender slice of lobster claw. "Do you have any pets?" He had no idea why he asked that. Bud shot him a look.

Sylvia lifted her attractive face, happy.

Colin answered. "I have a cat. Bullwinkle. He showed up at my back door one day and I took him in. I can't hear him purring, but by placing my hands against his ribs, I can feel him purring. Should we proceed to talking about why you are here? I would like Brandon to show you what he has done with his bedroom."

Everyone stood up from the table, Bud bending forward to stab his fork through a final cold shrimp.

They all followed behind Brandon as he rolled to a door a short hallway down from the kitchen.

Sylvia turned around suddenly, looking at Stan, who looked away.

Colin addressed Stan and Bud. "And this is Brandon's room, after he moved back in with me."

She signed some more to Colin, but Colin didn't say anything further.

Stan looked at Colin. "Was there something else Sylvia wanted to say?"

"It was a private comment meant for me."

Sylvia stepped back, dipping a hip, swinging her bare right arm forward, inviting Stan to enter first.

Slightly larger than most bedrooms. Tall, domed ceiling painted to look like a summer sky, lots of blues and clouds.

Stan's eyes darted around. It took a moment to register what was odd. "Why all the filing cabinets?

Brandon rolled past Stan's slanted pants pocket, doing a U-turn to face him. "They hold all my pictures of Olivia. My girlfriend."

Stan nodded. Mentally counted the number of tall filing cabinets lined up around three walls of the bedroom. "How many pictures of your girlfriend do you have?"

"Fifteen. I wish I had more."

"Well, of course."

Brandon talked to the filing cabinets. "So what I do is use those fifteen photographs as a means of making new photographs." Like a lot of shy people, his voice grew less hesitant now that he was speaking on a subject that obviously meant a lot to him. "In that first cabinet, that's photographs of Olivia I've cropped in lots and lots of different ways using Adobe Photoshop. So from each photograph, maybe I have thirty or forty versions of that photograph, cropped different ways to make it seem like a new photograph. Close-ups showing just her face, for example, cropping out the scenery, close-ups of just her eyes, or just her lips, etc., etc., etc. Then I also have photographs where I went back to the location where the original photograph of Olivia was taken, and I try to take the exact same picture, from the same height, the same angle, etc., etc., etc., but without Olivia in it now, of course. A lot of that is in the second filing cabinet. Then the third, fourth, fifth and sixth filing cabinets are where I take all those photographs, the originals, the crop variations, and the on location recreations of the photographs with Olivia no longer in them, and run them through different color filters. Red, green, pink, yellow, orange, blue, etc., etc., etc., and purple, a filter I've discovered brings out a lot of her skin tones. Who would have thought purple would be the ideal filter to bring out her skin tones? But I'm glad I have the photographs using the other filters as well.

"Filing cabinets seven through fifteen are me using a camcorder to film all these photographic interpretations of Olivia from different angles, panning across them at different speeds, different angles, with sound added. The cabinets I named have music on the soundtrack; cabinets sixteen through twenty-two use spoken word. I'm the one speaking."

Sylvia made some hand gestures. Colin turned to Stan. "My son really misses his girlfriend."

More signings. Colin raised his black eyebrows. "I tell him he should get out more often. Get back into the world. I don't want my son to be sitting in front of a computer screen all day."

Brandon wheeled around in his motorized chair. Obviously, this was a sore point between the two. "Well, I do get out pretty often, as I've said, Mother, by rephotographing the locations where I took the original fifteen photographs of Olivia. I'm working on a project right now where I'm going to use my camcorder to film the different locations where I took the original fifteen photographs of Olivia, then run those clips through different color filters, one set with music, the other with spoken word. I'm really excited about this new project. I plan on starting it once the next shipment of filing cabinets arrive."

Bud was walking down the line of gray filing cabinets, stooping over to read each drawer's typewritten label. Brandon rolled over, asking if Bud had any questions.

Sylvia, standing next to Stan, made some more signings, facing him, in such a physically restrained way that the hand and finger gestures felt private, whispered. Colin straightened his face on his neck. "Do you like my short-shorts?"

Stan blushed. "Guess you caught me."

Those fiery brown eyes looked right into his. More hands, fingers. "Are you married?"

She was standing close enough that he could feel the warmth of her body. "No."

A few more gestures, lazy this time. The fierce eyes still holding his. "Even if you were, that is okay with me."

Everyone trooped back out to the breakfast nook. Their plates had been cleared.

Bettina served coffee.

Stan took a sip. Strong, no sugar, but the sweetness of the half and half made it the perfect cup, like you'd get at a busy cafeteria in downtown Manhattan. He looked at Sylvia. "The Half-Haunted House."

Sylvia made a quick gesture, looking at Stan.

Colin nodded. "Hoover Manor."

Brandon, less shy now that he had done so much talking in his bedroom, picked up the thread. "Olivia was my only true love." His eyes teared-up behind his glasses. "You guys are older, but have you ever had a true love? An innocent love?"

Bud shook his head. "Confirmed bachelor."

Stan's country western singer's face lifted, with a smile. "I know what you mean, Brandon. Suddenly you understand what the point is to the world. It's her. Then when she's no longer in your life, the world has lost its magic. The leaves on the trees are just leaves again."

Brandon swung his face away, wounded. Took a moment. "Mom was opposed to her, but I didn't care. We rented an apartment together, by the Dallas zoo. At night, through the windows we'd leave open for the cool spring air..." He bent his head, remembering. "Through the mesh of the window screens, we'd hear the animals in their cages. Barks, screams, hisses. Giraffes, hippopotamuses, crocodiles, monkeys. After a while, lying side by side in bed, or lying wrapped around each other, like a Chinese fortune cookie—" he raised a defiant look to his mother—" we could tell which voice came from which throat.

"I used to play a game with her. Lying in bed together on a Saturday morning, watching TV, I'd glance over at her, see she was absorbed in what was on screen, then casually lift my hand above her hair, lower it, lightly touch her scalp. I'd watch, eyes slid left, how it'd take a moment for my touch to be felt. I'd see on her face how the touch registered. She'd distractedly raise a hand to investigate her scalp, get more focused as my touch increased, maybe a little alarmed, her hand would reach up more quickly, then I could see her remembering I'd play this trick before, the fronts of her fingers would meet my fingers as she twisted her face around on her pillow, looking up at me, giving me a, You didn't fool me look. It was a lot of fun. She thought she was in danger, but she wasn't."

Sylvia cut in, waving. Lowered, raised her fingers.

Colin cleared his throat. "They were so poor! Could barely pay the rent! I had to give Olivia my own dresses so she would have decent clothes to wear. I even had to provide her with my underwear. The panties and bras she wore, those were mine! The panties were too snug for her, her hips were too wide, and the bras were too big, she couldn't fill them like I can. This is his

9

soul mate? I always thought, maybe it wasn't his true soul mate. I tried to tell my son this, many times, but he would always argue with me! His mother!"

Brandon's face went rigid, ignoring his mother. Sitting in his wheelchair, in a controlled voice he said, "In Dallas, we have a shopping mall known as the 'Half-Haunted House'. It's the third most popular tourist attraction in Texas."

Bud nodded. "Right after the Alamo and the Sixth Floor Exhibit."

"Originally, it was the Hoover Manor. After Hoover died, owing a fortune in property taxes, it was purchased at auction by the City of Dallas. The city turned it into a tourist attraction. The bottom two floors were converted into a mall, with twenty-three commercial lessees. The top two floors were eventually considered undevelopable. Leaving the top two haunted floors of the mansion commercially unoccupied turned out to be a canny move. There are dozens of malls throughout the Dallas area, it's the "shop until you drop" capital, but only one that was half-haunted. People came to visit the haunted floors of the mansion, but then stayed to spend money in the restaurants, boutiques and sports shops on the first two floors. The Half-Haunted House in fact has the highest profit on return per square foot of retail space of any mall in the city.

"The second draw of the Half-Haunted House is that it is made entirely out of exposed wood. Logs and planks."

Stan glanced at Sylvia. Back at Brandon. "Don't be offended by this, but when I first met you, you seemed kind of…in your own world. But I just realized how intelligent and articulate you are."

Sylvia signed. Finishing, she slipped her bare right arm behind her son's shoulders, giving him a squeeze.

Colin vocalized. "Yay, Brandon!"

Looking at Brandon, Stan asked, "So what is it you want us to do?"

Sylvia began a series of finger moves, hand swoops.

Colin translated while she was still gesturing, in order to keep up. "The Half-Haunted House is believed to hold hundreds of ghosts on its top two floors. Perhaps thousands. It is thought to be a shining light for the recently departed. Many fly away after visiting the top two floors, but some remain. Brandon is hoping, because of the abruptness of her death, and her sorrow in not being able to live out her natural lifespan with my son, her ghost may be still wandering around the top two floors. I fervently wish this, for my son's sake!"

"And if she is still there?"

Colin started up again, eye on Sylvia's signings. "If she is not there, nothing can be done. Correct?"

"Basically."

"But if she is still there, I want you to bottle her ghost, so that my son will always have her, in one of your jars, in his room here in my home. "

"Brandon, how do you feel about this?"

"I don't want to keep her from passing on. I would never want to keep her on Earth if she's ready to go to Heaven. And I think maybe she's already in Heaven. But if she is still here, on this plane, then I do want to have her near to me, where I can look at her, and possibly she can look at me?"

"If you bottle her, she will be able to see you. And of course you'll be able to see her."

"That's what I want."

Stan glanced at Bud. Looked back at Brandon. "Do you understand though, ghosts don't behave exactly like they did while they were still alive? They have different concerns. Some parts of her you'll still recognize as, That's Olivia, but other parts of her, now, since her death, will seem unfamiliar to you. Even puzzling."

"I can accept that."

Stan hesitated. "I believe you that that's the way you feel. But just to be clear, because this is a "big thing" we're about to do, and we want to be fair with you, Bud and I aren't one of these "fly by nights", do you fully understand that even though she still loves you beyond the grave, and you'll re-experience that love once you die, that in interacting with her ghost while you're still alive, because her ghost is going through so many changes we can't comprehend on our plane, in addition to some signs of love from her, there may also be some signs of…." Stan shrugged. "It's usually expressed as, indifference."

"But it's not true indifference, right?"

"No. But to you, someone still on this plane, it may come across as indifference. Which can be disheartening. Obviously."

Brandon, in his wheelchair, long dark hair, eyeglasses, set his jaw. "I accept and agree."

Stan turned his attention to Sylvia. "All that's left to discuss then is our fee."

Sylvia, serious look on her face, signed to Colin.

"I am not a rich woman."

"Well, we're not rich men."

"The fee you mentioned in your email, ten thousand dollars, that seems like a lot of money. You'll only be here a few days!"

"Let me give you some background. Most of what Bud and I do is travel around the country, to different collectors, buying and selling ghosts. These ghosts have already been bottled. There's very little risk to us involved.

11

Occasionally, like in this situation, we are willing to bottle a fresh ghost ourselves, but there's a lot of spiritual danger to us associated with that. It's like buying and selling alligator shoes as opposed to paddling into a mosquito-filled swamp and capturing a live alligator. We have to be compensated for that risk. I can tick off on my fingers people who tried to bottle a fresh ghost, got in over their heads, and wound up in a place where even ten thousand dollars—one hundred thousand dollars—can't help them. If Olivia's ghost is somewhere on the top two floors of the Half-Haunted House, we'll make every effort we can, safely, to bottle it. If she's not there, we get one thousand dollars for our expenses. If she is there and it's not safe to bottle her, we get two thousand dollars. If she is there and we bottle her, we get the full ten thousand dollars. That's our offer."

Sylvia signed. Colin looked at Stan. "If she's not there, absolutely, one thousand dollars for your expenses. I can understand that! If she is there and you fail to bottle her, because of your safety concerns, that to me is still one thousand dollars. You have not done what I am paying you to do! If you do bottle her ghost, I can see, let's say, five thousand dollars. I am not a rich woman."

"Five thousand dollars doesn't cover our risk."

Sylvia's fingers. Colin's voice. "Name me a reasonable figure!"

"Eight thousand dollars."

"Still too high! I cannot afford it. Six thousand, or go home."

Stan and Bud exchanged looks. "Six thousand. We agree."

All five of them met the next morning in the parking lot of the Half-Haunted House Shopping Mall.

Colin slid the side door of Sylvia's silver van back, under the cobalt and pearl of the Texas sky, so Brandon could lower in his wheelchair to the parking lot's concrete pavement.

Stan winked at him. "Nervous?"

Brandon gave a weak smile. "All kinds of emotions."

Sylvia came around the front of her van, wearing a sleeveless blouse and a short skirt. Bare legs. Started signing right away, in charge. Colin, shorter than her, catching up, looked at Stan. "I thought we would start with having lunch. I have asked the manager of the mall to provide us with some information about the layout of the upper two floors."

As they walked towards the mall's main entrance, Sylvia thumped Stan's upper arm with her knuckles, fiery eyes, aggressive grin on her face. Colin gave Stan a dry look. "Is my skirt too short? Do you mind me showing so much leg? Do you like it?"

Entering the mall's wooden world was like walking into an enormous cabin, 52,000 square feet of logs and knotholed planks. They could hear hundreds of tiny creaks as shoppers walked the promenade, climbed up and down the wooden stairs.

Sylvia swung her head around, hair sweeping across her bare shoulders, looking for the manager.

A white-haired man scurried over to the group, blue bowtie with white polka dots. "The Doone group?"

She nodded enthusiastically.

"I'm Bert Lambert. We spoke on the phone. I reserved a table for you at Ping Pay."

Settled around the table at Ping Pay, across the courtyard from the miniblinds of an attorney's office, everyone but Stan looked at the green menu.

Sylvia signed to Stan. "You're not eating?"

"The day of a ghost capture, I only eat Saltine crackers."

Moving candle lamps and bottles of dark condiments, Bert laid a blueprint of the third and fourth floors of the Half-Haunted House on the table. "A couple of formalities we want to get out of the way. In Dallas, you're allowed to carry a concealed weapon if you have a permit. We do not allow any weapons, concealed or otherwise, on the upper two floors of the mall. No exceptions. Do any of you have a weapon?" The look he shot around the table was a lot more assertive than Stan would have expected from a guy with a polka dot bowtie.

Everyone said they didn't.

"Good. Also, management requires that every guest visiting the upper two floors sign a waiver of liability." He lifted the stack of stapled forms up in front of him on the restaurant's table, passing them around like menus. "Basically, you understand and agree that City of Dallas Recovered Properties Management, doing business as Preakness Investments, cannot be held liable for any injuries you suffer, personal or otherwise, while you are on the top two floors of Half-Haunted House, and further, that you understand and agree to indemnify Preakness Investments against any and all legal actions which may arise out of any injuries you suffer, whether those injuries are the result of your or Preakness Investments' negligence, gross negligence, or willful misconduct."

Stan signed his name in blue ink on the final page of the agreement. He and Bud should have held out for more money.

After Bert collected all the signed waivers, and secured them in a brown briefcase on the floor by his shoes, he slid the blueprints closer to the center of the table, so everyone could follow his right index finger as it

13

traveled down the white lines of the blueprint. "As you can see, the third floor was gutted, and store aisles put in, to increase retail space. However, while the developers were preparing the floor for retail use, the on-site contractor's crews reported so many incidents of paranormal sightings that retail use of the floor was eventually abandoned. No attempt was ever made to develop the fourth floor. It was too infested. We tried bringing in exorcists, mediums, and other spiritualists, but the infestation was just too extensive. The fourth floor remains as it was originally, mostly bedrooms and bathrooms.

"The wooden stairs leading to the third floor have been removed, to isolate the two halves of the mall. To travel from the second floor to the third floor, and from there to the fourth floor, you'll have to use the elevator. We needed to control who gets to the two upper floors, to make sure everyone who did access those floors had signed our liability waiver.

"The third floor has a strong presence of ghosts. The fourth floor has an intense presence of ghosts."

Bert's blue eyes, under his white eyebrows, looked around the restaurant table. "Put another way, metaphorically, the third floor has a lot of insects. The fourth floor has an overwhelming number of insects, and they're all really big. Almost none of our visitors go to the fourth floor. The ones that do, not all of them come back down the same person they were when they went up." He stood up from the table, bowed to Sylvia. "Good luck. I sincerely hope you find what you're looking for."

As the others were finishing their meals, Stan turned in his chair, facing Brandon. "I take it you weren't born paraplegic, right?"

Bud looked up from his Egg Foo Young.

"No."

"So what put you in a wheelchair?"

Brandon ran his hand through his long hair, moving it away from his eyeglasses. "Olivia and I got jobs near each other, so we could meet for lunch. Me walking through a crowd of strangers, southwards, eventually spotting, with a bump to my heart, her walking northwards through the mass of pedestrians. There was nothing like that experience of us spotting each other each work day in the crowds. My best friend! My lover!

"And then one day, around Christmas, we went shopping in the mall. Not this mall, but another mall. We never went to the Half-Haunted House mall. Olivia didn't believe in seatbelts or condoms, but she did stay away from Ouija boards, and anything else supernatural."

Stan conceded the point. "No one should ever use a Ouija board. They're incredibly dangerous. It's like living in a city and leaving your front door open at night."

"We had agreed to go our separate ways in the mall, something we never did, so we could buy each other a surprise Christmas gift. We met by the indoor skating rink at eight o'clock. Both of us smilingly noncommittal about what was in the shopping bag hanging from our hand.

"Holding our free hands together, we took the stairs down to the first floor, to enter the parking garage.

"And there at the bottom of the stairwell, a man lying on the concrete floor, on his side. I thought, Was it a homeless person? A drunk?

"Me being the man, I walked over towards him, handing Olivia my shopping bag, telling her not to look inside.

"He was wearing a dark suit. At first, I thought he had a rose pinned to the front of his suit jacket, but lower than a rose would normally be pinned. Then I realized the dark gray suit jacket had a large bloodstain.

"A businessman lying on his side on the cold concrete floor at the bottom of the stairwell, blood on his jacket.

"I turned back towards her in the bottom silence of the stairwell. I think he's dead. I think he's been stabbed.

"Are you sure? She came closer, down a step, down a step, out of curiosity, and to protect me.

"Now I saw there was some dark, dried blood on his lower lip.

"It was so hard to get it to register! To see what I had never, ever expected to see. A dead man lying on the floor, in a business suit. And especially, for some reason, during the Christmas season.

"While we were both in shock, gawking at his corpse, and it never occurred to either one of us to go back up the stairs, to call 911, to look for one of the mall's security guards, the steel door at the bottom of the stairwell swung open.

"And there was this tall, white guy with curly hair, a rope in one hand. He saw us, did a double-take, and attacked.

"I leaped to get between him and Olivia, but she leaped at the same time, out of love, getting between him and me. The last I ever saw her, alive.

"When I came to, I was in a white room. No idea where I was. Took about ten minutes—seriously, ten minutes—to realize I was in a hospital bed. I was so dazed. What happened came back to me. I tried getting out of bed to see where Olivia was, to make sure my best friend was okay, but when I tried to rise off the hospital bed, I fell on the floor, on my back and elbows, ripping out all kinds of monitoring devices and feeding tubes. My legs no longer worked. Later that day, I found out what had happened to Olivia. The hospital staff didn't tell me. The two detectives investigating the case told me she had been stabbed to death. She bled to death next to me while I was unconscious. She was conscious, dying on the stairs, unable to wake me to say goodbye.

"The detectives didn't want me to see her corpse. They wanted someone else to identify the body. But I insisted. They wheeled me into the morgue. I identified her myself.

"The coroner pulled the white sheet down off the hump of her head. Red stab wounds across the palms of her hands, her breasts, her face."

Bud raised his hand. "What present did you buy Olivia?"

Brandon's eyes reddened. "A stuffed bird. A cardinal."

"Did you ever find out what she bought you?"

"I eventually got her shopping bag back from the police. She bought me the same thing. A stuffed cardinal."

"Was there…"

"Every morning a pair of cardinals used to flutter down to the brick windowsill outside our bedroom. We'd leave out black sunflower seeds for them."

"Did you know cardinals mate for life?"

Brandon shot Bud an angry look. "Yeah. We did. That was kind of the whole point."

They went up the creaking wood stairs to the second floor. Made their way past the crowds of distracted shoppers, past the different storefronts, including a space called The Half-Haunted House Experience, to the rear of the floor. Stan could see where the staircase leading to the third floor had once been. Squares of wood on the floor and across the ceiling, where the support for the stairs once fastened, were paler. A large rectangle in the ceiling of a different wood, its grain in a different direction than the rest of the ceiling planks, had obviously been installed to plug the hole between the second and third floors.

At the rear of the second floor, on the left side, a line of people waiting to get approved to go beyond the metal detector, to the elevator leading to the third floor.

Bud nudged Stan. Pointed with his forehead at a large sign by the guard's station.

$50 per person. Nonrefundable.

NO children under 18.

NO adults under five feet tall.

"So who's going to pay the admission fee? Us or the mother?"

Stan made a face. "I'm guessing the mother. She's at the head of our group. I hope so. I'm already not liking the deal we made."

"The deal you made."

16

"Yeah. Well…"

"You think your son may be here?"

"He's gotta be somewhere, Bud."

"Or maybe not. Maybe he's in Heaven."

"Yeah, maybe. But I don't think so."

The people in line were for the most part the type you'd find queuing up to ride a roller coaster. Mostly under forty, happy, nervous, cameras and camcorders slung around their necks, craning their heads to see what was beyond the metal detector, but also a few old people here and there, by themselves or with a spouse, looking lonely and a little desperate amid all the young people, like the third floor was the final Lost and Found.

Stan let the guard pull everything out of the large black leather satchel he had slung over his shoulder, to the annoyance of the tourists who had joined the line behind him. With each item the guard lifted out of the satchel, he shot a more and more puzzled glance at Stan.

Bert came over, shaking his finger at the guard. "He's okay. Long as he doesn't have any firearms or knives in there."

The guard stepped back, hands gesturing down at the items on the examination table. "Did you see this stuff?"

"It's okay. I know what he's doing. Pack all the stuff back in his bag, let him through."

"How many visitors do you get to the third floor?"

Bert gave a happy chuckle. "Each weekday? Hundreds. Weekends? Even more. And it's all pure profit. This is better than Jesus Christ and a donkey on a tortilla."

Once they got beyond the checkpoint, the group made its way over to the one elevator.

A female employee with a whistle hanging around her neck organized the people into groups for each elevator boarding.

Stan, Bud, Sylvia, Colin and Brandon managed to get an elevator ride to themselves.

The elevator operator, a scary-thin black man, to where you could see too many bones under the skin, in a short-sleeved gray uniform, made sure they were all fully inside, pushed a button to have the two metal side doors of the elevator meet, then pushed another button to have the elevator rise.

Squarely surrounding everyone in the elevator, four mirrored versions of the six of them.

Stan smiled at the elevator operator. "What percentage of people, after they experience the third floor, go to the fourth floor?"

The man looked at Stan, no attempt to be friendly. "No percentage."

They could all feel in their bending knees the elevator arrive on the third floor.

The two metal side doors of the elevator slid open.

"Watch your step."

They all exited.

Stan had expected the third floor to look like the first two floors, individual glass storefronts on either side, but instead, the entire third floor appeared to have been optimistically built as one immense retail space. Aisles and aisles and aisles.

Each aisle was flanked on either side with empty shelves for merchandise, going about fifty feet deep into the space, at which point the aisles were crossed by a wider aisle, forming a grid of north-south and east-west aisles that filled the entire floor. It was like an immense, abandoned department store without merchandise or music.

A lot of the tourists seemed hesitant to venture down the spooky emptiness of the aisles, as if they might get lost. The mood was very different than it had been, waiting in line.

Except for the old people. Walking hand in hand, or if alone, walking alone, they gamely made their way down the first set of aisles, glancing at the shelves, even though there was nothing to look at on the shelves.

Stan set down his heavy satchel, away from the milling crowds.

Sylvia turned towards him, gesturing.

Colin once again earned his salary. "So how is this done?"

Stan pulled a large jar out of his satchel, about one foot wide, two feet high. Set it down on the floor. "This is a corking jar. It's what we use to capture ghosts."

Sylvia leaned forward, palms on her thin bare knees, root beer colored hair swinging down, to examine the jar.

"We have to put something pungent inside the jar, on its bottom, to attract ghosts. We use anchovy fillets mashed with minced scotch bonnet chilies, and some cat urine. It's worked really well for us. Then at the last minute we add something personal, that only the ghost we want to capture will recognize, so we don't cork the wrong ghost. In this case, it'll be a clipping of Brandon's pubic hairs, which you've provided.

"Once the ghost is lured into the jar, we screw down the top. At that point, we have the ghost. The glass threads at the mouth of the jar, and the metal threads of the top, are smeared with Vaseline and salt. The Vaseline is to keep the salt in place. Ghosts can't cross a salt barrier."

Colin channeled. "Fascinating."

"So what we have to do now is look for Olivia's ghost. We're probably going to see some ghosts anyway, but to see even more ghosts, and possibly Olivia's, we have to look at them through water." Stan pulled some square screens out of the satchel, each one foot by one foot, with wooden frames along the edges, the two plastic sides of each screen separated by an inch, the inch separation filled with water. "Just hold these up over your face, and you'll be able to see all the ghosts on this floor."

He passed around the heavy screens. One by one, Sylvia, Brandon, Colin held the squares of water in front of their faces.

Sylvia jerked hers down. Signed.

Colin: "I don't like this! I'm seeing terrible shapes."

The furrows on Stan's country boy face deepened. "Well, that's what ghosts are. If you don't want to look, don't. Bud and I can do the searching."

Brandon kept the water screen in front of his face. "I'll look. I don't mind."

Most of the young crowd had gone back down in the elevator. Not, it turned out, something they wanted to experience. The old people were far down the aisles, holding hands or alone.

The group made its way down the nearest aisle, towards the wider aisle that cut across.

They heard a scraping. Stan halted the group.

The scraping drew closer.

In that wider aisle, a tall, plastic trash can moved on its own, jerking forward, jerking forward, across the aisle.

Stan held the square of water up to his eyes.

Following behind the trash can, an old woman in a yellow and blue flowered dress that went down to her ankles. Twisting her white, wrinkly fingers off their knuckles, screwing them back on. Trailing behind her, men in business suits, little boys with tiny penises, pennies on their eyes.

They kept searching, aisle to aisle.

Just when they were about to give up, at the back of the third floor, Brandon stopped his wheelchair from cruising forward. Held the square of water up to his eyes.

"I don't like what I'm seeing!"

Stan hurried over, holding up his square. "Describe it."

"Dead women spreading their legs, masturbating each other, tongue kissing!"

"Pull the square of water down from your face."

Brandon held the square in place. "There's this one woman. She looks nothing like Olivia. Shorter than Olivia, dark hair, thin legs, small breasts. She's wooing me from the other side. Trying to seduce me with our common interests, her personality."

"Pull down the square of water. She's a malicious ghost."

19

"She's whispering things in my ear. I can feel her breath buzzing in my ear. Olivia wasn't my soul mate. This ghost is my soul mate."

Stan watched as other ghosts behind Brandon crept closer, changing form, becoming short, skinny, brunette. "Pull down the square of water!"

"She's got me in a fantasy where we're kissing. I'm kissing her white throat, I'm kissing the dark curly hair between her legs, her hands are holding her knees up outside my hips, spreading her thin legs, while I fuck her. We're talking about movies and songs and books Olivia and I never talked about."

Stan pushed the square of water down from Brandon's face.

"Don't consider that!"

Brandon's features were rigid.

The ghosts had got to him. Had got inside him. Frozen look on his face, as if behind bars.

"Brandon?"

Brandon, in his wheelchair, sobbed. Helpless, red-faced, head twisting, like a little boy. "She showed me what I always feared. Even while Olivia was alive. The ghost convinced me Olivia can be replaced. My one true love isn't unique after all. There is no such thing as a true soul mate!"

Stan put his middle-aged country boy's face in front of Brandon's. "Don't listen to her. She's a malicious ghost. We run into them all the time. She's trying to fuck with your mind."

Brandon, lost, furiously waved his right hand at Colin, to not translate. "She told me, You should masturbate thinking about me. And you should masturbate thinking about other, awful things."

Stan straightened up. "We're going back down in the elevator."

Stan gathered everyone up, led them down the empty aisle, back to the elevator.

Once on the main floor, Stan ushered everyone out to the parking lot.

Sylvia was signing to Colin, asking what had happened.

Colin was non-committal with his fingers, hands. A lot of shoulder shrugs.

Stan stood by the side of their van. "Listen, today's session did not go well. Tomorrow, Bud and I will return on our own, search the rest of the third floor, and the fourth floor if we need to, and see if Olivia's ghost is in there. Ghosts can be very malicious, and that's what happened today."

Sylvia angrily signed to Colin, who dutifully turned to Stan. "What happened?"

Stan raised his head. "We ran across a ghost who was very malicious. She put a lot of really bad ideas inside your son's head. We don't think your son should be exposed to that kind of influence again. Let Bud and me try to find Olivia's ghost on our own, we'll cork her, and bring her to you. If in fact she's in the Half-Haunted House."

Stan motioned to Bud to get the mother back in the van, and distract her.

He leaned over Brandon in his wheelchair. "I know you're paraplegic. Can you get an erection?"

Brandon, looking up, nodded.

"And can you masturbate to ejaculation?"

Another nod.

"It's really, really important you don't masturbate tonight thinking about that short, skinny brunette, or anything else she told you to masturbate about, that you're too embarrassed to tell me. The psychic power of an orgasm can bring all kinds of malign spirits into your head. Masturbation is like a Ouija board. It can invite a lot of malign ideas. So please promise me you will not masturbate tonight."

Brandon closed his eyes behind his eyeglasses. "I'm just really fucked up right now."

"I know you are! But you have to hang in there. I've never seen so many ghosts in one location. Unfortunately, the more ghosts there are, the more likely some of them are going to be malicious. That skinny brunette ghost is a loser. She gets off on creating negative energy, just like some men and women in real life get off on flirting with someone who has a partner. She's a loser. Don't play her game. She may not even be who she presents herself as being. She could be an old woman, or a man. Just make it through tonight, don't masturbate, and things will look so much better in the morning. I guarantee."

Stan and Bud were in their motel room, TV on, eating bratwurst grinders they got next door, roasted the old-fashioned way, over pine cones, then boiled in beer with sliced onions, stuffed into slit-open baguettes, slathered with mustard, draped with the limp brown onions from the beer boil.

The black phone on the night table between their two beds rang.

Stan wiped the delicious bratwurst grease from his lips. Picked up the remote, turned down the sound on Antiques Roadshow. "Never a good sign, when a phone rings in a motel room."

He lifted the black barbell receiver. "Hello?"

It was Colin.

Of course. It couldn't be the mother. Not over a phone.

"I have some very sad news about Brandon. He committed suicide."

"Repeat that?"

21

"Sylvia checked in on Brandon a few hours ago. She wanted to know if he was ready for his sponge bath. And he was on his back on the bed. He sliced his forearms lengthwise, instead of crosswise, so the arteries wouldn't close. Can you come out here?"

By the time Stan and Bud arrived, the police had left.

Sylvia was on her knees on the living room carpet, keening. In her grief, she didn't seem aware they were there.

Stan asked Colin if he could take a look at Brandon's bedroom.

The weight of Brandon's body had left an emboss on his white sheet, two arms, trunk, two legs, where he had been lying. A red Rorschach of blood by the end of each arm's imprint.

Around the emboss of the body, on either side, a total of five pools of pale crust. Stan shook his head. "I shouldn't have let him be alone. I should have known he would start masturbating, thinking about Olivia, to reaffirm his love, erase the arousal he felt in the Half-Haunted House, but then halfway through, the darker ideas took over." He examined each of the five ejaculations. "The first one? Olivia, the skinny brunette ghost. The second? Olivia, the skinny brunette ghost, his mother. Third, fourth and fifth? His mother."

Bud reached up, squeezed his friend's shoulder. "I was wondering about that."

"The poor son of a bitch probably thought if he could masturbate just one time thinking only of Olivia, their love would be safe. But each masturbation just turned him more and more towards his mother, until eventually he reached the point where he couldn't get hard enough to make another attempt."

Stan and Bud stayed in the kitchen, drinking coffee at ten p.m., when Sylvia showed up, standing by the stainless steel refrigerator in a black bikini. Her gestures were listless.

Colin raised his chin. "I went for a swim in our backyard, to clear my head. I want my son returned to me. I believe his spirit is very likely in the Half-Haunted House. I want you two to return there, find him, and bottle him. I will pay you twenty thousand dollars for this."

Stan glanced at Bud. "We'll do it."

"Where will you find him?"

Stan raised both palms, smoothed his hair away from his tired face. "I believe we'll find him on the fourth floor."

Going up in the Half-Haunted House's elevator, just Stan and Bud, without the others, was much easier. This is how it should have been the first attempt, Stan realized. Bad idea to let civilians get involved.

The elevator opened on the third floor. All the nervous tourists disembarked, eyes going everywhere.

The scary-thin black man looked at Stan and Bud still standing at the rear of the elevator. "Don't you want to get off?"

"We want to go to the fourth floor."

The elevator operator made an angry face. "You sure?"

"Absolutely."

The operator stayed by the elevator's console, not pushing the button. "For me to go up there, you got to pay me extra."

"How much extra?"

"Fifty dollars extra. Cash. I don't take checks."

Stan reached in his back pocket, pulled out his wallet, split it open, peeled off two twenties and a ten.

"We get to the fourth floor, the two of you get out in haste. I'm closing the door as soon as I open it. Just so you understand." He punched the round button for the fourth floor.

They rumbled up, no one talking.

In the elevator's four mirrored walls, as they rose, more and more faces emerged, staring at them.

The doors slid open.

"When we push the button to summon the elevator, you'll come back up here to take us down, right?"

"If you push the button. And if you pay me one hundred dollars in addition. I'm too old for this shit."

Stan set his black leather satchel down on the floor of the fourth floor as the elevator doors closed behind him, the operator making the sign of the cross.

Bud, hunched, looked around.

This floor hadn't been renovated. It was still mostly bedrooms and bathrooms, with a central hall. Far-off screams.

Stan got out his corking jar, its lid, and the ghost bait. His voice was subdued. "I'm guessing, if Brandon is here, and chances are he is, as a new ghost he's probably in one of the far rooms. That's where the other ghosts would have dragged him."

Bud, tense, looking around, nodded. "Probably right."

They started down the main hallway, towards the rear, the screams getting louder.

23

"Bud, I'm thinking maybe we should at least glance through a pane of water, just to see what we're dealing with. I know it's like turning on a bathroom light in the middle of the night in a jungle hotel, but we need to know how bad the infestation is."

Bud's shoulders were still hunched, eyes looking everywhere. "I'm seeing a lot of blurs. It looks like they can move really fast. Faster than us. If you want to look through a water pane, go for it. I'm not gonna do it. Sorry."

"That's okay." Stan quietly slid his water pane out. Held it up in front of his face.

They were everywhere.

Walking alongside them, staring balefully. Crawling on the floor by their knees, heads twisted backwards on their spines. Scuttling like huge cockroaches across the ceiling, with an extra set of legs.

A ghost stood in the middle of the hall in front of them, an old man with white hair, no eyes, just red sockets, arms waving sideways, blindly, ready to grab them. His yellow lungs hung on the outside of his gray vest, rotted with black spots.

"Step left. Far left."

A little girl walked on her hands towards them, bare feet up in the air, bad teeth, upside down face babbling.

"Now right. Far right."

Passing another bedroom door, Stan glanced inside through his pane of water.

A middle-aged man trying to rise off the bed, both arms and legs broken, sideways movements like a crab.

Something about him didn't look right.

Stan lowered the pane of water from his eyes.

He could still see the man.

The man wasn't a ghost.

He was a live tourist the ghosts had trapped up here.

The man rotated his face towards Stan. Glistening eyes, all hope gone. His lower jaw had been unhinged, yanked off, thrown away, exposing the half-moon of teeth on his upper jaw, like ugly pearls.

The ghosts were slowly pulling him apart.

"You okay, Stan?"

An immensely fat person waddled out from a bedroom door up on their left. Gave Stan a look of pure hatred. Heavy folds of flesh hanging from its face, abdomen. So obese it was impossible to tell the sex. Bracing its wide right foot forward, its left foot back, to balance, it bent over. Reached a hand up between its legs, face grimacing with pain. Up and up the hand went

24

between the legs. Once it was buried up to the wide elbow, it rolled its head back on its neck, gritted its teeth, and pulled down.

Out from between its legs splashed a slightly less obese person, covered in blood, and small dogs, slipping their black paws in the grease of blood, rising up, barking. The slightly less obese person glared at Stan. Still lying on its fat side, it reached between its own legs, yellow eyes rolling. Raised its right leg higher in the air, to get its hand in deeper. Yanked, and yanked, breath coming out in huffs, forearm sliding out, spilling out a third person, who lazily rolled over onto its hands and knees, amid more dogs dropping down onto the greasy pool of blood. Shot a look of roiling hatred at Stan. Crammed its hand up between its legs.

"Stan? You okay?"

"Bud, trust me, we have to walk much faster, all the way over to the right again. Press your shoulder against the right wall. That's how far right we have to get. But hurry!"

Something walking on Stan's right.

He turned his head, pane of water held in front.

A skeleton ghost.

Stan had heard about them. Never saw one with his own eyes.

The skeleton turned its tall eye sockets, like black caves in a green cove, in Stan's direction. Poked the articulated bones of its right index finger at Stan's shoulder.

Of course, Stan felt nothing, since it was a ghost.

He and Bud made their way farther down the hall, towards the door at the rear.

The skeleton kept a shuffling pace beside Stan, poking the bones of its index finger at Stan's shoulder over and over and over again, the phalanges compressing, springing back. The skeleton did it so many times, Stan started faintly feeling the impact of the pokes, as if his shoulder were numb.

This was not good.

They reached the end of the hallway, approaching the door to the bedroom farthest from the elevator. Ghosts on the ceiling behind them dropped down, rising to full height.

The screams were coming from within that bedroom. Echoing off the ceiling and walls, like screams at an indoor swimming pool.

Stan entered through the doorway.

The bedroom was humming with ghosts, hornets in a hive.

On the bed, a school of ghosts, wriggling inside a horse's bucking head, swimming up its nostrils, dark gray tails whipping left, right propelling the soft mouths deep into the blinded eyes.

The horse's head was Brandon.

25

Stan forced his way to the side of the bed, keeping his mouth closed.

To the ghost bait in the jar he added a lock of Sylvia's hair, to keep the other ghosts from swirling into the jar. Nothing worse than two or more ghosts in the same corking jar.

Tilting the opened mouth of the jar down against the horse's bucking head, Stan watched as its brown agony rose from the flared black nostrils, slid sideways across the air, pooling within the jar.

Stan quickly screwed on the lid, its threads sticky with Vaseline and salt.

The skeleton ghost's jabs were getting painful. And real. Physical.

"Bud, they're coming after me. We have to leave right now."

"I won't leave you behind, partner. Keep walking forward."

Back out in the hallway, the elevator a long, long distance away, Stan started punching the side of his face. He tried walking faster. "I'm getting taken over. I don't know, Bud. I'm really scared. I don't want to be trapped up here."

Bud got behind Stan. Shorter, but huskier. Putting his hands up into Stan's armpits, he propelled him down the corridor as fast as he could.

Stan kept punching his face. Switched angles, so his fists were bouncing directly off his nose.

By the time they reached the elevator, Stan's face bloodied and broken, the howls were so loud Bud had to slap a hand over one ear as he kept frantically hitting the button for the elevator.

The screams grew even louder, Bud holding both hands over his ears, bending over, teeth chattering.

Colin observed Sylvia's signings, turned politely towards Stan. "What happened to you?"

Stan watched Sylvia, dressed in a pants suit, set her cup of tea down in its bone china saucer. His broken nose had been set, held in place with white tape under his two black eyes. "It got pretty scary up there. The ghosts focused on me, because I was the one watching them, through a pane of water. I had to inflict pain on myself, to distract myself from what they were saying."

More signing. Colin: "But you did recover my son?"

"Yes."

Her hands and fingers flying. Colin: "Where was he?"

"He was wandering around the halls."

Sylvia made a gesture. Colin interpreted. "Was he upset?"

Stan looked at Bud. Shook his head. "No. He was just wandering around."

Sylvia signed some more. Colin raised his dark eyebrows. "This is wonderful news! And he is in that satchel?"

"He is. One thing I have to tell you, though. Bud and I aren't willing to go back up into the Half-Haunted House to cork Olivia's ghost. This one effort took too much out of us. There's just too much activity up there. But we can give you the names of people who have more experience in these matters. There's one man in particular, Clay, who can retrieve Olivia for you."

Sylvia opened her mouth in a soundless laugh. Touched Colin's knee. Signed. Colin raised his right hand. "But I don't want you to retrieve Olivia! That is what my son wanted, but it is not what I want. And now I am in control. This Olivia woman, I never thought she was right for my son! I will keep his jar in my bedroom, where I can see him every day, and he can see me. A mother and son, that is the most powerful bond. It cannot be broken by anyone! May I see my son now, please?"

Stan pulled the satchel across the carpet towards his shoes. Undid the leather straps at the top. "I want to warn you that he is, of course, a ghost now, so he's not going to look quite the same."

He pulled the sphincter at the top of the satchel loose. Lifted out the jar.

Sylvia, rearing back in her chair, clapped.

Hands reaching out, desperate to hold the jar with her son inside.

Sylvia settled the weight of the glass jar in her lap. Twisted the jar around, to see her son's face. Like seeing something from years ago, pale and sickly, preserved in formaldehyde.

Long hair, eyeglasses, trapped look in his eyes, as if behind bars.

Tears rolled down her cheeks. Hugging the cold jar, she leaned forward in her chair, ignoring Colin, looking straight into Stan's eyes as she opened her mouth and vocalized. "Yaw half maid maw drams coom trah. Than yaw!"

TINY DOORWAYS

Clay descended into Seattle early enough in the day to go straight down to the harbor.

Aitken Island sat ten miles off the coast.

A ferry ran out to the island every Monday, but this was Friday.

He walked around to some of the shore bars. In the third one, the bartender called over Sean, a tall, blonde-haired kid losing money at one of the pool tables.

They left at eleven, sailing north up Puget Sound under a beautiful, blue sky to Port Townsend, where they docked for twenty minutes so more of Sean's friends could get on board. Turns out they were all camping on Amber Isle, a few miles north of Aitken's Island, for a weekend of beer, beach cooking, and a Monopoly marathon.

Once everyone was on board, the sloop rounded Port Townsend and headed west out into the Pacific Ocean, full wind in the tall, white sails.

Clay made an effort to be sociable, holding the same beer bottle for two hours, his homely face laughing at everyone's jokes. He felt he owed it to his host.

As the mainland dropped behind them, he went to the aft, watching the smoke and planes of the city disappear, as if forever. Looking down into the sloop's churning wake, he saw faces in the soapy white foam, just like he saw faces in dinner plates, light bulbs, the clear plastic wrapping around a pack of cigarettes, and every other object in the world. All those silent gray mouths opening, all those black eyes staring.

Late afternoon, the blue and green pines of Aitken's Island slowly spread across the horizon.

As the island grew even larger, houses and roads magnifying, showing windows and cars, Sean angled the tall white sails of the sloop to slide into the marina.

Money had never been discussed, but Clay gave Sean a handshake of sixty bucks.

He walked with his backpack down the wide, gray-planked pier, passing men and women on either side with fishing poles.

Since it was Friday, there were a lot of families in the noisy confusion of the marina, kids and wives in shorts, husbands wearing captain's hats with

31

dark blue visors, white suntan protection greased over their noses. Almost more Styrofoam coolers than people.

The air was wonderful. Each inhalation felt healing.

Weaving through the impatient honks of the shoreline street, he found a phone booth on the other side, called the number in the email.

Nathanial Thorpe, on the other end of the line, sounded not entirely pleased Clay was on the island.

"Okay, glad your trip was all right. Give me ten minutes to get there."

He showed up half an hour later, his driver helping him out of the back seat of a black town car.

An old man in a dark gray suit, red tie, no socks.

He was shorter than Clay, slightly hunched. Clay could see down onto the thin white hairs neatly combed over Thorpe's pink scalp, with its brown age spots. Clean-shaven. Something every old man does before he goes out in public.

Thorpe turned around towards a restaurant two doors down, cardinals in the side yard of the restaurant flying back and forth through the joy of the water sprinkler. "Let's go inside so we can talk."

The staff knew him. He asked for a table at the rear, since the sun was setting through the wide front windows. The table was made of wood, knotholed and glossy, with a ceramic bowl in the shape of Santa Claus' jolly face, green and white, holding slim bottles of Tabasco and Worcestershire sauce.

Thorpe's weak eyes swung up as a favorite waitress arrived. Sitting up in his seat, raising what was left of his eyebrows, he asked her advice on what he should order. Clay was excluded from the conversation.

Once they had their drinks, Thorpe took a sip. His beaked nose, at this point in his life, took up half his face. Clay wondered, Does he know he keeps rubbing his lips together?

Thorpe avoided Clay's eyes. "I appreciate you coming out here." He kept staring off, loose-fleshed fingers parenthesing his glass. "I told you the situation with my daughter. The doctors don't seem to be able to help her. She's in a coma. They say she may die."

"I'm so sorry."

"Well. I'm desperate. Obviously. A friend of mine, who I trust, Jack Emory, said you might be able to help."

"I hope so."

"Yeah? What does that mean? You hope so?"

"From what Jack told me, and what you said in your email, during one of your last phone calls with your daughter—"

32

Thorpe raised his right forefinger, as stern a look on his face as an old man can muster. "Most recent. Not last. That's important."

"It seemed like the standard phone call the two of you have, but then she said, There's a boy living in my stomach."

Thorpe was embarrassed. "She's a corporate attorney. Bright as a tack."

"Did she say what color the boy was?"

His lower teeth jutted out. "What difference could that possibly make?"

"It makes a big difference."

"What color does the boy have to be? White? Black? Brown? Yellow?"

Clay stopped talking while the waitress, bending her knees, put their appetizers in front of them. Steamed Manila clams for Thorpe, Dungeness crab cakes for Clay.

"Cobalt blue."

Thorpe reared his old head back from the clam dripping off his fork.

Clay tried one of his crab cakes. It tasted like mud. "Tell me about your daughter. How old is she?"

"Forty-three."

"Any children?"

Thorpe stalled by eating another clam, face dipping forward so he didn't get any melted butter on his chin. That wouldn't look good, for an old man. Like showing up unshaven. While Clay watched him chew, he saw a change in Thorpe, a decision, out of love for his daughter, and fear for her safety, to swallow his pride, let down his guard. "No children. She's still a beautiful woman. You'll see, when we go up to the house. Her mother stayed beautiful too, until the chemo. I said to her, when she bought the house—" his eyes came alive, because he was talking to her now— "Why'd you buy a house with so many bedrooms? You only need one. But she said, Daddy, there are no houses with only one bedroom. I was kidding her." His lips went down in a shrug. "And maybe giving a gentle nudge from her father. Wouldn't mind being a grandfather. She's our only child. You have any children?"

"No."

Thorpe made an attempt at male bonding. "Never met the right girl?"

Clay realized he was being asked to share. "I'm not the best-looking guy in a room."

Thorpe's polite shrug did not disagree.

"I get girls occasionally. Believe it or not, there are some women who prefer homely men. I don't ask them why. But I'm one of those men who shouldn't have children. Each time I've gotten a woman pregnant, I've paid to have her get an abortion."

Clay's honesty hung between the two men sitting across from each other.

Finally, Thorpe went back to searching with his fork through his opened clam shells. "You could have just said it was none of my business."

Mia's home was a sprawling pink brick house, circular driveway out front.

Inside, the double front doors opened onto a three-story foyer with marble floor tiling, different doorways disappearing into rear rooms, a dark walnut staircase winding in a curve up to the second floor.

It was supposed to look impressive, but it looked cold and empty.

Thorpe, back hunched, lead them into an elevator at the rear of the foyer. Clay watched as Thorpe slid the elevator's black wrought-iron door across, the riveted compression expanding into diamond shapes. Thorpe forcefully tapped his middle finger against the 2 button. Probably having to forcefully hit the button because of arthritis. As the elevator shuddered, then rose, Clay caught Thorpe watching him out of the corner of his eye. This was a father impressed with his daughter's material success.

"I've made arrangements for you to sleep in the room next to Mia."

Clay took a chance, putting his hand on Thorpe's shoulder. The man didn't flinch, or pull away. That was good. "Thanks."

When the elevator adjusted its level to the second floor, Clay didn't help as Thorpe fumbled with unlatching the black wrought iron door, because he knew that would be taking power away from the father.

Thorpe, hunched over, led Clay down the red-carpeted hall to the white room at the end, pink and purple sunset in the windows.

A private duty nurse in a white cap stood up from the side of the bed, closing a crossword magazine. "No change."

Thorpe stood by Mia's pillow, hands hanging by his sides. "There's my little girl."

Clay stepped beside Thorpe.

Looked down.

Blonde hair, tall forehead, closed eyes, long nose, still lips.

Some women don't become truly beautiful until they're in their forties. Mia was one of those women.

White hospital gown, pink stripes. Like most patients, she showed more skin than she probably would have if she weren't in a hospital bed. Her small hands were raised up around her white pillow in a sleeper's position, exposing the pale undersides of her arms, all the way up to the hollows of her armpits.

"What I'd like to do is put my hand on her throat, and see what I can read."

"Candice, you don't have to stay for this."

"Canady."

Thorpe ducked his head impatiently, acknowledging the name correction. "You don't have to stay."

The nurse already had her crossword magazine in her hand. She walked out of the bedroom. She didn't seem to have a lot of affection for Thorpe.

Thorpe stood back, facing his bed-bound daughter, glancing at Clay. "Do what you have to do. God help you if this is some kind of con."

"I need a glass of cold water, for afterwards."

Thorpe went into his daughter's bathroom, came out, handed a glass of water to Clay.

After Clay placed the glass of cold water on Mia's bed stand, he took off his shoes. Got in bed with Thorpe's daughter, on top of the sheets, bending his knees so he didn't disturb her body. He placed his right fingers on her throat, lightly. "Most people assume the soul resides in the chest, but the soul is actually in the throat."

Thorpe said nothing. What could he say?

"Because she's in a coma, I have to lightly squeeze her throat. I'm not strangling her. I'm just trying to get in."

Thorpe looked skeptical. "I trust Jack Emory's word, but boy oh boy, you'd better be careful."

Clay placed his thumb on one side of Mia's throat, four fingers on the other side.

The skin of her throat was warm. The warmth of the skin, her exposed armpits, the helplessness of her, aroused him.

His thumb and four fingers squeezed her throat.

He was looking down into a toilet. Red blood. He squeezed a little harder. She walked backwards, got into bed. He let up on his squeeze. She threw the sheet off her body, thinking about coffee. Looked down, saw the blood and tissue between her legs.

His face twisted. Sobbing, she ran to the bathroom.

Sat down on the toilet.

The blood and tissue dropped out of her, splashing up onto the undersides of her thighs.

"Was she pregnant recently?"

35

The question caught Thorpe by surprise. "Not that I know."

Her horrible loneliness. Sitting on the toilet, face in her hands, sobbing.

Standing in her kitchen. Hollow eyes, pink nose. Cell phone to her ear, listening. A man's voice. "We have to talk quick, because Janice is walking Caesar, and he's already done his business. So it's gone? You're not pregnant anymore? Can you have sex again? How does that work?"

"Are you saying she was pregnant?"

"Just a minute, please."

She takes time off. Goes in her backyard each morning, with her coffee. Clay can see her tired face. She sits in a white wicker chair under the blue and green pines, hopeless, head lowered, holding her coffee in both hands, staring down at the grass. Should she quit her job? Call off the relationship with Morgan?

Thorpe shows up, in the backyard with her. Odd to see him the way she sees him. Taller, more energetic, kindness in his eyes. How much time has passed? It's definitely after the miscarriage. Children never tell their parents what's really going on in their lives. Thorpe is speaking, in the backyard.

"Probably put a birdfeeder back here. Hang it from one of these trees."

"I probably could! That's a good idea." First time Clay has heard her voice. It's musical, but trying to hide her sadness. Thorpe doesn't notice.

"At least then you'd have something to care for."

"That's right."

"Since you don't have any children."

"Let me think. Oh, that's right! I don't have any children."

"What's going on?"

"I'm reading her. Please be quiet."

Buying bird seed from the island's main supermarket. Standing in the aisle, dead, shopping basket full of single serving food.

Deciding to spread some of the seed on the brick window ledge outside her second floor bedroom.

"Are you learning anything?"

"Please. Be quiet."

It's night. She's upstairs, in her bedroom, after hours on the computer. Tired.

At first she thought there was a squirrel in her room, sitting by her window. Then she realized it was on the other side of the glass.

She walked over to the window, bending forward, mouth open.

36

The squirrel was perched on the pink brick of the outside ledge of her window, nervously picking up seeds, jamming them into his mouth.

Apparently, he couldn't see her on her side of the glass.

She was able to get right up to him, as if he were in an aquarium.

Never before had she seen a wild animal this close. His black eye, constantly roving while he ate. Each coarse strand of his black and brown fur. The black feet, with their long, inward-curving claws.

He kept jerking up, jerking down, snatching another seed, both front paws holding the tilted sunflower seed under his mouth as if praying, teeth rapidly nibbling off its husk, so he could gulp down the germ. Jerking down again, up again, in a start and stop series of clockwork motions.

Despite everything in her life, she grinned like a little girl. This was so cool.

Clay smiled.

She wakes up in the middle of the night.

Clay and Mia can hear the seed-crunching sounds coming from the opened window.

She gets out of bed in her pajamas. That's a surprise, that now she's wearing pajamas. Something to do with seeing the blood between her bare legs?

Do squirrels eat at night? And who's thinking that thought? Is it her, or him?

She's a little nervous, padding in her bare feet towards the opened window.

There's a shape on the other side of the gray wire mesh of the window screen.

It's not a squirrel shape.

But she can't tell that much about what is eating seed outside her window, in this moonless night. Except that it's larger than a squirrel.

She's little-girl curious.

Should she get her flashlight? But she doesn't want to scare it off.

She sits on the white carpet by the opened window, listening to the steady crunch of seeds, wondering what she should do.

Would the flame from her cigarette lighter be less upsetting to whatever was noisily eating outside her window screen?

She hurries quietly in her pajamas back over to her side of the bed, finds her orange disposable lighter.

Crouches by the screen.

The pad of her thumb rests atop the lighter.

Drawing in her breath, she rubs her thumb pad down against the notched metal wheel.

Yellow flame rises, waving.

In the flame's glow she sees, on the other side of the window screen, a naked boy, his long fingers picking up seeds, passing them between his wide lips.

His entire body is cobalt blue.

And transparent.

His round, black eyes jerk up. Stare right into her. Into Clay.

Clay yanked his hand off her throat.

Thorpe crowded Clay's back. "What's wrong? Did you hurt her?"

Clay got off the bed in his stockinged feet. "I have to urinate."

Thorpe leaned over his sleeping daughter, old mouth open, looking down at her face. "If you hurt her, there's going to be hell to pay."

Clay went into her master bathroom, closing the door behind him.

It looked like a woman's bathroom. Lots of pink, lots of soft textures.

Rolling his neck, he made his way over to the toilet alcove. Lifted the seat.

Looked down.

Realized this was the same toilet where she had seen all the blood in the toilet bowl.

Finished, he went over to the double vanity, which she didn't need, chose the sink closest to him. Ran some cold water in the marble sink, splashed it up onto his face. Thorpe knocking impatiently on the bathroom's door.

When Clay opened the door Thorpe backed up, squaring his thin shoulders. "What's going on?" His voice tried to sound tough, but it was too high-pitched.

Clay put a hand on Thorpe's shoulder. Given everything that was ahead of them, he needed Thorpe on his side. He also made a pragmatic decision not to tell Thorpe everything at this point.

"Your daughter encountered a Neek."

In his experience, that was usually the best way to start the discussion. Let Thorpe start asking questions, and take it from there.

Thorpe jerked his face forward, eyes blinking. "A what? What did you say?"

"A Neek."

"N,E,E,K?"

"Yeah."

Thorpe looked exasperated. "What's a Neek?"

"It's a thing, a creature, an entity, an energy, I don't know how to describe it. It's bad."

"What do we do? How do we get rid of it? Is that why my daughter's in a coma?"

"That's why she's in a coma, yes. To answer your last question first." He dunked the fingers of his right hand in the glass of cold water.

"Is your hand okay?"

"My fingers are burning. Like I've been cutting up a lot of hot chilies. That's an effect of connecting with someone, like I did with your daughter. Your fingers really burn afterwards."

"When does that go away?"

Clay looked down at his flexing fingers. "It doesn't, really." He glanced sideways at Thorpe. "You want to know about a Neek, right? It always takes the shape of a small boy, and it's always cobalt blue. I have no idea why. It seeks out seeds. That seems to be its sole purpose. It has to keep eating seeds, to stay viable. It's not like it has to eat seeds as often as we breathe, but I'd say it has to eat seeds as often as we drink water.

"Your daughter's big mistake was leaving out seed. Seed is the essence of life. From a quarter inch seed, a forty-foot oak can grow. Putting out seed is just asking for problems. You're luring entities. It's a way in, for them.

"I saw what happened, in your daughter's case. Her next door neighbor? He reseeded his lawn. All these thousands of seeds, out on the grass, attracting Neeks. One took. It came here, knelt on its hands and knees on the lawn while the sprinkler sprayed water over its blue transparency, picking up seeds from the grass, pushing them between its lips.

"Once it ate all the grass seeds, where did it go next? The neighbor across the street, who had a ten pound bag of rice in his pantry. Rice is seed. While that neighbor slept, the Neek gorged itself on the rice grains, blue and transparent in the pantry, but eventually, every last white grain in that big canvas bag was eaten, even the grains resting in the bag's sewn creases.

"So where does the Neek fly next?

"Your daughter puts out bird seed. The Neek eats and eats, long fingers lifting the bird seed from the brick ledge to its wide mouth.

"So what seed does the Neek eat next?"

Clay looked at Thorpe.

"Eggs are seeds. The Neek burrows inside your daughter's abdomen, starts eating her eggs. She told you she had a little boy in her stomach. That was the Neek, long fingers, wide lips, patiently eating all her eggs. A woman who so much wanted to have a child, and here was the Neek, eating all her eggs, all her potential babies. And there was absolutely nothing she could do to stop it devouring her chance of being a mother. She just had to lie there in bed, helpless, on her back, sunlight streaming through these windows right here, listening to the sound of her eggs being eaten. And that despair, that loss of her womanhood, is what put her in a coma. And putting her in a coma is what allowed the Neek to start eating her Plum. Because the Plum is also a seed. And for a Neek, a Plum is the sweetest meat, closest to the bone. A lot of terrible things happen in daylight."

Thorpe looked stricken. "What do we do?"

Clay looked out a bedroom window. The sky was dark, but the land was darker. "We can't do anything tonight. I'm too tired from connecting with your daughter. I need to rest. Rebuild my strength." Clay turned his homely face in Thorpe's direction, so the older man could see Clay's resolve. "Tomorrow, after a good night's sleep, and a hearty breakfast, we fight back."

Thorpe was deflated. "This island has always been so safe. I grew up here. We used to leave our dolls unlocked at night."

The cook served them breakfast at six the next morning, the time Clay and Thorpe had agreed on the night before.

Thorpe had a soft-boiled egg, served in an egg cup that featured a twenties flapper winking her eye, and some dry toast.

Clay had a huge mound of scrambled eggs mixed with sautéed onions, a thick slice of ham, cottage fries, lots of buttered rye toast, some fresh pineapple, and a tall cold glass of Clamato.

Thorpe dipped another modest, torn-off strip of dry toast into his egg's runny yolk. "That's a hearty breakfast all right."

"Did Mia become a lawyer because you were a lawyer?"

Thorpe's bent shoulders conceded the point. "It was important to her to please me. What a daughter does, for her father."

"Was she happy choosing your profession?"

Thorpe looked impatient. "I don't know. When she was a little girl, she wanted to be a ballerina."

"Did she take any classes?"

"Yes, she took the classes. For years. Years and years. It's not a serious profession. Strictly hand to mouth. But was she happy? As a lawyer? That was your question?"

He tilted his head to one side, as if thinking through the question, but Clay had the sense Thorpe already knew the answer, had known it all along. "The three of us were in Chicago. For her mother's chemo. Mia flew in from Seattle, after I called her that Sunday night, to let her know." Thorpe's voice was hoarse. "The chemo in Chicago was, basically, a last ditch attempt to save her mother's life. The cancer by then…in Raleigh they thought they had gotten it all, but during a routine check-up it turned out they hadn't, it had spread even more. Cancer always spreads upwards in the human body. Did you know that? I didn't know that." He stopped talking, following his own thoughts. Gave a snort of amusement.

"What's that?"

"I was—you know, you asked me about her mother's treatment, and I just remembered…" He let out a huge sigh. "Sitting in the fucking waiting room, the three of us crowded on a sofa, early for her mother's appointment with the oncologist, none of us wanting to read a magazine, we were just so disheartened, and there was a mother and daughter sitting in chairs on the other side of the room. The mother was obviously the one with cancer. A colorful scarf, like a gypsy's scarf, over her bald scalp. The daughter was around twelve. You could tell from her eyes she had been crying a lot. And, I guess to cheer her daughter up, or distract her, the mother said, I spy, with my little eye. The daughter ignored her at first, but the mother coaxed her, and eventually the little girl joined in. Between the two of them they spied an orange fish in the waiting room's aquarium, the oncologist's framed medical degree, a golf magazine, a man sitting in the corner who couldn't stop coughing.

"My wife was admitted to the hospital right from that visit. Mia and I stayed with her in her hospital room as long as we were permitted, then went back to the hotel. We sat in the room my wife and I had booked, to be together, though we didn't really talk. At one point Mia turned on the room's TV, and it was a Saturday Night Live show. Not very funny. Coincidently, Mia had just been made a partner in her firm. She said something curious to me. She had been drinking. She said, my initials are M.T. Empty." Thorpe looked at Clay.

"How did that affect you?"

"Well, to be honest, I kind of understood how she felt. I mean, I had always put work first, and I guess she did too, emulating me. But the thing is, if you put all your eggs in work, that's not as safe as putting everything in family relationships. A family relationship lasts forever. A work relationship can end tomorrow, if they think they can do without you. There's no loyalty. I remember about six months later, after Ann died, I was at a business conference. Afterwards, my boss came up to me and said, They weren't applauding because they thought you were great. They were applauding to get you to stop talking." Thorpe made a face. "Such a mean-spirited thing to say, regardless of whether or not it was true. Right then, I realized I made the wrong decision. I should have chosen love over success. But it was too late. Is my daughter losing her soul?"

Clay dipped another cottage fry into the pool of ketchup he had on one side of his plate. "No. You can't separate the soul from the body, until death. The soul is always safe." He took time out to eat the crisp square of

41

ketchup-draped cottage fry. It tasted like mud. "Every human being has five powers. The body, the mind, the soul, the Plum, and the Ansei."

Thorpe got that exasperated look again.

"Different entities can affect the body and the mind, but a Neek isn't one of those entities. No entity can affect the soul or the Ansei. A Neek is one of the few entities that can take someone's Plum. The Plum is the will to live.

"What the Neek did was take your daughter's Plum, and hide with it somewhere in this house. Wherever it's hiding, it's steadily eating your daughter's Plum. The more it eats of her Plum, the more likely it is your daughter's will power will give out, and she'll surrender her will to live to the Neek. The Plum is what the Neek is after. That's the ultimate seed. That's all it wants out of this."

"How would that affect my daughter?"

"Well, it would affect her significantly. When she comes back, in her next life, she'd obviously be very self-destructive. Because she lost her will to live. You hear about these people who are alcoholics, or drug addicts, or who don't take care of themselves? Those are all people who lost their Plum to a Neek in a previous life."

"So what do we do?"

"I walked around the rooms while I was waiting for breakfast. I noticed all the doorknobs in this home are very nervous. That suggests to me the Neek is in a house within this home. I'm thinking, a dollhouse, maybe?"

"I'll have Brenda look. How is it you have this power?"

Clay scooped a triangle of buttered rye bread under some yellow curds of scrambled eggs, flecked with moist squares of onion, transferred that steaming weight to his mouth, pizza-style. It tasted like mud. "When I was about eight, I had a dream. I was walking down a dirt road behind a housing development, and gasoline started falling out of the sky. Not waterfalls of gasoline, but droplets in the air. I knew it was gasoline, because it had that intoxicating smell. So what did I do? I lit a match. The flame from the match sparked all around me, sparked up over my head, sparks popping and crackling all the way up into the clouds. A moment passed, way up in the sky, there was a loud explosion. The gray clouds turned orange.

"Airplane parts started falling. I had to run under a tree to get away from the flaming debris, the body parts.

"Holding my elbows over my head, I thought, I blew up an airplane!

"I woke up. I saw the world as it really is. Everything swarming around us. And most of it is evil."

Brenda found a doll house in the attic.

She and Clay carried it down the attic stairs, to the second floor elevator.

Riding down, Clay was aware Brenda kept looking at him when she thought he wouldn't notice.

They set the doll house down on the marble floor of the front lobby.

Clay touched Thorpe on his shoulder. "Did you know about this?"

"No! I don't know why she had it. She certainly never mentioned it to me."

"Maybe she bought it in anticipation of getting pregnant?"

"I suppose. It's possible."

Clay got down on his hands and knees, in front of the doll house. It was constructed to look like a Victorian home, with a small white porch out front. The house itself was a yard high and deep, two feet across.

"Despite what you may have heard, most entities aren't strong enough to haunt an entire house, but they can haunt something as small as a dollhouse. Having a doll house in your home is dangerous. Like having a Ouija board in your home. You'd be surprised how many doll houses are haunted."

"So the house itself, Mia's house, isn't haunted?"

"Correct. What you have is a haunted house—the doll house—inside a regular, unhaunted house. Everywhere outside the doll house is safe. Everywhere inside the doll house is dangerous. The Neek is in there, with your daughter's Plum. We have to find out where the Neek is nesting inside the doll house, lure it out, and trap it. Then we can remove the Plum.

"The key to removing a spirit from a house, whether a doll house or full-sized house, is to first of all clean the house. Spirits prefer dust. If we clean the doll house, we'll start to loosen the Neek's grip on the house. Brenda? I need all the cleaning products you use, some rags, and as many Q-tips as you can find in the bathrooms."

Clay spent the morning stomach down on the marble of the lobby, extending wet Q-tips through the tiny doorways and windows of the Victorian doll house, carefully scrubbing the diminutive walls, floors and ceilings.

Once he had those clean, his Q-tips swept under the legs of the small furniture, rubbed along the picture frames of the landscapes and portraits, tilting them, removing dust.

By three in the afternoon, the inside of the Victorian doll house looked immaculate.

There was a large aluminum tub filled with heavy cream beside the doll house.

Clay lit a cigarette.

Thorpe, returning to the lobby periodically between business calls in his casual wear, dark gray sweater and black tie, lifted his wobbly chin. "I never approved you smoking inside my daughter's home."

Clay, lying on his stomach, holding a dentist's mirror in his other hand, looked up like an alligator. "Is that really an issue for you? Given everything else that's going on?"

"What are you doing?"

"Smoke can reveal where the Neek is nesting inside the doll house. I use the dentist's mirror to look around furniture and doorways I can't see from the windows. If it helps, this is not tobacco I'm smoking. It's oregano. God hides clues for us throughout the world. Green mold on bread cures infections. Smoke from oregano detects ghosts."

As Thorpe, standing, watched, Clay brought the cigarette to his lips, gently blew its smoke through windows, angling the dentist's mirror through the rooms, tilting it this way and that.

Gray translucencies floated within the walls, in mid-air, two black dots below their hoods, tattered robes drifting behind. "Ignore those. This is an old doll house, passed down through generations. A lot of dolls have died in here, but they're not related to what we're doing.

"There! Here! I found it."

Thorpe leaned forward.

"Come down here. Let me show you."

Clay's hands bracing the old man's bony chest, Thorpe got down on his hands and knees.

"I want you to look through this parlor window."

"This one here?"

"Right. As I blow the smoke into the corridor beyond the parlor, I want you to look into the dental mirror, which is going to reflect what's behind that open pantry door. Are you ready?"

Thorpe was breathing heavily. His face beside Clay's he said, "Yes. Go ahead."

Clay took a drag on his cigarette. Held it. Lowered his lips to one of the parlor windows.

Gently blew gray smoke through the window, against the small chairs and sofas of the parlor.

The smoke drifted across the palm frond and banana leaf patterns of the parlor's wallpaper, into the hallway leading into the kitchen.

Clay snaked his dentist's mirror along the narrow space of the hallway, angling it across the kitchen's entrance.

In the dentist's small, circular mirror, cigarette smoke drifting past, Thorpe saw the reflection of something cobalt, its mouth ferociously yanking up pink strands from a shape its blue feet had pinned to the floor behind the pantry's door. As Thorpe leaned closer, he recognized, under the gripping spread of blue toes, his daughter's anguished face, her eyes filled with tears, her mouth trembling, like when she was a child.

"Oh, dear!"

"He's pulling the Plum right out of her. And he won't stop, unless we make him stop."

"Look what he's doing to her! Do something!"

"I had Brenda go down to the village after breakfast and buy up all the heavy cream she could find. Neeks are highly acidic. We're going to pour a little bit of the cream into the doll house, to shock the Neek, then shake him out of the house, into this aluminum tub filled with cream."

"Then what?"

Clay's homely face. "Then I'm going to eat the Neek."

"What?

Clay unscrewed the red plastic cap atop a quart container of heavy cream. "Neeks eat seeds. I eat Neeks."

Thorpe and Brenda stood off to one side.

Clay lifted the front of the dollhouse by its white porch stairs.

Inside the house, an angry screech, as if from a large insect.

He carefully poured the quart of heavy cream through the small front door, angling the house so the cream flowed past the parlor, down the hall, towards the kitchen.

His circular dentist's mirror bumped rapidly through the rooms, knocking over tiny chairs, scraping down the hallway, to look behind the pantry door.

"Okay! It's on its back!"

Dropping the front of the dollhouse, he went around to its back. Lifted the house. Slid his hands underneath, halfway down the sides of the house.

Lifted the whole doll house in the air, its weight that much heavier, now that he didn't have Brenda's help.

Awkwardly tilted the house forward, arms straining, lower back aching, over the aluminum tub of heavy cream.

Shook the house, tilting it more and more forward.

Tiny tables fell out. Framed paintings the size of postage stamps. Little tea cups and a silver sandwich tray.

He tilted the back end of the house higher, the straight line of its rear foundation rising painfully up his chest.

Kept shaking the house. Shaking it.

When the back bottom of the house was up under his nose, there was a heavy splash, something blue landing in the aluminum tub of cream.

Clay threw the heavy house to one side.

The Neek rose out of the aluminum tub, dripping heavy cream.

A beautiful, cobalt blue transparency. Black eyes.

As the Neek stood higher, a line of sharp blades sprouted across its scalp, forehead to nape. The Neek's mouth opened, hissing, showing its red fangs. As the fangs spread further apart, a roar rose from its throat, loud as a lion.

The Neek lifted its blue knees, stepping out of the tub, swaying its head left and right, black eyes staring at Clay, wagging a long index finger at him.

Clay's left hand pushed the Neek's face sideways. He leaned in with his teeth, taking a bite out of the Neek's neck.

Pulling blue, transparent meat out of the Neek's shoulder, Clay chewed furiously, tripping the Neek at its ankles, dropping it to its side.

The cobalt blue hands punched Clay's ears while Clay bit down into the Neek's chest, yanking up flesh.

That loud insect screech rose from the floor.

As Thorpe watched, hand over his mouth, Clay's teeth went down again and again into the struggling Neek, each time pulling off more and more blue, until, after ten minutes, there was nothing on the floor but spilled heavy cream.

Clay stood up with a large pot belly.

Head tilted back on his neck, he rolled his eyes.

Thorpe made his way over, looking down so he didn't slip in the heavy cream on the marble. "So the Neek is dead now?"

"Let's go upstairs."

He and Thorpe rode up in the elevator.

Clay took his shoes off again, got back in bed with Mia. Positioned his right hand around her throat. Gave a light squeeze.

Thorpe stood by the side of bed, licking his lips. When Clay didn't say anything after a while, Thorpe, mostly to remind Clay he was waiting for an answer, said, "It's reassuring there are all these rules."

Clay took his hand off Mia's throat. "The Neek has left her."

Thorpe's shoulders slumped. "Thank God. So she'll wake up now?"

Clay looked up from the bed. "What?"

Thorpe smiled for the first time since they met. "My daughter? She'll wake up now?"

Clay got off the bed, standing in his stockinged feet. Looked Thorpe in the eye. "I don't think you understood what I can do. Your daughter is going to die. I can't reverse that. Unfortunately, she also had too much of her Plum eaten by the Neek. She will be self-destructive in her next life. I was here to stop further damage from being done, but I can't reverse the damage that was already done."

Thorpe backed up. "What?"

"She was infested with a Neek. It spread everywhere inside her. It's what Neeks do."

"My little girl's going to die?"

"Yes. I never said I could save her. All I can do is get rid of the Neek."

Thorpe's frail body trembled. "What good are you? Why should I write you a check?"

"I can't save your daughter's life. I'm sorry."

"And in the next life? She's going to be suicidal? An alcoholic? A drug addict? A wrist slasher?"

"I know you want the truth. In that life, and several more, until the effects of losing her Plum wear off, and she grows a new Plum."

Thorpe went into a rage, arms shaking. When words finally came out, they left spittle on his lips. "And there's nothing you can do? What the fuck good are you?"

Clay ignored the old man's anger. "There's only one thing I can do."

"Don't tease me!"

Clay avoided Thorpe's pathetic eyes. "I can eat your Plum."

Thorpe took a step forward. "Huh?"

"I can eat your Plum—your will to live—and put it in your daughter. The blood will match."

Thorpe shut up.

"If you want, I can do that."

Thorpe put a hand over his mouth.

"But...I believe the consequences, to you, are obvious. If they aren't, I can detail them."

Clay actually had no idea what Thorpe would decide. Sometimes, you can tell. With Thorpe, he couldn't.

Thorpe sat down in one of the easy chairs in his daughter's bedroom. His clothes looked too loose on his frame. "Do you have a cigarette? A real cigarette? Not one of those oregano things?"

Clay handed him an unfiltered Camel. Lit it for him.

After his first draw, Thorpe looked at the glowing orange end of the Camel. "This is the first cigarette I've had in thirty years."

Clay said nothing.

Thorpe smoked in silence. There was Mia lying in bed in a coma, Clay standing quietly in his socks, Thorpe sitting in the easy chair, exhaling gray smoke up towards the white ceiling.

Once he finished the Camel, Thorpe stubbed it out. His runny blue eyes looked up at Clay. "Let's do this thing."

"You're sure? You know what you're giving up?"

Even an old man can have balls. "Fuck, yeah. Let's do it."

Clay rubbed his nose. "Okay. It's probably easiest if you stay seated in that chair. Are those dentures?"

"What? No. You can't tell? How uneven they are?"

Thorpe watched, eyes fearful, as Clay walked over to the side of his chair, as if Clay were a dentist.

"Is this going to hurt?"

"It's going to hurt a lot. Unbutton the front of your shirt, please. All the way down to your waistband. Have you ever had any heart problems?"

Thorpe's loose-fleshed fingers started unbuttoning. "Noooo. Why do you ask?"

"A Plum is not physical, but it still has to drawn through your veins so I can extract it, and eat it. That's going to put a strain on your heart. Just so you know."

Thorpe's narrow chest was bared. Discolored nipples, sagging skin, wisps of Santa Claus hair. His voice was tight. "Okay."

Clay handed Thorpe a small wooden rod. "Place this between your teeth, and bite down on it now."

"Oh dear!"

"Changed your mind? Remember, the effect on you is going to be far worse than the pain you're about to experience."

Thorpe drew himself up in his chair, one of the last of the "greatest generation". Put the rod in his mouth. Took it out. "Do you have any more Camels?"

"Most of a carton, in my backpack."

"I'm going to need another one when this is over."

He put the wooden rod back between his teeth.

The way to do this is to do it quickly.

Clay lowered his head, biting into the sourness of Thorpe's chest. Thorpe's skin smelled of must and the gelatin caps used for prescription medications. Clay's teeth found a vein. Sucked. Sucked mightily, spitting the blood back into the vein, sucking and sucking and sucking until the taste of the Plum, salty as anchovies, entered his mouth. Thorpe screamed underneath him, body jerking in the chair in unbelievable agony. Clay's cheeks hollowed, sucking more and more of that saltiness into his mouth, ignoring the frantic punches to the top of his head. When his mouth was full, he pulled his teeth off Thorpe's chest with an audible pop, then hurried, bent over, to the sleeping Mia.

Using the thumb and forefinger of his left hand, he spread her pearly teeth apart, leaned over, his lips forming a seal over her lips, and dribbled the Plum into her mouth, the whole time massaging the front of her throat, to have her gulp it down, gulp it down, gulp it all down.

Clay took off his white shirt, lifting his arms, standing under the bedroom's ceiling fan, letting the sweat on his upper body dry. "You want that cigarette now?"

Thorpe nodded. He sat up in the chair. "Ow!"

"That's gonna hurt for a while, then it's gonna itch like crazy. When the itch really gets out of control, to where you want to take a knife to your chest, get to a shower and put the water on as hot as you can bear. Not scalding, but damn hot. Get in the shower, and let the steaming water wash the itch out of your wound. You'll have to do that about twice a day, for a couple of months."

Thorpe took a long drag on his Camel, letting his head lean back. "So now is my daughter safe?"

"Probably. She'll die tonight. Now that she has a Plum. As she dies, we'll know for sure if she's safe."

"You son of a bitch. I went through all this, all to come, and you still can't say for certain she's safe?"

"If I told you it was fifty-fifty, would you have done it?"

"Absolutely!" Thorpe took another angry hit on his Camel. "I don't know. Maybe. I see your point."

Clay and Thorpe sat on either side of Mia's bed during the death watch.

Thorpe chain-smoked.

Clay regarded Thorpe's nervousness. "I actually didn't think you were going to sacrifice yourself for your daughter."

"Why would you say that?"

"I don't know. You seem selfish."

"Maybe I am. In a lot of ways. But there's very little a father won't do for a daughter. That's kind of an unspoken promise a husband makes to a wife. Treat me however you want, but make her life better." Thorpe thought about that. "Make her not have to marry the type of man I married."

Mia died around eleven that evening. She never regained consciousness. When she was near the end, Thorpe held her hand. Clay went to hold the other hand, but Thorpe bared his teeth. "I don't want you to hold her. I want to be the only one holding her!"

Clay put his hands in his lap.

Her chest jerked up, her legs twitched, white bubbles popped between her lips.

And that was it.

Then there was just that long weight in the bed, devoid of spirit.

Thorpe raised his old face, tears streaming down the sides of his nose. "How do we know—"

On her bedside table, the lamp's bulb burst.

Clay let out a sigh. "She's safe."

"She's safe?"

"She's safe."

Mia's father sat back in his chair. "At least I did one good thing in my life."

It was too late for Clay to leave the island that evening, so he spent another night in the room next door. In the morning, the cook served him another hearty breakfast, but the father never showed up to share the meal. Why would he? Clay wasn't needed now.

After Clay waved away a refill of his coffee, everything on his plate gone but a yellow smear of egg yolk, some toast crumbs and grease from the small pork sausages, the father poked his head in the kitchen. "I've arranged for Burt to take you back to Seattle. So you don't have to hitch a ride. Here's your check."

Clay got up from behind the table, walked over. Accepted the check. Didn't look at it.

The father was obviously uncomfortable. Clay felt if he reached out to touch the father's shoulder now, he'd pull the shoulder back.

"Thanks. No breakfast?"

"I tried a shirred egg earlier. Didn't taste right." Mia's father avoided his eyes. "Thank you. Well, I have business to attend to."

"Don't let me keep you."

Clay watched the father start to leave the kitchen. "Now that you've found out what it's like to not have a Plum, do you regret your sacrifice?"

The old man turned around. Clay recognized the lost look in his eyes. "Nonsense! Of course not."

"I'm glad."

"I don't give a fuck if you're glad or not. It's just one more thing I've had to do. That's what life is. Just one miserable thing after another."

Clay shook his head. "Life is wonderful. For most people. But not for me." He folded the check, put it in his pocket. "And now, not for you."

A Woman Made Of Milk

Berlin Springs turned out to be a small town. Main drag and a few side streets under the Mississippi sun. One and two story buildings, giant ads for businesses that no longer existed fading on their brick sides.

Tilda had no trouble locating Lyle's Cafeteria, midway down the drag.

She slid her pick-up into a parking slot close to the entrance.

Got out, tall and thin, tangle of short blonde hair atop her bony face. Pulled on the ropes securing the boxes in the bed of her pick-up, their nautical knots lifting, to make sure nothing had come loose. One of the boxes had noises coming from within.

Two cigarettes later, a blue Subaru slanted into the slot next to her truck.

The driver kept the engine running, probably for the air-conditioning.

Tilda dropped her cigarette. Walked over, dipping her head. Couldn't see past the tinted glass of the driver's window, but she knew whoever was inside could see her approaching.

She waved her big hand at the tinted glass.

With a whirr, the window slid halfway down.

Behind the steering wheel, a man, probably in his nineties. Military crew cut, black-framed glasses, strong, square-shaped face.

"Merle MacDonald?"

"Ms. Clem?"

"Tilda."

"Let me get out of my car." He raised the window. Shut off the engine. Tilda stood back so MacDonald could swing his door open.

Standing in the road next to Tilda, holding onto an attaché case, MacDonald squinted up from behind his black-framed glasses.

Tilda anticipated the question. "Six foot seven."

He got a grin on his face. "Ever play on the girls basketball team in college?"

"I didn't go to college."

MacDonald kept looking up, with a salesman's inability to be discouraged. "Did you play on the girls basketball team in high school?"

"No."

55

"You should have."

"I didn't do well in school."

"If you got into sports, that probably would have helped."

She didn't reply. He seemed to realize he was getting off-track. "I appreciate you came all the way over from Mobile. Did you get your check all right?"

"I haven't cashed it yet. Wanted to see what the deal was."

They walked next to each other across the concrete sidewalk to the glass front door of Lyle's. Both a bit self-conscious. Tilda held the ding-a-linging door open for MacDonald. Ducked her head, following.

Inside, it was cooler from the overhead ceiling fans. Half the tables occupied.

MacDonald seemed to be disoriented, looking around uncertainly, fixed smile on his face.

The young black woman in blue plaid behind the cash register raised her voice. "Nice to see you out, Mr. MacDonald."

He whirled around. Set his jaw. "How's Esther doing?"

"The OB-GYN found another little tooth inside her."

"That's the damnedest thing."

At the back of the cafeteria they selected two hard plastic brown trays, a knife, fork, spoon set wrapped in a white paper napkin. Slid their rectangular trays along the steel tube counter that ran in front of the display cases of food sitting in metal tubs.

Half a dozen smiling women on the other side of the display case, white caps on their heads, clear plastic gloves over hands that held big metal spoons or tongs.

MacDonald leaned his stomach against the steel tubing counter, overhead lights haloing the white in his crew cut. "Let me have the American Chop Suey. But from the rear tub. Tilda, I don't know if you ever had an Italian beef sandwich before, but if you have and you liked it, Lyle has a new cook down from Chicago. They're messy, but they're good."

He seemed to feel a little awkward, playing host at a cafeteria. "And you should try the peanut butter pie. You won't believe how light it is."

Tilda put the tea saucer holding a triangle of the pie on her tray.

At the end of the line she stepped in front of MacDonald to pay for both their meals.

MacDonald set his attaché case down on the floor. "No, no. I got this." He reached into the sagging rear pocket of his pants.

They sat by the front window, on opposite sides of the small table, placing their brown plastic trays down on the red and white checked gingham tablecloth.

56

Tilda bent her head, whispering a brief prayer of thanks. Bit like a vampire into the tall, hot, moist side of her Italian beef baguette.

Once they were finished with their meals, the two of them sat back, a bus boy lifting away their trays and empty plates.

Tilda lit a cigarette, blowing her gray smoke out into the aisle.

This close to each other, sitting opposite at the small table, the distraction of introductions and exchanging small talk while eating gone, Tilda was able to examine MacDonald's face more closely. It takes a while to truly see someone else's face. Crow's feet, parentheses around his pale mouth from decades of smiling. Probably a strong, masculine face decades ago, but now in decline. Still, he looked more robust than most men in their nineties.

MacDonald drew in a breath to tell his story. She realized he had rehearsed his introduction many times, in anticipation of this meeting.

"Thanks for coming here.

"My wife, Liz, died six months ago. Okay?"

"Okay."

"We lived at Chatterton, which is an estate—a very large estate—that's been in her family for centuries. Since the sixteenth century. Could I, may I, have one of your cigarettes?"

Tilda passed him a cigarette. Put the pack on the table between them. Added her blue disposable lighter.

"Normally I only have one cigarette a week. Friday evening while I watch the market report."

A slight tremor in MacDonald's hand as he held the smoke-trailing cigarette.

"She had been coughing a lot. We thought it was a persistent cold, maybe walking pneumonia. So she made an appointment with her doctor. I was out in the waiting room, going through some old Readers Digests, when the inner door opened and there was my sweetheart. Is everything okay? Did they figure out what it was?

"She had lung cancer. Yup.

"She took the whole chemo course. I don't know if you've ever known anyone who's taken chemo?"

Tilda shook her head.

"I'd take her in each day for her chemo, then sit in the waiting room doing crosswords while they led her to the back, where the actual chemo took place. I never saw that area. A nurse would open a door in the waiting room, to the side of the receptionist area. Mrs. MacDonald? We're ready for you.

"After a week of chemo, she'd get three weeks off. It was a pattern. First week after chemo, she'd just lie in bed all day, sleeping and watching

TV. Lots of court shows and home designer shows. No appetite. Second week, she'd be more active, even go back to cooking some of our meals, with a chair by the stove in case she had to sit down while the onions were browning. Third week, it was like old times. But then of course, the fourth week, we'd be back at her oncologist for another round of the chemo.

"Losing her hair? That was frightening." He winced. "It would come out in clumps. Seeing long strands of it hanging off her fingers, it did make me think she was dying. That went on for six months. Then her new doctor decided they had got rid of the cancer.

"Our lives went pretty much back to normal.

"After a year of no chemo, we went back in for a check-up.

"Her lungs were still clear, but now it had spread to her brain. Cancer always travels up.

"Brain cancer, ask anyone, they'll tell you it's the most painful. My dad died from brain cancer. A plate he got in his head from World War One.

"So, back to the chemo. But this time, maybe we didn't have the same optimism. That second series, a year after the first, there was a tall, stout man who used to get his chemo the same time she did. We'd see him in the waiting room every day, just about. While he'd wait to be called in, he'd pull different-colored balloons out of his side pockets, dropping some on the carpet. Blow them up for everyone, as gifts. No one really wanted the balloons. What are you supposed to do with a balloon in a doctor's waiting room? Most people would just put their balloon on the stack of complimentary magazines. One morning, Liz leaned against my shoulder and whispered, He's terrified. Never found out what happened to him.

"Towards the end, she got weaker and weaker. She always handled the bills. I guess that's one of the first things a woman takes over, finding out where the money's going, but now, she taught me how to do them. Not that it was that hard to learn, but the fact I'd be doing them now, after nearly a half century, was her way of saying, I'm not going to be here much longer."

MacDonald snapped his head away for a moment, jaw clenched. Tilda watched his profile compose itself. Stay dry-eyed.

"She had to be on oxygen all the time. Big, silver cylinder on wheels we could roll across the carpets and wooden floors of our home wherever she went. Two clear plastic tubes leading from the tank to a contraption strapped across her face, so the two tube endings stayed in place up inside her nostrils.

"I moved our bed down to the first floor. Put it in the kitchen, so we could talk while I made dinner. Not that she ate much, anymore. She mostly slept. I can't tell you how many hours I spent sitting by her bed, watching her sleep, hearing shirt buttons hit against the inside drum of the dryer.

"She died in the kitchen. I went to the front door to answer the bell. It was the food delivery kids. We had all our household goods home-delivered at that point. I wasn't gone long, it was just a couple of minutes, maybe not even that, but when I shut the door, the Hospice nurse was already running down the hall towards me. She's gone."

His voice got higher. "I knew immediately what she meant, but I kept holding onto a hope that I had misunderstood. But I saw, when I hurried into our kitchen, her small body motionless across the sheet…she was gone."

His blue eyes looked directly into Tilda's. "I believe in life after death. Am I foolish?"

She glanced down at her large hands. "I've seen enough ghosts to know it's true. We're not dirt."

"But when someone dies, isn't her ghost supposed to come back from the other side, at least once, to say goodbye?"

Tilda put out her cigarette, feeling the crushed orange heat in her fingernails. "People say, my spouse died, my child died, my parent, my best friend died, and the next night, there they were, at the foot of my bed, real and wavery as a jellyfish."

MacDonald jutted his jaw. "It's been six months!" He gave a self-deprecating smile, hiding his pain behind humor. "It's starting to feel like an insult." His smile faded. "She was my wife. We loved each other. Why hasn't her ghost appeared?"

Tilda realized she was going to be able to cash the check, after all. "We need to go to the house where she died. The house always holds the answer."

Chatterton was ten miles outside town. Tilda followed behind MacDonald down the mud-rutted roads.

She was somewhat prepared by what MacDonald had told her over the phone two weeks ago when he first contacted her. But still, it was the strangest house she had ever seen. And she had seen a lot of strange houses.

She got out of her pick-up, slammed the door behind her. Walked down the wide green lawn to the side of the house, staring up at it, trying to figure out in her mind how it worked.

In front of her was a three-story home in a contemporary style. Red brick façade, big windows reflecting trees and sky, some nice architectural flourishes along the balconies and roofline. By itself, a fairly normal house commissioned by someone with a comfortable amount of money.

The rear of the house though was pressed against the front façade of a much larger home, a white stone mansion that rose higher and stretched wider than the contemporary in front.

As she walked closer across the grass, she realized the contemporary wasn't just built against the mansion—its red brick rear was actually built into the white stone front of the mansion, protruding into the mansion's large front foyer, as if the smaller contemporary had been snapped onto the much larger mansion.

Three mules were tied to stakes at the side of the contemporary. Dipping their large doll heads down, picking up from the grass and gulping, with their buck teeth, carrots.

"It was hard to explain over the phone."

"So how many houses are there?"

He gave a lopsided shrug, attaché case still in his left hand. "I don't know. I don't think anyone in the family did." MacDonald looked off, blue eyes lost somewhere behind his black-framed glasses. "Her father told me once there were two hundred and ninety three houses all together. The family had an enormous amount of wealth. This was the family estate. Each time they wanted to change where they lived, they didn't remodel their existing home, they just built a new one in front of it. Some generations built fifteen or more houses over the course of their lifetime. Multiply that by four centuries, and you have a series of homes connected to each other, front to back, that stretch deep, deep into the woods. I have no idea how many miles back they go. It's a centipede house."

Tilda, at her basketball height, looked down the receding depth of the houses' sides. "Couldn't you just travel outside the houses to get to the original house?"

MacDonald shook his head. "There's dense swamp half a mile in. No way to traverse it."

"How deep into the houses have you been?"

MacDonald swatted at a dragonfly buzzing in front of his face. "Maybe twenty houses. As you go farther into the depth, there's more damage from the weather, and of course decades of neglect. Centuries of neglect. Swamp critters have managed to get inside. That's why I asked you to bring a shotgun. You did, didn't you?"

Tilda nodded. "I have everything we need. Enough food and water for several weeks, flashlights, rope, axes in case we have to chop through any collapsed sections, two sleeping bags, two tents, plenty of sterno, some knives and chainsaws, a pair of shotguns, and a sidearm. I assume you've handled firearms?"

He swatted with the back of his hand at the irritating orbit. "More times than I care to remember. So how's this work?"

"In my experience, your wife is feeling enormous guilt because she died without saying goodbye to you. In those circumstances, the ghost often loses track of what she's supposed to do next. She just focuses on the 'mistake' of dying without you."

MacDonald looked stricken. He must have seen a lot of his wife suffering while she was in the end stages. He didn't want to think of his wife still suffering, after death. "So what do we have to do, as a practical matter, to end her suffering?"

"Ghosts go through three stages. First stage, they come to grips with the fact they're dead. You can imagine how confusing that is. Like looking in the mirror and seeing an elephant. That's me, now? Second stage, they understand. That's when they visit loved ones. They've passed to the other side, but they come back. At first, maybe it's to help themselves accept. Soon enough, it's to help the loved one. Remind them how good life can be. Third stage, usually seven years after their death, they flow upwards. No more visits. Until the loved one dies, and they're reunited.

"Chances are, your wife, like most ghosts who have guilt, hid somewhere in the home you shared. Normally, they're not that difficult to find. Just look at a place farthest from household activity. The attic, the cellar. In this case, her ghost may have wandered miles back into these connected houses. Hopefully not. But that's why we need to journey into the houses, to locate her ghost."

She looked up at the position of the sun. "What we should do, if you're ready, is load up the mules with our supplies, then try to get at least a few houses in today."

Transferring all the supplies from the back of her pick-up to the mules, and securing them in place, took several hours. By the time they were ready to go in through the front door of the contemporary, it was close to dusk. She could hear that most Southern of sounds, the thrum of cicadas in the darkening tree tops.

As MacDonald held the walnut and stained glass front door of the contemporary open, Tilda trooped the three mules through. Slapped their haunches to get them to march straight from the foyer into the high-ceilinged dining room, and past that, into the large kitchen jigsawed with granite counters, stainless steel appliances, cherry wood cabinets. The bed Liz had lived and died in had apparently been removed.

Before they started on their journey, both had switched to sensible shoes. MacDonald walked in blue sneakers, which made him look younger than ninety something, over to the built-in wine cabinet. "Did you think to bring alcohol?"

Tilda filled one of the stainless steel kitchen sinks with water, stepping back so the mules could quench their thirst. She was hoping some of the plumbing would still hold up, fifty or sixty houses in, so they wouldn't have to share their water with the mules. "Few cartons of cigarettes, but no alcohol. Wasn't sure how you'd feel about that."

MacDonald stood alongside one of the gulping mules, cramming tall bottles of red and white wine down into their packs. "Might as well bring all our vices along."

"Somehow I didn't take you for a drinking man."

"I saw all kinds of men get green with demons growing up during the Great Depression. I spent a lifetime drinking water and milk. After Liz died, I figured, why not? I'm too old to do any real damage. I don't drink hard liquor though. Whiskey's not my friend."

Tilda looked around the large kitchen. "If you have anything we could eat for dinner in one of these refrigerators, that'd help. All the provisions I have are canned."

Moving around the kitchen like he must have for all the years he and his wife lived in the contemporary, he made them four ham sandwiches. They ate two of them in the kitchen, stepping away from the mules, who had defecated on the cherry wood floor after drinking all that water. The other two sandwiches MacDonald put in a zip-lock plastic bag with an ice pack, to have later in the evening.

Around eight o'clock, they passed through the back of the contemporary into the foyer of the white stone mansion.

The foyer was four stories high, cathedral ceiling made of marble.

Tilda slapped at the mules to keep them moving forward, lighting a cigarette. She craned her neck back to look up at the concave ceiling. "Did your in-laws build this?"

MacDonald shook his head. "We did. Liz and me. There was this familial one-upmanship with the Berlins, generation to generation. My house is going to be bigger and better than your house. The houses sometimes did get bigger, but they didn't really get better. Those circular support columns under the second story wraparound balconies? They look like old, veined marble, but they're really faux marble. Further into the houses, a couple of days from here, you'll see real marble columns, like they used to have in churches."

They traveled four houses in their first day. Decided to camp in that mansion's library, the size of some modern homes. The gleaming black piano at one end of the library was still in tune. Tilda played a few bars from

Waldstein, then stopped, it occurring to her MacDonald might think she was showing off.

The tall, narrow windows in the library were dark.

They ate their remaining ham sandwiches in front of the library's main fireplace, which they didn't bother to light. MacDonald uncorked a bottle of wine. He had forgotten to pack wineglasses. Tilda got out a pair of white Styrofoam cups.

Once they were finished with the meal, they both realized how tired they were. Tilda tethered the three mules to the strong black legs of the piano.

The tents weren't needed yet, so Tilda unpacked the sleeping bags. She and MacDonald slept ten feet apart, on the library's floor.

Every once in a while during the night, rolling over in the canvas smell of her sleeping bag, Tilda could hear one or another of the mules braying.

She woke up the following morning to the smell of strong coffee.

MacDonald had found one of the cans of coffee, and the metal coffee pot. He dumped in enough grounds, then filled the pot with water from a nearby bathroom with gold fixtures. While Tilda slept, MacDonald started a fire in a small corner of the massive main fireplace, hanging the pot above the red and yellow flames.

"May I say that I'm impressed?"

MacDonald grunted, hiding his pride. The heat from the white Styrofoam cup, rising as he sipped, steamed his black-framed glasses. He took them off, wiping the twin lenses on the front of his shirt, rippling the small white buttons. "I want you to know a little bit about her. Since you're on this journey with me."

"Okay."

He lifted his left haunch. Clumsily pulled out of his hip pocket a doubled-over black wallet that looked like it was older than Tilda. "Here's a picture I took of her about half a century ago. Happier times."

Tilda leaned sideways to take the photo.

It was in color. The picture wasn't meant to be a sexy pose, but it was sexy because she was in it. Lying on her stomach on green, green grass from fifty years ago. White slacks, calves raised behind her, crossed at the ankles. Red high heels. Red and white checked blouse. Just one button undone, at the top. Dark hair to her shoulders. Face cradled in her palms, dark eyebrows, dark eyes looking up at the camera. An open, girl next door face, confident and sensual.

"I got lucky."

"Any kids?"

MacDonald kissed the photo, carefully slid it back into the wallet. "I sired six children with Liz. Three of them are in Heaven. One of our boys died in Vietnam. The other son died with a needle in his arm. The daughter died from liver complications."

After their coffee they decided to move on.

Getting the mules to trundle the weight of their packs room to room, house to house, became routine. MacDonald helped quite a bit, getting on the side of the sour-smelling animals opposite Tilda. If the animals tried to stray off the straight path, he'd slap their large profiles.

By mid-day they made it through another dozen houses.

They stopped in a kitchen, this one larger than where they ate the night before, but of course not as modern. Tilda test-opened the refrigerator. Inside, the wire racks lit up. Good. They still had electricity.

"Do you remember any of this from the time you and Liz made your journey inside?"

"I do remember these avocado appliances. We probably went another five or ten houses deeper inside."

Flipping open the blue cabinet doors under the counters, Tilda found an aluminum pot with a blackened bottom. Washed it out in the sink. Put it on one of the stove's circular electric coils. Switched on the heat, watching the black coils turn orange.

"What are we having for lunch?"

"Thought we'd go with a big can of Campbell's Chicken Noodle Soup. And I have a box of Saltines." She noticed a floor to ceiling break in the side wall of the kitchen. Walked over while the yellow soup heated.

Tree branches crowded the rupture. Mud had been tracked in, sideways slides across the kitchen's black and white floor tiles. "Something fair-sized broke into the house here. Could have been a year ago. Could have been last night. I only have the one side arm, but you see where the rifles are sticking up out of the mules' packs, right? Both rifles are loaded. Just in case."

They ate standing up.

Using his thumbs, MacDonald broke more Saltines into his bowl of soup. "So how do we know when we're near?"

"There'll be signs. Birds, mostly. Their nests. Once we get deep enough inside, and I get a sense of getting near to her ghost, I'll break out my secret weapon."

"Does that have anything to do with the cardboard box on that mule there that has all those tiny scrabbling noises inside?"

"Matter of fact."

"And what's making all those scrabbling sounds?"

"Cockroaches."

MacDonald stopped chewing on a Saltine. Started chewing again. "Serious?"

"Cockroaches scream when a ghost is near."

"Say that again?"

"It's not a very loud scream, but when you put thousands of them together in a confined space like I have, their collective scream is deafening. We may have to use hand signals at that point to communicate."

MacDonald rested his lower back against the edge of a counter. "I was going to say, I've seen a lot of cockroaches but I never heard one scream, then I realized you'd just say, That's because there weren't any ghosts near. Are they just loose in that carton?"

"I have them in a cage. Made out of a wood frame with window screening on all six sides. The mesh is fine enough they can't squeeze through the small squares. Plus the cockroaches themselves are quite large."

"Liz never liked them. Course, I wasn't too fond of them myself. Before she'd cook any meal, I'd have to slide open the cutlery drawers for her, to make sure there wasn't one scurrying over the knives and forks. Sometimes, there would be, and I'd have to pull out all the drawers, place them on the kitchen floor to find out where it was hiding behind the shelves."

"I'm not a fan myself. But I have to work with them, so I try to make my peace. They are life. Killing a cockroach is killing an extremely tiny part of God."

MacDonald set his jaw. "Honestly, I've never speculated about that. I see a cockroach, I kill it. With a fly swatter. Easiest way to do it."

"Cockroaches are smart. That's why we fear them. An ant or a beetle, you spot one, you can just step on it at your leisure. You see them, but they don't see you. But cockroaches, they're the only insect that runs away from us. They perceive our presence."

The next day, they pushed deeper into the houses, trying to get through twenty by lunch. The mules, used by now to the routine, cooperated.

They stopped in the ruins of a ballroom, half its tall ceiling lying on the marble floor. The far exit to the ballroom was blocked by criss-crossing tree limbs.

They ate tuna fish sandwiches while sitting on the floor, Tilda unscrewing the blue top off a jar of mayonnaise, a small, sample-size jar, since they'd have to throw it out once it was opened.

After eating, she got one of the chainsaws going, little puffs of gray exhaust rising from the rear like smoke signals. Walking over with its loud vibration hanging from her right hand, she placed the spinning chain against the nearest tree branch blocking the exit to the ballroom. Let the weight of the chainsaw carry the rapid teeth down into the wood, sawdust spraying up, whine of the chainsaw rising as the teeth spun down through the limb.

Stepping back, she let the severed limb fall. The asymmetry of its branches caused it to shift on the marble floor, as if it were still alive.

Looking over her shoulder at MacDonald, she shouted above the noise of the chainsaw. "If you could move each limb to the side so I don't trip over it and have a very painful accident, I'd be much obliged."

Working together, they cut a passageway through the mess of limbs in an hour.

Tilda opened her mouth to say something. Instead, dropped the chainsaw on the floor, letting it spin around, still alive. Pulled her side arm. Aimed and shot in front of her.

Ran through the passage, poked her head in a nearby bathroom, reared her head back, fired into the bathroom five more times.

MacDonald crept through the carved-out tunnel, past the thick white cuts of tree branches, a rifle from the mule pack in his hands. His face was flushed.

Tilda had her revolver flipped open, thumbing fresh bullets into the cylinder. "It's dead."

MacDonald peered into the Art Deco bathroom. The alligator had collapsed with its spine against the tiles of the rear wall, exposing its pearl underside. Long jade tail in the bathtub, one front claw in the bathroom sink, scrabbling gray streaks in the white porcelain. Its triangular head rested against the medicine cabinet's circles of shattered mirror.

Blood leaking from six small holes.

Tilda dipped down her right hand until she had the rhythm right, then hoisted up the spinning chainsaw. "You know how good alligator tail is. I could saw off the best part of the tail, wrap it in that shower curtain, and we'd have fresh meat tonight. You game?"

MacDonald gave an amused shrug. "Okay. Sure."

Tilda stepped into the bathroom with her chainsaw, poking its round tip at the alligator's scaly stomach, just to be sure. Positioned the buzz of the saw above the thickest part of the tail, watery pink blood spraying up onto the geometry of the shower stall's white tiles, the plastic curtain's cartoons of smiling goldfish.

They built a fire that night in the middle of a downstairs bedroom.

MacDonald, cradling a shotgun across his forearm, foraged outside, finding some wild thyme, a huge bush of cultivated oregano that must have been from a garden planted a century ago, and some swamp onions.

Tilda sat cross-legged on the floor near the fire, using a large Bowie knife to patiently carve chunks of alligator meat away from the bone of the tail, and its tough skin. "I have plenty of salt. By any chance are those pink peppercorns growing over by the bureau?"

They could have made stock from the tail bones, and that would have been nice, but it would have taken too long. Instead, Tilda opened a couple of cans of Campbell's Chicken and Rice soup, strained out the rice for a side dish. Put a large pot on the fire, letting its bottom get hot, then made a roux with oil and flour. Once the roux went past the stage where it smelled like popcorn, to where it was as dark as melted chocolate, she dumped in all the spices and herbs they had found. Let the roux seize up, then added the raw rectangular crocodile pieces. Stirred them around in the rising smoke. Everything seared, she poured in the soup liquid, plus a few cans of water.

Once the gumbo thickened, and cooked for twenty minutes to get rid of the raw flour taste, she poured each of them a big bowl. Pulled some baguettes out of a mule bag, a bit stale after so many days, but not too much.

They ate side by side on the floor.

The mules kept wandering over.

"We probably shouldn't camp here? This part of the houses seems invaded by a lot of outside animals, and we don't want the smell of our meal to lead them to us."

MacDonald wiped a shaky forefinger across his lips. "We get bear down here, sometimes."

Tired as they were after eating such a large meal, they slapped the mules another few houses deeper, until they reached a laundry room with old-fashioned washboards lying in large tubs.

More of the rooms were ruptured this far back into the swamps, ceilings gone, walls collapsing, large paintings face-down on the floors, so instead of sleeping bags, they slept in separate pup tents.

Long after dark, Tilda woke to the sound of rain falling against the soft green slopes of her tent.

She unzipped the front, poked out her head.

Thunder and lightning, indoors.

MacDonald had his head outside his dripping tent. "Are we safe here?"

Tilda played the big yellow circle of her flashlight across the ceiling. Seemed secure enough. Baring her teeth, she shouted back. "We're safe."

It rained off and on the next three miserable days.

Their progress slowed to four or five houses a day, and even that was a struggle.

The morning of the fourth day, an inch of water across the walnut floor of the massive foyer they had just entered, the floor itself severely buckled from past floodings, they decided to take a day off.

She had no idea when this particular house had been built, but evidently it was before the general use of electricity, because there were no wall sockets, and all the lamps knocked-over around the foyer were kerosene lamps.

She didn't want to tie up the mules on the first floor, because that would keep their hooves in cold water all day, which would surely lead to diarrhea, and maybe even the trembles. One by one, she and MacDonald pulled and shoved each mule up the curved flight of stairs in the rain to the first landing, where Tilda knotted them to an oak banister. The landing was fairly dry, since the ceiling above it was still intact.

Once they had the mules tethered, the two of them grabbed some food, wine and rifles, and continued up the staircase to the second floor.

After so many days traveling through half-destroyed rooms, it was nice to find quarters untouched by the years.

They wandered down the central hallway, glancing in the different bedrooms, like home buyers.

Some still had the beds made.

"I wouldn't pull down that bedspread if I were you. You never know."

MacDonald shot his shoulders up, backed away.

One room had chairs lined up around the bed, like the bed was a dining room table.

Halfway down this section of the second floor was a large, open space that had evidently been a Florida room, if that term was used back then. Outer wall filled with large square windows to let in the sunshine, several skylights above them.

Lots of pots around the space, ceramic and clay, still holding dirt. But whatever plant was once growing within their circular rims had long ago shriveled and blown away.

They sat on a striped pink and white settee facing the windows. From this height, they could see black clouds, distant lightning strikes, trees swaying.

The yellow appearance, disappearance of fireflies floated in the room's air, circling below the tall ceiling.

MacDonald, placing the round bottom of a bottle of pinot noir between his bluejeaned knees, twisted down the metal pig's tail screw into the cork. Yanked up.

They drank out of white Styrofoam cups.

Leaning forward on the settee, holding his half-full cup not too far from his lips, MacDonald jerked his jaw at Tilda. "So, are white Styrofoam cups really cheap where you live? You actually smiled!"

Tilda's mop of blonde hair was even more tangled atop her head. MacDonald never saw her brush it. "I guess they're cheap just about everywhere. I bought these at Wal-Mart."

MacDonald regarded her as she took another deep swallow of her wine. "What's your story? Are you married? Do you have a regular job?"

This conversation usually happened at some point. She knew that after so many days, the older man was beginning to wonder if Tilda was, in fact, legitimate.

She looked down at her bony hands. "I've lived by myself since I was fourteen."

"What about your family?"

"My daddy was a real so-and-so. I was always tall, so soon as I could, I lied about my age and got a job working on an Alabama shrimp boat."

"Do you still do that?"

"No. I have a small construction firm. We do a lot of tear-downs and renovations."

"I don't know what you call it. A gift? Have you always had this gift?"

"I don't call it a gift, but yeah. When I was real small, I thought everybody had it." Looking off, she rubbed one hand atop the other. "Took me a while to realize I was the only one."

He focused on her albino eyelashes. "In the world?"

Shook her head. "But where I grew up. Later on, I met other people like me. We meet, occasionally, in different motels across America." She looked across at MacDonald's elderly face. "You understand, or maybe you don't, this is gonna go where it goes?"

"Yeah. I guess." MacDonald gave an uncomfortable laugh. Tried to cover it up by assuming a comical prosecutorial tone. "What exactly does that mean, Ms. Tilda, that it's going to go where it goes?"

"Most times, people like me see what a person wants before they see it. That's what I meant."

MacDonald scratched the side of his neck. "Like a lot of men, I lived my life knowing no girl could ever beat me up. But you could probably beat me up."

"We're deep enough inside these houses we could probably do a test to make sure we're on the right track. Would you like to do that?"

She could see she caught the older man off-guard. "Well, yeah, sure." He gave a nervous laugh. "What kind of test exactly?"

69

"I have it here in my pocket." She pulled out two squares of fabric, plus a zip-lock bag filled with fur.

MacDonald crossed his arms. "Are we going to see ectoplasm?"

"Huh? No." Tilda shook the fur out of the baggie onto the pink and white stripes on the settee beside her, like shaking out marijuana. Distracted as she divided the fur into two puffy piles she said, "Ectoplasm only occurs during séances. The ectoplasm itself? It's made out of fingernails. Fingernails are the most psychic part of a person's body. Except it's soft, like fungus. You can learn a lot by tasting it."

MacDonald's voice was quiet. "What's it taste like?"

She slanted her bony face, as if she had never before been asked that. Shoulders lowering, thinking about the question. Those albino eyelashes, and floating within, blue irises, black pupils. "Slightly chemical. Similar to grape leaves. It's an acquired taste."

Tilda unfolded the two squares of fabric. Animal prints. She handed one over. A cheetah print.

Spreading the square in his hand, MacDonald realized it was a faux print. "It's not important to use real animal skins?"

"It's not about the skin. It's about the pattern."

Tilda smoothed her own faux print, a tiger's, across her drawn together knees. Watching, MacDonald did the same with his print. Tilda handed him one of the two piles of fur.

"This is cat fur, isn't it?"

"Yeah. What you need to do now is rub the cat fur lightly over the animal print, so the fur covers some of the print, but not all of it."

"Like this?"

"What we're going to do now is bring our face down close to the print, try to unfocus our eyes, and start randomly moving the fur over the pattern. So we're concealing parts of the pattern, revealing other parts. We're going to just keep on doing that, looking at what's being exposed and covered, but trying to keep our eyes unfocused. What we're trying to do is self-hallucinate."

"And what will that accomplish?"

"After you feel like you can't see straight, you can only see these changing arrangements of fur on the print, I want you to look up, keeping your eyes unfocused. Don't look up until you're absolutely certain your eyes are seeing double. Don't be afraid by what you may see."

MacDonald ducked his head to himself, a little overwhelmed. "Okay. I guess."

They both leaned forward over their laps, staring down as they casually moved the cat fur over the patterns of the jungle cats, trying to unfocus their eyes. Tilda raised her head first, after a minute.

Five minutes later, MacDonald raised his head, black pupils dilated. He let out a back of the throat moan.

"Tell me what you see."

"I'm scared, Tilda."

"That's okay. Do not focus your eyes. Just tell me what you see."

His voice went up high. Came out as an old man's voice. "I see what looks like three hyenas, standing upright on their hind legs, their faces are really, really ugly, especially with their forward snouts. They're shaking their shoulders in unison as they step unsteadily closer towards me. Tilda, I'm about to climb over the back of this settee."

"That's okay. Focus your eyes."

He dipped his head, rubbing his eyes with the heels of his palms.

Looked up, scared.

Reassured.

"They're gone."

"That's good." Tilda rubbed her own eyes. "Those are siliths. They always appear in threes, and they always synchronize their movements. I don't know what their purpose is. They're not ghosts. They're something else."

"But will they harm Liz?"

"They don't interact with the dead. Or the living. I don't know what they interact with. But that means we're getting closer to your wife's ghost. Siliths hang out near the same psychic space as ghosts, like it's a watering hole."

"Are they still here? Even though I don't see them since my eyes focused?" He looked over his shoulder.

"Yeah. But they can't hurt you. I went to a dentist once, and he scraped my front teeth, carried his dental pic into another room where there was a microscope. Rubbed his pic on a glass slide, then asked me to look down into the microscope. I saw all kinds of things floating around, wriggling under that bright white illumination. He expected me to freak out, I could tell, as he no doubt had gotten other people to freak out, probably for the amusement of his dental assistant, who was leaning in the doorway, but I didn't freak out. I just accepted there's all these invisible life forms all around us. And death forms too."

The next day the rain let up, so they clomped the mules down from the stair landing and continued deeper into the houses.

Around noon Tilda got the mules to stop their slow, dumb-eyed forward march.

MacDonald watched her go over to a bookcase against one of the mahogany walls. Bouncing her right foot on the first shelf of the bookcase, testing the strength of the shelf, she climbed her tall body up the shelves ladder-style, books falling. At the top, she reached over the decorative scalloped border of the bookcase, retrieving something about the size of a hat.

Holding the object in her right hand, she balanced herself down the shelves, using her two feet and left hand to keep from falling.

She brought it over.

As she carried it closer, MacDonald realized it wasn't a hat. It was a bird's nest.

Tilda passed it to his two palms.

Looking down at what was cradled in his hands, it looked like a regular bird's nest to him, except the twigs were oddly shaped.

"Look closer."

"Oh! It's not twigs. Is it bones?"

Tilda nodded.

Frail bones wrapped around each other in a circular weave to form the nest. At one part of the weave, towards the bottom, MacDonald saw what looked like a small pelvis bone. As if from a squirrel.

"Is this a sign?"

"Your wife's ghost is near. These nests are made by bone birds. That's what most people call them. There's a much longer, Native American word for the birds, but it's hard to translate."

"Obviously, they're called bone birds because they build their nests out of bones?"

"They build their nests out of bones, but not bones they find on the forest floor. They attack other animals, tear the fur and flesh off them while the animals are still alive, with their beaks and talons, then carry the sticky red bones up to a high spot, where they weave their nests."

"Can I put this down now?"

She took it from MacDonald, rested it lopsidedly on top of a nearby blue and yellow globe of the world.

"So what do we do?"

"We're going to spend the night here, in this library. It's likely the room will get cold as your wife's ghost approaches, so it would pay us to start a fire in that fireplace. We can use all these books on the shelves for fuel. They're old, so they'll burn bright."

72

Once the fire was roaring, red and yellow behind the blue marble of the fireplace, Tilda led the older man to a sofa in front of the blaze. Sat next to him.

"She'll likely come in through that far door."

"When will that happen?"

"In order for us to see your wife's ghost, we're both going to have to believe her ghost is, in fact, in this room. That's where my cockroaches come into play. Is your love for your wife unqualified?"

MacDonald seemed surprised by the question. "God, yes."

"That's going to help. Later on. Remember when you wanted me to know a little bit about your wife? You showed me her photograph?"

MacDonald, uncertain, nodded.

"Now I want to know a little bit more about you."

The old man looked at the mules. "May I ask for what purpose?"

Tilda, so tall sitting next to MacDonald, turned her gaunt face toward the smaller man. "It'll help me. With this process. Doesn't have to be your whole life. Just your childhood."

The old man's face went inward. "Okay. I was born poor. My daddy had died, leaving behind a wife and lots of hungry mouths. In the 1930's, while the USA was in the Great Depression, I was driving on U.S. Route 25 down from Akron, trying to find work, and I stopped one evening in Corbin to load up on gas. A young man there pumped it for me and he knew just about everything about which roads were open, and especially the condition of the roads going from 25E down through the Smoky Mountains to Asheville, a great town, incidentally, and 25W through Knoxville down to Atlanta. Told me he drove those routes himself every so often to see if they were improved. This was valuable information to me, and I thanked him for it.

"He had a little place to eat next to the gas station, just a one-room shed with a dining room table in the middle of it where everybody sat, that maybe fitted fifteen people, but he got puffed-up and called it a restaurant." MacDonald smiled. But it was a tighter smile than it would have been if he were with family and friends. "Anyway, the food he served there was quite good, like maybe you'd get from a fat aunt. Lots of potatoes with nice thick gravy poured all over, plenty of cracklings, chicken with all kinds of spices and herbs they'd be dipped into before frying. Big, soft, heavy biscuits that'd get my fingers greasy just handling them. Bowls of pole beans. Cobbed corn plucked right out of the field, so sweet you'd taste the sun in those kernels. Plus he wasn't the type of man who got shy about butter. It felt like Sunday dinner no matter what day of the week it was you pulled in there.

"Well, after a while I'd hit that little place every time I was on the highway passing through Corbin, and I want to tell you, I never met a woman who cooked as good as he did."

MacDonald looked up from under his white eyebrows at Tilda. "You know who that man was?"

"Do you actually expect me to know?"

"That was Colonel Harland Sanders himself."

"Colonel Sanders? The man who founded Kentucky Fried Chicken?"

MacDonald nodded. "The one and only. And I got to sample his cooking back when he did it himself, long before some kind of corporation took over. And we all know how it is now, but back then he was always carrying a tub of chicken to a table full of tired truck drivers, offering them as many repeats of the meal they wanted, wearing all white with an undershirt underneath.

"I used to watch him haul that big deep tub from chair to chair, wondering how many chickens he had to chase to get so many drumsticks in there."

"You knew Colonel Sanders? Really?"

MacDonald was having a good time. "Old people always have one or two interesting things to say. If they decide to share." He looked out over the room. His eyes went inwards. "I was on the road a lot in those days. A lot of miles between jobs. And many days behind the wheel from sunup to sundown, staring at the white lines. So when I got out of my truck, I wasn't one to talk much. But the Colonel, maybe he sensed how far I was from home, and how often. After me catching him just quietly watching me a couple of times from the far corner, he started speaking to me each time I showed up, took to inviting me out back after my meal to listen to the crickets while we sat side by side in folding chairs. He drew me out to where I'd talk some about my concerns . And every time after we talked, he'd give me encouragement to keep on keeping on, that one of these sunny days I was gonna find what I needed on that long road.

"God bless that man. He set me on the straight course. Just like a hundred other boys back then, driving across the thousands of miles of America, crying against their steering wheel, trying to be Daddy.

"A long, long time after that, after I became successful as a salesman, I met Liz at a church group."

Tilda went over to one of the mules, its big white teeth gnawing the marble feet of a statue.

Using a pocketknife, she slit open the cardboard box filled with scrambling sounds.

Hands dipping inside, she pulled out a cube one foot square made out of window screen.

Lifted out of the cardboard, the scrabbling noises got much louder. MacDonald swallowed.

She placed the wire cube on the library's floor.

Went back to the mule. Slid a wood broom handle off the mule's pack.

The far end of the handle had holes drilled through it.

Rummaging through the mule's pack, Tilda retrieved a thick circle of heavy gauge wire, the lift out of the pack causing it to start uncoiling.

MacDonald watched as if what she was doing was the most normal thing in the world, like watching a mechanic change a tire.

Tilda threaded the wire gauge through the end of the broom handle. She raised the broom handle, with its squid's worth of hanging wire. Placed that end on top of an edge of the wire box. Tied the wires to the box, pulling tight on the wires, until she had a secure fit.

Standing, she grasped the rear of the handle. Hoisted the wire box full of live cockroaches up into the air, about waist-high, testing the knots.

MacDonald took a step back. "How many cockroaches are in there?"

"I never counted. Be kind of hard to do. I fill the box according to weight. There's four pounds of cockroaches inside this mesh. And each cockroach, big as it is, doesn't weigh that much."

She rested the box back down on the floor. Went back to the mule's pack. Took out a jar of peanut butter. Using her pocket knife, she swirled a thick curl of peanut butter onto the side of the blade. Balanced that light brown swirl over to the top of the box. Rubbed the peanut butter across the top of the screen, sideways-held knife blade grating against the hatching.

The dark mass within the box rippled over itself, in a frenzy that rose from the bottom of the box to its mesh top.

The peanut butter was gone before MacDonald could swallow twice.

"Now we wait. Her ghost will come. Because you're here. Her ghost will waft into the room like the scent of something cooking on a stove in another room. We'll know when her ghost arrives because the cockroaches will start screaming. Once they start screaming, I'll locate her ghost within this room. I'll try to make it as exact as I can. It'll be up to you to actually see her first. I can't see her until you see her. That's the way this works."

MacDonald, blinking his eyes, offered an old man's smile. "Then what?"

Tilda avoided his eyes, fussing with the box of cockroaches. "Then, you know, we'll correct things."

They sat in front of the fireplace, Tilda occasionally rising to her full basketball player height to toss a few more books on the flames. While they waited, they passed a bottle of pinot noir back and forth, neither bothering to wipe the top of the bottle clean before drinking. Every half hour or so, MacDonald bummed a cigarette from Tilda.

About two o'clock in the morning, MacDonald became aware of a background noise. Like an air conditioner hum. "What is that?"

Tilda rubbed the heels of her hands over her bony face. "That's the sound of agitated cockroaches. Whatever happens, it's gonna happen very soon. Do you have faith?"

MacDonald jerked his head up, frightened. "I want to say, I think of you as my daughter. All these talks we've had."

She got up, grabbed the end of the broomstick handle, hoisted the weight of the wire box of cockroaches up into the air. "I don't think of you as my father. This is just a job."

The scrabbling increased. The agitation of so many legs and long antennae sounded like rain, but not really.

Swinging the wire box at the end of the broom handle as though it were a divining rod, she advanced right, away from the fire. "Nope. Getting cold."

She swung the wire box to the left. The scrabbling increased. Like a tea kettle that suddenly starts whistling, the thousands of cockroaches inside the wire box began screaming, in a high-pitched rasp that held some intelligence.

Tilda swung a little more to the left. Little more to the right. The screams multiplied. She had to shout over the voices rising from thousands of yellow-black throats. "I need you over here!"

MacDonald got unsteadily to his feet. Didn't want to look inside the wire box as he passed it, but of course did. A huge, writhing mass of cockroaches pressing in fear against the back of the box, using their six legs and long antennae to push the ones in front of them further forward.

"She's there." Tilda lifted her right hand off the broom handle, the wire box lowering, pointing her index finger at the shadowy corner of the library. Most of the corner's lower shelves were empty, their books used for the fire. "Can you see her?" She quickly wrapped the fingers of her right hand back around the broom handle, lifting the wire box again, the cockroaches' screams rising, as if they were on a roller coaster.

"I…" MacDonald stared where Tilda had pointed. So after everything, what was this? A con? He didn't see anything.

Tilda shouted again over the deafening scream of the cockroaches. "Do you see her?"

"Honestly, I---" He froze. Blue eyes staring.

Liz. On her hands and knees. Backing herself into the corner. Frightened.

"I know you see her, because I see her."

He lifted his old shoulders. "I…This is too much. Why is she so afraid of me?"

Tilda tossed the wire box and its broom handle to one side, like a torch. She came up next to MacDonald. "The dead fear the living. We're too huge with life. For them, it's like being in the same room with a lion. Plus her ghost is filled with guilt over dying without you being there. This is your chance. Your only chance. If you want to make peace with her, this is the time."

MacDonald kept swallowing. "I don't know what to do, this is too intense, I--"

"Call her! Call her or regret it the rest of your life."

His lips parted. "Liz? Liz?"

The ghost put its forearms over its head, cowering.

Tilda shouted over the screams of the cockroaches. "Get down on your knees. Call to her!"

The old man went down to the carpet on shaky knees. Held his right hand out. Offering his hand to her. Now, finally, the tears down his face. Finally understanding it wasn't a con. "Liz? Can you hear me?"

Still the ghost cowered, a woman made of milk.

"You have to remember a time when all was good. A moment when the two of you were happy, and in love. Think! Think hard. She won't stay forever."

And a moment did pop into MacDonald's head. Oh, what was it? Five years ago? Maybe more? Before the diagnosis, before the quiet final evenings, the long talks in the kitchen where they worked together, gently, with some tears, to understand their marriage. They had just bought tomato plants at a local nursery. The two of them wheeling the metal cart from the register to their car in the parking lot. The sound the wheels made, passing over the uneven tar of the lot. The smell of the tall, green tomato plants jittering in the cart. Hot sun on their forearms, scalps. Sweat droplets between their eyebrows. And they were so happy!

The milk moved closer towards him.

"You have to let her be the one to approach you. Like you have to coax a cat to approach you."

MacDonald stretched his right fingers further out, moving them. "Come on, Liz. Come on."

"Whatever moment you're thinking of, remember more detail."

MacDonald sobbed.

The way the wind blew her hair out of its brushstrokes.

The calmness of her voice.

The shape of her teeth.

The milk went to him. He put his arms around the milk, sobbing, putting his arms not around his dead wife's body, because she no longer had a body, but instead putting his arms around her smell.

He held her scent close to him. Then the scent stood. He stood with it. Stared into the scent. "I love you. I love you!"

The milk rose.

Nothing in front of MacDonald but the empty corner again, the empty bookshelves, a few opened books sprawled like fat dead moths on the floor.

He let out a half year's worth of held breath. "She's free now."

"No. She's still here. She's on the ceiling."

MacDonald craned his head back.

"I don't see her."

"She doesn't want you to see her. She's still ashamed. Now you have to decide. She's stuck on earth because she believes she let you down. Eventually, she will be free, but it will take a long, long time. But you can free her ghost tonight, if you want."

Tilda drew a long, thin knife from her waist.

MacDonald took a few steps back. Looked at the exits. "By killing myself?"

"You can't commit suicide. That's forbidden. But you can allow me to kill you."

MacDonald let out a breath. Couldn't think of what to say.

"I can do a quick plunge down the side of your throat, opening up your carotid artery. The pain will be brief. You'll bleed out quickly. You'll feel light-headed, have trouble moving your hands, then you'll be dead. The freshness of your ghost, joining hers, will raise you both to Heaven. Two balloons, pink and blue, floating up around each other, into the white clouds."

MacDonald made a noise.

"This is the only way. You knew her ghost was in trouble, because it never appeared to you, despite the intense love between you. This is what you need to do to free her ghost."

She watched as MacDonald agonized. "I want more than anything for Liz to be free. But everything we've always believed is that we can't kill ourselves, or allow ourselves to be killed. That was our faith!"

"What would Liz want you to do?"

The older man sobbed helplessly. "I'd give my life for her in a moment. But I know she doesn't want that."

Tilda hefted the knife. "So what do you want to do?"

"Goddamn you! You should have told me! I can't go against what she would want!"

"So you don't agree to letting me kill you?"

The old man's eyes grew bitter. "You fuck! You tricked me! You let me get this close to helping her, knowing I couldn't go against her wishes!"

"Do you want me to kill you!"

"Goddamn it! No!"

Tilda tapped MacDonald on his left shoulder. As MacDonald's stricken face turned towards his left shoulder, Tilda slid the long, thin blade down the right side of MacDonald's neck.

The old man's chest bumped against Tilda's breasts. His eyes stared up, into Tilda's.

Tilda dipped her knees, slicing the femoral arteries inside both of MacDonald's thighs.

MacDonald sagged against Tilda's embrace, bloody teeth, old hands around Tilda's shoulders.

Tilda held the side of MacDonald's face, wrist and palm wet with blood.

She felt the warm spray of femoral blood urinate against the front of her trousers.

Steadying MacDonald's face, she watched as the blueness of his eyes paled. "You're safe. You forbade me to kill you. You have no sin. You can rise with Liz."

MacDonald looked up, dying.

Tilda lowered the body to the library floor.

Up above, on the ceiling, rich, thick cream swirled into the milk. Together, they both rose. Vacuumed up.

Tomorrow, she'd pick axe the library floor, bury MacDonald's body. Toss his attaché case atop the corpse.

There'd only be one person traveling back, so Tilda could afford to give the mules some of the bottled water.

She unscrewed the cap on a blue plastic bottle, going over to the front of the first mule. Wedged the circular tip of the bottle between the mule's gray lips, its buck teeth. The mule suckled gratefully, brown hooves clomping.

She liked that about mules. They aren't like dogs. They don't care.

GREEN WITH DEMON

"When something dies, it's dead. Why make a big deal about it? The marriage is over. And she should not be speaking to my family. I could speak to her family, tell them what a fucked-up, worthless, passive-aggressive money-eating cunt she is, but I'm trying to take the high road."

Mel tripped over the length of his green bathrobe, falling forward, elbows out, eyes widening. As his face bounced off the carpet, the cell phone jerked out of his hand.

Cursing, he rose up in the robe to his knees, crawled forward to retrieve the phone.

"Wait a second."

He got clumsily to his feet, swaying in the green folds of the robe.

"My mother has Alzheimer's. I don't need her calling my mother at her nursing home and dumping all these false allegations about me on some poor woman who doesn't even know her own name anymore." He twisted his head around, trying to figure why each step forward was pulling the robe off his shoulders, realized the terrycloth belt had wrapped around his ankle. "God damn it!" He yanked the strap free. "She was never, ever, a good fuck. Did you know that? Every time in bed she was like a deer in headlights." He screwed his face up in imitation. "Oh, well, if you want me to get in this position I suppose I could, but it is kind of uncomfortable. Can you imagine trying to fuck that? And all the time we were married, every time we got in bed together, she'd have a fucking balled-up Kleenex in her hand. What the fuck are you doing? Stop grabbing a fucking Kleenex every fucking time before we start making love."

Short black hair, middle-aged face, Mel opened his front door to get the morning paper. "And confirm the invite to Juno's party on the fifth. And get some plumber out here to fix my showerhead. Every time I take a shower, the showerhead falls off, hitting me on my head. I don't know what—"

Mel stopped talking.

Scattered across the concrete of his front patio, hundreds of tiny black balls. He stepped out cautiously in his slippers, bathrobe bending forward as he peered at the balls.

Tiny transparent wings motionless, stingers stiff. Bodies curled inwards, like cooked shrimp. Dead bees. Hundreds of them. Why would that be?

"Yeah, I'm still here."

He looked up at the white soffit of the roofline. Nothing unusual. Where did all these bees come from? Why were they dead?

Carlos' crew was mowing the front lawn.

Mel stepped out beyond the concrete patio, onto the wet green grass of early morning. Birds flying in and out of his ornamental trees, cardinals, blue jays, red-headed woodpeckers. Other crews on other lawns in this neighborhood of West Covina, across the street and down the block, shouting to each other in Spanish.

Large black pick-up truck parked by the curb, Carlos' men walking back and forth behind lawn mowers. Carlos was on a phone by the pick-up's passenger door.

Mel strode across his lawn to the truck, muttering to himself.

"Hey, Mr. Wilson." Carlos said something in Spanish to the phone, lowered it from his ear.

Mel elbowed himself up from the damp lawn, spitting out newly-mown grass blades, swearing. Yanked the length of his robe up to his knees, as he stood. Held the hem at his knees, walking the rest of the distance to Carlos. "Did you see all the dead bees on my patio?"

"No, Mr. Wilson. I sure didn't."

"Would you take a look at them?" Mel started back across the lawn, slanting his bathrobed body towards the porch, looking at Carlos to follow him, which of course Carlos did.

"Oh my goodness, that is certainly a lot of dead bees."

"Have you ever encountered anything like this before?"

"Honestly, I have not, Mr. Wilson." Carlos tiredly raised himself up to full height. "But I will have my men use a leaf-blower to roll all of them off your patio, before we leave. Your concrete will be spotless."

"Where are they coming from?"

Carlos turned around as the background buzz of the mowers died, to confirm his men were finished mowing. "I don't know, sir."

"And of course this is the master bedroom, as you can tell by its size, and the coffered ceiling, where the Sheik of Araby has no pants on."

The husband, in a black t-shirt, short and stout with gym muscles, looked around at the walls. "Is there a flat screen TV that comes down from the ceiling?"

"Even better." Mel, who didn't have the same perfectly-sculpted body, but did have a solid frame that made him look like someone who would win most bar fights, picked up the long black remote from the bedside table. Aimed it at the wall across from the bed's walnut footboard. The knuckle of his thumb went down as he depressed a blue button.

A large, rectangular TV rose noiselessly from the floor, to eye level. "Cool, huh? Just like the Radio City Music Hall stage at Christmas. Great to have something in a bedroom you can rely on to rise when you need it. Right, Mrs. Littlefield?"

The blonde wife, taller than her husband, went over to the sliding glass doors leading out to the balcony. Great ass, but the face looked old. Too many years of wearing too much makeup, and boozing. Turned back to her husband with a mournful announcement. "You can't see the ocean."

"Well, we're a few miles from the ocean, but you can smell it." Mel sucked breath in through his nostrils, tilting his head back, smile spreading across his lips.

The wife's worn face, lonely face, looked dubious.

"Give it a try! I can smell the salt, the rawness. And that's what counts, healthwise. As long as you can smell the ocean, you're getting all the beneficial medical effects of living near the ocean. It'll clear out your lungs, and this air is great when you're working out in your own gym. Can you smell it, Tony?"

The husband, holding his arms away from his sides, as if his forearms were as big as lobster claws, sniffed. "I don't know."

"Speaking of the ocean, let me tell you this joke. I'll clean it up. This guy and his dog go sailing one day. A big storm rolls in. I have to take this."

Mel's cell phone continued playing the opening bars of "When You're Smiling."

Raised his right index finger. "Won't take but a moment."

He walked across the bedroom to the glass doors, slid them open, went out on the balcony. Reached behind him to slide the doors closed.

Outside, on the balcony, smog, palm trees, Spanish tile roofs, empty driveways.

"What is it?"

Vickie exhaled into the phone. "Why is it so hard to get in touch with you?"

"Well, you're in touch with me now. What do you want?"

"What do I want, Mel? Well, it would have been nice to have a caring husband who was supportive of my career."

"Didn't happen. So why are you calling me? And why are you calling my mother, who has Alzheimer's, and my kid sister, who wants nothing to do with you?"

"It's just so sad, Mel. You're so sad. You really are."

"Well, fuck you too. What's this call about?"

Vickie sighed over the connection. "I know we agreed you would get the mansion if you paid me the three million dollars, but more and more I'm thinking, why should I be put out of my home? How cold is that, to evict your wife from her home?"

"I didn't evict you. You left. If you want the house you can have it, but then you don't get the three million."

"Hardly seems fair. I contributed to our two years together. Why shouldn't I get my fair share of the rewards? Michael would have never taken this tact."

"Well, Michael is dead. And he dumped you before he died. So I don't see why you're bringing your ex-husband into this."

"That was a real man. Not only a physician—"

"A chiropractor. Not the same thing."

"— but a gourmet cook."

"He bought a bunch of fucking truffles. That made him a gourmet? Maybe I'll buy a truffle, and get a James Beard award."

"I guess he was the only true love of my life. Especially after you had so much trouble performing in Paris on our honeymoon. I remember at the time wondering if you were a closeted homosexual. Since you could only get…I don't know. Wobbly? Is that a word?"

"I'm showing a house. I can't talk to you now."

"Be as sad a little man as you want to be, Melvin. Anyway, just wanted to call to let you know if you try to get in touch with me the next few days, I'll be on vacation with my girlfriends in Cancun. Woo hoo!"

"Why wouldn't I be able to get in touch with you? They have cell phone service in Mexico."

"Oh, and why else was I calling you? Oh, that's right! I've instructed my lawyers to subpoena your mother for a deposition."

Mel turned around on the balcony in tight, angry circles. "What?"

"Yeah, I'm going to have your mom testify at my attorneys' office. In downtown Los Angeles. I hate that downtown L.A. is so busy and noisy and potentially confusing for someone in your mother's fragile mental state, but I have a right to protect my interests. She was witness to a lot of your outbursts whenever we'd visit her in the nursing home. I still can't deal with how furious you got that time I asked one of the nurses if they could get me some coffee."

86

"My mother has Alzheimer's. She doesn't remember shit."

Vickie kept up her fake cheerful voice. "Oh, well. We'll see." Her voice got serious. Quiet. "And Mel, I will never, ever forgive you for—"

"You cunt. You worthless piece of—"

" La la la la la. I can't hear you! Well, gotta get packing for Cancun now. Woo hoo!"

That's the thing about a cell phone. You can't slam it down in anger. All you can do is press a little button to disconnect the call.

He punched his fist against the balcony railing.

Slid the glass doors open with his other, uninjured hand.

Silence and open doorways. The Littlefields were gone.

Mel pulled out of his garage in his bottle green Jaguar.

On a hunch, got out the driver's side door. Let the car throb, deep breaths of a big cat, while he walked across the windowed front of his home, pleased he couldn't see inside any of the windows, to his front door.

More dead bees on his front patio.

Hundreds of them.

"Look at you! A little gray hair never hurt anyone."

Mel hugged Juno back. Told himself to stay pleasant. "Yeah, if you had any idea the hell I'm going through with this divorce, you would be fucking stunned my hair isn't as white as Colonel Sanders."

Juno shimmered her long black hair away from her tight face, her roasted eggplant breath. "Well, at least you're back on the market."

"I'd love to be back on your market."

"Mingle!" Juno brought her fingertips together over her head as if they held finger cymbals. "Shake off that married man reticence. It's okay to touch single girls on their shoulders again. Rejoice!"

Juno abandoned him, swimming off into the crowd of shoulders in her living room.

A tall young male, blonde hair tucked behind his perfect ears, slid over to Mel's side. His green eyes teased. "You look like you need a cold drink in that mitt."

Mel didn't look at him. "I'll have a Manhattan. Make it a double. Whiskey, not brandy."

While Mel was still glancing around to decide what conversational group to stand on the outskirts of, until he had earned the right to contribute a comment himself, the tall blonde server returned, holding out the glass. "I took a sip, since it was overflowing. I hope you don't mind. I'm Derek, by the way."

"Thanks, Derek. I'm gonna need some more of these, so please keep an eye on me."

Mel waded into a group by the fireplace talking about communications with the dead.

He started off just standing a little outside the group, listening. Then he began nodding at what people said, grunting agreement. After five minutes, he laughed out loud at one person's comment. The others turned towards him, joining in the laugh. He raised his black eyebrows. "Do you mind if I ask a question?"

The man who had been speaking, an art history professor from Jordan, who looked like he hadn't bothered to shave for the party, shook his head. "Let's hear from you."

"I'm getting like, hundreds of dead bees outside my front doorway every day. Does that mean anything to any of you? Does it have anything to do with the dead?"

The Jordanian professor seemed disappointed. "Honestly? For me? It means nothing."

The others in the group, taking the professor's lead, shook their heads. Turned their backs, continued talking, in even lower voices, about pulling 35mm film out of its spools, laying the dark brown strips across living room carpets, to see if anything showed up on the strips overnight. Mel no longer existed.

He drifted away from the group, looking around angrily for Derek, who was actually watching Mel from across the crowd. Mel held up his glass, ice still blocky inside, but no more whiskey. Shook the glass as if it were a bell.

Derek weaved his way past party-goers' spines with another double. "Struck out?"

"Once I started talking to them, I realized they were a bunch of God damn fakes."

"In the midst of a painful divorce?"

Mel chose not to answer.

"I can tell by the suppressed anger. This is probably not the best venue? If you do get a woman to go home with you here, it's going to be like eating a pickle. You should go to a nightclub. Don't be too much of an asshole, and you can go home with a Big Mac and fries, a bunch of ketchup packets in the bottom of the bag."

"I don't like nightclubs. Everyone thinks they look sexy while they're dancing. Have you ever heard anything, at parties, about people who have hundreds of dead bees outside their front door?"

"That is so absolutely gross. Dead bees? Hundreds? Did you spray an insecticide? Do you know that's a real problem now, so many bees dropping dead? It may affect crop production."

"This isn't about insecticide. And at this point in my life, crop production is really low on my list of things to worry about. Maybe even lower than dolphins getting accidently caught in nets meant for tuna."

"I'll ask around. Shouldn't be a problem. This is Hollywood. People are incredibly wealthy. Everyone loves talking about spiritualism. Do you want me to just automatically come around with a fresh double every twenty minutes, judging by your drinking rate?"

"That would be grand and glorious."

Mel positioned his body above the toilet in one of the downstairs bathrooms, face numb, right hand holding his cock away from his opened zipper, desperate to make sure he didn't urinate on the front of his pants.

Like a lot of times drinking, he hadn't had to use the bathroom the first two hours, but now had to go every ten minutes.

After wiping the head of his slack cock with a square of white toilet paper, to absorb any moisture still beaded on the slit, he zipped up. Turned around in the small bathroom, unlocked the white door.

Noise, sweat, smoke.

A short Mexican woman with thick eyebrows reached up her brown hand, waved it in front of his wet face. "Are you the guy who found hundreds of dead bees in his swimming pool?

"Not in my swimming pool, but yeah."

She looked up at his drowned eyes. "I had the same problem! It turned out a ghost was trying to leave my home. The bees were sacrificing themselves to keep the ghost inside."

Mel reached his left hand behind him, to steady his upright self against the wall. "Why would bees do that?"

The short Mexican woman sucked in breath. "I don't know! But does it really matter?"

Mel felt too much tingling in his head. Why did he ever drink more than three Manhattans? How many Manhattans did he drink?

"There is a good man, a man from Ireland, who can take care of your problem. I've written down his name and telephone number. Here it is."

Mel looked down, head spinning, at the white piece of paper she held out.

"Put it in your pocket. When you wake up tomorrow, and have had some coffee, and a decent breakfast, with lots of proteins, call him. He may be able to solve this problem of yours."

He had houses to show the next day, a closing to go to that afternoon, and an open house he had to host the day after that, and he still hadn't bought the cheese and fruit for the showing, so he didn't call the number until Sunday morning.

Mel used a silver spoon to dump glistening blueberry jam on the split halves of his hot, buttered English muffin. He'd eat once the phone conversation was over, as a reward. Took another relaxed sip of his coffee, which spilled all over the front of his sailboats pajamas. He stood up, disgusted at his clumsiness. Pulled white squares of paper towels off the silver spindle, blotted at the hot brown stain.

Once the call went through he spoke as if the man were a plumber, and Mel had a leak. "Here's my situation. I'm getting hundreds of dead bees on my front patio. The gardening guys blow them away, but then the next day, hundreds more dead bees show up. Are you familiar at all with that kind of situation?"

"I have to say, unless there's been some insecticide use—"

"There hasn't."

"Well, then that could indeed be evidence of a haunting."

"How, exactly? That's what I don't get."

"It is possible the dead bees were trying to protect you? Insects do that sometimes. I've seen it as well with ants and cockroaches. Insects, despite what we think of them, are usually good at keeping spirits inside homes. They're very territorial, that way?"

"That's what happening here? A ghost is trying to leave my house? Why wouldn't I want a ghost to leave my house? How is that protecting me?"

"Well, I don't know. I haven't been to your home to take a gander. The insects may be trying to alert you to the presence of this ghost."

"Insects would do that? Seriously? There's like a, I don't know, committee of cockroaches that meet once a week inside the walls, looking after my spiritual growth? That sounds fucking crazy, Patrick."

"Insects are extraordinarily complicated. You would be stunned by some of the tales I could tell you. Would there be a reason why a ghost would be trying to depart from your home?"

"None! I bought this house eight years ago, and as far as I know, the owners are still alive. No family members have died. It's just me and my wife. Actually, just me. I threw my wife out of my house just recently."

"And she's still alive?"

"Unfortunately."

"Would you be wanting me to come out and take a look?"

"That was a joke, when I said 'unfortunately'. I didn't hear you laugh." Silence on the other end. Mel made a face. "How much would that cost?"

"Goodness me. Let's calculate this. You're in West Covina. I'm in North Hollywood? I could come out and look around your home, get a reading, for, let's say, one hundred dollars? If I find a problem, then of course it would be more to correct it. Getting rid of a ghost can be expensive, you know."

"How expensive?"

"Ten thousand dollars to forty thousand dollars? Depending on the type of infestation."

Mel looked at his jam-topped English muffins. "Really? That much?"

"It depends on what's trying to leave your home. It may simply be a lost ghost, or it may be a purposed ghost. There's really no way for me to tell without coming out there, and walking through the different rooms."

Mel didn't have any meetings scheduled for Monday morning, so he asked Patrick to come out at eight o'clock in the morning. Might as well get this taken care of right away.

Promptly at eight, his front doorbell rang.

Standing on his front patio, a man taller than him, thinner, with an onion-shaped face, short curly brown hair. "Mr. Wilson, is it?"

"Yeah."

Patrick turned around, as if he were going to leave. "Well, I certainly see the evidence of the dead bees." Behind him, on the concrete of the front patio, hundreds of dead black bodies, curled up.

"Have you seen dead bees like this before?"

Patrick's pale blue eyes looked over Mel's shoulder, into the interior of Mel's home. "I certainly have. May I come in?"

Mel followed the taller man as Patrick walked quietly through the different downstairs rooms, in his baggy trousers, looking at walls, ceilings. "Well, I can tell you, if there is a presence, it's here on the first floor."

"Okay."

"This is your master bedroom? Where you sleep every night?"

"Yeah."

"And here's the master bathroom, off the master bedroom? Let's go in there. Ghosts love bathrooms."

Mel, apprehensive, skeptical, followed. "And why would that be?"

Patrick turned his face around, pale lips smiling. "The tile, sir. Ghosts can soak into wood, and plaster, but it's hard for them to soak into the hardness of tiles. It's a more solid surface, that they tend to rest against."

As they entered the master bathroom, Mel following Patrick, the shower in the stall suddenly came on. Shooting down water at a slant.

Mel jumped.

Patrick looked at the downpour within the glass. "This does help us. Do you see anything in the slanting water?"

Mel stood next to Patrick, staring at the water spraying down from the silver showerhead. Steam rising inside the shower's cubicle. Suddenly glad Patrick was here. His voice was hoarse. "I see a body standing in the water of the shower. Not a full body. Just the back, and the nape of the neck."

"Has that ever happened before?"

"No!"

"This will occur sometimes. The ghost realizes I'm a sensitive, and he or she sends out a sign. You only see one body in the slants of water?"

"Yes."

"Okay, then. Let's go outside, to your back yard."

On their way to the swimming pool, they passed, between two tall crepe myrtles, a small alcove that had been set up as a Zen garden, its sand raked in different curved directions. A white Styrofoam cup blew across the sand.

Mel shook his head, walked over to the edge of the garden. "I keep getting these Styrofoam cups in here. I don't know what it is. I don't know if it's from the gardeners, or they're blown over here from one of the other back yards, or if someone on a plane passing over this area of California keeps flushing them down the toilet."

Staying on the edge of the sand, so as not to step on the curved rakings in the sand, he tried reaching out to grab up the cup, his fingers straining. Just as the tips of his fingernails touched the rim of the cup, the cup lifted away, skittering a few more feet away.

"Son of a bitch!"

A long rake with stiff wooden prongs was propped by a nearby Rose of Sharon. Mel snatched it up. Clumped across the serenity of the curves drawn in the sand, thumping the end of the rake against the sand, trying to stab the white cup. The cup flew easily away from the thrusts, floating in its immortality. One last attempt, the handle of the rake, under Mel's fury, snapping in two.

He waded out of the sand, frustrated. When he stepped off the sand, he looked back. Saw how messed-up the garden was, a trail of his hourglass footprints across the timeless wavy lines. The white Styrofoam cup touching back down in the center of the sand. Biting his lower lip, he smacked the half handle still in his hand against a branch of the crepe myrtle, punishing the branch. "You fuck! You fuck!"

He flung the half-handle at the cup. It struck the sand and bounced back, like a boomerang, thumping against his right ear.

"Fuck!" Raging, one hand over his ear, he grabbed up the handle, tried to snap it in half across his knee, lost his balance. Landed on his side in the grass.

Breathing heavily, he got back to his feet. Touched his fingers to his injured ear. Pulled his hand away, saw the blood on his fingertips.

He walked over to Patrick. Angled his head so Patrick could see the ear. "Is it a bad cut?"

Patrick shook his head. "It's superficial."

They sat across from each other at a round, glass-topped table by the swimming pool. So many happy times at this table for Mel years ago, and now here he was, not only getting fucked up the ass by divorce lawyers, but having to deal with ghosts. Jesus fucking Christ.

Patrick inclined his onion-shaped head towards Mel, in a courtly manner. "I didn't see a body in the steam of the shower, at all. You did tell me no one you're related to by blood or marriage has died in the past year?"

"Absolutely not."

"That is odd. Normally, it's me that's seeing the ghost, not my client. Tell me about yourself."

The question caught Mel off-guard. "Tell you, like what?"

"About your life. Were you born in California?"

"No." Mel shook his head. Realized by the patient look on Patrick's face he was expected to elaborate. "I was born in Nebraska."

Patrick folded his hands on the glass top of the table, head tilted to one side. Said nothing.

Mel shifted in his seat. "What do you want, the whole biography?"

"Please."

Mel looked off, at the smoggy California sky. "I was a choir boy. And I used to do the whole Meals on Wheels thing.

"And I used to be in a rock and roll band in high school. The Gentle Tones. We played at parties, then we got some gigs at Omaha clubs, mostly weeknights at first, then weekends. The year we graduated, we took the summer off before college to tour the Midwest. Why not, right? This guy, Frank, he was a regional booker, he had seen us at one of our club appearances. He bought us all drinks after our set, said he could book us some dates. So we decided, you know, to give it a try. I think all of us kind of thought, Why the fuck not? If we do well, maybe we won't go to college in the fall. Maybe we'll just keep touring. None of us really wanted to go to college. None of us wanted to sit in a class room anymore, staring up at words and arrows getting drawn on a blackboard.

"So anyway, we did a bunch of dates that summer, traveling around in this beat-up van, and we were getting better. Two of the band members, Andy and Steve, they started writing songs. And the songs were pretty good. We wound up in Chicago in August, played some clubs there, and one festival in a park. Frank introduced us to this guy, Abby, who wanted to record some of our songs, at his expense. The idea was he'd shop the demo around to some record companies, and in the meantime, we could sell CDs of the demo at our concerts, and pick up more money that way. Do you have a cigarette, by any chance?"

Patrick reached into his jacket pocket, pulled out a half-empty pack of Dorals.

Mel pulled off the light brown filter, dropped it on the glass surface of the table, put the cigarette between his lips. Patrick handed him a Bic lighter. Mel drew in that first dizzying inhale. After a long moment, he sighed the smoke out through his nostrils.

"Man, I don't know if I can ever get to the point where I can truthfully say, This is the last cigarette I'll ever smoke. Is that the same with you?"

Patrick gave him a pleasant smile. "I don't attempt to quit."

"I had the same thought the first time I got married. Really? I'm never going to kiss another girl again? For the rest of my life? Sixty years or whatever? Never going to fuck another girl? Scary. Are you married?"

"No."

"Ever been?"

"No."

Mel took another pull on the cigarette, getting a bit more aggressive. "I mean, I'm sharing. Shouldn't you share?"

Patrick sat back. Pale blue eyes. "Have you ever employed the services of an electrician?"

Mel set his jaw. Gave an exaggerated blink. "Sure."

"When he arrived at your doorstep, did you describe the electricity problem you were having in your home?"

"Obviously."

"Did you ask him what electricity problems he was having in his own home?"

"It's like that?"

There was a loud splash in the pool.

Patrick rose up out of his chair faster than Mel would have expected. Strode over to the wet edge of the pool, under the blue California sky.

Mel joined him.

"Do you see anything in the pool?"

"No. But shouldn't you be the one who sees something, if you're the expert?"

"Not necessarily. But you did hear the splash?" Mel nodded. He watched Patrick as the taller man studied the green surface of the pool.

"What does it mean?"

"I don't know. But it is interesting that there have been two manifestations while we've been together, once in the shower, and once here in your pool. That could be significant. That both are associated with fluid."

They sat back down at the table.

"Was Abby able to find a recording contract for your band?"

Mel didn't answer at first. Took his time finishing his cigarette, ignoring Patrick. Once his cigarette was finished, he crushed the hot orange end against the side rim of the table top, dropped the white butt to the green grass. "What was your question?"

Patrick said nothing.

"The recording contract. Yeah. He had all the band members sign this contract that said in exchange for him recording the songs, we'd get a royalty, but he'd own the copyrights to the songs, and all licensing rights. We agreed. What the fuck. We figured we're just starting out, we got a thousand fucking songs inside us.

"I still have some copies of that demo CD. It was four songs. Three of them, I don't know. But one of them, that I wrote, Just For You, it was a pretty fucking good song. Upbeat." Mel jutted his jaw. "You ever hear it?"

Patrick thought a moment, head tilted, pale blue eyes looking upwards. "Perhaps I did, at one point, and I just don't remember right now."

"You're very polite, aren't you?"

"I suppose I am."

"Just For You was a radio hit in the Chicago area, and the Midwest generally, so Frank and Abby arranged for us to fly out to California. Not take that shitty van. Fly. In an airplane. Decko Records was interested in meeting us. Maybe for a recording contract. We went back to Omaha. They treated us like fucking rock gods. Almost every bar we went to, the drinks were free. And like the proverbial saying goes, I got more ass those two weeks before we flew to California than a God damn toilet seat. The girls in the bar gave me a nickname. Double Rubber. "

"What does Double Rubber mean?"

"I'd wear two condoms instead of one."

Mel shook another cigarette out of the red and blue pack, without asking if he could.

"We get out there, meet with the record executives, it goes really well. I can tell they're really impressed. They take us to dinner afterwards.

The bill came to hundreds and hundreds of dollars. Bill fucking Murray is sitting at the table next to us.

"The next three months, it's like a movie, and we're the stars. I start combing my hair differently, get contact lenses, and grow a moustache. I take a stage name. Mule Winston. We're playing clubs in Hollywood, working in the studio on our tracks, posing for the album cover, and when the record's finally released, we do all these crazy early morning radio interviews with L.A. DJs, appear at different record stores, everything.

"And, it's, you know. What the fuck. The record doesn't sell that well. We were supposed to appear on David Letterman. Then our appearance was canceled. I still see the album for sale on ebay sometimes."

"Did you go back to Nebraska?"

"No. Everyone else in the band did. I couldn't. It would be too humiliating." Angry look on his face. "Hey, folks, here's your rock god, bagging your groceries, pumping your gas."

"What did you do?"

"I was the drummer in the group. I managed to get some session work in Los Angeles, playing on other people's records, then I drifted into stand-up comedy. Wound up in real estate. Where I made a fortune. I was a failure. That was my one shot in life at turning into someone else. To not be Mel Wilson anymore. To be someone new. And I failed. I thought I was going to be someone like Don Henley, and instead, I was just another kid with drumsticks and a bad haircut. Is that enough?"

"For now. I appreciate your honesty."

"You want a drink?

"I don't drink."

"Afraid you'll develop a drinking problem?"

"It's already fully developed."

"You mind if I drink?"

"Not at all."

Mel pulled out his cell phone, called his house. Twisted around in his chair, listening as the phone sounded inside the house. "Rosie? Bring me a double Manhattan on the rocks, and a glass of ice water?" He looked at Patrick, who nodded.

"So what do we do to get rid of this ghost, and how much is it going to cost me?"

"Well, I would say the first step would be to ghost-proof your home. We sink two-by-fours all around your house, down to a depth of thirteen feet. Leave them there eight days, then pull them up to see if the ends have any discoloration. Usually, only one treatment is needed. It leaches out the ghost into the porous wood of the two-by-fours. If we need a second treatment, we do it."

Mel glared at Patrick, holding his head still. "Why thirteen feet? Why eight days?"

"Ghosts can't survive to thirteen feet underground. That's where thirteen as an unlucky number came from. Why eight days? Because a week has a mystical property. You do it one day past a week, and you've defeated the ghost."

"How much is this going to cost me?"

"Sixteen thousand dollars. Your house has a big 'footprint'. That's a lot of holes that have to be dug down thirteen feet. But there's something else I want to discuss with you."

Mel took another draw on his cigarette.

"You're green with demon. I saw it when I first met you. Your eyes, the way you hold your body."

"What with who?"

"Green with demon. Did you know that as soon as we're born, as we inhale our first breath, we draw bacteria into us, which we absolutely need to survive, to digest?"

"Yeah. I did know that."

"Well, with that first breath we also draw in our own, personal demon. Which we also need to survive. To digest, spiritually. Most of us learn to control that demon. To fight it. Some, such as you, don't succeed. You surrender to the worst that's in you. People like me, we call that being green with demon."

"Well, thanks, Patrick. I guess you're saying I'm doomed."

Patrick brushed the knee of his crossed trouser legs. "I'm sorry to say, I do think you're doomed. I think you started out all right, a choir boy, Meals on Wheels, probably lots of other good works, but then over the years, with each set back you experienced, which we all experience, instead of rising above the situation, you gave in. To anger and fear. And that caused the demon inside you to grow. You could have starved it, but instead you fed it."

Mel shot Patrick a look, right eye skeptical, left eye frightened. "Seriously? I'm doomed? I thought this was a bad cold, but it's inoperable cancer?"

"I hope not. We'll run the ghost test. See if that works. But whether it works or not, I'm afraid you may be too far along. Thoughts can't be taken back. Words can't be taken back. Actions can't be taken back. As attorneys say, You can't unring the bell."

Patrick arrived with his crew Wednesday morning. Lots of trucks and cars parked at the curb. Mel met them as he was leaving for work. "This is going to solve my problem?"

Patrick was wearing protective glasses. "It should. If it's a ghost issue."

"And if it isn't?"

Patrick tilted his onion-shaped head to one side. "Almost everything that troubles us in life is a ghost-related issue. Give me some time to banish whatever ghosts are in your home. We can methodically eliminate the reasons why you're being haunted. If this doesn't work, there are other steps we can take."

"For additional money."

"It can get expensive. It's not easy to get rid of a ghost."

When Mel came home around eight that evening, the trucks were gone, and the tops of two-by-fours were sticking up around his house on all four sides of his property. He stopped counting after one hundred.

Patrick didn't call Mel during the eight-day waiting period. There was probably no reason for Patrick to call him, they had to wait to pull up the two-by-fours to see the results, but still, it bothered Mel that Patrick hadn't made any contact. Sitting at his computer late one night, sipping still another Manhattan, even though his scalp was already tingly, he brought up his online banking site, saw that his sixteen thousand dollar check had already been cashed.

On the sixth day Mel called Patrick's number, but just got a recording. "I am presently out of the country. Please leave your name and phone number, and I will get back to you shortly." He felt a twinge of jealousy. Was Patrick helping some other ghost victim? Was he going to forget about Mel's problem?

But on the eighth day, stepping out of the shower, Mel heard the noise of machinery outside his home.

He toweled off quickly, not taking time to dry between his legs or under his arms, wrapped his green bathrobe around himself, headed out the front door.

Somehow tripped over his own Welcome mat, spilling forward, landing in a sprawl across the concrete of the front porch. Got up, swearing, red scrapes on the palms of his hands, elbows, forehead.

Patrick was on the front lawn, directing the workers.

Thirteen-foot long two-by-fours lay across the green grass.

Mel went up to Patrick. "So what have you found?"

Patrick led Mel over to the pile of lumber.

In this quantity, the wood, piled up criss-crossed, had its own smell, strong as tobacco. The tip of each two-by-four was pale yellow. The rest of the length, having been submerged for eight days in the ground, was darkened and damp.

"If there were a ghost in your home, the bottoms of these two-by-fours would be blackened, as if dipped in tar. But do you see how there's no greater discolorations at the bottoms than there is along their lengths?"

Mel, unhappy, nodded.

"There is no ghost in your home."

"So I just paid sixteen thousand dollars for nothing?"

"Well, your sixteen thousand dollars has confirmed your home is not haunted. That's something."

Mel snorted. "But what about all the dead bees? What about what I saw in the shower, and that splash we both heard in the pool?"

"Where'd you get that red abrasion on your forehead?"

"I tripped on the way outside."

"Have you been tripping a lot lately?"

"Maybe. Does that mean something?"

"Have you been having any other slapstick-type accidents?"

"Is this just going to be something where you keep asking me all these stupid questions and I keep writing checks to you?"

"I understand your frustration. But this is how the process of freeing you from a supernatural presence works."

Mel made some fists by his hips, consciously turned them back into flat hands. "I guess, yeah. Lately, when I reach up to move the hair away from my face, I've been poking myself in the eyes with my thumbs. I've been stubbing my big toes a lot more than usual. Spilling liquid on myself. Accidently hitting my humerus bone against the edge of the kitchen sink. Last night I was crushing some ice cubes in the blender for a lime margarita, and the plastic top of the blender flew off, hitting me under the jaw." Mel made a sour face, looked at Patrick to make sure he didn't laugh.

"The presence is being playful with you. In an immature way."

Mel tried to control his temper. "So, does that mean something? Does anything you say mean anything?"

"I'm not entirely sure. But I have some thoughts."

"Well, good for you Patrick. And when will you share these thoughts with me? And how much will these thoughts cost me? Jesus, you know after I got your name I called around, and everyone gave you glowing recommendations, but I have to tell you, if it weren't for all those testimonials, I'd be really starting to wonder whether you're just taking me for a ride."

"We're not dealing with a ghost as such. I believe this might be a case where you're being interacted with by a different type of presence. I think I should spend the night with you. We'll stay up all night, sitting in chairs. It might help solve the problem."

"And how much will that cost?"

"A thousand dollars."

"Really. And do you guarantee a cure by the time the sun comes up?"

"Absolutely not. But I do think it would be helpful."

Mel and Patrick sat in Mel's living room, chairs facing each other. It was nine o'clock at night. Given it was summer, the windows surrounding them had only recently turned dark.

"So we just sit here? And now I lay me down to sleep?"

Patrick sat with his forearms comfortably lying atop his chair's arm rests, his stupid onion-shaped head held straight on his neck. "Tell me more about yourself. About your mother."

"Are you qualified to give a psychiatric evaluation of my relationship to my mother?"

"I'm not a psychiatrist. I'm a death sensitive. A Ghoster."

"My mother is a good woman. She was always very nervous. I'd be talking to her, and she'd suddenly apologize for something trivial from years ago. Give you an example. I had visited them, had a tuna fish sandwich for lunch, and she hadn't had a pickle to give me. Years later, I'm talking to her on the phone about this and that, and out of nowhere she blurts out an apology for not having a pickle that day. I could tell the fact she hadn't had any pickles in the refrigerator that day was something that had been gnawing at her all those years, until she finally just had to let it out." Mel wiped at his eyes. "Do you have any idea how disturbing that is, for a son to hear his mother say something as bizarre as that? She's my mother! And all of a sudden, holding the phone to my ear, I realize there's something not right with her. She's not normal. And she wasn't. She had emotional issues. Five years ago, she was diagnosed with Alzheimer's disease. She's in a nursing home. I pay her monthly institutional fees."

"What about your father?"

Mel took another gulp of his drink. "My father. How much time do you have?"

Patrick gave a polite smile. "All night."

"He was very demanding."

"Of you."

100

"Of everyone. Let me correct that. Everyone in our family. Within our home? He was a tyrant. His eyes were always angry. He used to cut his own hair, in the bathroom mirror, and it always turned out crappy, some locks longer than others. I was just a little kid. My sister was even smaller. He'd get into these murderous rages. Throwing chicken legs against the windows, punching the doors off our kitchen cabinets. The dogs would run out of the room." Mel twisted his head to one side, imitating, pain in his eyes. "Supper isn't ready yet? Get off that God damn phone before I knock it out of your hand."

He raised his face, eyes glistening. "But outside our home? Men used to mock him. To his face. I went with him to work once, when I was still a kid. The men he worked with? Coming up to him, knowing he wasn't going to do anything, calling him 'Shorty'. 'Hey, guys, look. Shorty brought Little Shorty to the office with him today.' And my dad would say nothing. He would be fucking meek. This meek little, I don't want any confrontations, shit-eating smile on his face as he tried to get away from his tormenters. This short, cowardly, pathetic little man. And they would laugh in his face. The taller men would follow behind him and me, cracking more jokes. Even younger, shorter men would join in, and my dad would just take it. I couldn't believe it. He was this angry giant at home, but here at work, he was a fucking midget. And you know what I did during that visit? I started laughing along with the men. I started calling him Shorty myself, in front of him, in front of all the men gathered around with their Styrofoam coffee cups. At one point, and it was extremely, incredibly gratifying for me, I even knocked my father's coffee cup out of his hand. Me, eight years old. And all the men my dad worked with fucking roared!"

Mel dumped the rest of his drink down his throat, angrily biting through the ice. Got up to make another.

"But he went to work every day?"

At the living room bar, Mel turned around as he poured in the whiskey, no longer using a shot measure. "Of course he did. What's your fucking point, Patrick?"

"If his working environment was that hostile, why didn't he just get another job?"

"He couldn't!" Mel shook in some Angostora bitters. Took a long sip. Stayed at the bar, swaying, ready to make another drink after this one was gone. "This was a position he had worked himself up into over twenty years. If he left, he'd have to start at the bottom again, for minimum wage. He didn't finish grade school! He dropped out after seventh grade. Do you have any fucking idea how embarrassing it was for me to have friends over, and to hear him mispronounce so many words?"

"So he stayed at the job, with all its humiliations, in order to keep a roof over his family's head, provide food for the table."

"Shut the fuck up! He wasn't some..." Mel wiped the spittle off his lips. "He wasn't a hero. He was a God damn weakling! Do not! Try to portray my dad as sympathetic. I vowed. I fucking vowed I would never, ever let anyone take advantage of me like what happened to my father." He raised his voice, terrified. "If someone tries to take advantage of me, I split their fucking head open."

Patrick let a beat go by. Let Mel catch his breath. "Is he still with us?"

The heavy whiskey bottle, as Mel tilted it to make another Manhattan, fell out of Mel's grasp. As it rolled across the bar top, leaking whiskey, Mel grabbed it up, let out a frustrated cry, and hurled it against the nearest wall. "No problem. I have plenty more bottles of whiskey."

Patrick watched as Mel, back to him, pulled another bottle of whiskey down from the wall of bottles behind the bar, twisted off the top.

"And is he still with us?"

"I was fourteen." Mel stopped talking, carefully constructing another Manhattan, one eye squeezed close. "Fourteen." He made an elaborate, meandering gesture with his right hand in the air. "Playing in the back yard. Killing ants or worms or a bird or something. I look up at one point, and there's my dad. On the roof! Two-story house. All the way up, at the top. By the chimney." He waved his limp right hand in front of his face. "As you may imagine, I'm thinking, What the fuck? Why's he up there? Why's he fucking up there? And..." Mel lazily spread his arms apart. "He swan dives off the roof. Splat! Right onto our driveway. Concrete. I'm running into the house. Getting my mom. 'Dad jumped off the roof!' It takes a moment to register with her. She comes out. We run over to the driveway. My mom is crying out of control.

"That's when I saw how my dad was. And what I was becoming. It had to stop."

"A man and his dog decide to go sailing. A storm blows in, they get lost at sea. Swim to a deserted island. There's a fresh water spring on the island, so they have water. Lots of coconuts and bananas, so they have food. Using palm fronds, he builds a lean-to for him and his dog. So they have shelter. But after a few days on the island, the man gets really horny.

"He notices there's a flock of sheep on the far side of the island. So he goes over there, huge hard-on in his pants, and walks among the herd. Picks out one sheep that looks better than the others. Gets behind it, holds its tail so it doesn't wander off while he unzips his pants, lets out his throbbing cock.

"Just as he's about to slide his cock up inside the sheep, his fucking dog comes running down the hill, barking. Yap, yap, yap! So he puts his cock back in his pants, leaves.

"Next day, he gets up early, while his dog is still sleeping. Sneaks back over to the herd. Locates the sheep he likes, unzips his pants.

"Just as he's ready to slide his aching cock up into some moist sheep cunt, here's his fucking dog again, racing down the side of the hill, into the herd, bark, bark, bark.

"So he puts his cock back in his pants."

Mel had slept for an hour, while Patrick sat quietly in his chair.

The windows in the living room were now fully black. Moon and stars.

"He's incredibly frustrated sexually. He's walking along the beach, and up ahead he sees this figure lying at the shoreline. Gets closer. It's a human! Closer still. It's a woman! In fact, it's a teenager, long blonde hair, blue eyes. She's wearing a black neoprene scuba diving suit.

"Is she alive? Dead? He gets down on his knees by her head, starts giving her mouth to mouth resuscitation. She stirs. Spits out sea water.

"Oh my God! You saved my life!

"She's gorgeous. That type of incredibly healthy California face, with the widely-spaced blue eyes, you only see in expensive magazines.

"She looks up at him as she starts to pull the zipper down the front of her black neoprene scuba diving suit.

"He realizes she's stark naked underneath.

"You saved my life, she says, pulling the brass zipper further down, exposing her beautiful breasts. I owe you my life. I would do anything for you. She pulls the zipper further down, baring her incredible stomach.

"He arches an eyebrow. Anything?

"She yanks the black neoprene suit down to her waist, slipping it off her bare hips, down off her long, shapely legs until she's nude. Her big blue eyes look up at him. Anything."

"He sucks in his breath, incredibly aroused.

"Would you watch my dog for five minutes?"

Around midnight, Mel excused himself to load the dishes in the dishwasher.

Patrick stayed in his chair, pulling out his phone, paging through messages.

In the too-bright kitchen, Mel lowered the front door of the dishwasher. Reached into the left side of his stainless steel sink, picked up two dirty drinking glasses.

Using the bottoms of the glasses as substitute hands, pulled out the top drawer of the dishwasher.

Went to put the glasses in the top drawer. Stopped. Peered at the dirty dishes and cups already in the dishwasher.

Saw, across the surfaces of the plates and cups inside, the mosaic of a human being.

Dropped the glasses in his hands on the bamboo floor. Ran out to the living room.

Patrick followed behind him, back into the kitchen. Squinting at the bright light.

Mel stood by the opened dishwasher, shaking. "There! Do you see the ghost inside my dishwasher?"

Patrick walked over, bent his knees, pale blue eyes looking inside, at the top rack, bottom track. "No."

"No?" Mel got angry. "Are you blind? You don't see the ghost inside the dishwasher, arms and legs folded over itself?"

"I honestly don't." He gave Mel a mild look.

Mel was astonished. "It's right fucking there!" He pulled out a plate, pointed to the wet sheen on the plate. "You don't see someone's knees reflected in that plate?"

Patrick shook his head.

"You don't see someone's fingers across this coffee saucer?" He pulled out a coffee cup. "Look! There's a concave face inside. A girl's face. You don't see that?"

Patrick took the coffee cup from Mel, tilted it around in his large, freckled hand to see the interior from all angles. "I don't see anything."

Mel, furious, frightened, threw the cup against the stainless steel sink, where it exploded in white shards. "How the fuck are you a 'death sensitive' expert if an ordinary civilian like me can see this ghost, and you can't?"

"Mr. Wilson, I don't see a ghost. I don't know what you're seeing. But I don't see it. And yes, I am an expert. How old is the person you're seeing?"

Mel stepped back. Shrugged unhappily. "I'd say, young."

"How young?"

"I don't know. What the fuck does it matter?"

An hour later, back in the living room, Mel announced he was hungry.

"There's a pizza place that's open all night. You want a pizza?"

Patrick sat up in his chair. "I would."

"You can get whatever the fuck you want on your side of the pizza. I'll get what I want on my side. What do you want on your side?"

"Mushrooms would be nice."

"Seriously? Are you kidding? You can have anything you want. Caviar. Abalone. Kobe beef."

"I just want mushrooms."

Mel angrily punched the numbers to the pizzeria into his phone. "Oh, really. Is this like a thing? Like, I'm an asshole, so you're only going to order mushrooms? To show me up? By the way, your half? That's coming out of your own wallet. You're already getting paid a thousand dollars for doing nothing. You can pay for your own fucking pizza. Yeah. Hello. I want to order an extra-large Pizza Country pizza. Mushrooms on one side. Taramousalata, caviar, and quail eggs on the other side. And hey! Bring a quart of spumoni, too."

After Mel hung up the phone he made himself another Manhattan. "You know, I may just put a stop payment on the one thousand dollar check I wrote you tonight. In fact, I think I will. You don't deserve it. I saw those body parts in the dishwasher, and you saw nothing. I think you're a fraud. I don't think you know shit about the afterlife. Come to think of it, once this pizza arrives, I want you to get the fuck out of my house with your half of the pizza. But you have to pay me first for it. Cash on the barrel. Get your wallet out, you stupid, ugly, onion-headed, money-eating freak. And you're not getting any of the spumoni, even if you're willing to pay for it. And this place makes the best fucking spumoni in the world. They import their pistachios from Italy."

Patrick smiled. "Why did your wife leave you?"

"Huh?" Mel slurped his Manhattan, whiskey running down his chin. Patrick waited.

Mel got clumsily out of his chair, made another drink, whiskey spilling across the bar's countertop. The outside of his glass was so wet, dripping whiskey, he decided not to use it. He returned to his chair, settling down heavily, holding the bottle of whiskey in his right hand by its neck. Took a swig, then settled the bottle between his legs. He made a vague, mid-air gesture. "Is there a doctor-patient confidentiality here?"

"I'm not a doctor."

"I beat her up a few times. Big fucking deal. Once while she was pregnant. I felt I had to do it."

"I didn't realize you have a child."

"I don't." Mel took another long swig of the whiskey. Glared at Patrick, eyes challenging. Sitting in the chair, Mel clasped his hands together, stiff-elbowed, holding his knuckles down below his knees. "When something dies, it's dead. Why make a big deal about it? She left me after that incident, a couple of weeks ago."

"That joke you told earlier."

"My favorite story. I fucking love telling that story. It's funny!"

"And it is. But did you ever think, it's a story about a man who's lost his way?"

Mel snorted. "What?"

"Normally, the man in the story would much prefer to have relations with the young woman who's washed up on the shore, but because he thought for so long the only avenue available to him for carnal relations was the sheep, he no longer saw this far better option, the young woman, right in front of him. Isn't that where the humor in the story derives?"

"I don't know what the fuck you're saying."

"The man couldn't escape his past."

"Whatever. Stupid potato head fuck."

"Remember when I said I saw you as being green with demon? The demon is coming out of you. I can see it emerging from the holes of your body. I'm sorry for you, Mel. I truly am. That's the real reason why I wanted to stay tonight. To help you when your demon emerges."

The doorbell rang.

Mel stood up lopsidedly. "Our pizza."

He weaved his way to the front door. "You better pay me for your half of the pizza, Patrick. Cash on the barrel."

Mel yanked the front door open.

Shoved the young pizza guy to one side. "Out of my way!"

Stared at the concrete patio outside his front door. No bees.

The pizza guy looked at Mel resentfully. "I don't like getting shoved."

Mel pulled out his wallet. "Well, you're a pizza guy, so I'm sure there's a lot you don't like. I'm not responsible for your bad career choices. What do I owe you?"

"Hey, man. Fuck you."

Mel reared up. Those blue eyes clouded over. "Seriously? Fuck me? A pizza guy is telling me to go fuck myself?"

The pizza guy stood in front of Mel, in the darkness of the front porch patio, holding the pizza horizontal in his two hands, thumb above either side. "You're being rude. For no reason."

Patrick walked quietly over to the confrontation at the front door, saying nothing, doing nothing.

"I'm being rude? You're telling me to go fuck myself? I'm being rude?"

"It's thirty-five eighty. How do you want to pay?"

Mel swayed in front of the pizza guy. "How do I want to pay. How do I want to pay. Well, I guess I'll pay by giving your mom an extra tip next time she gets down on her tired old knees and sucks my cock. How does that sound?"

The pizza guy, tall, curly hair, backed up with his pizza. Looked directly into Mel's eyes. "Fuck you. Do you see what I'm saying to you? Maybe you're too old, or too drunk, to get it. But just stare into my eyes. Fuck you."

Mel gave a loud, helpless laugh. "Really? Fuck me? Some young punk who thinks he's a good guy is going to tell me to go fuck myself? After all I've been through, this is what I get? Some worthless piece of shit telling me to go fuck myself?" Mel swung his right hand up, knocking the square box of pizza out of the delivery guy's hands. It sailed backwards, landing on its corner, top opening, triangles of pizza spilling out onto the porch's concrete, uneatable. "You're going to tell me to go fuck myself?"

Patrick bent his head.

The pizza guy made a fist. "You're going to pay for that pizza."

Mel let the fury overwhelm him. "Really? I'm going to pay for it?" He lashed out, fists, teeth, knocking the pizza guy back. The pizza guy was probably stronger, and certainly younger, but he didn't have Mel's fury. He tried at the last minute to back up, away from the attack, but lost his balance. Once Mel got the pizza guy on the ground, he climbed on top of him, bouncing his fists off the screaming face.

Out in the street, a car stopped. "I'm calling 911!"

Mel looked up, still sitting on top of the pizza guy's body, blood splattered across his neck, cheekbones, hair. "Go ahead and call 911! Come up here and say that to me, faggot! Pretty easy to be brave when you're out in the street, locked in a car. Come up to where I am and say that to my face, you limp-wristed faggot!"

Mel rose off the twitching body, looking down at it, at the pizza triangles scattered across the patio's concrete. Wiped his face with the back of his right hand, glanced down at his knuckles, seeing the blood.

Eyes staring, he walked back inside the house. Left the front door open, the pizza guy lying outside on the patio.

Blood speckling his face, he looked at Patrick. "Well, I guess that's it. I always knew this day would come."

Police sirens sounded in the distance.

Patrick put his hand on Mel's shoulder. "I see the presence now."

Mel looked up at him, desperate. "You do? Finally?"

"It was released by your second act of violence in this home. You know who it is, don't you?"

Mel wandered around the living room. Looked at the bar. In a defeated voice he said, "It's that fucking fetus, right? The miscarriage, when I punched Vickie in her stomach?"

Patrick nodded. "You can only become a ghost if you've been born. That's why I never saw it before."

"So what is it?"

"It's a soul. The soul of the fetus you killed."

"Oh, this is so bad."

The sirens wailed closer.

"It's right here. Do you want to hold it?"

Mel dipped his hip. "Oh, I don't know. This is so bad! I know I did bad things in the past, but I never did anything really bad, until then."

Patrick walked over to Mel, his arms cradling.

"I don't see anything."

"All souls are invisible. It's about to be released. To leave. Do you want to hold it?"

"Why did it stay here?"

"It wanted to leave. All those dead bees. But at the same time, she wanted to help you. You're her father. She loves you."

Mel let out a sob. "It was a girl? A little daughter?" The tears ran down his face. "This is so bad! I wanted to be a good guy. I really did." His middle-aged face looked desperately at Patrick. "I started out as a good guy."

"I believe you did."

Mel was silent a long time. When he finally opened his mouth, his voice was quiet. "When I knocked the Styrofoam coffee cup out of my father's hand? And the men laughed? One of them said, Way to go, Little Shorty." He tilted his head to one side. "And I said, No, I'm not Little Shorty. I'm Bleach. That was the nickname I was trying to get known by, as a kid. You know how kids do that sometimes? Try to create their own nickname? But one of the men, he just said, Okay, Little Shorty. And I said, No, seriously, everyone calls me Bleach. And that man, he looked down at me, and he said, If you say so, Little Shorty."

Patrick stood in front of Mel, arms cradled. "Hold her before she leaves. The rest of your life is not going to be good, Mel. Do this, hold her, to make that long, long time ahead of you a little easier."

Mel accepted the invisible bundle from Patrick.

The weight was small, active. Although he couldn't see it, he could feel, on top of his forearms, the warmth, the muscles moving. He started petting the soul's invisibility. Heard a pleased purring.

Mel's blood-covered face looked up, teary-eyed. "It's purring, like a cat purrs!"

"Souls often do, when they're happy. She's reunited with her dad."

Mel started crying uncontrollably.

A big man, helpless now. His legs gave out under him. Knees going sideways. He sat down hard.

Stayed slumped on the floor, face covered in blood, tenderly petting the soul, stroking its warmth, babbling apologies to his daughter.

The police sirens shut off on the street outside his front door.

WARFARIN

The livestock guy pulled into the property Clay was renting at three o'clock, right on schedule.

He hopped out of the truck, short and old in blue jeans, walking down the length of the trailer he was hauling, to where Clay stood.

Blue sky, tall trees at the perimeter of the property, dirt driveway.

"You Clay?"

"Thanks for showing up on time."

"Told me you were on a tight schedule?" He squinted up at Clay's homely face. "You don't look like a horse person. I don't know."

Clay shrugged. "I'm not."

"No? What you gonna do with this horse? You gonna ride it?"

Clay walked over to the rear of the trailer. Inside, behind the trailer's back gate, a large shadow moving, the sound of clops, snorts.

"For what I'm paying you, do you care?"

The livestock guy ducked his head. "That horse in there, Aloysius? I was in the barn the night the mare gave birth. He licked the palm of my hand. Guess I've always had an affinity to him since? So, you want him for what?"

Clay stepped up onto the back fender of the trailer. Lowered his eyes to see, through a gap between the horizontal metal slats, the horse's rear haunches, switching tail. He clucked his tongue. The horse, deep inside the shadows of the trailer, turned its head so Clay could see its profile, its long face.

"You need to sell this horse, right?"

The livestock guy backed up. "Well, strictly speaking. But I want some reassurance he isn't gonna be abused."

Clay dropped back down to the dirt of the driveway. "Do I look like a guy who would abuse a horse?"

"Well, I can't be sure. People today aren't like people fifty years ago."

Clay glanced at his wristwatch. "I'm fixing to open up a petting zoo right here on this property. Ol' Aloysius, he'll be the star attraction. We'll have little kids riding him, wearing candy necklaces. For a fifteen year old well broke trail horse, I think three thousand dollars is a fair price. Plus another three hundred to rent this bumper pull livestock trailer for a day. That's three thousand, three hundred dollars I can count out right now into the palm Aloysius licked. That's a pretty tall stack of hundred dollar bills."

The old livestock guy scuffed his sneakers in the dirt. "So he's gonna strictly be a petting zoo type animal?"

Clay looked him right in the eyes. "Absolutely. He's gonna go into old age with a big smile on his face."

"Well, that's what I wanted for him."

Clay touched the old man's shoulder. With his other hand, he pulled out a thick wad of bills. "That's what we want for all our loved ones, right?"

Once the livestock guy unhitched the trailer, said goodbye to Aloysius by reaching through the metal slats for one last pat on his haunch, lowered himself back down to the dirt of the driveway, blinked a few tears, trudged back to his truck, pulled out onto the paved road, honking as the truck disappeared behind roadside bushes, Clay was finally able to get in his rented pickup, left hand on the steering wheel, right arm thrown over the rear of his driver's seat, face turned around as he maneuvered the rear of the pickup against the hitch of the trailer.

Although the pickup had a radio, Clay didn't turn it on as he made his way onto the highway, keeping to the middle lane. After an hour he got off at the Fairleigh Street exit, just as the late afternoon rush hour traffic was starting.

Brinebarn was a fairly small town in western Tennessee, main drag alternating fast food joints and gasoline stations, lines of cars under the green and pink of the evening sky. Most of its farms had been developed into housing tracts. It would have been much easier if the Eisenberg house was out in the country, no neighbors in sight, where he could stake the horse on the front lawn, but Eisenberg lived on a suburban street where the lots were only one acre, meaning Clay would have to bring the horse inside the house before starting.

Once he found Eisenberg's house, he pulled ahead of the driveway entrance, then carefully backed the trailer up the driveway, until its rear gate was only ten feet from the garage door.

Turning off the loud engine, he lowered himself out of the pickup, a woman already coming out of the house's front door, heading across the lawn towards him.

She was overweight, as wide as she was tall, dressed in white with a nurse's cap.

"Clay? May I call you Clay?"

The hand she held out was larger than Clay's. "I'm Mrs. Ritchie, the afternurse." She stood back, grinning. "Big fan of your work."

Clay smiled. "While we're out here alone, without family around, why don't you tell me what the situation is?"

She sucked in air through her nostrils. Face blushing. "You know this is about Harold Eisenberg, right? He's been in hospice care for over five months now. I'd say we're looking at only a few more days before he goes. His daughter, Ruth, contacted me through the hospice program because it was obvious he was infected with Smudges. She didn't know what Smudges are, she only knew he was going through extreme emotional issues. Lots of unresolved conflicts. I didn't really get into the whole Smudge issue with her, just came out here to assess him, and there were just too many Smudges for me to handle. Which is when I thought of you, based on your reputation. "

Clay nodded. "How many Smudges have you identified?"

"Thirty-three!"

"So there's probably three times that number inside him."

"I would think so. I sat beside Mr. Eisenberg's bed each day, and with his help drew sketches of the different Smudges' faces." She beamed at him, proud. "I got twenty-eight sketches." She thrust her sketchpad out at him.

Clay took the sketchpad, flipped through the pages, glancing at the different pencil-drawn faces. Decided it was time to give her a pat. He'd need her later on. "These are really well-drawn. Almost like police sketches. That'll help me a lot."

"I hope so." Her voice rose. "May I say, it's an honor to work with you."

"How am I going to get this horse inside their home without the neighbors noticing? I want it to end up in their living room, which is the closest to their front lawn we're going to get."

"We can bring it in through the kitchen, through that red door up there by the side of the house, then we just have to lead it down a short hall, to the living room."

"Let's go inside. I want to talk to the daughter before I drag a horse through the house."

The daughter, Ruth, was standing in the middle of the living room, not pretending to be doing anything other than waiting for Clay to walk inside.

She had one of those faces that even in its age showed a memory of the beauty she must have been. Still had her long black hair, though it was shot through with gray. She looked like a sincere, down-to-earth woman who was sad her dad was dying. She was wearing blue jeans, and sneakers.

"Do I call you Ruth?"

115

She bobbed her head. By the way she held her angular body, ready for a fight, Clay picked up skepticism.

"Do you understand why I'm here?"

The daughter decided this would be a good time to assert herself. Hand on her hip. "Not really." Eyes steady. "I mean, what are you again? Some kind of medium?"

Clay put a smile on his homely face. This was always the unpleasant part, having to deal with the family. "I can't communicate with the dead. What I can do, is assist the living as they go into death. I've done it many times. In your father's case, your hospice nurse has seen some signs in your dad that suggest he has a lot of unresolved issues about some of the people he's met in his life. 'Unresolved' meaning he's had a number of encounters in his life with strangers where he feels he was bested by those strangers. They took advantage of him. His good nature, his reluctance to make a scene, whatever. Each of us, in our lives, encounter people, however briefly, who are negative. It could be someone who pushes ahead of us in line, or flirts with our significant other in a store, says something sarcastic to us on the street, or otherwise acts in a rude way in our presence. A lot of people, women particularly, are able to accept that momentary rudeness, and move on. Some men can't. It bothers them that they were treated with disrespect by these strangers. It bothers them so much that even years later, decades later, they still replay these encounters in their mind, trying to imagine a way in which they triumph over the offender. But these recreations wind up as an endless loop. They may spend every day of their life repeatedly replaying these encounters from decades ago, trying to resolve them in their minds once and for all, but there is no once and for all with Smudges.

"In our profession, that's what we call these persistent replayings. Smudges. Mrs. Ritchie has identified thirty-three Smudges bothering your dad. Living inside him. Preventing him from dying happily. My task is to find a way to leach those Smudges out of your dad, so he can transition to death untroubled."

"And how much is this going to cost his estate?"

"I don't bill estates. I bill people who can hand me a check the evening I arrive. A check that won't bounce when I deposit it."

"You're asking me to pay you before I see any results?"

"You've already incurred about five thousand dollars in expenses. You're going to have to add another twenty thousand for my services going forward. Twenty-five thousand dollars total. You're going to have to write me a check, now, for that amount."

She lifted her chin. "What if I don't?"

Clay looked into her eyes. She took a step back. "I didn't call you. You called me. I interact with demons. Do you really want to fuck with me?"

He watched as she decided how to react.

She shook her head.

"The after--" Clay shut his eyes. Opened them. "The hospice nurse told me you love your dad very much."

Ruth nodded, tears rolling down. There wouldn't need to be any more discussions about payment.

"I know you don't want to see him pass while he's still in a state of emotional agony. You want him to die in peace, right?"

Tears down her face. "Yup."

"That's what I'm here to do. Did you contact the list the hospice nurse gave you of other people I've helped?"

"Not all of them. But enough of them that you seem reliable."

"I'll be back in a minute or two."

Clay stopped himself on his way out of the room. Turned back around. "You understand I'm bringing a horse into the house now, right?"

She looked like she could really use a drink. "The hospice nurse mentioned that."

Clay went outside, leaving the red door to the kitchen open.

Unlocked the back gate of the horse trailer.

Slid the inclined wooden ramp into place against the back of the trailer.

Looked around, at the darkening trees and shrubs. Yellow rectangles of distant windows floated behind the branches, but it was unlikely any neighbor would see what was going on, especially if the transfer was swift.

He walked up to the top of the ramp, grabbed the horse's switching tail. Pulled on it, hard.

The horse in the trailer, feeling the pain, reared its head in the trailer's shadows, ninnying.

Clay yanked even harder on the tail, forcing the horse to back out of the trailer, hoofs clip-clopping.

A moment of four-legged panic for the horse as its rear hoofs clapped down onto the inclined slope of the ramp, searching for a level ground that wasn't there.

Still pulling on the tail, Clay yanked the horse backwards out of the trailer, the horse high stepping backwards down the ramp, clomping onto the tar of the driveway.

Twisting the end of the tail around his left hand, like a leash, he slapped the horse on its haunch, propelling it forward, towards the opened kitchen door.

Getting the long face inside the open doorway wasn't difficult, but getting the wet noodle of the horse's resistance to pass its body through the doorway required strong slaps against the horse's left profile.

"There you go, Allison. Trot inside."

Once the horse's body was completely inside, large black eyes panicking at the bright overhead lights of the kitchen, Clay leaned his shoulder against the horse's rump, pushing the horse's head against the white stove, which rocked backwards at the impact.

He shut the red kitchen door behind him.

The horse reared up, big stupid eyes panicking, front hoofs kicking against the kitchen counter, the refrigerator, denting its door. Photographs and Christmas cards taped to the door fluttered down.

Still grasping the tail, grabbing it tighter with each attempted escape, Clay slipped a noose over the horse's nose, slid the circle of rope up the long face, pulled it down the back of the head until it was around the base of the horse's thick, muscular neck.

Now I've got you.

Letting go of the tail, Clay pulled the rope taut.

The horse tried to rear up on its front legs. Clay pulled even tighter on the noose, the rope twanging, forcing the horse back down on all four hoofs.

Another attempt by the horse to rear up.

Another tightening of the noose.

Huge exhale through the horse's black nostrils.

Those big black eyes went inwards.

The horse ducked its long head.

Clay led it through the short hallway, the horse trotting behind obediently.

Once in the sadness and furniture of the living room, Clay tied off the end of the rope around the iron radiator standing between the two front windows.

The afternurse brought Ruth back into the living room, so she could see the horse clopping around by her sofa.

Clay looked Ruth up and down. "Never thought you'd have a horse in your house, right?"

The daughter said nothing, staring at the animal.

"Would you like to try to calm it down? Maybe talk to it, scratch its forehead?"

Ruth went up on tip toe. "Actually, if it's all right, I would."

Why do they always want to pet the horse? But at least it distracts them.

While Ruth stroked the horse's head, bending in her blue jeans to look up into the horse's huge eyes, Clay glanced at the afternurse. In a quiet voice he said, "You hired a woman to obtain the sperm sample?"

She nodded. "Alice. She'll be here by the top of the hour. I already have the urine sample." She grinned at Clay. "That one's always easy to get."

"How old is Eisenberg?"

"Ninety-one."

Clay raised his voice. "Ruth? I'd like to meet your dad now, if that's okay. Would you prefer to be present?"

She tore herself away from the distraction of petting the horse. "Absolutely!"

The daughter acted as hostess, leading Clay and the afternurse into a back bedroom.

As she passed through the doorway into the bedroom she said in a high, tiny voice, "Hi, Daddy."

He was lying on his back in bed. Sheet pulled down to his chest. Wearing blue-striped pajamas.

Clay walked over to the side of the bed for a closer look.

A shriveled little man. Liver spots on his hands and balding skull. Big ears, white hair growing out of each, like something leaving. Large moles on his neck.

His wrinkled eyelids were almost fully closed. Clay, looking down, could see the milky eyes shifting within, like two slow fish.

The father's breaths were bigger than his lips. Infrequent. The afternurse was right. He was slowing down.

Behind the bed, up on metal poles, the cheerful blue and green lines spiking across the screens of the monitoring equipment, beeping steadily.

"I used to always know what my dad was thinking. Just from being so familiar with that face! Now I can't tell. That's what dying does. They're somewhere else. When he holds his hand out, for the first time in my life I don't know what he wants. For me to hold his hand? For me to give him a glass of water? To turn on the TV? I'm no longer sharing with him. I'm just observing."

"Did he eat today?"

Ruth hugged herself. "Half a sardine sandwich, while he watched The Dick Van Dyke Show." She pulled a white Kleenex out of the bright teenage colors of the cardboard dispenser by the side of the bed. Wiped her father's wet nostrils, reversed the Kleenex, wiped his lips.

119

"What's he dying from?"

"Originally it was cirrhosis of the liver. When they started running tests to come up with a treatment plan, they realized he had lung cancer. So technically, that's what's actually going to kill him."

She was trying not to cry. "I want to tell you something about my father. I don't want this to just be an anonymous job you do. Okay?"

Most people need to share, at this point. He looked sideways at her. "Okay."

She picked up her dad's limp left hand, large blue veins streaming across the tendons of the back of the hand. Held the big bony knuckles of his fingers. "He was the youngest of seven children. All the rest of them got jobs working for the city, or as night guards, but he went to college and became a biologist. He worked all over the world. When I was growing up, my mother and I would get postcards from Brazil, and Hong Kong, and Sweden. I used to look up the entries for the different countries in the local library's Encyclopedia Britannica. I'd read about the populations, and major exports, and average rainfall. It was all so exotic! He was a really great dad." She tried to raise her chin up out of her grief. "He let me know that I can do anything I dream I can do.

"After he retired, he started making dioramas, wooden boxes with the front open, where you can see a scene inside. There's one over there."

Clay walked over, bent his knees to look inside. The diorama was the size of a shoebox on its side. Past the Saran wrap stretched whitely across its front, with some diagonal wrinkles, he could see a small jungle tucked rectangularly within, green tinsel for the rain forest floor, upwards-spreading tiny trees, minuscule butterflies and flying beetles suspended by the thinnest fish line.

"That's beautiful."

A daughter's pride. "It really is. I'm thinking of using some of the estate money to have his collection permanently archived at the local college. Except for some dioramas I want to keep for sentimental reasons."

Clay let a beat pass. Turned to the afternurse. "How did he do on the alternatives test?"

Mrs. Ritchie glanced at the daughter. "Not so good. I got him to talk about one case where years ago he and his wife were waiting at a bus station because their car broke down, a tire rolled off, and this other man at the bus depot, younger than him, kept staring at his wife's legs. She was wearing shorts."

"Did the younger man interact with the wife?"

"Not verbally. But apparently he kept staring at Mrs. Eisenberg's legs, and would occasionally try to catch her eye."

120

"Did he do anything in real time?"

"No. But afterwards, he had a fight with his wife on the bus back home. Questioning whether she was flirting with the young man, either consciously or subconsciously."

"How did the alternatives go?"

"When he replayed the scene in his mind, several times a day over the past fifty years, it would always end with him standing over the younger man, eventually gouging out the young man's eyes with his thumbnails."

Clay turned to the daughter. "That level of violence in revenge fantasies is fairly typical," he said, to reassure her.

"I got him to recreate the scene thinking of what a more reasonable response would be. In one recreation, he glared at the man, but then the scene eventually led to him getting off his bench, gouging out the younger man's eyes with his thumbnails. In another recreation, I had him walk over to the younger man, asking him to not be rude, to respect the fact he and his wife were married, but it ended with him gouging out the younger man's eyes with his thumbnails. I tried different scenarios where he and his wife moved to a different bench, or he put his shirt over his wife's legs, or gave the younger man the finger, or stared at him with hostility, or tried to reason with the younger man's rudeness, or tried to befriend the younger man, or threaten the younger man, or complain to the bus station personnel about the younger man, or stand aggressively directly in front of the younger man, shifting his body to block the man's view of his wife's legs, or stare at the man while he put his hands on his wife's bare legs, like you can look all you want, loser, but only I get to actually touch her legs, and fourteen other variations, but they all ended with him gouging out the younger man's eyes with his thumbnails. He definitely was stuck in the replay rut.

"There were also a lot of masochistic embellishments, where Mr. Eisenberg and the younger man got in a verbal or physical confrontation, and the younger man bested Mr. Eisenberg."

"And how many times has Mr. Eisenberg replayed the incident since its original occurrence?"

Mrs. Ritchie put on a conscientious face. "I'm estimating, over the past fifty years, he replayed the incident in his head approximately fifty thousand times. Although Mr. Eisenberg tried many, many times to come up with a satisfactory solution that would not be violent, all of the replayings ended with Mr. Eisenberg gouging out the younger man's eyes with his thumbnails, and none of the fifty thousand replayings gave Mr. Eisenberg any sense of closure or peace."

"And you say there are probably thirty-two other Smudges Mr. Eisenberg would struggle with each day, trying to resolve an unpleasant encounter from his past?"

"At least. Over the past fifty years he's probably reenacted encounters with Smudges, trying unsuccessfully to resolve them, at least one hundred times a day. It must have been exhausting."

Clay turned to the daughter. "You understand, the best response to an encounter with a jerk is for your father to eventually realize he doesn't control how other people behave, and other people may in fact be behaving in a way he's misinterpreted, in that their behavior may not be as antagonistic as your father may have initially perceived the behavior to be. In other words, 'It's not all about him.' And that in any event all of us in life encounter people who are unpleasant, and we just need to put those encounters in context with the more important anchors of happiness we have in life. But some people, and certainly your dad, become so obsessed with these instances of perceived disrespect that they can't shake it. It drags down their life."

The front doorbell ding-donged.

Clay smiled at the daughter, who looked uncomfortable. "That's probably Alice. She's come to spend some time with your dad."

"And do what?"

Clay stood up from his chair. "She's here to help us prepare the Warfarin."

He and the afternurse held back as the daughter headed towards the front door. Clay looked at the nurse. "You're sure Alice will be able to get a sperm sample from Mr. Eisenberg?"

"She's a pro. She could get a sperm sample from a corpse."

Ruth opened the front door. Clay couldn't see what Alice looked like, because of Ruth's eclipsing body.

Ruth's voice was tense. "Come on in. There's a live horse in the living room, so just be aware of that."

Ruth backed-up as Alice entered.

"What a lovely home." Her voice sounded light, musical.

"It's my dad's home. I live in Nashville."

Alice stepped around Ruth, recognizing Mrs. Ritchie. She was short, middle-aged, bit on the heavy side, yellow blouse, purple slacks. The type of thick-lensed glasses that make the face a mask.

Clay shook her hand. "I'll show you where our patient is."

Ruth reared her head. "What exactly is she going to do?"

Alice tilted up her eyeglasses. She squeezed Ruth's upper arm. "I'm here to give your dad a foot massage!"

Mrs. Ritchie raised her eyebrows. "We want your dad relaxed."

Clay, Mrs. Ritchie and Ruth sat in the living room while Alice was in the back bedroom with Ruth's dad.

Mrs. Ritchie cleared her throat. "Is Nashville a nice place to live?"

Ruth, one ear cocked to pick up any sounds from the back bedroom, ran a thin hand through her hair. "It's okay."

"Lots of barbeque joints, I'm sure."

"Did you bring any food to feed the horse? It looks hungry."

Clay glanced at the afternurse. "Mrs. Ritchie, did you explain the Warfarin process to Ruth?"

"I did, yes. Ruth, you do know what's going to happen, right?"

"Well I guess I do. Somewhat."

"Did Mrs. Ritchie share with you that this horse is not going to survive the night?"

Ruth's wet eyes looked from the horse, snuffling the TV set, back to Clay. "Somewhat. I mean, of course the actual, physical horse wasn't here when she did. Is it absolutely necessary to kill him? Isn't there any other way?"

"No. If you want your dad to pass from this life a less tortured soul than he is right now, hoping that that will make him less susceptible to Smudges in his next life, we do have to slaughter this horse. If you're not okay with that, we need to know right now. Because then you've wasted our time."

Ruth was teary-eyed. "Well of course I don't want my dad to suffer. But do you kill the horse quickly? Is he anesthetized before you kill him?"

"The horse is going to go through a lot of pain. That's why I tied him up, so he can't break free."

"I don't know why helping my dad has to involve torturing a beautiful animal."

"Well, it does. And you're going to have to be the one who tortures it. Can you do this?"

Ruth looked helpless. "I mean, I love my dad. I want him to be happy. I just want him to die in peace."

"Then this is what you have to do."

"But how do I live with that? What does that do to me?"

"So you're backing out?"

"No. But give me something to cling to."

"What's more important? Your dad being happy, or what happens to an animal you never knew existed until an hour ago?"

Alice walked into the living room, beaming. "Your dad loved his foot massage."

Clay accepted the plastic baggie from Alice. Wiping her right hand with a perfumed wet nap she asked, "May I stay? I love this shit."

Clay added the father's urine that Mrs. Ritchie had collected to the baggie, then spit in the baggie.

Ruth, hugging herself, came closer. "What is that?"

"The sperm is death. The urine is life. The spit? That's me."

"The sperm?"

He massaged the sides of the baggie, getting all three fluids to mix. "We have to move quickly."

He strode over to the horse. Reached his left hand into the baggie, scooping up the yellow, gelatinous mixture on his fingers. Bonked the horse on its black nose, getting it to open its jaws in protest.

His left hand snaked down the maroon throat of the horse, elbow resting on its big teeth, smearing the horse's esophagus.

The horse reared back, lifting its front hoofs.

Clay moved in aggressively, circling his left arm around the back of the horse's head, forcing its long profile down, right hand massaging the throat to get the horse to swallow the mixture.

Once he released the horse from his strong grip, the horse backed up in the living room, beautiful tail switching, snorting through its nostrils.

"Okay."

He handed a knife to Ruth. Stared into her eyes. "This is what you're going to do. You can think about what you did this evening the rest of your life, but for right now, I don't want you to think at all. I just want you to do what I tell you to do. Unless you want your dad to live in the hell of his own memories."

Ruth, sniffling, nodded.

"Everywhere I tap on the horse with my right index finger, I want you to stab the knife into the horse at that point, up to the depth of the black magic marker line I've drawn on the blade. Do you understand?"

"I had no idea that—"

"Do you want to save your dad?"

"Yes, of course, but—"

"Then just fucking do it. Don't think. Just stab. Or your dad is going to a hellish afterlife. Here!"

Clay tapped a stretch of muscular brown flesh just behind the horse's head. "Stab!"

Crying, Ruth lifted the knife. Made a few feints. "I just can't, I—"

The afternurse got behind Ruth, banged her meaty palm on the back of Ruth's clenched hand, the impact punching the knife deep into the brown flesh of the horse. The blade didn't quite sink into the horse up to the black magic marker line, so the afternurse pounded the side of Ruth's hand again.

All the way in.

The horse reared up, Clay holding onto both sides of its brown mane, its black nostrils flexing, eyes panicky, mouth opening in big-toothed pain.

Ruth was shaking, snot dribbling out of her nose.

"It's a fucking animal! Do you love your dad? Do you truly love your dad?"

She reared up the knife, plunged it where Clay tapped his finger. The afternurse took over holding the horse's head down by its mane. Clay made a slow circuit around the horse, tapping here, tapping there, Ruth raising the knife, terrified face speckled with dark blood, plunging the blade down, into the horse's meat over and over and over and over and over and over again as the horse bucked its head, hooves drumming on the living room carpet, anus under the tail dribbling pungent-smelling feces, long face screaming in agony.

Once they had completed the circuit, Clay took the knife away from Ruth. She turned around clumsily, staggered away, threw up on top of the TV set. Threw up again. Sparks fireworked from the set as it short-circuited, screen going black, smoke rising from behind.

"Okay." Clay handed Ruth a wet paper towel. "Wipe your mouth. And your nose. This is just the beginning. "

Ruth's black and gray hair hung in front of her face. She spoke in a hoarse voice. "What do I have to do? What does this entail? I want to save my dad, but I want there to be something of me left after I do it!"

"We're going to bring out the Smudges now. You have to confront them, shout them down, convince them your dad is a good person. This has to be done by someone who truly loves him, and it looks like you're the only person who did. This can't be done by friends, or neighbors. This has to be done by someone who no matter what, loved him unconditionally. His wife is dead, you're his only child, so it's on you. Can you do this?"

She stood in her blue jeans in the middle of the blood-splattered living room, a fifty-five year old daughter, shoulders swaying. "Let's do it. He's an old guy." Her nose scrunched up her face. "I love him."

By this time, pink cones had sprouted from each knife wound, like dunce caps. Clay stepped in, rubbing rancid butter over each cone, like greasing dozens of penises.

As he stepped back with his homely face, as he watched, small men erupted from each cone, up to their waists, as well as a few women, little heads turning around, surprised at where they were, small arms waving.

Dozens and dozens of them, malicious.

Ruth touched her fingertips to her lips. "Are they demons?"

Clay shook his head. "They're just ordinary people. It's your dad who thinks of them as demons. These may not even be bad people. But your dad thought they were, because of a chance encounter. Maybe if he had gotten to know them better, he might have actually become friends with some of them. But the thing with Smudges isn't who the people actually are. It's what your dad perceives them to be. So we're not exorcising the people. We're exorcising your dad's opinion of these people."

Clay shot her a look. "You have to understand, chances are there are a lot of people walking around in the world who hold your dad as a Smudge. It's all interconnected."

He moved her in front of the bleeding horse. "Listen to what the heads are saying. Refute each one."

Ruth, standing, swayed. Blinking her eyes, she stared at the heads.

One of the heads, young male with long hair, struggling to pull the rest of its body out of the brown side of the horse, unsuccessfully, glared up at Ruth. "Pretentious shit. Never said more than hello to me all the times he'd show up at my window to deposit his checks."

Ruth shifted her feet, like playing a game of catch. "My dad was shy! If he didn't talk to you it was because he couldn't think of what to say to someone from a different generation than him."

"Blah, blah, fucking blah."

Mrs. Ritchie showed Clay and Ruth the pencil sketch she had done that matched the Smudge's face. "Eisenberg—your dad—told me he hated this guy, Mike, because Mike kept asking him for his driver's license, even though he had been coming to Mike's teller window at the bank for four years. He felt Mike was doing that to make him jump through loops. Like he wasn't important enough to remember from each visit. A passive-aggressive thing."

The Smudge's head puffed with fury. "I heard that! I have to write the driver's license down on each check I receive! I did it for everyone! Did he never notice that? Did he really expect me to memorize the driver license numbers for all my hundreds of customers?"

Ruth stepped in front of the little Smudge. "But he never knew that! You never told him that!"

"Well…"

"My dad was a good person! I loved him. Why couldn't you have been kinder towards him?"

The Smudge said nothing. Its upper body went limp, hanging sideways. Clay, using the knife, lopped it off the horse's side. The Smudge fell heavily onto the living room carpet, limp as a small, dead octopus.

Clay bumped Ruth's shoulder, moving her to the next Smudge.

"This one's right here." Mrs. Ritchie flipped to the relevant page in her sketchpad. "Eisenberg and your mom went to dinner at a North Hollywood restaurant when your mom's cousin was in the hospital. The Smudge was their waiter. He ignored your dad throughout the meal, speaking only to your mom, flirting with her. Your dad got incredibly jealous. Wanted to kill the waiter, smash his face down on their table, lift the face up so the waiter could spit out teeth, then smash his face down again."

"Why would you be so disrespectful? My mother and father were in a tense time. Her cousin was dying. Why couldn't you have picked up on that, and not just be some oily waiter with all this resentment over his station in life who tries to score on the men he has to wait on?"

The little head raised his face, tiny arms waving furiously. "I'm gay! I don't like talking to straight men because they always put me down! Score laughs off me. So of course I only talk to the ladies. What did I do wrong? I brought over exactly what your dad ordered, and even got the cook to make up horseradish sauce, which the restaurant doesn't normally serve, for your dad's prime rib dinner. And for that he wants to break my mouth apart?"

"He didn't know you were gay. All he saw was a man leaning over his wife constantly, speaking only to her, ignoring him. Why couldn't you have been more open-minded? Why would you immediately assume my dad was this homophobic type you're talking about? Why didn't you even give him a chance?"

The Smudge opened his small mouth. Shut it. His head, arms went limp, hanging sideways off the horse's brown flesh. Clay lopped him off.

Mrs. Ritchie flipped through her sketches. "Okay! This one here, sticking out of the horse's haunch. With the spiky black hair and the tattoos on his neck. Your dad was trying to start his car one morning outside a Seven-Eleven, and the motor wouldn't turn over. This Smudge came out of the store holding a container of coffee. Once he realized your dad couldn't get his car started, he stuck his head through the rolled-down passenger window, it was a warm day, and started mocking your dad. Calling him an old man who couldn't even start his own car. Couldn't get it up."

"Why would you say that? What did my dad do to you?"

"Fuck you!"

"But why did you say that?"

"Fuck you!"

Clay touched Ruth's shaking shoulder. "This is a malicious Smudge. They're the worse. The confrontation isn't based on a misunderstanding. Malicious Smudges are infested with their own Smudges. Think about this: A lot of times, when someone insults someone, they're calling that person what they fear they are themselves. "

"Do you have a girlfriend?"

The head sputtered. "Fuck yeah!"

Ruth drew herself up to full height. "Is she faithful?"

The tiny hands gestured down at the little waist high body rising out of the horse's haunch. "What bitch wouldn't be faithful to this?"

"So, on some frightened level you know she's fucking other guys, right? Is it a neighbor? A coworker? The guy who gave you those tattoos?"

The face reared up on its neck tendons, screaming at Ruth.

Clay lopped off the teary-eyed Smudge.

By the time all the Smudges had been cut off the horse, brown clumps across the carpet, staining it, everyone in the living room was exhausted.

Clay sat on the sofa. Looked up at Ruth, who was still side-stepping, even though there were no more opponents. "On this night of all nights, I hope you don't mind if I smoke a cigarette?"

She looked like she would object, automatically, but then the rising breath went out of her, and she didn't.

He gestured with his lit cigarette at the floor. "You're going to have to replace the carpet, if you want to sell this house after your dad dies."

Face flushed, she looked down. "You don't think I could just rent a rug shampooer machine at the supermarket?"

Clay scrunched his eyes. "It's actually going to get messier by the time we're finished. I don't think a rug shampooer could do the job."

She plunked down next to him. Accepted a cigarette, a light. Exhaled smoke towards the agitated horse. "You know, the thing is, your dad is dying, and you think that's going to be a memorable event in your life, something special, and spiritual, but then all these other realities encroach on that. I would love this to be something like in a movie, where I journey to my dad's house and hold his hand as he peacefully passes on, then I spend a day in his empty house just walking through all the rooms, filled with memories, but the truth is I've had to devote almost more time to my dad's finances, and mine, as I have to his actual dying.

"After I pay you, I'm broke. My dad doesn't have any money. He refinanced the mortgage on this house two times, to help cover medical costs when my mom was dying. So there's no money there. Given the economy, I'm probably going to end up owing money once we sell the house. Plus I have to pay funeral costs, and burial costs, and thousands of dollars to an attorney to get everything through probate. I'm not rich. I'm not even financially stable. I live paycheck to paycheck. What little money I have in the bank after I pay you and the funeral home and the cemetery and the attorney I'm using to get my dad's dioramas accepted by a local university. I have no one left now. If I lose my job in Nashville, I'll lose my apartment. I'm fifty-five. It sucks I haven't saved up much money over the years, but what am I supposed to do?

"My job is not secure. I helped make my company as big as it is. I was one of the stars. But there have been so many lay-offs over the years, and so many younger people brought in at lower salaries, that I no longer know half the people there. I called the other day to say I would be late, I was meeting a client off-site and the meeting had gone longer than scheduled, and the receptionist at my work had no idea who I was. Plus there's this new woman there, Cheryl, who's half my age, and I just know she's gunning for my job. I hired her! But then I found out she was saying things behind my back. I tried to befriend her, take her to lunch at Pavor's, which is an exclusive club in uptown Nashville, but I could tell she saw that as weakness on my part. And you know what? It was."

She started crying.

"I go down to the break room and she has her own little clique of women her age. When they see me, they shut up. I even feel nervous now when we're in the same meetings. There's always those little digs at me, big innocent smile on her face, in front of everyone.

"What am I going to do? My dad's dying. He's the last person in the world who really knows who I am. Who I could call up at ten o'clock at night to talk about these things. What's going to happen to me once he's gone?"

Clay waited a beat. "Sounds like you have some real problems. I have to finish with the horse now. You did a great job confronting the Smudges. You may not want to be here for this next part."

She finished her cigarette. "Oh, what the fuck. I might as well see it all. I'm paying for it."

Clay stood in front of the bleeding horse. The afternurse brought his long black canvas bag over.

The horse's big dark eyes, moist with misery, watched as he pulled out a long, shining blade.

As the horse started to rear its profile, Clay's sword fell hard across the back of its neck.

The first blow cut clear through the neck bones.

The long face drooped down, hanging off the neck by the skin of the throat, mouth opening, blood spilling over the lower teeth.

Clay raised his arms again, slammed the sword's blade back down into the widening wound behind the neck.

The horse's head fell off its shoulders. Landed sideways on the white carpet, gushing blood.

The horse's beautiful body, headless, backed up blindly.

All of them in the living room, Clay, Ruth, Mrs. Ritchie, Alice, watched the muscular legs stilt around aimlessly, gore dripping out of the neck hole, tall legs stumbling against the furniture, looking for a way out of a situation that had no way out.

Just when it seemed the staggering would go on forever, the four knees buckled. The animal fell over, legs stiffening, sticking out straight. A painting of a sunlit cottage in the woods fell off the wall. The large black chest heaved a few final times, blowing pink bubbles out of the neck hole, then everything was quiet, motionless.

Ruth, hand to her mouth, looked like she was going to break down in tears, but she didn't.

Clay moved quickly. He filled the horse's mouth with sea salt.

Gouged out both eyeballs with a tablespoon. Filled the red sockets with more salt.

Went around back, lifted the stiff rear leg, and with a long knife sliced off the horse's cock and balls. Filled the dark red hollow with more salt.

Still on his haunches, wiping his bloody hands with paper towels, he looked up at Ruth. "I'll haul off the horse. Because we cut off all the Smudges, it's spiritually infected. It has to be burned, then its black bones ground to dust. The dust has to be combined with salt, and thrown into the ocean."

She nodded dumbly.

"That's included in the price."

"Okay."

He stood up. Raised his eyebrows. "It's time to let your dad go. While the Smudges are silent."

"Okay, so now we go in the bedroom?"

"Yeah."

Clay stopped Alice at the bedroom door. "I don't think you need to be present for this part."

She raised her eye-glassed face. "Oh, but I want to be!"

He put his right hand on her yellow blouse, stopping her from moving forward. "In other words, you need to leave."

Alice swung her face to Mrs. Ritchie. "I was hoping I'd—"

Mrs. Ritchie stood in front of Alice. "I'll call you in the morning, babe. We'll have lunch! But for now, you have to leave."

Clay turned to Mrs. Ritchie. "You too."

She seemed genuinely surprised. "I usually stay, in case—" But she didn't finish the sentence. "It was a great pleasure working with you."

"Those sketches really came in handy."

After both women were gone, Clay and Ruth entered the bedroom. Eisenberg was still on his back, the way they had left him.

His claws clutched the top of the white bed sheet.

"Say your last goodbyes, please."

Ruth's face was red, puffed. Eyes popping out of the face, from so much sadness. "This is it? This is final?"

"Yeah."

"No more calling him on the phone? No more planning for a visit from him? Getting a hug? Hearing his stories?"

Clay didn't answer.

Ruth leaned over her dad's face. Put her fifty-five year old palm against the side of his face. His eyelids fluttered.

"Daddy? Can you hear me? I love you, daddy. I'll see you and mommy someday soon. Then we'll all be happy again, like we used to be."

"Finished?"

She backed off, childish look on her face.

"Don't touch him from this point forward. It's too dangerous."

Clay stood by the brass headboard, behind Eisenberg's head. Snaked his left hand down. Using his thumb and index finger, he pinched the old man's windpipe closed, way up under the soft skin of his jaw.

Eisenberg's hips rose slightly.

"You can look away if you want."

She shook her head left, right. "I don't want to."

Eisenberg's claws lifted away from the white bed sheets, but they stopped mid-air.

Clay continued shutting off Eisenberg's windpipe, with a casualness as if checking his pulse, looking up at the ceiling.

Ruth lifted her elbows, keening. "Goodbye daddy! I love you!"

The weak shifting of the limbs, the body's struggle to keep the life force, ceased.

Clay held onto the windpipe a moment longer.

Let go.

"You can touch him now."

Ruth kissed his forehead, tears dripping on his frozen face.

They went back out to the living room.

Clay got on his cell phone, arranging to have people he knew come out to get rid of the horse.

"I already spoke to the town's Medical Examiner. They understand these situations, especially in the South. There won't be an autopsy. Your dad died of natural causes."

Ruth bobbed her head up and down. "I don't—I'm not sure what good manners are in a situation like this. Do you want something to eat? There's still some pastrami in the fridge." She shrugged.

"Thanks, but no. Everything I eat tastes like mud. I have to get going."

"Oh! Okay. Wow, we've been through this life-altering evening together…"

Clay packed up his equipment. "I have to return the horse trailer tonight. It's a rental."

She followed him to the front door. "What happens if I have Smudges when I'm near death?"

"Do you have any children?"

She shook her head.

"That does make it more difficult." He reached in his shirt pocket. "Here's my card. When the time comes, give me a call. I'll see what I can do."

He unlocked the front door.

"Okay. So, this is it?"

Clay turned back towards her. This was always the part he hated, the human-interaction part. "Your father will have a less-troubled life next time, thanks to you." His homely face smiled. He was actually a little shorter than her. "Congratulations."

This Old Haunted House

His grandfather's car was gone.

Jonathan didn't want to park in the same place where the silver Lexus would normally be, right by the front door, so he pulled further along the curve of the circular driveway, by one of the drive's drainage grates, under the blue San Diego sky.

Radio off, engine off, he rose out of the driver's side door to a green neighborhood ticking with quiet. Trees quiet, pavement quiet. Not even bird song.

The lawn leading up to the porch was still neatly-mowed and edged; the pink and yellow rose bushes flanking the walk still held dark green leaves free of black spot. He could see fresh, slanted pruning work on branches whose flowers had faded.

For the first time in his life, he had a key to his grandfather's front door.

He eased the key's tiny mountain range of serrations into the lock's brass slit. Twisted right.

Still hard to believe his grandfather wouldn't be waiting for him inside. White moustache, eyeglasses hanging on a chain below his jaw.

The tall interior was as silent as the outdoors.

He started by just walking through the downstairs, like a ghost, remembering his grandfather in each room, the good times, the bad times, the occasional nights the old man had had too much scotch.

No one would ever believe the kitchen belonged to a seventy year old. Poured concrete counters, herb gardens basking with three shades of green under the sunlight of every window, all the latest stainless steel gadgets.

Out of curiosity, Jonathan opened the door to the refrigerator.

The food hadn't been cleared out. Apparently that was his job. Mushroom soy, tall as a wine bottle. Pale knobs of ginger, noses pointing in different directions. Seaweed wrapped in plastic, the plastic overlaying silver triangles across the dark, dried jade. Two fresh water chestnuts, bobbing in a tub. Unopened package of tofu. Squat glass jar of unpasteurized caviar. The long body of a duck, with its pale skin.

Jonathan lifted out the jar of caviar. Unscrewed the lid. Sniffed the tiny black eggs inside. Something he never would have done while his grandfather was still alive, he submerged his index and middle finger down

135

into that cold, rolling-away wetness. Scooped out a tall clump. Slid it between his lips.

Still fresh!

He moved the dark mass around in his mouth, teeth and tongue feeling the small pops of the eggs.

That wonderful, briny taste of raw ocean.

Granddad.

On the pink marble floor in front of the stainless steel stove, the punctuation of a big red comma, where his grandfather fell backwards, died.

He spent a little more time downstairs, reminiscing, but he knew what he really wanted to do, and that looking at the geraniums in the sun shot study, feeling the fur of their leaves, which he loved to do as a kid, and lifting through the stack of magazines in the living room, with their white address labels, was just a way to delay his real interest. What he wanted to do, with this new freedom to snoop, was go upstairs and, for the first time in his life, enter his grandfather's bedroom.

As a kid, when he had stayed over, his grandmother still alive, caramelizing onions in a black iron skillet, he would be put in the room next door. Its postered bed too big for a boy, always having trouble getting to sleep between unfamiliar sheets, overhearing the deep rumbles of conversations, and snores, through the wallpaper's watercolors. And always, after the short black hour hand, with its filigreed pointer, jerked from twelve to one, while his snub-nosed profile tried left, right on his pillow, the long, distant moan of a train would start up, from the darkness beyond the black and silver mesh of the window screen, garlic in beef stock. That train signal was the voice of the night, its animal wail so evocative, so lonely, so romantic, he knew it was a train chugging him to his future, away from this town, away from this family, this bedroom.

He stood on the threshold to his grandfather's bedroom. Had to actually reassure himself granddad was dead, it was okay to finally enter.

Most of the room he had, of course, glimpsed as a child as he passed by it, eyes sliding left, shoes slowing, towards the upper room's nearest bathroom.

The bed he knew. It was right in front of the doorway.

Dresser on the left? Had seen it, but only from outside the doorway.

First surprise. There was a closet on the right. Over two decades, and he had never known that, because the angle of the opened bedroom door would always cut it off.

And on the wall opposite the bed, only visible from within the bedroom?

Paintings.

Three of them.

Each looked a hundred years old.

A skating scene, on a blue pond. A cottage tucked in the woods, orange windows. A green field, overgrown, the eye travelling up the paint to a yellow sun.

The closet held about a dozen of his grandfather's dark suits, smelling like him, on hangers, plus one pink and white flowered dress, and, hanging at a slant, a large hat box. Inside the hat box, nothing but scent.

At the bottom of the closet, shoes. Propped against the back wall, a shotgun. On the wooden shelf above the hangers, old newspapers. Jonathan went through them, curious, yellow pages cracking apart into jigsaw pieces, but nothing in them seemed relevant.

The bureau held socks and underwear, none of which Jonathan touched, plus one drawer down handkerchiefs, bowties and cufflinks, one drawer lower pajamas, and in the lowest drawer, nothing, just a thin sheet of beige paper meant as a lining.

Three hours after he shut off his car's engine in the circular driveway, he was down in the dark basement.

It stretched on forever.

As he advanced into it, he had to pull down more and more hanging chains, to have the latest naked bulb light a wider yellow glare of subterranean clutter, like working his way through the solar system.

Far from the wooden stairs, by now just floating horizontal lines behind him, he came across several large beige boxes.

Fearful of spiders, he ripped the top off one of the boxes.

Squinted down into the shadows.

Rounded gleams.

He pulled one free.

It was a Chinese metal serving bowl, with a lid. The type of metal bowl that would be brought to your table at a Chinese restaurant, with a metal hood. You'd lift the hood, and inside there'd be the steam of Sweet and Sour Pork, or Egg Foo Young, or Orange Beef.

He rummaged through the rest of the boxes, finding dozens and dozens of the same bowl and lid combinations.

The contractor he hired was supposed to show up at eight o'clock. Jonathan arrived in the circular drive with all his blue-inked notes on his yellow legal pad at seven-thirty, white-capped cup of coffee from McDonald's in his car's molded cup holder, in case the crew arrived early, but the orange pick-up truck didn't turn into the bottom of the drive until a quarter to nine.

"Did you have trouble finding the place?" Standing outside his car, in a dress shirt and tailored trousers, watching the three t-shirted men approach. His way of letting them know he knew they were late, without being confrontational about it. At twenty-four, and with a law degree, he had a lot of confidence, but he had never overseen a house renovation before, didn't know a lot of the technical terms, and the foreman he had selected was twice his age.

He wanted to show his father he was an adult, he could handle this type of project.

"Sorry about that, Mr. Wilson. It took a bit longer than I expected to round up the crew."

They all trooped through the downstairs, Jonathan pointing out the changes he wanted. Red tape meant remove and toss in the commercial trash bin he had rented, and had had towed to the site, a giant green coffin parked by the holly bushes. Yellow tape meant leave as is. Blue tape meant, change.

Jonathan, Dan the foreman, and Dan's two-member crew, Abbot and Costello, were in the library. "Pack up all the books in cardboard cartons. You don't have to catalogue them. Put the boxes in the center of the front hall, where I'll go through them later. Strip off all the wallpaper, prep the walls, then paint them Seashell Blue, using this paint sample. Pull up the carpet, put down this carpet in its place, Corn Husk, here's the sample."

And so on.

It took two hours. Dan asked a lot of questions, made lots of notes, which was reassuring.

Jonathan took a seat at his father's dining room table, halfway down one side, his fiancé, Jordan, lowering herself into the chair next to his.

His father, John, waited while the family butler, Orendo, poured pinot noir into the tall wine glasses, walking behind the chairs, tilting the wine bottle forward each time, like lighting candles. "Let's take the time to do this. A toast to Jack, my late father, your grandfather. Salute, Jack!"

Everyone took a sip. Jordan took a long swallow.

John rotated the bottom base of his wineglass against the white tablecloth. "Jonathan, I dropped by the house yesterday, and I didn't see a lot of changes."

"They peeled off all the seashore wallpaper in the rear sitting room, and painted the walls yellow."

"I didn't see that. I went out at three in the afternoon, and the wallpaper was still up."

"That's ….impossible. I was out there at noon, and the peeled-off wallpaper was lying in a big, curled heap in the middle of the room. They had two of the five walls painted."

"Didn't see it. You have to stay on top of these people." His father looked at his wristwatch. "If that's too much of a challenge, tell me now. I'll take over the supervision, even though that means I'll have to reschedule my court appearances."

"That's not necessary, dad. I'm on top of this."

His father used the undersides of the fingers on his right hand to make sure his moustache still felt groomed, pale eyes looking upwards, away from Jonathan. "If this contractor is leading you around by your nostrils—"

"—I'm handling it!"

"I didn't raise my son to be a figure of fun for a curly-haired contractor and his crew. Do you know how to bring out the whip, or do I have to leave my office, go down to the site, and bring out the whip myself?"

Nene, Jonathan's mother, beauty parlor hair, took another sip of her wine, choosing not to enter the conversation.

"I told you. I'm handling it."

"I got a big whip, son. You want me to whip it out, you just let me know."

"It's not necessary, dad. I've got this."

"We'll see. I better not catch you out there, during the workers' lunch break, stooping from man to man, patting the corners of their lips with a handkerchief. That's all I'm saying." He leaned back in his chair, holding up both palms like he was being robbed. "A new tradition I'm starting tonight?" His right hand ripped at his neck, pulling, flinging away. "No more bowties! Your grandfather always insisted I wear one, but I'm my own man now." He reached in the side pocket of his suit jacket, pulled out the snake of a red and black rep tie. Looped its length under his collar until the black and red diagonals fell just right in front of his shirt buttons.

Orendo came out with the main course, duck l'orange.

Jonathan, angling his gold fork, lifted the dark meat away from the ribs, put it in his mouth. Chewed.

"I supervised the preparation myself. Of course."

"It tastes different this time."

"I marinated the duck in teriyaki sauce. Pretty good, huh?"

"What made you decide to do that? To add an Asian treatment to duck l'orange?"

His father snorted. "There's nothing Asian about teriyaki sauce. This is ten times better than that Mexican crap you serve us whenever we visit."

Jonathan tried another forkful. "Dad, seriously, if you're concerned about the progress on the renovation, why not stop by tomorrow at the house? I'll show you what I've done, room to room." He looked away, shy. "I could cook you some breakfast. Just you and me. Scrambled eggs, slice of ham, cottage fries."

His father reared up in his chair, gray moustache rising. "Don't call them cottage fries. They're home fries. Your grandfather didn't live in a cottage. He lived in a magnificent home. Just like your mother and me live in a magnificent home."

Jonathan arrived at his grandfather's home the next morning at seven-thirty. His father's car was already there, in the spot where his grandfather used to park.

Jonathan pushed open the front door. "Dad? Hello?"

He found his father at the back of the house, in the rear sitting room, laughing on his cell phone.

The seashore wallpaper was back up on the walls. As if the walls had never been touched. As if his grandfather were still alive.

What?

His father slammed the phone shut. Shoved it back in his front pants pocket. "Is this the room where you told me they stripped off the wallpaper, put up yellow paint?"

Jonathan, despite himself, took a step back. "Yeah! I mean, they did. I saw it with my own eyes."

His father, shorter than him, got in his face. Past the point of polite distance, to where it was intimate. What a son fears, when the father's bloodshot eyes are looking directly up into your eyes, disappointment in those eyes you know too well. Like an older, less gentle form of you. It reminded him of that time, years ago, when Jonathan was dating that blonde girl trying to make it as a jazz singer on the local scene, and his dad, right under Jonathan's face, asked him if he needed some rubbers, he had them in his pocket just in case.

"Are the walls painted yellow, Jonathan? Simple question."

"They were. I don't know what—"

"Let me tell you something I have never told you, or anyone else, before. Out of shame. Your own mother doesn't know this story."

Jonathan tried backing up, but his father's harsh eyes telescoped forward.

"I was in grade school. There was a bully in my class. I watched, from my school desk, as he gradually got all the other boys to do what he told them to do. Give him their lunches. Kiss the sole of his shoe, which he'd slap up on their school desks. Carry his books. I tried to avoid any contact with the bully, by keeping my eyes down, pretending to be absorbed in my lessons. If the bully was humiliating another boy in class before the teacher arrived, looking around at the rest of us to see our reactions, I'd laugh out loud at what the bully was doing, just like the other kids. I was weak. I was frightened. I was intimidated."

Jonathan glanced again at the seashore wallpaper, trying to understand how it had got back up on the walls.

"Then one day, the bully came for me. He took my lunch out of the bag that your grandmother had prepared. Looked inside at the contents, then ate the peach she had put in there for me. Right in front of my face. Juice dripping down his chin. All the other boys laughing at how frightened I was. Then once he was finished with the peach, he held the pit out to me, and told me to eat it. To eat the pit. And I did. Do you have any idea how hard it is to gnaw your molars around a peach pit, trying to scrape off enough with each effort to be able to swallow? But I did it, and I did it, and I did it, until I finally swallowed the last shard, even though it hurt the back of my tongue. I did it because I was a coward. I was intimidated by another boy. I allowed another boy to rule what I did.

"You know what your grandfather, my father, did once he found out about that?"

Jonathan, uncomfortable, said nothing.

"Do you know?"

"No, I don't know."

"Your grandfather, my father, went out. Which he never did once he had arrived home for dinner. Windows in the living room filled with night. When he came back, he had a shopping bag with him. It said Eileen's on the outside of the shopping bag. I remember that. Didn't let me see what was inside.

"But the next morning, he showed up at the bathroom door while I was brushing my teeth. 'I laid your outfit out for you on your bed. The outfit you're going to wear to school today.'

"I finish brushing my teeth, already feeling ashamed for letting my dad down. Go into my bedroom, and there, laid across my made bed (I had to make my bed each morning before I went to the bathroom, even if I had a full bladder, or digestive problems), was the outfit your grandfather, my father, bought for me to wear to school that day. A pink dress, with pink stockings, and laid on the blanket above the dress, two long pink ribbons."

His father stopped talking. Stared up into Jonathan's eyes.

The silence made Jonathan uncomfortable. Blushing, he broke it. "What happened?"

141

"What do you think happened?"

Jonathan fidgeted, blinking, five years old, three feet tall. "You stood up for yourself? You refused to wear the dress?"

"Your grandfather, my father, told me to wear that dress!

"The girls at school howled behind their hands. Even the ones I secretly liked. I learned a lot that day. The boys? Do you want me to tell you how the boys reacted, Jonathan?"

In the near distance, Jonathan could hear the familiar thrum of Dan's pickup enter the bottom of the circular driveway.

His father leaned his face even closer. "Like hyenas." He pulled his face back. "Yup. Uncontrollable laughter. But with the laughter, the idea they were going to descend on me during recess. Tear me apart. Maybe not physically, but emotionally.

"So my first class, the bully walks in. The teacher is always late. May he rot in hell, for leaving children alone with each other, unsupervised. All the other classmates, by this point, are the bully's sycophants, because they've been broken by him.

"He starts off by calling me 'Joanna'. The other boys are leaning sideways out of their school desks, tears in their eyes from laughing so much. The girls? They're whispering behind their fingers, tossing white notes to each other, jiggling their crossed legs.

"So the bully comes down the school desk aisle towards me, real slow, real heavy, like he's a statue. His voice is a drawl. Mocking in its casualness. So show us your titties, Joanna. And you know what I did?"

"Is this like that song, A Boy Named Sue, where your dad forced you to defend yourself?"

"I don't understand what the fuck you're talking about, son. You know what I did?"

"No! I don't know."

"I got my thumbs under the pink shoulder straps of my dress, and I lowered those pink shoulder straps until the bully could see my nipples."

"What?"

"I was terrified of him! He could easily beat me up. I was afraid of the pain, the knocked-out teeth, the broken nose. And after that day, he never bothered me again, well at least not that much, because I was no longer a challenge. He knew I would never, ever rise up against him."

Jonathan heard the front door swing open, Dan and his crew arriving.

"Dad, I don't understand. What's the lesson you're trying to teach me?"

"Don't give in to bullies! When this contractor arrives, this Dan, I want you to march right up to him, punch him in the face. Or you're no son of mine."

Dan found Jonathan and his father in the rear sitting room. "Hey, guys!"

His father glared at Jonathan. "Are you a man? Are you my son?"

Dan walked over, extending his hand to the father. "Mr. Wilson?"

Abbot and Costello looked around at the seashore wallpaper.

The father shook Dan's hand. "I believe my son wants to have a word with you. Jonathan?"

"Dad…"

Dan pulled his face back on his neck. "Why'd you put the wallpaper back up? How were you even able to do it?"

"I didn't. I assumed you did."

Dan brought his eyebrows together. "No." He grinned. "We're the guys who tore it down, remember?"

"Jonathan?"

Jonathan, uncomfortable, unhappy, looked at the wallpaper, back at Dan. "Someone put it back up."

Dan laughed. Swung his face from son to father. "Wasn't us!"

"Are you my son, Jonathan?"

Jonathan curled his right hand, hanging by his side, into a fist. "It had to be you. Who else would have done it?"

Dan's face lost its joviality. "Hey. I told you. We didn't do it. If you want it removed for the second time, and the walls repainted for the second time, that's gonna be extra."

His father got up close to Jonathan, their chests touching, for the first time ever. His father whispered in his son's ear. "That's their scam. Tear wallpaper down, put it back up, tear it down again. So they can inflate their original quote. He's playing you for a fool, son."

"I'm paying you to remove the wallpaper. I'm only paying once. Remove the wallpaper, put up the yellow paint. Like you were supposed to."

Dan spread his shoes apart on the carpet. "I told you. We removed the wallpaper. You saw it removed."

His father's chest rubbing again against Jonathan's chest. "He's leading you around by your goddamn nostrils. You don't think they were laughing about this in the pickup on the way over? How he'd cow you into submission?"

"You're going to remove the goddamn wallpaper, put up the goddamn paint, and you're not going to charge me one goddamn cent for doing that."

143

Dan stared at Jonathan.

Jonathan opened his mouth to say more. To be a little conciliatory. Dan raised his hand. Jonathan closed his mouth. Dan's throat was red. "You listen to me, sonny. I don't know if you're trying to show off in front of your dad, or if you're just some fucking asshole, but I'm gonna make this real clear for you. You are going to get out your checkbook, and you are going to write us a check for the work we've already done on this house, through today. Then you are going to hand me the check, you are going to apologize to me, and me and my crew—"

Jonathan's fist bounced off Dan's nose.

The older man backed up. The punch appeared to have had no effect on him whatsoever. "The fuck?" He reached his right hand up. Jonathan noticed Dan's hand was much larger than his. Pinched the bridge of his nose with his thumb and forefinger. Wiggled the two fingers, to see if the nose was broken.

Stepped forward, made a fist, the knuckles standing up like hard ridges.

"Chief!" Abbot stepped behind Dan, looped his forearm under Dan's right armpit. "Not worth it. Creep's a lawyer."

Dan shook himself out from the forearm. Weathered face, laugh lines around the eyes and mouth, but now, set in disgust. "You write me a check right now, sonny boy. Add a thousand dollars for pain and suffering."

His father, on the sidelines, mimed throwing another punch.

Jonathan got out his checkbook.

After Dan and his men left, Jonathan, staring down at his shoes, lifted the weight of a sad glance, to his father's eyes.

"So now you have to start all over, son. Maybe find a contractor who doesn't intimidate you so much."

"That wasn't it."

"Looked that way to me." His father kept the left side of his mouth closed, opened the right side of his lips, letting out a loud cluck. "I was thinking it, wasn't going to say it, but here goes. Thank God Jordan wasn't here." He raised himself up on the fronts of his shoes. "Not a good thing to have your fiancé watch another man emasculate you. Can create some problems in the bedroom. Who's she really thinking about when the two of you are in bed? You, or the masterful contractor guy?"

"Fuck you, dad."

His father laughed, but his eyes were glistening. "Know how many times I'd say those two words to my own father, your grandfather? Know what he'd say right back at me? When you say that to someone, 'fuck you' means 'I'm impotent.' We might as well eat, since no work is going to get done today. I bought lunch for us. I thought it would be a celebratory meal, but clearly it isn't. I picked it up at a French bistro a few blocks from here."

"I thought I was going to cook some ham and eggs for us?"

His father lifted some wide, white Styrofoam cartons out of a pair of paper bags.

Jonathan flipped the lid on his container, steam wisping upwards, accepting the plastic spork and knife from his father.

The food inside was so soft he didn't need the plastic knife. Just cut off a square with the side of his spork. While his dad dug in, Jonathan held the sporked bite under his nose. Put it in his mouth, tasting egg, pork, cubed carrots, a soy and beef stock sauce.

"Delicious, isn't it?"

Jonathan swallowed. Looked sideways. "Dad, this is Egg Foo Young, isn't it?"

His father nodded while he ate.

"I thought you said you got it at a French bistro?"

"I did! French food is all I eat. The French know how to cook food. No one else does. Period. Certainly not the Mexicans. End of sentence."

It was uncomfortable having a meal with just his father. Without his mother or his fiancé present to distract, with their own conversation, from how little he and his dad spoke to each other.

"I thought you were going to stop wearing bowties."

"I am!"

"But you have a bowtie on now."

"What? I always wear a bowtie." His old fingers touched his blue bowtie, the white polka dots. Puzzled look in his eyes.

"The other night at dinner you said you were going to stop wearing bowties. You were going to be your own man."

He slammed down his spork. "I'm not my old man!" He made a dismissive face. "I didn't look familiar to myself with a regular tie. My father, your grandfather, wore a bowtie, and so do I. Means nothing. I'm certainly not my 'old man' as you seem to think. Nothing could be further from the truth. Eat your oeufs. Bon apetit!"

After his father left, Jonathan sat by himself in the kitchen for a long time, watching the sunlight slant through the window over the sink, how it slowly advanced across the marble floor, wishing he was a smoker, so he'd have something to do.

Why did he never have a conversation with his dad where he felt good afterwards? Is it like this for all sons? But he knew it wasn't. He knew his friends had much better relationships with their own fathers.

After a long time, the sun on the marble in front of the side-by-side, he went into the rear sitting room, picked up a can of the yellow paint.

The can was half empty, so obviously it had been used.

The kitchen had rich cherry wood paneling on the walls.

He walked over to the wall by the side-by-side, paint can dangling in his left hand, paint brush grasped in his right hand.

Dipped the paint brush into the can. Just an inch.

Held the brush in the can until it stopped dripping. Raised the brush out of the can, its front edge banana yellow.

Applied strokes up and down over the wall, bristles bending, coating a square foot of the cherry wood with banana.

Sat back down in his kitchen chair. Stared at the wet yellow square on the wall, trying to be as optimistic as the new paint smell.

Here I am, the kids I grew up with, went to school with, getting ahead in life, becoming adults, lighting their log fires with hundred dollar bills, and here I am, literally watching paint dry.

And it did eventually dry.

And it did eventually turn back into the rich cherry wood.

Once the regression was complete, he got out of his chair. Rubbed his palm over the square where the paint had been. No stickiness, no reside, no paint. Just cherry wood.

On the poured concrete island, a small cardboard box of brass pull knobs he bought online to replace the wooden pull knobs on the kitchen drawers.

Unscrewing each wooden knob, window over the kitchen sink darkening, he screwed in the replacement brass knobs.

Sat back down in his chair, facing the knobs.

Got up at one point, peeing on tip toe into the kitchen sink, eyes sideways at the brass knobs, because he didn't want to miss the transformation.

Sat back down after running the hot water tap in the sink.

The drawers' brass knobs had returned to wood knobs.

Remaining calm, he went down into the basement, where he remembered seeing a heavy mallet, with a long handle, propped against the side of the stairway.

Brought it upstairs, into the kitchen, dragging its heavy head, as if it were anesthetized, across the marble floor.

Wrapped his hands around the cobwebs on the handle.

Raised the mallet.

Smashed it down on the stove, black burners levitating. Against a door of the side-by-side, crinkling a waist into the stainless steel. Surprised the kitchen faucets, water jumping up like a scream. Smashed and smashed and smashed, smashing his father's face, his face, his life, until he was too spent to smash anymore, chest heaving, heart beating so loud it frightened him, and he collapsed on the marble floor.

When the slant of sunlight woke him up the next morning, limbs stiff from lying on the cold marble all night, the kitchen was back to the way it had been.

A boy with long red hair skateboarded past the parking meters, palms stretched out in crucifixion, balancing his height above the whirr of the skateboard's rolling wheels.

A green pick-up parked in an empty slot in front of the Bama Seashore Motel.

Tilda rose out of the pick-up to her full six foot, seven inch height, tousled blonde hair curling in the ocean breeze.

Smells of cotton candy, fried clams, sun tan oil.

Kids screaming, car passing behind her with a bad muffler, faraway boom across the seaside cove of a male announcing over a loudspeaker the roller coaster is now open!

She made her way down one side of the motel's black tar lot, long white lines marking parking spaces, looking at the black numbers on the aquamarine doors, until she reached 111.

Knocked.

From behind the door a muffled, "Just a minute!"

When the outside brass knob finally rotated left, a gaunt man, beige bathrobe wrapped around his body, stood back, inviting admittance.

She ducked her head so her height could enter the motel room, quickly swinging the door partially shut to look behind it.

Nobody with rope behind the aquamarine door.

The man shuffled back to the standard motel room circular table, resuming his seat. Curled his hand back around a cardboard cup of coffee, like palming the hot cup restored whatever strength he had left.

Motel bed, unmade. Stormy sky of yellow sheets, brown blanket suggesting it had not been a restful night.

The TV on top of the credenza was tuned to a local morning show about fathers and sons hunting together.

Tilda stood in the middle of the room. "Are you Jonathan?"

He nodded.

She left the front door to the motel ajar. Sat down in a chair opposite him. "Do you remember contacting me?"

A nod.

147

"So what do you have to show me?"

Jonathan pointed at the credenza. "Have you noticed how well made it is?"

Tilda got up, pulled out the top drawer. Rapped her knuckles against the interior side of the drawer. Solid wood. No veneer glued on particle board. Looked at where the front of the drawer met the two sides. Tongue in groove construction. "Okay. No motel could afford to put this piece of furniture in each room."

Jonathan sat up in his seat. "Exactly! When I first checked into this room, there was a different credenza under the TV. The cheap, slapped-together piece of furniture you see in any motel nowadays. Any home. But that credenza, the one that's here now, that came from an earlier era."

"I agree."

"Let me show you something else. Are you willing to go into the bathroom with me?"

"Okay."

He led her into the bright overhead light of the small bathroom, the cheap mirror, the plain toilet. "See that bathtub? Tell me the fucking motel paid for that."

Tilda advanced on the bathtub, where normally, in this type of motel, you'd find a plastic shower stall.

The bathtub was a standalone, with four gold feet, an elegant, curved white porcelain body suggestive of a woman's shape, gold fixtures.

Jonathan clutched his bathrobe tighter around him. "That bathtub followed me here. Just like the credenza. Just like some of the paintings on the wall, just like the expensive lamp on my side of the bed table."

Tilda raised the front part of her height up from smelling the bath tub's gold fixtures. "I agree. So what are you saying?"

He rubbed his nose, eyes shooting around. "Everywhere I go, and I've been moving from one motel to another across the United States, this furniture follows me. I checked into a motel in New Mexico, it was the typical cheap room made to look like an executive suite where an important person would open his suitcase, and the next morning, when I woke up, I had this tongue in groove credenza, this gold faucet bath tub where the night before had been a hard plastic shower stall, these different paintings on the wall. Same thing when I drove to motels in Dallas, New Orleans, Biloxi.

"All this furniture is from my grandfather's house in San Diego. My grandfather's house in San Diego is a haunted house that's following me across America. It won't let me drive away from it."

"What's your grandfather's name?"

"Jack Wilson."

"And your father's?"

"John Wilson."

"Jack is a nickname for John?"

"Well, yeah."

"Is your name Jonathan, or John?"

"Well, it's actually John. Everybody in the family called me Jonathan, to distinguish between me and my father."

"So, you're John Wilson III?"

"I suppose. I never really thought of it that way."

"Did your grandfather have any facial hair?"

Jonathan, looking gaunt, nodded, "He had a moustache."

"How about your father?"

"He has a moustache."

Tilda held out her palms. "And of course, you also have a moustache."

"Well, yeah. I just started growing it."

"Why?"

"I don't know. I just did. I see what you're saying. But the three of us are actually really different in all other ways. For example, we went out in completely different directions, career-wise."

"Like how?"

"Grandfather was in criminal law. My dad's in family law. I chose real estate law."

"Let's go back out to the living room."

Jonathan gestured at the kitchenette that came with the room. "Would you like me to make you something? I went to a small Mexican market earlier today. I can make you this terrific traditional Mexican dish, tofu sautéed in truffle oil."

Tilda shook her head.

"Look at that!" He got excited, like pointing at a shooting star.

Tilda turned around, at the wallpaper behind the bed.

As she watched, the wallpaper changed, shadows and lines shifting, country cottages enlarging into seashore cliffs.

Jonathan looked frightened. "That's the wallpaper from my grandfather's house. That's the first time I've seen it in one of these motels I've been renting. The haunted house is catching up to me. I've been in this motel too long. Should I check-out? But where would I go? Overseas?"

"The house would eventually find you. London, Tokyo, Cape Town, Buenos Aires, International Space Station."

A full-grown man, although a young man, not yet used to what life can do to you, he fell apart into tears. His red face looked at her for help.

"What am I supposed to do? I'm just starting out in life! I went to school, I got really good grades, I met a wonderful girl, I've been faithful to her, I've saved up money so we can buy a nice home of our own, I give to charity. It's not fair! Why do I have this problem, and no one else does?"

"If I had some Kleenex I'd offer them to you, but I don't carry Kleenex with me. That may have come out a little condescending, but I didn't mean it that way."

Jonathan took the hint. Went back to the bathroom. Returned with a white roll of toilet paper. Unraveled some squares. Blew his wet nose. Refolded the squares. Blew again. "Sorry."

Following Tilda's example, he lowered himself to his seat at the round table.

"You said no one else has this same problem, but it does show up from time to time. To varying degrees. In its mildest form, its most common form, children find themselves living with some of their parents' belongings in their house once the parents have passed. Some of those belongings they've physically brought into their home, but other belongings arrive in the home through supernatural agency. The children don't notice, because it's not that obvious. There may be a clothes hamper in their home from a spouse's childhood. It transferred on its own, supernaturally, from the parents' house, but since their own home also has other articles of furniture from the parents' house, they just assume it's something they themselves saved from the parents' house, like they saved a dining room hutch, some expensive skillets, or an easy chair.

"Your case is more extreme. Less common."

Jonathan reached for his roll of toilet paper. "I'm feeling really scared right now. Like I'm at a proctologist, and I've been putting off the exam for months because of fear, but now I have to know if…"

"…It's just a pimple, or if it's cancer?"

He nodded, eyes big.

"I understand. It's cancer."

"What?" The circles under his eyes started twitching. "I'm going to die?"

"Not physically. But who you are? That will die. Jonathan will go away, bit by bit, until Jonathan is gone, and what's left is Jack. Your grandfather."

"But I don't want to go away." In a tiny voice he said, "I want to stay me."

"We'll talk about that later. Tell me a little bit about your grandfather. What was his state of mind towards the end?"

150

Jonathan tossed more toilet paper in the wastebasket underneath his side of the table. "He was deteriorating. Mentally."

"How so?"

"He suffered from depression the last year of his life. One time when I was there, near the end, when he started drinking a lot more scotch, out of the blue he went into this monologue, both of us sitting in his living room, no lamps on, not even looking at me, about how he was trying to track his depression. Apparently, he felt depressed most of the time, but there were some times during the day when the depression just really hit him. Really dragged him down. And it wasn't consistent. It wasn't like, every day at four in the afternoon the really heavy depression would come. The arrival times would vary, and the duration would vary.

"So what he did was, he started tracking his incidents of heavy depression, on a chart. I'm sure if nothing else, it made him feel like he was fighting the depression, by trying to understand it. I've started doing the same thing with my own depression.

"Over time, he came to believe this form of heavy depression was actually a separate entity inside him. A psychic entity that lived in his mind. He believed it woke up at a certain time in his mind each day, not always the same time each day, then floated inside his consciousness for so many hours, before going back to sleep until the next day. He seemed to really believe very strongly in the existence of this entity. That it was something parasitical that had somehow swum its way into his thoughts from outside him. He described it as looking, he thought, like a jellyfish—in other words, something that floated inside him, with rippling sides.

"He was a brilliant man. He really was. I could show you some of his legal briefs. His theories are cited time and time again in case law. It must have been horrible for him to realize he was slowly losing his mind, and trying to fight that." Jonathan sat quietly in his chair. Tilda said nothing. After a few moments, he spoke again. "I see that same trait in my father. He's begun going through these spells of heavy depression as well. Just like my grandfather. Some of the things my dad's said lately, things he's been confused about, cuisine and everything, I worry that he's starting to get the same way as my grandfather."

"And maybe you are too?"

"I don't think so."

"The entity you're describing inside your grandfather? It's known as a Mouth. And yes, it is parasitic. And it is independent from its host. Unfortunately, it's transferrable from father to son. Or in your case, from grandfather to father to son."

"So there's a Mouth in me?"

151

"Probably a small one at this point. But it will grow."

"How did my grandfather get it?"

"I don't know. No one does. They're out there. They select certain hosts."

"Out where, exactly?"

Tilda made a face. "There's the earth, and then there's the universe. In the same way, metaphorically, there's our consciousness, and then there's out there.

"The thing with your grandfather is, once he died, he became what we call a Domino Ghost. Someone who has such strong feelings about himself, and such little empathy for others, once he does die he transfers his personality down the line to his male children and male grandchildren. And even male great-grandchildren. And so on. That's why you're seeing his house as it was while he was still alive reassert itself during your renovations. Assert itself in all these motels you've been fleeing through. His ghost is chasing after you. He has such a high regard for himself, he can't accept he's no longer relevant. So his ghost, instead of leaving, stays here, invading his offspring. You've seen that influence in your own father, but eventually, that influence will move entirely to you, grow even stronger, until it overwhelms you."

He slumped in his chair. "Why wouldn't it be my father he attacks? Why me?"

She shrugged. "Think of it like electricity. Your grandfather is holding your father's right hand. You're holding your father's left hand. Your grandfather touches a live wire. The charge passes from your grandfather through your father, to you. You're the one who gets electrocuted, because you're the final person in the hand-holding connection."

"So how do I stop that? How do I get rid of the domino effect, and the Mouth?"

"You can't get rid of the Mouth. Sorry. Once it wiggles its way inside you, it's in you for life. But you can stop the domino effect of your grandfather's influence."

His thin face nodded. "That's what I want to do. It's like old time dancehall music that keeps playing over and over in my mind, twenty-four hours a day. I've lost twenty pounds in the past week. I want to be my own man. Whatever that takes. I don't want to be my father, or my grandfather. I hate that musky smell. My dad gave into it, but I don't want to. I want to be me."

"Do you have any children?"

"What? No."

"Good. Because if you did, you'd have to kill your children."

"What? Why?"

"Because the Domino Ghost can exist—the haunted house following you around everywhere can exist—only if you have children, or have the potential to have children. The Domino Ghost exists only if its influence is open-ended, to continue passing its influence down through the generations. If you end the possibility of that happening, of future generations of males happening, the Domino Ghost goes away."

"So how do I do that?"

"Referring back to the cancer metaphor, it requires surgery."

"Like, psychic surgery?"

"No. Real surgery. Physical surgery. To your body."

Jonathan opened his mouth to ask a question. Closed his mouth.

Tilda glanced around the ceiling for smoke alarms. "You mind if I light a cigarette?"

"I was in such a state when I checked in, I didn't notice if I got a smoking room or non-smoking room."

"Well, one way or the other, you're going to be moving out, right?" The flame of her lighter flared up in front of the white-circled brown tip of her cigarette. "Do you understand what I'm saying to you?"

"Could you spell it out?"

"Since you don't have any children, you don't have to kill them. That's the good news. But you do have to eliminate the possibility that you'd ever have children."

"Okay."

"And, obviously, you have to do that surgically."

"Meaning?"

"I would have to perform surgery on you."

"Physical surgery?"

"Yes."

"What type of physical surgery?"

Tilda exhaled smoke. "I'd have to castrate you. I'd have to remove your testes. I'd have to take a knife, cut into your scrotum, and surgically remove your testes. Your balls."

Jonathan watched the TV show for a minute. Upright rifles getting loaded, long bullets slipped into the chambers. "So, you'd have to do what? What did you say?"

"I'd have to cut off your balls. Geld you, like a bull."

"I don't. Are you a doctor?"

Her tall height, evident even while sitting. Her blue eyes, pale nose, pale cheekbones. "No. But I've castrated a number of men with my knife."

He ducked his head. "Let me just...What would you have to do?"

"I'd have to cut off your balls. That's the only way of assuring you'd never have children. If I remove your balls, the Domino Ghost will realize there's no lineage left to him. He'll disappear, and his haunted house following you across America will go away. Forever. You'll become your own man. Live your life, instead of someone else's life. You'll be free. No longer be tormented by your father's influence, or your grandfather's."

"I'll be cured?"

"Yes. Of the domino effect. The Mouth will stay inside you. I can't help you with that. No one can."

"It's just so…radical. So final." He dissolved into tears again. "Why is this happening to me? It really isn't fair."

"No, it's not. But."

He had his forehead in his palms. Shoulders shaking. "I just want this to end. I've been thinking these thoughts, like…Maybe I should end my own life."

Tilda said nothing. While Jonathan's head was bowed, she glanced at her wristwatch.

He collected himself. Unspooling more toilet paper. "And that would definitely cure it? Absolutely?"

She nodded.

"What if I decide not to do that?"

"What you know as 'Jonathan' will die, and you'll become possessed by 'Jack.' You'll no longer be you. You'll be someone else, your grandfather, living in your body. The issue really is, Do you want to be you, or do you want to turn over your mind, your body, and your life to your grandfather?"

They agreed she'd come back tomorrow to the motel room, with her knife.

When he opened the motel room's front door to Tilda, it was clear from the circles under his eyes he hadn't slept well.

He had some coffee going in the kitchenette.

"Do you remember me telling you not to eat anything?"

"I didn't. I remembered."

He kept stirring his white Styrofoam cup of coffee with a white plastic spoon.

On the motel's TV, an old black and white Frank Sinatra special.

She squinted at the ornate antique mirror over the credenza. "When did that appear?"

"What, what?"

"The mirror."

Sitting at the round table, he swung his head around, smacking his lips. "That's always been there!"

"Yesterday, you had a plain, rectangular mirror on the wall."

"I don't think I did."

He looked down at his bathrobe. "I'm naked under this."

"Well, really, you don't need to be entirely naked. Just your genital area. Would you like to put on some pajamas? I'd just need to have you lower your pajama pants, and lift the bottom of your pajama top, for the procedure."

"I'm fine." Swung his head around and up, at the clock on the wall. "I thought about getting a prostitute last night, to have sex one last time, but I didn't know how to find one. I called some escort service, but I guess I was too specific about making sure I'd be getting someone who would have intercourse with me, so they thought I was a cop." Frightened grin. "Wow, the silence in this motel room is deafening when I'm not talking."

Tilda smiled. "Are you absolutely certain you want to go through with this?"

Jonathan nodded.

"No second thoughts?"

"I can't keep living like this. And knowing it's only going to get worse."

She let out a sigh. "Well, then, why don't we retire to the bathroom?"

He stood out of his chair, chair falling backwards. "That's where we're going to do it?"

"Mm-hmm."

Keeping his bathrobe pulled around him, heading towards the back of the room, he glanced down at her purse. "And everything you need is in there? I'm surprised."

She followed him into the bathroom. The overhead light was already on. She flicked the other wall switch to turn on the ceiling fan.

He stood by the toilet, clutching his robe. "So, how do we, where do you want me…"

"Because this isn't your home, where it wouldn't matter what kind of mess we make, it's best if you get inside the bathtub."

Jonathan's head swung to the standalone white porcelain bathtub with gold feet that had journeyed to this motel room from his grandfather's house. "Makes sense!"

"It's an easier clean up."

"Should I? Do you want me to get into the tub now?"

"Why don't you? Then we can get started."

As she watched, Jonathan stepped his bare right foot up over the curled white rim of the tub, setting his instep down inside, toes splaying from added weight as he swung his other foot off the floor of the bathroom.

"Remove your robe, please, and sit down in the tub. You can sit on your robe, if it's a robe you don't mind throwing away afterwards. That might be more comfortable for you, so you're not sitting on the cold, hard bathtub interior."

Standing in the tub, he raised his eyebrows. "I think I might do that. Thanks!"

Self-conscious, he bent his head forward, underside of his jaw resting against the top of his rib cage, like a kid would do buttoning his shirt front. Untying the cloth belt, he let the robe open naturally. Curled his hands around both soft lapels. Pulled the robe off his shoulders, down his arms. Naked, he held the robe out. "Do I just hand it to you, or…?"

"Were you going to sit on it?"

He ducked his head, snorting. "Right. Completely forgot."

Looked down at his naked body. Sucked in his stomach.

"You don't need to do that."

After he was sitting on his folded robe in the bathtub, Tilda, kneeling, put her purse on top of the closed lid of the toilet. Reached her left hand up, twisting on the hot water tap in the sink.

Unrolled squares and squares of toilet paper, like bunting, arranging their quadrupled layers across the bathroom floor until she had a large, white, puffy square.

Pulled her purse closer to her across the toilet lid. Reached in. Took out the spaghetti of some wobbly orange rubber tourniquets.

Reached back in. This time, her pale hand came out with white, coarse-weaved surgical gauze, and a spool of tape.

Hand back in. Lifting out a spool of thick white thread, a sewing needle, a tiny pair of silver scissors.

Placed beside them on the toilet paper a small vial with a red rubber top, a syringe.

Hand back in. A small Tupperware container, hard blocks knocking against each other inside.

Last item: A long, skinny knife with a black plastic handle.

Face flushed, he watched her add the knife to the other items on the toilet paper. "Wow. For whatever reason, I thought you'd be using a scalpel."

She pointed her right index finger at each item on the spread toilet paper, making sure she had everything she needed. "I don't like them?"

Sitting in the bathtub, naked, he tried to keep up his end of the conversation. "Really?"

She reached into the breast pocket of her blouse. "They can snag sometimes. It can make the incision messy. Here." Out of her breast pocket she pulled a small red pill. "Place this under your tongue. Let it dissolve naturally."

He took it from her, feeling her fingertips in his for a moment. Smooth, dry, warm. "What does this do?" He opened his mouth, eyes terrified. Placed the pill under his tongue.

Tilda picked up the syringe, and the small vial with the red rubber top. "It's a powerful sedative. It'll relax you, confuse you, make you not care about what I'm going to do. You don't need to talk at this point. You might dislodge the pill from under your tongue. I want the sedative to get into your bloodstream as quickly as possible."

While they waited, Tilda pulled a pack of Dorals from her purse, and a lighter. Lit her cigarette. Took a few deep drags.

Still smoking, she leaned her head over Jonathan, looking at his pupils. "Pretty relaxed? You can talk now."

"Yeah."

"That's good. Look right into my eyes."

Jonathan looked right into her eyes.

"Here's what I want you to do now." With the palm of her right hand, she banged the left curved rim of the standalone bathtub, banged her palm against the right side. "I want you to hook your left ankle over the left top of the bathtub, hook your right ankle over the right top of the bathtub."

His bare feet lifted, waving upwards.

She helped him get the bony ankles where she wanted them.

Lying inside the bathtub with his ankles hooked over either side, as if in stirrups, his scrotum was raised to a position of easy access.

"How you doing, Jonathan?"

He was staring up at the bathroom's plain ceiling. "Doing fine. You have really nice lips. Did I say that already?"

Reaching over the rim of the bathtub, she popped the syringe's slanted steel tip through the red rubber cap of the vial. Drew up all the paleness inside. Held the syringe needle end up. Pushed the plunger just a quarter inch, to squirt out all the different-sized air bubbles.

Went around Jonathan's genitals, sticking in the needle, lowering the plunger an inch here, an inch there, over and under the curly black hair of his genitals, into the meat, until all the drug inside was injected.

"Did you feel anything?"

"I did? But I didn't care."

"Excellent." Selecting one of the rubbery lengths of orange tourniquets, she tied it expertly under his balls, around the top of his cock,

157

finishing with the small bowtie of a square knot. Watched as his cock and balls turned pale.

Placed some of the surgical gauze under his balls, in front of his asshole.

"How you doing, Jonathan?"

"Doing great."

Took another drag on her cigarette.

"What are you doing?"

"Just getting ready. Do your cock and balls feel numb?"

"Yeah!"

She held the skinny blade of her knife under the hot water tap, sterilizing its reflections.

Pupils dilated, he grinned at her. "What's everyone else in the world doing right now?"

Satisfied the blade was sterilized, she opened the square top of the Tupperware container. Her fingers lifted out an ice cube.

"Hold this."

He took the ice cube from her. "Cold!"

"If you start to feel nauseous at any point over the next half hour, I want you to press this ice cube against your lips. Do not put it in your mouth. Just press it against your lips. Do you understand what I just said to you?"

Holding the ice cube, which was starting to drip down his knuckles, he nodded.

"Here's something else which is also very important. I want you to rest the back of your head against the rear rim of the bathtub. Do that now, please. Good! I want you to look up at the ceiling. I want you to never remove the back of your head from the rear of the bathtub until I tell you to. Also, I don't want you to look down at your body, at what I'm doing, at any point. Swear to me you won't look."

"Swear. Pinky swear. Whatever."

Holding the sterilized knife in her right hand, she reached down with both hands into the tub.

Her left thumb and forefinger pinched the top of his scrotum, pulling upwards on it, so his two balls were pointing forward.

"Did you feel anything?"

"Nope!"

Holding the knife blade-up at the bottom of his scrotum, between the heavy sag of his two balls, she pushed the tiny tip of the blade against his skin, denting the skin, denting it deeper, until the tip popped through. Drops of bright red blood dribbled out.

"So, what's your fiancé like?"

Jonathan kept staring up at the bathroom celling. "She's really nice. She's the only person I can call and just say, It's me, and she knows who that is."

"Are you in love with her?"

He smacked his lips. "My dad doesn't like her. She's a dental hygienist. But I do love her."

"Well, that's all going to change. You won't care what your dad thinks in a little while. Just what you think. Do you have a favorite memory of her?"

"I guess."

"What's your favorite memory of her? I know you have one."

"Yeah, I do. One day, we were over her apartment, it's a really nice apartment. Lots of potted plants, like girls do. Her bed sheets are really nice. They smell really nice. And her hair smells really nice. When she's just finished washing it. Her hair smells like chocolate. Like when you take the wrapper off a Hershey's bar? It smells like that. And her skin smells really nice, too. Her skin smells like artichokes."

Tilda slowly raised her right hand upwards between his thighs, slight sawing motion. "So what's your favorite memory of her? You haven't told me yet."

"I went over her apartment this one time? And she cooked me spaghetti carbonara and it was really good. She served it with a salad but I didn't eat much of the salad. It had gorgonzola cheese in it which I had never had before, but I didn't really like the taste. It was kind of like a chemical taste? And we got in bed afterwards and made love. And I was really happy. And we fell asleep together in her bed. And I didn't wake up until the next morning. And she kissed me, she was really happy like I was really happy, and she got out of the bed to pee, and there was a window on her side of the bed, and when she got out of the bed, the sunlight outlined her limbs. Like she was an angel. And that's my favorite memory of her. I'm not just a lawyer. I'm a lot of other people too. Will she still love me when this is over?"

"I don't know. Does she want to have kids?"

"Yeah."

"Then she might not. You may have to find a new fiancé."

"Okay. It feels funny down there."

He pressed the ice cube against his lips. Spoke against the melting ice. "What are you doing down there?"

Her pink-slicked steel blade finished its ascent, just below the base of his limp cock. Both halves of his scrotum, cut free from each other, sagged apart, widening the red incision.

"Are you doing okay, Jonathan?"

"I guess I am. Can I lower my eyes to see what you're doing to me?"

"No. That would be a bad idea. You swore you would keep looking up at the ceiling. Remember?"

"Yeah, I remember, but…"

"Keep looking up. You promised me."

She removed the blood-soaked surgical gauze from in front of his asshole. Heavy now that it was so saturated. Put a new pad of white surgical gauze in its place, but bloody already with her fingerprints.

"You like Mexican food, right?"

"Oh, yeah!"

"So what's your favorite Mexican dish?"

"I gotta think about that one."

"Take your time."

Her little silver scissors poked its points into the left side of his bisected scrotum, behind the outer raw chicken skin and springy black pubic hairs, to the blood clots and ivory shapes within, snipping.

"My favorite Mexican meal. That's a tough one."

Head down. Snipping, snipping.

Putting her thumb inside the sac, peeling the pink underside back, reaching with her scissor tips behind the ball, snipping, snipping. The pale fat ball drooped forward, away from the wall of tissue that had been snipped.

"You know? To me it may very well be chili rellenos."

"And what are those, again?"

"You take a poblano chili, and you roast it under the broiler until its skin is black and blistery, then you peel off the skin, like peeling off sunburn blisters on your shoulders. Then you put it on a cutting board and slice down one side of it, open it up, and pull out the seeds, and membrane."

"Okay." Tilda wiped the small blades of her scissors against his black pubic hairs, belling them red. Sunk the tips of the scissors back inside. "Then what?"

"Then, you roll different Mexican cheeses into a torpedo shape, and slip it inside the poblano. Then you use toothpicks to close the long slit you made."

Tilda lifted both pale balls out of his sac, holding them in her left palm like water chestnuts. "That sounds delicious."

"It is!"

Tossed them in the toilet, where they bobbed.

"And then you eat them?"

"I don't think so! No. Then you make a batter with the beaten egg whites, and you fold the yolks in, and some flour, and salt, and maybe some ground pepper, and you roll the stuffed poblanoes in that, then fry them in hot oil in a skillet."

Tilda reached for her needle, her white thread. "Wow, that sounds really good!"

"So what are you doing down there?"

"Can you feel anything?"

"No."

"Good!" Her right hand raised in a salute out of the bathtub, silver needle pointing upwards, white thread twanging behind. "Do you use a sauce for the chili rellenos?"

Jonathan kept his happy face pointed up obediently at the celling, blissfully unaware of the red mess below his belly button. "Well, yeah! The easiest sauce you can do is an enchilada sauce, which is a bunch of spices, including a lot of red chili powder, cooked in chicken broth. Then you thicken it."

Tilda finished sewing crisscross stitches up Jonathan's scrotum, like sneaker shoelaces. Gathered the tall flab of excess scrotum skin above where she had tied-off the final stitch. Using her paring scissors, she cut across the bottom of the upward-stretched excess skin, the skin rippling away from the ever-advancing snips, until it lifted free from the scissors, hanging in her left hand.

"I have to say, that sounds delicious!"

Jonathan, back of his head still lolled against the white rim of the bathtub, raised his eyebrows. "It really is. People just don't understand how important capicin is. And it's healthy for you!"

"Okay, I think we're finished here."

"Already?"

"Yeah. Let me just clean you up a bit." Toilet getting flushed, flushed again, balls and excess chicken skin swirling under, sucked down into the general sewer system flowing with the world's bad decisions, drugs and torn-up notes and failed meals and baby crocodiles and baby people.

"Stay where you are, while I wipe down your body."

He looked up at the bathroom's ceiling.

Lots of lots of wet toilet paper going from his naked body to the toilet. Flush, flush, flush.

"Okay, why don't you try standing up?"

He did, unsteadily. Rising up out of the wide porcelain tub with gold feet from his grandfather's house into a cheap motel shower stall, plastic sliding door. Still some blood around his toes, but that was all right.

"Are you nauseous?"

"No, not really."

"Are you in pain?"

"I don't think I am."

She led his naked body, like a nun, into the bedroom. "Do you want to lie down in the bed?"

"I think I can sit in the chair. By the round table."

No droplets of blood from the door of the bathroom, across the living room carpet, to the chair. Her sewing had been really tight. She kept getting better at castrations.

They both sat back down at the round table.

The TV was still on. Amazingly, it was still the Frank Sinatra TV special.

He was back in his bathrobe. Looked down at the table. "You have really nice hands. They look really delicate. The fingernails, the knuckles."

"How do you feel?"

"I feel really good. I mean, considering."

He looked around the motel room. The expensive, rich walnut credenza was gone. Cheap piece of shit furniture in its place. The mirror, which looked like it had taken a half dozen craftsmen to fashion, was gone. Cheap rectangular mirror stamped out one after the other in a factory in its place. The painting on the wall was no longer something you'd remember for years, at the oddest times. It was just a cheap knockoff.

He was no longer surrounded with beautiful, expensive works of art. He was in a cheap motel room filled with junk.

But then a cool breeze blew in through the opened front window. And doesn't a cool breeze always do it?

"I want to take a nap, then I want call my fiancé, then I want to walk to one of the local fish shacks and have some dinner." His young face looked at her. "I feel really good. Free. I don't have any balls, and the world is mine. Is that the sedative talking?"

Tilda smiled. "It's not the sedative talking." Patted the top of his hand. "It's you."

IF HE HAD WINGS

Tom, tall, blond, pale, sat at the kitchen table, red tie loosened but suit jacket still on, watching as Jen placed his beer in front of him. The one alcoholic drink he permitted himself each week, Friday night, in celebration of a job well done.

Time for fun.

Jen uncapped the Miller Light bottle. Stood back with a smile. Watched as he took his first sip.

"Is it okay?"

"Why are you wearing short-shorts?"

Jen glanced down, as if she forgot she had them on. "Just felt like it. You know."

His mouth twitched. "Basically. The one last week was colder, though."

She lifted her slim shoulders. "So how was work?"

"What's for dinner?" He sniffed the air, but he was never any good at identifying smells.

"Your favorite!"

Wiped his mouth with the side of his thumb. No doubt a habit from childhood. Right hand larger than his left hand, because he used a calculator all day. Fingerprints nearly nonexistent, from handling so much paper. People make fun of accountants, without realizing what they sacrifice. "Okay. Good."

"Tommy Junior's at taxidermy class. They're having a special session on eye socket enlargement. Jen-Jen's in her room, pinning butterflies she bought. Plus I rented your favorite video. I thought us and the kids could watch it after dinner."

"Patch Adams?"

"Yeah."

"Is dinner ready?"

"It will be in about twenty minutes." Gave him a humorous bow, the good wife. "So you have time to finish your beer."

He took another sip from the bottle. "Yeah, it was a rough day today."

Still standing, she put her left sneaker up on the seat of her chair opposite his at the kitchen table. Rubbed some white skin cream along the horizontal length of her bare left thigh. "Really?"

"The capitalized expense for the Nox project is going to have to be amortized over a longer period of time than we originally projected. Since we aren't expensing them as incurred, those expenses are probably going to negatively impact our tax position."

Her brown eyebrows drew together. "I'm so sorry!"

"I told Dick, You really don't want to expense these as accumulated, but he was too distracted, watching his secretary's rear end as she left his office."

Her fingers slowly massaged the white skin cream into the long muscles of her bare thigh. "He's such a, I hate to use the word, but a jerk. These new exercises I'm doing? I think they've really toned-up my thighs. What do you think?"

"The development costs for Nox are only going to run for about six quarters. But, of course, Dick thinks he has all the answers."

Her lips blew upwards at her light brown bangs, lifting them. "How did he ever get to be president?"

Tom clenched his right hand. "One never knows."

Jen sat opposite him at the kitchen table. Forearms and bright green eyes. "I had a weird day today."

"Of course, there is some non-operating income associated with the project. Once it's completed, we'll fire all the analysts we needed to test the project's deductive paradigm, to account for the outliers."

Sympathetic sigh. "Well, there's that."

"I'm going to spend some time tomorrow in the garage."

"Absolutely! On the bookshelves?"

He lowered his head, eyes tilting up. "Once I'm finished with them, the next step will be to figure out what to put on the shelves."

"Do you have any ideas?"

"One step at a time."

"You'll never guess what happened today."

Tom lowered the beer bottle from his lips. "You didn't try a new recipe for the meatloaf, did you?"

"No! It's just ground beef." She reached both hands up, smoothing her long brown hair away from her cheek bones, breasts lifting, elbows jutting at him. "That other recipe? With minced vegetables and torn-up bread and herbs? I threw it away."

166

Tom raised his right hand, slicing the air. "Meat loaf is just ground beef, and nothing more. You don't need to add all these other ingredients, like onions. The French are cowards. Look at World War Two."

"But something interesting did happen to me today. I got a phone call from a family member I haven't spoken to in years."

His eyes went suspicious. "Who?"

"Wally Walczak!" She sat back in her chair, as if re-astonished by the sudden, out-of-the-blue call.

"Who?"

"My cousin!"

"What did he want?"

"Well, Wally, he called me, and he asked if he could visit with us next weekend!"

Tom lowered his half-empty bottle. "Visit us? What does that mean? He's going to eat Friday dinner with us?"

"Well, actually, he asked if he could stay with us for a few days. Like, the weekend."

"Where would he sleep?"

"In the guest bedroom."

"He'd stay here? In our home?"

"Yeah. He'd be our overnight guest. For a couple of nights." She put a smile on her girl next door face. "Wow, that meatloaf sure smells good. And did I tell you? I don't think I did. I got your favorite ice cream, Rocky Road, for dessert. We can eat it while we watch Patch Adams. Later on, once the kids are in bed, we can go to bed ourselves. Maybe stay up for a while? You and me in bed?"

Tom lowered his forehead. "Wait a minute. Wait a minute. Why is your cousin staying with us? Did you invite him?"

Jen weakly lifted her shoulders. "He kind of invited himself."

Tom was the first to take his seat at the conference table, while all the other executives stood around by the windows, talking and laughing with each other. He set his coffee, in a single white Styrofoam cup, down next to his stapled paperwork. A lot of the others had their coffee cups placed inside a second white Styrofoam coffee cup, as insulation, so the heat of the coffee wouldn't be so intense when they picked up the double cups. An absolute waste of supplies. Tom had suggested the outer white Styrofoam cups be kept so they could be reused, to save the company money, he even wrote a company-wide memo about it, but no one had listened to him. After each Friday department head meeting, the trash cans were filled with the doubled white Styrofoam coffee cups.

All those doubled white Styrofoam coffee cups in the trash cans seemed to be meant as a challenge to his authority. To test if what he said could be ignored.

He was a good person. One of his recurring fantasies was of walking down a street, passing the mouth of an alley, and coming across three or four white kids bullying a smaller black child, who was just trying to get home to his grandmother. In his fantasy, Tom pushed the white bullies away from the black boy, lecturing them on doing the right thing. At the end of his fantasy, the white kids grudgingly thanked Tom, and the little black boy was able to continue his journey home, unmolested.

Dick, the company's president, finally sat down at the head of the conference table, left forearm in a white sling.

He gestured with his big face at the sling, black hair falling sheepishly across his forehead. "Took the Farber people out golfing. Drank a little too much. Fell over on the seventh hole."

The others around the table, except Tom, gave appreciative laughs.

Dick ducked his head. "Well, you know. Have an adventure a day." He raised his black eyebrows. "Did we get the account?" His blue eyes swept across the seated executives. Dramatic pause. "Fuck yeah we got the account."

Everyone around the conference table, except Tom, cheered.

Tom bent his head, baring his teeth. He reached for his white Styrofoam cup of coffee, but its curved sides were still too hot to hoist.

"So that means we don't have to close the Inglewood branch after all. All those employees and their families continue to have a steady income." He lifted his slung left forearm as high as he could. "It's a good day."

Dick jerked his jaw up at Tom, halfway down the conference table, giving him the toothy Dick grin. "How we doing with the black and red numbers, Tom?"

"It's looking even worse for our amortization for the Nox project. I warned about this. Stephen would have never approved this amortization."

Dick, at the head of the table, raising his big face, spoke in a mild voice. "Well, except that once our acquisition by Blending Corp was announced, Stephen ran away like a little boy in shorts when he found out he was no longer the big watermelon."

Clark gave the affable shoulder shrug of someone who knows nothing about details, and could care less. He looked around the table for support. "Is that really an issue? Don't we have to amortize any new project?"

Tom rolled his eyes to himself, although of course everyone sitting around the long table saw. "No, we don't have to 'amortize any new project.'

That's not the only way to do entries. We do do expenses as incurred expenses."

Sally, in Marketing, near the top of the conference table, snorted. "You just said 'do do'."

Everyone around the conference table, except Tom, cracked up. Even Dick.

Tom cruised slowly along the curb outside his home, passenger side window down, making sure the mowers had done a good job, which they had, after him speaking to the crew boss last month.

He rattled up the garage door, far off cries down the street curves and tall elms of the neighborhood, kids getting called in for dinner. Each evening he alternated between rolling up the garage door with his left hand or his right hand, so one arm wouldn't get more developed than the other arm.

Jen wasn't at the back of the garage like she normally was, holding up his bottle of Miller Lite.

He parked the car inside the garage, advancing the front tires until they touched the two by four he had placed across the garage floor at its rear, to assure the car was parked lengthwise equidistant between the rear and front of the garage, so he could easily walk around the car. Rolled down the garage door, slid the bolt left to lock it.

To the right of his car's ticking hood, sitting on spread newspapers, his finished bookshelf. Ran the tip of his index finger along the lowest shelf. Turned his finger around, to look. No sawdust.

He passed from the utility room, with its washer and dryer, some of his white shirts on hangers above the dryer, into the kitchen, hearing voices and laughter.

What the heck?

A strange, dark-haired man with a moustache sat in his chair at the kitchen table. Dark beer bottle by the man's large right hand.

His Friday evening Miller's Lite was nowhere in sight.

Jen stood up from her chair at the table, holding a bottle of the same dark beer. "Hey, honey!"

Smile on her face, she gave him an awkward embrace, holding the beer bottle behind his back.

What was going on?

Stepping back from the circle of his wife's arms, he spread his shoes apart on their kitchen floor. Stared at the dark-haired man. "Who are you?"

Jen was still holding that beer bottle. She never drank. "Tom, honey, this is Wally! Remember I told you he'd be staying with us?"

Wally lazily raised his hand from the chair where Tom normally sat. "Hey, Tommy!"

"Where did this beer come from? Why are you drinking?"

Jen backed up, embarrassed. Holding Tom's stare, sliding her eyes, a wife's signal, at Wally. "Come on, Tom. Wally brought the beer. I haven't seen my cousin in years, so I thought maybe tonight, for once, I'd kick up my heels a little. Okay?"

Tom looked in the trash can by Jen's side of the kitchen table. "How many beers have you already consumed before I came home?"

Jen got a sad look on her girl next door face, tried to shake it off. "Only one other. Or two. It's a special occasion, Tom. Okay? Do this for me?"

Wally, still sitting, took another long swig, staring at Tom over the upraised bottle. Lowered it with a slight bang onto the tabletop. "It's cool, Tommy. Hey! It's Friday night, right? We can all get a little fucked-up."

Jen moved in front of Tom. In her quietest voice she said, "Do this for me? Please? Come on, Tom."

Tom tried to adjust to this indignity. He looked at his wife. If she had any idea how his day had gone…But he'd fill her in on that later, once Wally was in their bathroom. "So, you're Jen's cousin?"

Jen gave Tom a grateful dip of her shoulders.

Wally jerked up his head. "Yeah. We haven't seen each other in a lot of years, though."

Jen, happy, led Tom to her chair, not his normal chair, which Wally was occupying. "Sit down, babe. Let me get you your beer."

Tom decided he was going to be his wife's hero, this one night. He sat down in her chair. "Where you from?"

"All over. I live in my car."

Jen brought Tom a cold bottle of the dark beer.

"I'd like my Miller Lite instead."

Jen massaged the back of her husband's shoulders. "Wally drank those? But this beer tastes really good!"

Tom, holding his emotions inside, took a sip of the dark beer. It was much stronger than what he was used to, and more bitter.

"So, what are you, Tommy? An accountant?"

"Yeah. And you are?"

Sloppy grin. "I guess I'm a free spirit."

Tom's mouth twitched. "Really. How interesting."

Jen sat down in one of the chairs by the side of the kitchen table, where Jen-Jen normally sat. "Wally's worked in all different businesses, he was telling me. He was even a security guard once, just like you, while you were going to college."

"That a fact, Tommy? You were a guard?"

Tom tried another sip of the dark beer. Didn't like it almost as much as the first sip. "For a year. My junior year."

"Did you get to carry a gun?"

"I didn't need a gun."

"Yeah? I always had a gun. What were you guarding? Little girls' pageant dresses?" Wally raised his dark eyebrows, smiling.

Another sip. He preferred his Miller Lite, but this beer wasn't too bad. "Archived company records. What did you guard?"

"Human organs."

Jen sucked in her breath. "I didn't know that! Is that why you needed a gun?"

Wally shrugged, finishing the bottle, tossing it in the trash can, where it collided against others. "Just about every security guard carries a gun. I never heard of one that didn't, until Tommy here." He shoved himself up out of his chair, which was really Tom's chair, walked with an air of careful nonchalance to the refrigerator. Yanked the door open, lifted out another beer.

Tom burned his eyes at Jen.

Jen pyramided the tips of her two hands in front of her, silently asking Tom to be a good host.

Wally sat back down, heavily, in Tom's chair. Used a flat bottle opener to flip off the metal cap on his bottle of beer, the cap bouncing across the table, falling on the floor. Wally didn't bother leaning over in his seat to retrieve the cap. "So did they give you any kind of weapon, Tommy? A slingshot?"

Jen pulled the top of her bottle out from between her lips. "Wally! Be nice."

"They gave me the best protection of all. Appreciation for the job I was doing. That year I worked for them, I got three raises."

"Wow."

"How many raises did you get?"

"Not that many."

"Any?"

"Not at that job."

"So you just worked for minimum wage? Maybe even worked sometimes when you didn't get paid, just to keep your job? Because they knew they could get away with that with you?"

Wally put a bored look on his face. "Whatever."

"I guess that's the 'free' part of 'free spirit'."

"Tommy was also the CEO of his own landscaping company for a while."

"Does a 'landscaping company' really need a CEO?"

Jen lightly slapped her palm on the kitchen table. "Tom, why don't we show Wally our home?"

"And this is our living room." Tom made a self-conscious sweep, with his right palm, feeling feminine, of the walls, furniture. One thing he could do is meet secretly with the executives at Blending Corp, and suggest Dick be removed, and he be put in Dick's place as president. There'd be a lot of firings, especially in Sales and Marketing, but it would be for the best of the company.

Wally strode over to a grouping of family pictures on the wall. Eyes moving from frame to frame. "Ever see a haunted house movie? Where the new family moves in, and they find some photographs of the prior family? That's what these pictures look like."

"Those are Tom's pets."

Wally squinted at the aquarium, his moustache making him seem even shorter. "These are your pets? Fish?"

"Tom can sit and watch these fish for hours."

"If you watch fish in an aquarium too long, you turn into a fish. You're sitting in your chair, just swimming left and right over and over again."

Jen touched her cousin's shoulder. "Let me show you your room!"

Wally, following her, ignoring Tom, spoke up. "I've been a guest in a lot of homes, so there are certain standards I expect."

She stood back from the doorway. "We're putting you next to our son. He likes to stay up late working on his taxidermy, but it's a very quiet hobby."

Wally walked into the guest bedroom, glancing around with an unhappy look on his stupid face. Small bed, a bunch of empty bookshelves on the walls. His moustache raised above his teeth. "This is my bedroom? I'd like to see your bedroom. I'll bet it's larger. And where's my bathroom?"

"You can use the one in the hall, Wally."

Wally sneered at his cousin. "Seriously? I have to leave my bedroom to use a bathroom? Even in the middle of the night? I'll bet your bedroom has a connecting bathroom. Am I right, Tommy?"

Tom twisted his head on his neck. "All our guests—well, we've never had an overnight guest—but this is where they would stay. It's a guest bedroom. No one's ever complained."

"Honey, I know he's not easy to take, but he's my flesh and blood." She studied her nude body in the bathroom's full length mirror, pink curves, maroon nipples, trimmed brown pubic hair. Bare-footed back out to the bedroom, where Tom was in his side of the bed already, wearing long-sleeved striped pajamas. "We'll put up with him a day or two, then he's gone. Probably forever."

Pretty little pirouette on the white carpet by his side of the bed, showing him her nakedness. Not looking to see his reaction, she strolled over to her side of the marital mattress, head down, eyes thinking private thoughts.

Once she was in bed, she slid her body over against his. "It's only two days out of the thousands and thousands of days we have together."

He stared up at the ceiling as her hand reached down below his stomach. "I don't like that we put him next to our son's bedroom. What if he's a child molester?"

She started as she always did, lightly stroking. "Oh Tom, come on! Why would he be a child molester?"

Tom spread his striped pajama legs apart. "He's short. Most child molesters are short."

"Not all of them! I remember I saw a child molester on the news once and he was over six feet tall! They couldn't get him in the back of the police car without banging his head against the top of the car."

She pulled harder, watching Tom's face.

"I don't know where he got that crazy theory about watching fish in an aquarium. It doesn't make any sense."

"Well, he's not the brightest bulb in the box."

"I'll say!" Lying in bed, getting his length jerked-off, he punched the side of his head once, twice, three times. Hard. Fist bouncing off his temple with each impact.

"Don't do that!"

"This is my home! He's in my home, acting disrespectful towards me!"

She slipped the pajama pants off his legs. Went to work with both hands. The right hand that pulls up. The left hand that caresses underneath.

Jaw lifting, nostrils widening, he spread his bare legs. "Dick continues to just blithely ignore all common business sense. And he has a cast on his forearm! From falling down while he was drunk! On a golf course!"

Jen, keeping the top sheet across her back, like a white cape, the way Tom preferred it, the top sheet staying up by their shoulders, not exposing anything below their necks, climbed her thin knees around his hips, right hand aiming the heavy height of his cock, with the concentration of a little girl's tongue between her lips, sliding that rigid length up, up, up inside her, deep inside her, her eyes rolling up.

Left hand on his throat, right fingers between the top of her own thighs, masturbating, she rode him slow, head bent. As they both got closer, her hips rotated faster, girl next door face rising, shut eyes opening their light brown eyelashes at the last possible moment, bright green eyes staring up gratefully at the white, white, white texturized celling.

"Who burnt the eggs?"

Jen put plates down in front of the kids, crowded together on one side of the kitchen table, getting into elbow wars, to accommodate Wally's fifth chair on the other side. "Tom likes our eggs cooked-through, so there's no slime."

Her husband ate silently, like an old man in jail, staring straight ahead.

Still holding his knife and fork in the air, Wally snorted. "Just flip 'em over. That's what happens when you serve eggs sunny-side up. You have to burn their bottoms. Here. Let me show you." He jerked his chair back, the four wooden legs making a screech on the tile floor.

Jen, at the stove, ready to fry her own eggs, looked over at Tom for guidance.

Tom shoveled the last yellow, black and white remnants of his egg into his mouth. Chewed quickly. "You're supposed to serve eggs sunny-side up! Have you never seen a freakin' picture of eggs in a magazine?"

Tom Jr. and Jen-Jen sat bolt upright in their chairs, scared glances to each other at their father's language.

Wally, at the stove, took the two eggs from Jen's hand. She stepped back, flustered by his rudeness.

"Hey kids! Put your forks down for a second and watch this."

Infuriatingly, both of Tom's children obeyed Wally, placing their knives and forks on their plates.

As if performing a magic trick, Wally showed them the two eggs in his right hand. Holding his left hand up, to prove he was doing this one-handed, he brought the fingers of his right hand together with a quick snap that split open both hard white shells. Before the cracks widened, he moved his hand over the hot butter in the skillet, staring at the children with a goofy grin on his face as the eggs, unseen by him, oozed out of their cracks, drooping into the skillet.

He tossed the two empty egg shells at the aluminum sink, some ten feet away, missing.

Brought the skillet over, so both kids could see that the eggs had landed intact in the skillet. "And no egg shells! Let's see your Daddy do that."

The residual heat in the skillet turned both egg's albumen white, but since the skillet was not on the stove, held mid-air in front of the kids, it made the cooking seem all the more magical. "Now watch." Still holding the skillet out in front of him, he jerked his right elbow back.

The two eggs, which had siamesed as they cooked, rose up in the air, turning over with a double-yolked grace, plopping back in the skillet upside down. Tom Jr.'s eyebrows shot up. "Wow!" Jen-Jen laughed out loud, applauding.

Tom, trying to ignore what was going on, picked up his coffee cup, tilted it to his tense lips, but the cup was empty. His pale hand reached up to the side of his skull, which was still tender from his punches.

"Madame, would you take a seat, *s'il te plait?*"

Jen looked at the two joined eggs on her plate. They were fully-cooked, but pure white. The side of her fork pierced one of the fat egg yolks. The rich, golden-orange yolk oozed out, onto her white plate. "Oh! Look, Tom!" She slanted her plate towards his averted eyes, as if showing him Jesus. "The yolk isn't hard. You can sop it up with toast!"

Tom, who had already eaten his eggs, and drank his coffee, had nothing on which he could pretend to be concentrating. He sat, trapped, head down, staring at his empty plate, throat getting red.

"Uncle Wally, will you cook my eggs that way next time? Please? Please?"

"Our visitor won't be able to cook any more eggs, because he's leaving tomorrow before breakfast. He's going to eat somebody else's eggs on the road. And that time, he's going to have to pay for the eggs out of his own pocket."

Tom Jr. looked like he was about to cry. "What? He just got here! I haven't shown Uncle Wally my animals yet!"

"Tom, could we—"

"Tell you what, kids. Tonight, dinner's on me. Your parents and me are going to the supermarket, and I'm going to cook both of you—and your mom and dad—the best meal you ever had in your lives! Know what I'm going to make you?"

They both shook their heads, eyes rapt.

"I'm going to make you…Chicken Wally!"

Jen-Jen shrieked. Tom Jr., palms rising, parenthesized the sides of his astonished face. "You have a dish named after you?"

Tom cut that off right away. "I don't want my children exposed to giddiness. My father broke my nose the one time I got giddy. It was the best thing he ever did for me."

"Well, regardless, I'll make a list of what we need. Jen, what do we have in the way of fresh vegetables?"

Jen backed her head on her neck. "We don't have any."

"You don't have any? Not even onions?"

"No."

Wally let his jaw drop. "Really? You don't have any onions in the house? Not a single one?"

Blushing, Jen shook her head.

"My God. What about spices and herbs?"

She glanced nervously at Tom. "We have salt. And a jar of dried parsley we bought years ago, by accident."

"Well, that just won't do!"

Tom couldn't help speaking up. "What do you need vegetables and spices for if you're cooking chicken? Chicken is chicken." He let out an angry snort, looking at his family for support.

Wally put down his pen, next to a blue-inked list that had already lowered to about a dozen grocery items. "Oh, I think I've upset your Daddy. You're upset, aren't you, Daddy? Because I made better eggs? Really?"

Tom shifted in his chair. "No. I'm not upset."

Wally, looking at the kids, giving each one a wink, squinted his eyes at Tom, skeptical. "I did upset you, didn't I?"

"Not at all. Kids, go play in your rooms."

Wally examined Tom's face a moment longer, tilting his head to one side, Tom blinking rapidly under the close scrutiny. Finally, inspection concluded, doubt gone, Wally nodded his head decisively. "Yeah, I upset Daddy. I can tell. Daddy's not used to being questioned."

Wally was in the kitchen, preparing Chicken Wally, chopping vegetables by the side of the stove, while Tom and Jen sat at the kitchen table.

"He has to leave tomorrow morning."

"Tom, really?"

Looking into each other's eyes, they both became aware that Wally had switched to chopping the vegetables very quietly, so he could eavesdrop on their kitchen table conversation. Which was kind of creepy.

"Well, we have to tell you know who tomorrow about him having to leave."

"I don't know if you know who has anywhere else to go."

"I don't give a nectarine. You know who has to go. That's final." Tom's face went red, his lips drawn back from his teeth. "I don't get any respect at work! And now I can't get any respect in my effing home?"

The meal was a huge success. With the kids. And with Jen. Tom took an angry bite, declared the chicken breast on his plate, draped with a stock-based sauce speckled with onion, bell peppers, celery, Anaheim chilies, jalapeno, and garlic, blended with sour cream, heavy cream and two types of cheddar cheese, to be inedible.

All the other family members scraped their plates clean with the sides of their silver spoons, but Tom pushed his moist dinner away after the first bite. Looked at Wally's left ear. "You ruined five chicken breasts."

Wally spread his hands apart, tilting his head at Tom. In an overly-reasonable voice meant to be maddening he said, "Let's take a vote. Kids? Do you think I ruined your chicken breasts?"

Tom threw his plate at Wally. "You ruined my fucking chicken breast!" The porcelain plate fell off Wally's shirt, yellow and green mess down the white buttons.

The kids screamed.

Jen drew her thin hands up to her lips, as if Tom had pulled out a knife.

Tom and Jen went out with their two children to church the next morning, dressed in pastels, except Tom, who wore black. Wally stayed home, to sleep late. "Church? Not my thing."

The family went to Louie's afterwards, for their traditional ham and eggs breakfast. Usually, it was a lot of fun. Who doesn't like ham?

Tom Jr. deliberately circled the wrong answers on the multiple choice quiz on his kid's menu. What animal has the biggest nose? His green pencil passed by Anteater, circled Cat.

Halfway through slicing his ham, fork and knife still in his hands, Tom looked at his two sad children sitting on the other side of the booth, picking at their food. He stared at his son. "Once we get back home, maybe you could show me that eye socket enlarging trick you learned at taxidermy class."

The little boy kept his head down, pushing the tined top of his fork into his ham, over and over, forming dozens of dotted lines. "Don't want to."

Jen touched the top of Tommy Jr.'s other hand, the one not raising and lowering the fork. "Sweetie? Your dad is really proud of what you do to animals. Wouldn't you like to show him how you make their eye sockets bigger?"

"Yeah, well, maybe I'll show Wally. Maybe I won't show anyone else."

When they arrived back home, the first thing Tom noticed was that Wally's beat-up Camaro was missing from the curb in front of their house.

He hurried inside their home, raising his jaw, to see if Wally's clothes were gone from the closet in the guest bedroom. They weren't.

Jen noticed the tiny red bulb on their phone in the living room was flashing.

Tom banged down on the message bar, sneering. "Let me just guess. Oh, my car broke down across town because I wasn't responsible enough to keep it well-maintained."

But in fact, the message was just a man's voice, leaving a phone number, asking that he be called back.

Tom picked up the receiver. Punched in the numbers. "I don't think we should have to pick him up somewhere. If this is a bartender, let him get Wally a ride home. Well, not home, but here."

Tom listened as the phone on the other end of the line rang two times.

"No one's answering."

Across the miles, the other phone was picked up. "Officer Klenghorn."

"Hello?"

"This is Officer Klenghorn. To whom am I speaking?"

Tom kept the phone to his ear, circling around to look at the others, circling back. "I'm returning your call. This is Tom Dunning." He thought, we are not bailing him out of jail. This may just be the lesson he needs. Spend some time behind bars, with the other races, start learning some respect. This is a good thing.

Jen, blue eyes frightened, stood next to him. "Who is it?"

Tom mouthed, The Police. In a quiet voice he added, "Apparently, he's been arrested."

"Oh, my God!"

"Not a surprise. Frankly."

"Mr. Dunning, what is your relationship to Mr. Walczak?"

"He was staying with us. For a visit that's ending today."

"Is he a blood relation?"

"Absolutely not. He's my wife's cousin."

"Mr. Walczak was involved in a one-vehicle automobile accident about two hours ago."

"We can't be held liable for any hospital bills. If he doesn't have any health insurance, and he probably doesn't, you're going to just have to treat him as an indigent. We do not accept any responsibility for his medical costs."

Jen was crying. "Is he okay?"

The two kids were looking at each other.

"Mr. Dunning, I'm very sorry to tell you the automobile accident was, unfortunately, a very serious accident. I have some very sad news to tell you. Mr. Walczak died as a result of the injuries he suffered."

"What?"

"Mr. Walczak perished in the accident. He's dead. We need someone to come down to the local station to identify his body. We went through some of the paperwork in his car, and it would appear he was from out-of-town? That you were the only ones who knew him here?"

"I guess. That's probably right."

"Would you or your wife be able to stop by the station sometime in the next hour to identify his body?"

Tom held the phone to his ear, back to his family.

"Mr. Dunning?"

"Okay. All right. Do I ask for you?"

"If you come down here in the next few hours, yes. Otherwise, you can ask for the morgue attendant."

"Okay. That's what we'll do then. Goodbye."

Tom hung up the phone.

"Is Wally okay? Is he in trouble with the law?"

Tom didn't answer, taking a breath. How was he going to phrase this? This important information he, and he alone, had to convey to his wife? "Kids, I need to talk to your mother."

They slunk off, looking back.

"Tom? Is my cousin okay?"

Tom looked at the aquarium, trying to find some peace in the back and forth swimmings of the fish. "It was a police officer. He had some very bad news about Wally."

"Oh my God! Oh my God! What?"

"He...died this morning in a car accident."

He reached his hand out to his wife's shoulder, but she shook the approach off, ran away a few feet, head bent, elbows up above her ears, terrified.

"Jen, I'm really sorry."

Her voice was high. "He's dead? Really?"

"I'm so sorry. He was in a car accident."

"What happened?"

"I don't know. The officer wants us to come down to the station, to identify him."

"I don't know if I can do this!" She burst into fresh, helpless tears. "Really? He's dead? You're not just making a cruel joke?"

That angered him. "Is that what you think of me? That I'd make a joke about your cousin dying?"

The two of them drove into town, Tom looking straight ahead, Jen in the passenger seat babbling, Kleenex over her eyes. Pulled into the police department parking lot they passed by at least once a day, without ever before entering.

Tom opened the front glass door of the station for his wife, letting her go first.

He expected the police station to look like it did in movies and on TV, a cavernous room with bench after bench against the walls where prostitutes and dope dealers sat handcuffed, a tall desk at the rear, but instead it was a small room with a few chairs, a sliding frosted glass partition at the back, much like a car rental office. To the right of the frosted glass partition, a closed metal door.

The frosted glass partition was slid shut. There were several small notices taped to the right, fixed half of the partition, typed instructions for parking tickets, home alarm renewals, bail arrangements.

Not sure what to do, he knocked on the frosted glass.

Nothing for about a minute, to where he debated if he should knock again, then he saw a shadow behind the frosting. The left half slid open.

A heavyset black cop in blue uniform looked through the partition's space at him. "Help you?"

"Is Officer Klenghorn available?"

He swiveled around on his stool, calling to the open doorway behind him. "Is Pete K. on duty?"

A man shouted something from beyond the doorway. Tom couldn't make it out. The policeman turned back towards Tom. "What's your business with Officer Klenghorn?"

"He called me twenty minutes ago about a fatal car accident my cousin, Wally Walczak, was involved in."

"Was Mr. Walczak the fatality, or did he cause someone else's fatality?"

"He was the fatality."

"Hold on." The cop slid off the stool, wandered through the back doorway.

Tom looked at his wife, who was bent forward, face scrunched, eyes still red. "He's checking."

After a minute, the cop returned. Tom noticed he had a gun strapped to his hip. The cop didn't say anything, didn't look at Tom, until he sat back down on his stool. "Go down to the end of the hall. Ask for Officer Mundy."

He reached his right hand under the counter.

The metal door to the right of the partition buzzed.

Tom walked over to the metal door, tried twisting the knob. It wouldn't turn. Frozen in place. The attempt to twist the knob clockwise hurt the undersides of his fingers.

"Try again. Turn the knob while it's still buzzing."

This time, Tom rotated the knob as soon as the buzz started.

Beyond the metal door, a narrow hallway that stretched deep inside the station. No benches, no people.

He walked down the corridor, nervous, Jen behind him.

At the end of the corridor, to the left, a small clearing. A policeman, crew cut blonde hair, blue eyes, stood holding a manila folder with pink and green strips of tape across its front.

Beyond the cop, a clear glass partition, large office space behind, men and women working at desks. Muffled sound of phones ringing.

"You're here to identify the Walczak body?"

"Yes."

The cop smiled at Jen. "Who's going to do it?"

Tom stepped forward. "I will."

Jen sniffed. "Are you sure?"

"You shouldn't have to see him like this."

The cop looked Jen up and down. "You can have a seat right here, Ma'am. It doesn't normally take too long."

Tom followed behind the cop, who was taller than him, more muscular than him. He resented the once-over the cop had given his wife, the idea that in the police system that kind of attitude was somehow appropriate, but said nothing. He just wanted to get this over with. He visualized himself back at home, building more bookshelves in the garage, Wally no longer in their house. Maybe he'd have another Miller Lite once this issue was resolved. Then he remembered Wally drank all his Miller Lites that first day.

They stopped in front of a numbered door. The cop knocked. Turned with a smirk towards Tom. "This your first body identification?"

"Yes."

"If you need to throw up, use one of the waste baskets. I'll point one out to you when we go inside. Don't throw up on the mortuary floor. Then

181

they have to shut down until the floor's decontaminated. That takes a long time."

The door opened. A black woman in street clothes smiled at the cop. "Wendall? Why aren't you home with your kids?"

Wendall shrugged his broad shoulders. "Double duty. Gots to pay for that new car somehow."

He and Tom walked into a medium-sized room, four long gray metal tables inside, all of them empty except one, a white plastic sheet draped across its body.

The cop nudged Tom, pointed at a metal waste basket next to the scissored legs of the occupied table. "Throw up in there."

The female coroner smiled up at Tom. She was pretty. Tom wondered if her long black hair held any extensions. "This isn't so easy, huh? But we're gonna walk you through it. People usually wonder, how much of the body do I have to identify? But what we're going to do is, I'm going to take you over to that table there, then when you tell me you're ready, I'm gonna fold the plastic tarp down just from his face. If you can identify him just from that, that's fine! If you aren't sure, and if you're aware he has any tattoos, or surgical scars, then what I'll do is unfold the tarp from just that small area of his body, just a peek, so you can tell me if this person is the person you know. I'm going to be right next to you while you do this, and I'll even hold your hand if you like. Are we okay? Are you ready to approach the table?"

Tom didn't want to look weak in front of her. "Sure."

"Well, let's do this then! Why don't you give me your hand, and I'll hold onto it, you know? Just in case. It's not easy looking at someone who's dead. That's a hard thing for someone still alive to do."

Hand in hand, Tom and the black coroner walked over to the table.

"Okay, with my free hand, I'm gonna fold the tarp back from his head. Now, I just want to warn you, he was in an automobile accident, so he did sustain some serious damage to his face and head. It's not pretty at all. What I tell people, pretend you're not looking at the real person you knew. Pretend you're looking at a horror movie, where the makeup people have created this fake mask for an actor. All you have to tell me is, Is this the person you knew? Are you ready?"

On the underside of the white plastic tarp, by the hump of the head, dark blood clots, like red jellyfish. Tom felt frightened. Sick to his stomach. He held onto her hand. "Yeah. Let's get it over with."

"Okay, then! See my hand at the top of the tarp? I'm gonna just unfold it a little bit at first, like this, just so you see the top of his head."

Her free hand slipped its knuckles under the top of the white plastic tarp. Curling the fingers down, she pulled the top edge of the tarp forward.

Tom saw hair. About the color of Wally's hair? Could he identify him just from that?

Mixed in the hair, something that looked like clumps of hair gel. Why would he have that much gel in his hair? It didn't make sense. Plus why was the gel so red?

The coroner pulled the tarp further down, resting the top edge of the tarp just below the corpse's flat eyes, the eyes that no longer looked at anything.

Tom's knees dipped. Tongue sliding across his pale lips.

"His eyes are gonna look different now, of course. Unlit, because the spirit's left him. Let's see the rest of his face. You doing okay, Tom?"

Tom nodded. Looked down, sideways, to locate the metal waste basket.

"I know how hard this is. Years and years ago I had to identify my own mother on a table like this. And I didn't even like her at that point. That woman got lost, filling herself up with all kinds of junk." She pressed the side of her body against the side of his body, not in a sexual way, but a human way. Feeling the warmth of her body against his gave him strength.

She exposed the rest of the face. Tucked the top edge of the stiff white tarp under the different directions of the chin.

Tom let out a moan. The coroner squeezed his hand.

Breathing heavily, heart beating in both wrists, Tom looked down at the chaos of the broken face, the red furrows, the gray flesh, the frozen agony of the opened mouth.

"That's him."

"You are absolutely positive."

"I am."

She threw the top of the tarp back over the head. "You're all finished here then. You done good, Mister Tom. Forget what you saw here. Erase it from your mind. That's something just us professionals have to remember. There's a wastebasket right next to you if you don't think you can make it to the bathroom."

Again outside the numbered door to the coroner's room, Tom rubbed both sides of his face. Wiped his palm across the sweat on his forehead.

The cop smirked at him. "Looked like you're were going to toss your brownies in there."

"Yeah, well. I didn't." After he caught his breath, Tom stood in front of the cop. "You have kids? You're married?"

The cop's eyebrows went up. "Yeah. Three kids. I'm divorced. So?"

"So don't look my wife up and down when we go back out to the waiting room. She's not divorced. She's married to me. And she just lost her cousin."

"Wow, we got a tough guy on the premises."

The two of them went back out to the waiting room.

Jen, sitting at the edge of a bench, fingers clutching each other, praying, stood up, hands falling apart, looking hopefully at her husband.

"It was him. He's dead."

She went into his arms. He held her while she cried, smelling her hair.

She pulled her sad, flushed face back, staring up into his eyes. The question everyone asks, fearing the answer. "How did he look?"

"Very peaceful. The coroner said he died instantly. Never saw it coming."

The cop, inspecting his fingernails, gave Tom a grudging look of respect.

Tom rolled over in bed.

Outside, in their dark backyard, a high-pitched screech, big as an airplane landing.

Followed by another plane landing. Another.

Each filled with frightening, uncontrollable rage.

He lifted his head off his pillow, realized he had been dreaming.

Did he dream the screeches, or was he hearing them while he was asleep?

He stayed silent on his side of the bed, not moving, heart thumping, Jen exhaling, waiting to hear if more planes landed. He was terrified they would.

He waited half an hour, a long time to be alone in darkness. At one point, the sound of water in the walls, the ice maker in their refrigerator dropping more ice. Which was reassuring.

Eventually, not meaning to, he fell back asleep.

Thursday night, the screeches woke him again. Again, he convinced himself it was just something he had dreamed.

Just as he was drifting back off, another screech rose outside. Louder than the others. Angrier.

Closer.

He sat up in bed.

I'm awake. I'm not dreaming this.

What should he do?

It took everything he had to get out of bed. Trembling. Crawl on his hands and knees over to the mini-blinds.

What if, parting the blinds, even just a half-inch, he drew attention to himself? Let whatever it was in their backyard know where he and Jen were?

But finally, shaking, he did peep through the blinds. He had to protect his family.

Within the dark shapes of bushes and trees in the backyard, the screech rose to another crescendo.

Forearms and back of his neck goosebumping, he stared outside for any sign of shadowy movement. Although if anything had moved out there, walking in the darkness, his heart would have stopped.

But no movement. No movement at all.

He stayed sitting on the carpet, pale face, watching. Wished he had a cigarette. That small, dog-like companion would have really helped.

After a long time, eyes closing, popping open, he got back in bed. But didn't fall asleep until the digital alarm clock on the table read four o'clock.

The alarm woke him, as it always did, at five-thirty.

He got out of bed quickly, because he knew otherwise he'd fall right back asleep.

Time to make the coffee.

His head felt heavy from lack of sleep. He stumbled around the dark kitchen, getting the coffee carafe out of the pulled-down door of the dishwasher, feeling the coolness of the tap water slide over the knuckles of his right hand as he filled the coffee pot at the kitchen sink.

Driving into work, he kept slapping his forehead to stay awake.

Even though he left home the same time he always did, he was ten minutes late at work.

As he walked down the carpeted corridor to his office, yawning, Meg from Sales, approaching from the opposite direction, holding a bunch of files, said, "Hi, asshole."

She was past him before it registered. He turned around in the corridor. "What? What did you call me?"

Still walking away, she twisted her upper body around, giving him the finger.

What?

Gloria, his secretary, a middle-aged woman who always wore a black wig, stood in front of the door to his office. "Dick wanted to see you as soon as you come in."

"Well, I need some coffee. And I have some reports I need to check."

"He wants to see you right now. He asked me to call his secretary as soon as you get in, which I'm about to do. You better see him immediately."

Looking into her stubborn eyes, he realized she had never liked him. A year ago, at the Christmas party, he had overheard her refer to him to Debbie, Dick's secretary, as cold.

"I don't take orders from a secretary. Get me some coffee. I'll go to Dick's office in a little while."

She blocked his reach for the doorknob with her body. "He wants to see you right now. Not after you've had some coffee."

Tom backed off. Didn't want to get into an embarrassing physical confrontation with this older woman.

She stood her ground, her own hand on the doorknob so he couldn't turn it.

Face red, he walked away from her, down the hall. Turned around. "You just sealed your fate. Update your resume."

He headed towards Dick's office.

"Debbie? Dick wants to see me?"

"Take a seat, please."

He sat in a chair outside Dick's office. Through the glass partition, which turned Dick's office into a fishbowl, he could see Dick inside with Owen, from Marketing. It didn't appear like anything important was being said. The two men just seemed to be shooting the breeze.

Tom was made to wait ten minutes. Long enough for him to start nodding off a couple of times in his chair, head jerking up each time.

Finally, the two men inside made their way over to the office's front door, but even then, they stopped at the door, not opening it, talking some more. With an easy camaraderie Tom had never known with anyone in his life. Why didn't people like him?

As the door opened, Dick, no longer wearing a cast on his arm, lifted his jaw at Owen. "You tell Yvette no matter how bad she thinks she looks in a bathing suit, she's gotta wear one. It can be a one-piece! It's not a pool party if people aren't wearing swimsuits."

So that's what this was. Dick inviting him and Jen to his latest party. He couldn't just send an email to everyone? Tom had work to do.

Owen, walking backwards away from Dick, ready to turn around at the corridor, yukked it up. "Let me work my magic."

Dick, tall and broad-shouldered, dipped his knees in his dark suit pants. "You do that!"

As Owen headed down the hallway, Dick lost his smile. Looked over at where Tom was sitting. "Come on in. Deb? No calls."

Tom followed Dick into the office, leaving the door open.

Dick, lumbering to the chair behind his ridiculously wide desk, which the company had to pay for after Dick decided Stephen's old desk wasn't impressive enough, raised his eyebrows. "Let's shut the door, shall we?"

Which meant, Tom had to walk back and shut the door. Plus Dick, who Tom suspected had barely made it through college, was now affecting airs, saying things like, 'shall we'?

Once both men were settled in their seats, Tom raised his right hand. It was hard to keep the condescension out of his voice. "Jen and I would normally agree to go to your pool party, but Jen just lost her cousin, who was staying with us. He died in a violent automobile accident. But thanks anyway."

Dick, astonishingly, offered no condolences. Like Tom hadn't spoken. "Tom, I'm reorganizing the executive staff, and as a part of that reorganization I'm letting you go as Chief Financial Officer."

Tom said nothing. Dick waited.

Nothing.

Dick looked down at some papers on his desk. "Human Resources has put together a package I'd like you to review, which includes your severance pay and COBRA options." He lifted the thin sheaf, placed it at the front of his desk, within reach of Tom.

"What did you say?"

Dick stared at Tom from across the boss side of the desk. With a look of enjoyment he made no attempt to conceal. "I'm letting you go. Effective immediately. You no longer work for the company."

Tom still hadn't picked up the packet placed in front of him. "Can you do this? Do you have the authority?"

Dick, surprised, laughed. "I'm the fucking president! I can fire anyone I want."

"You're firing me? Seriously?"

"Yes! You're out."

"Now that I think about it, Jen and I probably could attend your pool party."

"That has nothing to do with this."

Tom stared at Dick's big face. "How are you going to manage without me? Who's going to oversee the amortizations? Or keep track of—"

Dick raised his voice. "Tom, you're finished here! You're out!" In a quieter voice, face less angry, he added, "I'm promoting Jim Spritz to CFO. I believe he's a couple of years older than you? So no legal challenges there? Meet with him before you clean out your desk. Bring him up to speed on your projects."

"Jim Spritz? Jim Spritz is going to replace me? Are you frigging kidding me? When it comes to crunching—"

"Tom? Read your disemployment package. Tell me if you have any questions. Then we can both go about our day."

"Why are you firing me?"

Dick hesitated. It was obvious there was a lot he wanted to say. Instead, he glanced down at a sheet of paper on his desk, reading. Looked back up. "If you wish to have an extended conversation about your firing, I'll bring in the acting head of Human Resources, Crystal, to be present during that discussion, as a witness to what we say. But really, I don't wish to comment on why you're being fired. Texas is a 'work at will' state, so I'm not obligated to provide you with any details as to why you're being let go."

"Crystal is acting head of Human Resources? What happened to Agnes?"

"I spoke to her earlier this morning."

Jen placed a cold bottle of Miller's Lite in front of Tom at the kitchen table. "How was your day?"

Tom took a long swig. Put the bottle back down on the table. Avoided Jen's eyes. "Pretty much the same. The usual problems."

"Is the beer cold enough?"

"Yeah, it's fine. Why are you upset?"

She was surprised he noticed.

"Is it because your cousin's dead?" He took another long swallow.

Eyes red, she let out a sigh. "I bought something today."

"Jen—"

"Some flowers. For his grave."

Tom banged his beer bottle down on the kitchen table. "We already had this discussion!"

She reared her head at him, furious. "Because I wanted to!"

"I'm not made of money. We have to keep expenses down."

"It's my money too."

"It's my money!" Caught his breath, chest tense. Wobbled his head on his neck, trying to relax. Couldn't. "Not your money. You don't earn money. Tom Junior has a paper route. He earns more money than you do. "

She made a hurt, angry face, eyes blinking. Swallowing.

"I'm doing a new budget. Right after we eat. We need to cut down on everything."

"Why do we need to cut down on stuff? We're already—"

He slapped the half-empty beer bottle off the kitchen table. "Because I said so!" He jerked himself up out of his chair. Forming fists at his sides.

188

She backed up.

"I just spent ten thousand dollars on your cousin's goddam funeral!" His voice broke. He wasn't used to shouting. "I'm never gonna get that money back. It's gone. Forever! And now you turn around behind my back and spend even more money on him? For flowers?"

"Tom, listen, we have to be able to discuss this as a married—"

His pale skin pulled back on his skull, blue eyes popping. " You…thief!"

He stormed out of the kitchen.

Once he burst into the living room, he paced around for something to break.

Something of hers.

But almost everything in the living room, the house, was his.

On the wall beside the brick fireplace they never used, a black-framed photograph of her and her mother.

Snarling, he swiped it off the wall, as if it were a big bug.

Looked down at his right hand. Red gash across the creases in his palm, from the nail head.

Great! Friggin' great!

Pain in his chest, he collapsed into his easy chair. Tried watching his fish, to relax.

Pulled his notebook out of the inside pocket of his suit jacket. Flipped to the Wally section he had started. At the bottom of the list of how much Wally had cost him—food, alcohol, his share of the mortgage and utilities for the time he had spent in their home, funeral and cemetery expenses—he added at the bottom of the list, Flowers. He'd have to get the cost from Jen later, after she had cooled down.

Staring at the aquarium, it dawned on him there were ten fish swimming.

He only had nine fish.

Counted them again, not easy to do, since they kept moving. But definitely, ten.

Got out of his easy chair. Stood, knees bent, in front of the glass.

The first few fish in an aquarium are always easy to count. One, two, three, four, five. That one over there, six. The two in the lower corner. Seven, eight. The black and blue one, nine.

Another one, behind the rocks, just its top fins visible, rippling, as if it were hiding from him.

Ten.

How could that be?

That can't be.

He turned around to sit back down, try to figure this out in his head, but he couldn't sit back down. Because Wally was sitting in his chair.

"Just follow me in here and then I'll explain!"

Once she was in the living room, he let go of her tugging hand. "Look!"

He was afraid Wally would be gone, but there he was, still sitting in the easy chair.

"What am I—?" She brought her fingers to her mouth. Walked over to the carpet by the wall, stooped over, which made her look older, tired, and picked up the picture of her and her mother he had thrown off the wall. The square of glass covering the photograph was cracked. A shard had torn across the picture it had been protecting, putting a white ripple across her mother's face.

She turned towards him, tears on her cheeks. "Why would you do that? You know I don't have a negative for it. It was my favorite picture of me and my mom."

Pale face flushed, he moved his hands around in front of him. "I don't…I'm sorry. I was angry. Jen-Jen can Photoshop it. But look at the easy chair!"

She was crying again. "Why do you do these things?"

"Just look at the easy chair!"

She looked at the easy chair. "What?"

He thrust both his hands forward, exasperated. "You don't see him sitting there?"

That got her to stop crying.

She looked at her husband.

Looked back at the easy chair.

"See what, Tom?"

"See him! Your cousin! He's sitting in my easy chair!"

Looked at the far away front door. Back at him. Looked at the phone sitting about ten feet away, on a side table. Looked at the heavy brass pot holding the fireplace tools, about five feet from her. Looked back at her husband.

"You don't see him? Come on!"

Shoulders rising, she squinted her eyes at the chair, to show him she was trying to cooperate.

His voice broke. "He's right there, for God's sake!"

She drew her eyebrows together, still squinting. Walked sideways closer to the heavy brass bucket. "Yeah?"

"Jennifer, come on! Are you blind?"

She stopped beside the brass bucket, hand still holding the torn photograph of her mother. Looked at him. "What's he doing?"

Tom snorted. "He's sitting!"

"Is he talking?"

Tom lost some of his steam. "No. He's just sitting, staring straight ahead." He closed his eyes, drowning in his own mind, as he thought of what next to say. Jen carefully watched his face.

"You don't see him?"

"I honestly don't, hon."

Gestured with his right hand, embarrassed. "He's right there."

On impulse, Jen left the brass bucket, walked over to the easy chair, Tom's eyebrows alarmed. Sat down.

"Is he still in the chair?"

"He vanished. Get out of the chair, please. He may get on you."

"Do you see him anywhere else?"

"No. Please get out of the chair. I don't know what happens when you sit on something like that."

Since he was getting more and more agitated, which in a way showed he still cared about her, she stood up prettily, walked away from the seat cushion.

"Now he's back in the chair."

Jen didn't feel the need to stand by the brass bucket anymore. "Can you talk to him?"

Tom kept staring at the empty chair. "I don't know."

"Would you try talking to him?"

"Oh! Okay, I see what you mean." Still standing, he thought of what he should say, just like at one of the meetings at the company where he no longer worked. "Wally, why are you sitting in my chair? You're dead."

Jen waited a moment, looking, despite herself, at the empty chair. Glanced at her husband. "Did he say anything back?"

"No. He's just staring straight ahead, like he was before."

"Can you see through him? Like a ghost?"

"No. He looks solid."

Dr. Krowski waved a small, smoking bundle of dried sage around the living room. It smelled nice, like barbequed ribs smell nice. His bearded face swiveled towards Jen. "Another room where I feel a presence!"

Tom looked at Wally sitting in the easy chair, staring straight ahead. "Can you tell what the presence is?"

191

"Can I tell what the presence is." The doctor concentrated, lateral wrinkles on his forehead. "I sense…a person. A person who has departed. Did someone die in this room?"

Jen shook her head. "Not in this room. But maybe someone who died somewhere else, his ghost is in this living room now?"

The good doctor, head bent, eyes closed, raised his right index finger. "Exactly! That is what I was sensing. There is a ghost in this room, of someone who died. Is that correct?"

She nodded, then realized she had to vocalize, since the doctor's eyes were still closed. "Yes."

The doctor raised his face, opening his eyes. "Exactly what I thought! A family member? A friend?"

"Family member."

"Aha! A close family member, or someone visiting?"

"Someone visiting."

"A family member visiting. But, I sense, not a close family member. Maybe, an uncle? An aunt?"

"No." Jen made a face. "My cousin."

"Your cousin! Good! Male or female?"

Tom interrupted, looking at the easy chair. "Can you see where the ghost is?"

Dr. Krowski didn't answer at first, head bent down, to where Tom thought maybe he hadn't heard his question. The doctor breathed in through his nostrils. "He is…flitting around. Restless! Very restless."

Tom's eyes consulted with Jen's. The silent exchange reminded him of when they first started dating. "We're paying you five hundred dollars for this. If I give you an additional five hundred dollars, can you give me the name of someone who actually knows what they're doing?"

Jen stepped forward. "We appreciate your help. This has been really impressive! But this sounds like we need someone who's an expert in the particular field of lingering ghosts. Do you know someone like that?"

Dr. Krowski tossed the smoldering sage bundle into the fireplace. "Sure, I can do that. Although that kind of referral fee is actually seven hundred and fifty dollars additional." Sideways glance at Tom, to see how he reacted. "There's a small group of people who have…stronger ties to the first world. They call themselves Ghosters. They're not especially nice people. I'm thinking of one in the group in particular, who's not too bad."

"But for an additional seven hundred and fifty dollars you'll give me his name, and his phone number?"

Dr. Krowski, leather patches on the elbows of his hounds tooth sports jacket, shrugged. "Sure. What the hell."

"Are you positive you can take all this time off from work?"

Tom, sitting tensely in his chair at the kitchen table, coffee cup empty, nodded.

"Won't Dick get mad?"

Tom let his head sag sideways on his neck. "It's not all about Dick."

"No, of course not!"

"I'm my own man. Dick's a drunk, and a salesman. He's not part of the core group of people who keep the company running, and he never will be."

"Absolutely!"

The front doorbell rang.

Tom, rising up out of the chair as if he had a sword in his hand, strode to the front door, hoping his brisk stride would give him more confidence, but his right hand still shook as it reached out for the doorknob.

A man taller than Tom stood on their welcome mat. Light gray suit, blue tie. Next to him, a young black man, shorter, in a suit slightly too large, as if he were wearing his father's clothes.

The tall man bowed his onion-shaped head. "Are you Mr. Dunning?" His eyes went left. "And Mrs. Dunning?" His large right hand curled towards his ribs. "Patrick Kelly."

The four sat around the kitchen table.

Tom spoke first, to gain control of the meeting. "I asked you to come out here because as ridiculous as it sounds, we suspect we may have a ghost living with us. Well, he's not living, he's dead, but we suspect we—"

"Would we be talking about the ghost in the living room? The one sitting in the easy chair?"

Jen sucked in breath. Tom opened his mouth, but nothing came out.

"By the way, this is Matt." The young man with the shaved head nodded to both Dunnings, serious look in his eyes. "Matt is an apprentice." Patrick gave a courtly lift of his broad shoulders. "It's my hope you don't mind if I use this meeting as a training session for him."

"Do we get a discounted price for that?"

"The discount is already figured in. Matt, can you tell the ghost's name?"

"I was thinking it's an end of the alphabet name."

"Good!"

Tom and Jen both stared at the black youth's face as his dark eyes went into themselves.

"Clear your mind, then just guess."

"Wallace."

"Wally. Is that right, Mr. Dunning?"

"Well. It may be." Tom took a gulp. "It is. Yeah."

"All right, then. Matt?"

Matt's right middle finger started drawing small invisible circles on the kitchen tabletop, alarming Tom, fascinating Jen. As they watched , the circles lengthened to loops, zigged into cross-overs.

"Matt is in the early stages of learning how to access his talent, and often in those early stages, it's easier to write what he sees first, rather than just vocalizing."

Tom nodded, eyes glazed, thinking, What has happened to my life? When did everything go so wrong?

Matt's eyes slid to Patrick's patient face, intern looking at his mentor, middle finger still creating, even though he was now looking away from the circles and cross-overs. "Blood relation. Not a parent or a child. I'm sure of that."

"No up or down energy."

"Definitely not. I'm sure of that." Matt looked to Patrick, but Patrick's impassive face chose not to confirm or correct. "Maybe a brother but I don't think so." The middle finger continued moving its neatly manicured nail over the table. "Further removed."

"Which would be?"

Broad smile on Matt's face. "He's a cousin." A bit more middle finger writing. "Her cousin."

"Mrs. Dunning's cousin. Not 'her' cousin. Social graces, Matt." But it was a gentle reprove.

"Sorry, Ma'am."

Jen, flustered, shook her head, lifted her palms. "None taken!"

Patrick folded his large-knuckled hands on the tabletop, blue eyes looking from Tom to Jen. "And which one of you will tell me about Wally?"

Tom raised his hand. "I think I should."

Patrick didn't seem surprised.

"Wally contacted my wife after years of silence—I had never heard of him, she had never told me about him—and basically announced he was going to come stay with us, free of charge. I was at work when she talked to him on the phone, so I wasn't able to take part in that decision. If I had been able to take part, he would not have been coming here.

"Anyway, it turned out he was a freeloader. Drank all my beer—he was a heavy drinker—ate all our food, slept in our guest bedroom, used a lot of hot water to take a shower, etc., etc., etc. He was also a very, oh…what's the word? Disruptive influence on our children."

Patrick watched Tom's down-turned face while he talked, eyes sliding left occasionally to see Jen's reaction to what Tom was saying. Matt kept his attention on Patrick.

"So anyway, we came back from church Sunday, and there was a message on our answering machine from a cop who said Wally died in a car accident. We had to go to the police station to identify the body. Actually, I identified the body. Oh! And I had to pay for his funeral and burial, which came to ten thousand dollars, money we'll never see again. After which, my wife decided to buy flowers for his grave. Could her buying the flowers have caused his ghost to show up?" He glared at Jen.

"No."

"All right. Well." Tom looked embarrassed. "Do you need more information?"

Everyone at the table waited for Patrick to say something. Tom realized he had lost control of the meeting. Didn't know when he had lost control.

Patrick bowed his head to Jen. "I'm sure, despite what you've said, Mr. Dunning, that Wally must have had a good side to him as well, though?"

Tom reared his head back. "Not that we saw."

"I've been told more than once that a flaw of mine is my reluctance to speak ill of someone, that I always look for the good in them. Can it not be that despite some annoying aspects to the man, he was still essentially good?"

Tom's neck got red. His voice was flat. "I don't think you understand. Here's the problem. Let me repeat it for you in case you didn't grasp it the first time. This bum showed up on our doorstep expecting a handout. Which we reluctantly gave him. But all we wanted was for him to leave. Once he did leave, we felt relief. He's finally gone. But now it turns out he isn't gone. He's still here. We can't get rid of him. He's the unwanted guest who won't leave, even after he dies. So how do we get rid of him for good, and how much is that going to cost me?"

Patrick smiled. "It will cost you three thousand dollars."

"What?"

Patrick said nothing.

Tom shot his wife an incredulous look. "Why would it cost that much?"

"Like any fee, part of it is to cover operating expenses, part of it is the profit I expect to receive from performing this service for you."

"Can you itemize that for me?"

"I don't itemize."

"That's...ridiculous. You had to pay for a flight out here, and a motel room, but how much is that? I'm not paying his travel and lodging costs, because he's an intern. You don't need him to do this job for us."

"My fee is three thousand dollars. If you don't wish to pay that, we can leave right now, and you owe us nothing. I'll pay the travel and lodging costs for this meeting out of my own pocket."

"Tom, honey, should we maybe consider—"

"What exactly are you doing for us to justify that kind of fee? Can't you just wave a chicken bone or something and get rid of him?"

Patrick lay his left palm on the kitchen table. Rested his right palm on top. "First, we have to find out where the ghost is in your home."

"He's sitting in the freakin' easy chair! You said so yourself!"

"That's just the manifestation of the ghost. It's not the ghost's actual location." Patrick switched to talking to Jen. "Let me put it this way. Have you ever heard a noise, but you're not sure where it's coming from? Then eventually, you track down the source of the noise? That's like this situation. What is sitting in your chair is the noise. What we have to do is track down the source of that image. If you hear a noise, you can't stop the noise just by grabbing the air in front of you. You have to stop whatever is causing the noise, which may be in another room, or outside."

Tom rolled his eyes. "How do you do that?"

"Have any of your clothes been different, since Wally's death? Maybe different buttons on your shirts, or more pockets on your pants?"

Tom looked stunned. "What? No!" But he looked at Jen, for confirmation. "Have you noticed anything?"

She shook her head.

"Has food tasted like there's much more salt in it?"

"Jen?"

She looked helpless. "The food's been the same. Tom doesn't like salt. He says it keeps him up nights."

"Have you noticed any lights playing across your ceiling."

Tom was getting impatient. "No."

"Any loud, angry screeches at night, usually coming from outdoors." "No!"

"Are you seeing any images in water. For example, in the shower, or the dishwasher, or rainfall."

"Screeching? Is that what you said?"

"Matt, take over please."

Matt, sitting, leaned towards Tom, eyes flicking at Patrick. "You've heard screeching? At night?"

Tom looked rattled. "Yeah."

196

"Is it very angry-sounding?"

A shudder. "I suppose it is."

Matt, proud, glanced at his mentor. "Insect manifestation."

"What?"

"Mr. Kelly?"

"Please. This is a perfect opportunity to work on your interviewing skills."

"Certain ghosts can be discerned through insects." Matt lifted his head, proud to be able to participate in the meeting, maybe even show off a bit in front of his teacher. "There is passive discernment, where we become aware of a ghost's presence through insects rallying to defend the house from the ghost, which doesn't seem to be the case here, and then there is active discernment, where the ghost overwhelms insects, using them to announce its return. Which appears to be your case. What you were hearing—and I assume you're not hearing the angry screeches anymore, ever since you saw the ghost in the easy chair?"

Tom wondered if he should be taking notes. "That's correct."

"What you were hearing was the ghost overwhelming the insects in your backyard, and in particular cicadas. This type of active insect manifestation ghost possesses a cicada, gets it to screech until it dies in exhaustion, then passes to the next cicada to continue the screech, and so on and so forth. It can go through a hundred insects in that way, to sustain its screeching. Think of it like someone blowing out speaker after speaker after speaker."

Tom's face was pale. "Why?"

"To let you know it's back. And it's angry. Often, very, very angry."

Jen, scared, reached out, touched her husband's tense forearm. "Pay them the three thousand, Tom. I don't want this ghost around our kids."

Tom shook off her touch. "Do you mind? I'm still negotiating." He ignored Matt, turned towards Patrick. "So what do you do?"

"Matt?"

"Well, as Mr. Kelly said, first we have to locate where the ghost is in your home. Since this is an active insect manifestation, we place sugar cubes throughout your home, on coffee saucers, douse them with gasoline, then ignite them. Blow them out about halfway through the burn. Let the blackened cubes sit on the saucers overnight. The next morning, we should have an ant trail leading to the saucer closest to where the ghost is. We then set new sugar cubes on new saucers around that approximate spot, ignite them with gasoline, and further pin down the ghost's exact location, triangulating like a cell phone signal, until we know precisely where the ghost is hovering. Then we confront it, and remove it from your home."

After Tom wrote a check for three thousand, Patrick and Matt went out to their rental car, came back with sugar cubes and saucers, and a plastic squirt bottle of gasoline.

They placed four or five saucers in each downstairs room, depending on the room's size, dripped a little gasoline on each white cube of sugar, lit the cube with a match, watched the burning, melting, blackening, then puffed out each blue and yellow flame.

Patrick rose from his knees off the carpet after blowing out the birthday candle of the final sugar cube. His onion shaped head swiveled from Tom to Jen. "We'll be back early tomorrow, around six in the morning, to set out the new traps."

Tom didn't sleep well. He woke up, hands waving in front of his face, around four a.m.

Wandered in his pajamas out to the living room, carpet undulating with the bright blue light from the aquarium, to see if Wally was still sitting in his easy chair, and he was. Of course, he would be, since he hadn't yet been persuaded to leave. He expected to see a lot of snaky ant trails across the living room carpets, but there weren't any.

He should never have written out the check in advance. Never pay a contractor until he completes his job, and then try to renegotiate him down, since the work is already completed.

His wide-awake head told him it would be useless to slip his knees and shoulders back under the covers. No more sleep for him this early morning. So he flicked on the overhead kitchen light, eyes photophobic as the large, rectangular light blink-blink-blinked bright. Opened the refrigerator door, spilling out its surgical light, measured out coffee into the coffee machine. Carried back to the coffee machine, from the kitchen sink, the glass coffee pot heavy with water.

Noticed an ant trail from the utility room door, across the kitchen floor, to under the kitchen table.

Leaning over in his pajamas, mouth open like an old man who lived alone, he traced the knotted trail of ants to the melted sugar cube in the saucer underneath the chair at the back of the kitchen table.

Where he normally sat, but where Wally had sat that first evening.

Which did make sense. Wally's ghost probably would appear where he first asserted himself over Tom.

Patrick and Matt, arriving an hour later, carrying cups of MacDonald's coffee, and each holding their own brown paper sack, stood beside the trail in their big black shoes. Patrick raised the rolled rim of his paper cup to his lips, took a sip. "This makes our job a lot easier, it does. Who here is going to be the one confronting the ghost?"

Tom, in his pajamas, stepped forward. "But I want to get dressed first."

Patrick nodded. "Of course. Clothes give confidence."

By the time Tom stepped back out into the kitchen, after having shaved and showered, Jen was also awake, padding out of the bedroom in a tee-shirt and panties, not aware Patrick and Kelly had arrived. She stopped brushing her hair, retreated to the bedroom.

Patrick looked at Matt. "Never, ever."

"Understood."

Tom, knotting a red tie around his neck, looked to Patrick. "So now what?"

"Sit opposite the ghost."

Tom sat in what was normally Jen's chair.

Patrick, taking another hot sip of his coffee, reached into his brown bag. Dumped a small sack of white flour on the kitchen counter. Added to it a tin's worth of black pepper. Set his coffee down. Using his ten fingers, he scooped through the pile, mixing the black with the white.

Jen came back out, slacks and a blouse.

Patrick lifted two palmfuls of flour and black pepper, carrying the mix like cupped water over to the kitchen table. Threw the mixture across the table, above the opposite chair.

As the white flour and black pepper fell, the fall outlined the ghost of Wally sitting in the chair. The ghost shifted, angry, eyebrows and mouth visible.

Tom, seated in the chair opposite the outline, reared back. Patrick put his large hand on Tom's shoulder.

Jen sneezed. Sneezed again. Left the kitchen, headed back into the bedroom, still sneezing.

Tom sneezed. Reached into the pants pocket of his suit, sneezing.

The white-dusted ghost sitting at the far end of the kitchen table opened its black mouth, screaming silently.

"Tell it to leave."

"Leave!"

"What's it saying in reply?"

"You can't hear? He's really loud. Self-righteous."

Patrick leaned in his light gray suit over Tom's shoulder. "Only you can hear. You're the designated lightening rod. What's it saying?"

"He's saying, He's in a bad place. He doesn't have anywhere to go. His life's been a real mess. He's saying he was one step away from living in his car. Listen, Wally, I feel sorry for you that—"

"Don't apologize! He's trying to lure you. Ghosts are better at arguments than we are. Tell him to go fuck himself. Tell him!"

"Fuck you!"

"Tell him, he chose his life. "

Tom slapped his elbows on the table, leaning forward. "Fuck you. What you did with your life, those were your decisions. You were weak! You made a decision each time to drink, even though you knew you had a problem!"

"That's good! What's he saying in response?"

The ghost raised up out of its chair. Shook its floured fists at Tom. "Can he hurt me?"

"Mrs. Dunning? We need you here."

Jen walked over beside Patrick, eyes on the white ghost swaying on the other side of the table.

Patrick put his big hand on her shoulder. She was surprised how strong the hand felt. Patrick's blue eyes looked down into hers. She blushed. "I need you to walk to the other side of the table."

"Where my cousin is?"

Patrick nodded.

"Is he dangerous?"

"Not to you. He loves you." He took his hand off her shoulder.

Staring at the white form, she moved around the near edge of the table.

Glanced back at Patrick.

"Keep going."

Moved around the far corner of the table.

This close, she could see the thousand speckles of white flour and black pepper on the invisible form. The dusted head turned in her direction. She could recognize the contours of her cousin's face, the way he combed his hair. Could see the white lumps of the two eyes.

"Mr. Dunning, what's he saying?"

"Nothing. I just hear him breathing."

"Mrs. Dunning, do you love your cousin?"

Jen looked at Tom for permission. Before Tom could reply, she said, "Yes. Yes, I love my cousin. We used to play together all the time when we were kids." She wiped her eyes, defiant. "He'd pour mud on my head. One time he threw a praying mantis at me. He gave me candy corn. I had never seen them before. He told me they were clown teeth. He wore my prom dress on Halloween, and got chocolate all over it. Tom, we should have treated him nicer! He was my cousin!"

"Spit on him."

"What?"

"I need for you to spit on him."

"I don't—"

"Mrs. Dunning, do you want him to leave?"

"I don't know!" Her face got red, eyes watering. "Can't he just stay here? You're the only one who sees him."

"God damn it, Jen! Why are you always like this?"

"Mrs. Dunning…"

Tom reared up in his chair. "Spit on him! Spit!"

"Tom, I can't just—"

"Spit on him, you fucking cunt! Spit!"

She swung her head side to side, hands on top of her head, sobbing. Swished in her mouth, shut her eyes, spat into the white dust of her cousin's face.

She stood by herself on the far side of the kitchen table, all alone in her own home, shoulders shaking. Lines showed up on her face where future wrinkles would be. Even her eyes looked old. The elderly lady next door. "Are you happy now? Did this finally, finally make you a happy person?"

The flour-covered form stretched its black mouth wide. No sound came out, but Tom clamped his palms over his ears, wincing.

The spit, from where it landed on the outline of forehead, trickled slowly down the floured eyebrow, eye, side of the nose.

"Matt?"

With hesitation, but moving quickly to try to hide that initial hesitation from the others, and especially from Patrick, Matt, holding his paper bag, strode around the table to where the white form stood.

Opened the saw-toothed top of the bag. Pulled out a bottle of extra virgin olive oil, a container of salt.

Poured the extra virgin olive oil over both his palms.

Lifted up the metal spout atop the supermarket blue and white cylinder of iodized salt.

Shook the salt over both palms, until they were covered in the crystals.

Criss-crossed both black hands on top of the shape's white-dusted head.

Pushed down, rising up on tip toe.

Kept pushing down, cords in his neck sticking out.

As Matt increased his pressure, pushing down, the ghost started lowering, white arms flailing, empty mouth stretching open.

Jen spun around, ran over to the refrigerator. Yanked open the door, lighting the inside. Crying. Her thin hands rearranged the lonely cartons and jars inside.

Once Matt had the ghost pushed down to the level of the table, he was able to lean forward, hands still criss-crossed on the struggling head, and use his weight to push down even harder.

As Patrick and Tom watched, Matt's upper body slowly bent all the way over, elbows disappearing below the table top.

When he stood back up, his face was slicked with sweat. He puffed out a breath, grinning at Patrick. "I know I shouldn't use profane language in front of a client, so…Darn!"

Patrick raised his eyebrows. "Darn, indeed."

Matt reached down, picked up off the floor a compacted mass about the size of a sandwich.

"You've done well, Matt."

The white mass in Matt's hands rippled. He continued holding onto the square, held it tightly, but it was clear the movements felt by his fingers were making him queasy.

Patrick lifted his jaw. "Not everyone is a ghost-eater. Back at the motel there's waiting for you a lovely bottle of whiskey, and for me an endless supply of tap water. If you're up to it, lad, if you firmly believe this is who you are, this is the time. Just recall, a ghost you eat can never be shat out, pissed out, sweated out, bled out, or vomited out. "

Matt, holding the sandwich in both hands, its square pulsating, stared back at Patrick.

Sucking in breath, he opened his mouth, bit into the side of the sandwich. Pulled away with his teeth something half-white, half-invisible. Chewed. Swallowed. Lurched his incisors forward again. Bit again. Dragged more flour outline and invisibility from the still-writhing square. Chewed, swallowed. Within his lower face, protesting punches, like tent poles, pushed out his cheeks. Leaned his teeth forward, bit again.

Jen, who had returned from the refrigerator, backed away, eyes huge, colliding into the floor lamp, knocking it over. It fell across the table top, bulb bursting.

Tom, looking nauseous, watching Matt's Adam's apple bob with the final swallow, lowered his hands from his ears.

Jen put the side of her forearm in her mouth. "Do I need to be here?"

"Not anymore."

But she stayed.

When Matt was finished, he licked his lips, black face proud.

His head bent sideways, panic in his eyes, ear resting against the top of his shoulder, stare as flat as a fish gaze. His mouth yanked open. "Fuck you say, Tommy? Treat me like this? Help me back up. All I asked. Jen! Where are you? Leave him! Why hast thou forsaken me? Then they came for me. That's it. There's nothing more. I apologize, Mr. and Mrs. Dunning. I think he's gone."

Matt rubbed his palms over his young face.

Patrick handed him a small jar filled with a brown, grainy liquid. Matt uncorked it, drank it down.

"Is that to, I don't know…neutralize the ghost inside him?"

Patrick shook his head. "There is no way to neutralize a ghost inside you. I have dozens and dozens of ghosts living inside me, like tapeworms. The brown solution is an antiemetic, to keep him from vomiting. If he vomits, we have to start all over again."

Matt sat down in the same chair where the ghost had been. Pulled a white linen handkerchief out of his pocket. Wiped his wet face.

Patrick lifted his jaw. "You did well. I'll tell Clay."

Tom's eyes were everywhere. He leaned sideways, threw up into the wastebasket. Threw up again. Head still below the table top, his hand reached up, waving its fingers around to find the box of Kleenex. Pulled out a few puffed-up tissues, flew them under the table.

When he straightened back up in his chair, mouth wiped, he winced. Put a palm against his abdomen. "I think I pulled a muscle, throwing up sideways."

No one said anything.

He glanced at Patrick. "So the ghost is gone?"

"Indeed."

Jen stared down at her husband. "You called me a horrible word."

Tom admitted to it, nodding. "I was wrong to do that. It was a tense situation."

"Can you understand I loved him? I want to just love you, but I don't know if that's wise, Tom."

Tom sat in his chair, actually Jen's chair. If he had wings, they would be slumped to the floor. "I lost my job. A couple of Fridays ago. Dick fired me."

It took her a while to say anything. "Where have you been going?"

"I get an Egg McMuffin at MacDonald's. Then just sit in the parking lot most of the day. I drive home really slow."

"Are you going to get another job?"

"Yeah." He started crying. Knuckles against his forehead.

She stood her ground a moment, then the tip of her nose got red. She leaned over, hugged her husband. "It'll work out."

Where does that faith come from?

"We're going to leave, Mrs. Dunning. Our work is done."

She walked them to the front door.

Matt glanced at her. "Your husband seems like a very troubled man."

Eyes hollow, she nodded. Crossed her arms over her breasts.

"If you don't mind me asking—"

"Matt, I think we've taken up enough of Mrs. Dunning's time."

She looked over her shoulder, back at the distant kitchen. "He never says." Nodded to Matt. "I think most troubled people probably never say what it is they're troubled about." Nodded again.

Out by the curb, in the twilight, street lamps not yet on, sounds of kids in the suburban distance, Patrick unlocked their doors. "Are you okay?"

Matt scrunched his eyebrows. "Why does she stay with him?"

Patrick shrugged.

Matt glanced back at the silent house. It looked like every other house on the street. He couldn't tell from its windows and roofline what had just happened inside. "It seemed like there was a genuine breakthrough in their relationship at the end. Do you think things will work out for them?"

Patrick, opening his driver's door, laughed. "Seriously? No."

Inside the rental, Patrick slid the key into the ignition, setting off a comforting ding, ding, ding until he pulled his driver's door shut.

He started up the low thrum of the engine. "She'll kill him."

"What?"

"The demon inside him is stretching its arms, wiggling its toes. That's something else Clay or myself will have to teach you to spot. He'll try to kill her, and she'll kill him in self-defense. She'll probably call us back at some point, this time to exorcise his ghost."

"Can we do anything to prevent that?"

"Well, I don't know, Matt. Would you like to go back inside, ask if you could live with them? Maybe in Wally's guest bedroom?"

Matt, embarrassed, looked out his side window.

Patrick put the car in gear. "Maybe you're not right for this life. Maybe I shouldn't call Clay."

WE DON'T KEEP IN TOUCH ANYMORE

Stan stood in a brightly-lit supermarket in northern Nebraska. All around him, people he didn't know. How he preferred it. Just a stranger passing through. He and Bud had rented a hospitality suite at a local motel, meaning they'd be able to cook in their room. Off-season so they got it cheap. After so many restaurant meals, on the road for two weeks now, in a state eight colors away from their own, all they wanted was some homemade cheeseburgers.

Bud was off in the produce section, gathering lettuce, a tomato, red onion, couple of russet potatoes for French fries.

Stan was in charge of getting their meat. He figured in Nebraska, the rolled-down side window of their van letting in the smells of field after field of grazing cows, factory after factory of slaughterhouses, there might be a chance to get some really good ground beef.

Flipping through the pink packages he saw one he liked, twenty percent fat, looked for the sell by date, and instead saw the weight.

One pound, seven ounces.

His left eye always teared up first. He wondered why that was.

Turning away from the meat bin, locals milling around him, the living dead with shopping carts, he twisted his face left, right for somewhere private.

The frozen food aisle was almost empty. A college boy at the lower end, near the cash registers, comparing two pizzas.

He yanked open the glass door of the nearest upright coffin, cold air escaping. Reached into the metal shelves of the display case, dozens of different frozen dinners displayed. Grabbed the package closest to him, bent his head, pretending to look at it. Tears fell on the bright red photograph of the serving suggestion, freezing like Salvador Dali dimes.

The door held open so long, its glass began to ghost with vapor. Don't cry. Please don't break down. They're strangers, but you don't want to be the crying man in a supermarket.

By the time Bud caught up with him, package of hamburger buns, American cheese, ketchup sharing his hand basket with the produce, Stan had wiped his eyes, gone back to the meat bin, reached behind him and grabbed a different package of ground beef, one that weighed a different amount.

Stan tall and skinny, Bud short and stout, they made their way to the registers.

Waited in line by the nostril-filling smells of fresh-baked Italian bread.

Stan had nothing to say.

Bud knew his moods.

He woke up underwater.

Bottoms of row boats above him.

Holding his breath, cheeks puffed out, he swam through the living room where he used to live, bare feet kicking off the top of an easy chair.

Trying to get to the surface.

Fish all around.

His lips parted, big bubbles rising out of his mouth, as he reached the surface. Grasping the life preserver of his pillow, body bobbing on the white motel sheets.

Eustace Jones lived on a farm outside town.

He had clicked on Stan and Bud's website, liked what he saw, called the toll-free number. Toots talked to him for an hour, getting as many details as possible about his inventory. When Stan checked in with her by phone while he and Bud were in Missouri, hunting down mob ghosts, she told him it sounded like Eustace might have one of those legendary caches of bottled ghosts you hear about on the road, collected over a lifetime, but not yet visited by a dealer.

Eustace was interested in selling his collection because he had been diagnosed with acute lymphocytic leukemia, and he had waited too long to receive treatment. According to him, his doctors gave him a prognosis of only a couple of months. He wanted the money so he'd have something to donate in his will to a nearby no-kill animal shelter.

After they drove a dozen miles down a country road, no other cars, they came up on a dirt driveway, beat-up mailbox on top of a post. No name or number on the mailbox.

From the road they could see, far back from the mailbox, amid the blond and black and green of the farmland, a house and some outbuildings.

Stan was in a better mood today. He loved these old-timey ghost collectors. "What do you think?"

"No harm driving down to the house. Even if it's not his house, the owner can probably tell us where Jones' place is."

Stan turned their white van into the driveway, tires raising orange dust as their treads wobbled over the dried mud ruts. The fields on either side weren't plowed. Filled with the different colors and heights of Indian mallow, goat grass, wild onion, bluestem pricklepoppy.

"Surprised to find a farm in an area like this that gets harsh winters where the farmhouse isn't right by the road. Most farmers don't want to clear two miles of snow from their driveway in order to get into town."

Bud held out his right hand, grasping the dashboard in front of him, so he wouldn't get rocked side to side as much. "Mr. Jones likes his isolation."

Having been to so many farms over the years, they anticipated someone showing up on the front porch long before they reached the house, possibly with a shotgun.

Stan braked their van in front of the porch. On either side of the steps, pink blossoms of Joe Pye weed. Waited a moment, watching the screen door, expecting to see a shadow behind it.

Nothing.

Turned off the engine.

"Toots knows where we are, right?"

"I sent her an email just before we left the motel."

He let his driver's door creak open, swing all the way out. Amid the silence of the farm, it was a loud noise. Gophers lifted their heads, one mile away.

They kept a Springfield automatic in the glove compartment, seventeen rounds in the clip, because you never know.

Bud tossed his now-empty bag of popcorn over the top of his passenger seat. "Want to mosey up?"

Smell of spice in the air.

The porch steps needed replacing. Both had to look where they placed their shoes.

The screen door was shut, the front door behind it wide open. Stan could see, through the hatching, a front hall, room on the right with furniture.

He knocked on the screen door's frame. "Hello?"

Inside, the scrape of a chair getting pushed back.

"Here we go."

A short figure appeared at the back of the hallway.

"Mr. Jones?"

The figure came down the hall. Nothing in either hand.

"Are you Mr. Jones?"

The man lifted his chin, still approaching. "You the ghost collectors?"

"Yeah. We are."

Jones made it to the front of the hall. Talked through the screen door. "I was just finishing up breakfast."

"Did we get out here too early?"

"Doesn't matter. Let me get this door unhooked."

The three men standing inside the hallway, Jones, in his eighties, white hair, sagging blue overalls, looked up at Stan. "You boys want some tea?"

One thing Stan and Bud had learned over the years, especially with the old-timey collectors, is that you're going to get the best deals if you speak to the owner for a while first. Especially with someone living this far out from town. They like to talk.

The kitchen was an old-fashioned country kitchen, bigger than most living rooms.

Bud looked down at the kitchen table, the half-finished red mess on the farmer's white china plate. "What kind of breakfast is that?"

Jones shuffled with his tea pot over to the sink. Turned on the tap. "Eggs in Purgatory. You boys ever eat it?"

"Can't say I have, because then I'd be a liar."

"It's a nice dish to have when you're feeling low."

Stan took a seat at the table. "You been feeling low lately, Mr. Jones?"

"You heard I'm dying of leukemia, right?"

Stan shut his eyes. "I'm sorry. Just trying to get that thread started. Wasn't thinking. Sorry."

"I'm feeling damn low. Anybody in this room got a right to feel low, it's me."

Bud joined Stan at the table. "Is it just you, now? If you don't mind me asking."

Jones stared at the tea pot on the electric burner, waiting for it to boil. "Lois died about ten years ago."

"Sorry to hear that."

"Yeah, it was a slow death." He said nothing for a long time, the three men in the kitchen, the tea pot that hadn't whistled yet. His crows' feet deepened. "She was a real rapscallion."

While he waited for the water to come to a boil, Jones dropped a couple of slices of bread in his toaster, pressed down on the black bar.

The water came to a boil.

He made two trips from the kitchen counter to the table, one to bring their teacups, one to bring two small plates, one in each hand, a slice of hot buttered toast on each plate.

Stan picked up the pepper shaker, shook black pepper on his toast. "Thank you, sir."

Jones dug back in to his Eggs in Purgatory. "Can't eat in front of someone who isn't."

After breakfast was finished, Stan helped Jones carry the dirty dishes to the sink, where Jones rinsed each plate.

"Toots told us you have a large collection of bottled ghosts."

Jones sat back down. You could see the eighty years of life in his face. He smiled for the first time. "Your gal gave me your street address. Know what the street address here is?"

"One Willow Lane?"

"Yours is 343 East South East Boulevard, Suite 300. That's a long address. Sounds like you live in a metropolis. Like where Superman lives."

"It's a long address, but it's a small city. Suite 100 is a sandwich shop Bud and I go to most days when we're in town, and Suite 200 is a comic book store."

After some more small talk, Jones pushed himself up out of his chair. "Well, I guess we best get down to business."

The three of them went outside through the front door.

Jones paused once they got off the porch. Pointed around. "I don't keep any ghosts in the house. Just seems like a bad idea. Over there, in the barn, I got a lot of them. That outbuilding there Lois and I used to dry meat, but now it's mostly ghosts and memorabilia. The smaller outbuilding beside it, with one side falling down, I got my most expensive ghosts in there. And then there's the root cellar, over there by that stand of blue mustard. That's where I keep my special ghosts."

They started in the barn.

A couple of rusted cars on blocks, from decades past. "Don't do a lot of driving anymore."

Most of the dirt floor of the barn was filled with American memorabilia. Coca-Cola signs, old-fashioned gas pumps from the twenties, taking up as much space as the cars, presidential campaign posters, boxes of sheet music, toys from decades past.

Bud went over to one of the tables, slid a large tarp off the shape. "Look at this, Stan."

A red Buckeye root beer fountain dispenser with black logo from the nineteen-thirties.

Jones cleared his throat. "Look what's next to it."

211

A ceramic container, two feet tall, roughly hour-glass shaped, with the words GrapeKola written across the top curve; red grapes amid green leaves painted on the bottom curve.

"That's one of my pride and joys. From 1896."

Stan touched the smooth, hard upper curve of the container. "You have some real finds here."

"I'm having a couple of Americana people come out next week. But they're gonna have to give me a real good price to get that piece."

"You said there are some ghosts in here?"

Jones raised his jaw. "I keep them in the loft."

Stan climbed the wooden ladder, rising through the shafts of sunlight, to the hay loft. Bud below him.

"I'm not gonna come up myself. Not at my age, in my condition."

All the better. They could snoop as much as they wanted.

The bottles were set apart from each other on the hay loft's floor. Best way to store them. Not a good idea to let bottled ghosts see each other.

Stan walked over to the first glass bottle, about the size of a modern water cooler bottle. Got down in the dust on his knees. Used the fingers of his right hand like a windshield wiper.

The darkness inside, aware of the inspection, twisted its head and neck, like a horseshoe crab, banging its hair against the bottle's top seal.

"Mr. Jones? I got a woman with a red-checked blouse."

From the bottom of the wooden ladder, Jones' voice welled up. "That's a prairie woman I got in Kansas, mid-seventies. The owner told me she was from the eighteen-sixties."

"How much you want for her?"

"I don't know. Maybe one-eighty."

"Okay. Can we put her on a back burner and revisit?"

"Fine by me."

Bud pointed to a nearby jar. Squashed black face, large dark eyes stuck to the inner curve of the glass like two jellyfish.

"Does he have the letter "J" burnt into his forehead?"

"Appears to."

"Oh, that's an African slave. That's one of my oldest. Late sixteen hundreds. I can't possibly part with it for less than three thousand."

"Okay. We'll keep it under consideration. I see a dark-faced woman with braids on either side of her head, one of her lower front teeth missing."

"That's my squaw. She's kinda rare. She's from the Apache tribe, late eighteen hundreds."

"So after the Apaches were more or less domesticated."

212

"Well, I guess that's true. But still, you don't see that many Indians on the market. I'd have to get at least eight hundred for her."

At this point, Stan and Bud didn't agree to any of the prices. The best way to bargain with these old-timey collectors was to identify the ghosts the two of them wanted, then offer a single price for all those bottles, combined. You could save hundreds of dollars that way, instead of buying them individually.

To keep things friendly, Stan mentioned in a loud voice, so Jones at the bottom floor of the barn could hear, that a lot of times, the only way they could date bottled ghosts was by the clothes they were wearing.

Jones' voice floated up. "I suppose that's true. I was in World War II. The Pacific. Always surprised me what I'd find in an enemy's pocket, while we were stripping the corpses. Back then, maybe still today, you were allowed to keep whatever souvenirs you found. Teeth, pebbles, bits of colored paper. One thing I'd almost always find in the pockets though would be a picture of a woman. Not too many pictures of children. Guess they were too young to have their own family yet."

More bottled ghosts in the outbuilding next to the barn, where Jones and his wife used to dry meats. Still a barbecue smell inside, after who knows how many years. But the ghosts weren't anything special. Mostly day-laborers and farmhands, none of them more than a half century old.

"You say your most expensive ghosts are in that run-down building next door?"

"That's where I keep 'em."

The three men entered the structure. One side of the building had fallen down, gray planks in a chaotic pile, roofline sagging.

The collapsed wall let in much more sunlight than the other structures. Indian goosegrass grew in the center of the interior, long, spindly seed heads rising like hands.

The bottles were off to one side, in the shadows.

"Okay if I drag one of these out into the sunlight, Mr. Jones?"

"Long as you drag it back, and don't break the bottle. You break it, you bought it."

Stan leaned over, grasped the largest bottle by its top. Dragged it at a tilt, leaving a rut in the dirt.

Wiped dust from the curved glass.

Inside, the ghost looked out at him, squinting in the bright light.

A white man, long hair pulled back from his face, knotted below his nape.

Stan peered left, right into the bottle. "What's this on his face?"

"Cancer."

"Who is it?"

"That's Caesar Rodney. He was one of the signers of the Declaration of Independence."

Stan shot a look at Bud. "Are you serious?"

"Damn straight I'm serious. Born 1728, died 1784. He was a High Sheriff in Kent County, Delaware. Got elected to the Colonial Assembly, then the Continental Congress. Fought in the war. Finished his life as President of Delaware, and a member of the Upper House of the State Assembly."

Bud, standing next to Stan, leaned over, looking in at the man's large eyes.

"Forty-eight thousand. Firm."

Bud reached into his satchel. "Okay if I take a picture?"

"I don't mind, and I don't care if he does."

Bud steadied his camera right at Rodney's face. Turned off the flash feature, because it would put a glare on the glass.

Pressed down.

He and Stan looked at the image together. Lot of good details.

Stan got to his feet. Stretched his arms back. Turned to Bud. "I dragged it out. Could you drag it back? Do you mind? Mr. Jones, you say forty-eight thousand is firm, and I respect that. To be honest with you, that's way outside our budget. But here's what I'd like to suggest. And which we've done before. We can contact some of the private collectors we do business with, and see if they'd be interested in this kind of find. We'll handle all negotiations for you, arrange for the transport, present you with a cashier's check. We do all that for ten percent of the purchase price."

Jones stayed noncommittal. "I'll think about it."

"I hope you do." He hesitated. Tried to think of the most tactful way to put it. "Since time is of the essence here, it's not a bad arrangement."

Bud, back from dragging the bottle to where it had been, brushed his palms against his knees. "One of the worst things we see, Mr. Jones? A great collector like you passes on, and whoever gets this land, whether it's a distant relative or the bank, has no idea what these bottles are, and just trashes them. They end up in a landfill."

"We would tell the potential buyer he'd have to identify the ghost as being from the collection of Eustace Jones."

"I said I'd think about it."

They decided to take a break.

The three of them sat in rocking chairs on the ground in front of the front porch steps.

"You boys like something to drink?"

Jones went through the front door into the interior darkness. Came out a minute later with a jug and some glasses.

Back in his rocking chair, he leaned forward, plowed the curved rim of each glass in the dirt by his feet. Handed a glass to Stan, glass to Bud. "Use your fingers to rub the dirt around the insides, like an abrasive, to remove any grime. Dirt's dirt, but it's a cleaner too. I won't use my own fingers on your glasses because you might not cotton to an old man's fingers inside your glass. Especially an old man who's dying."

Once they spilled out the dirt, Jones poured an amber liquid into each glass. It caught the sun's rays.

Stan took a sip. Winced.

Jones, waiting for the reaction, grinned. "It ain't apple cider."

"You have any children?"

Jones looked down at the glass held in his lap. "A worthless son."

"You don't love your son?"

"Love him. Don't like him. The boy never had any imagination. He could see the tree in the acorn, but he could never see the chairs and bureaus and park benches and rowboats and toothpicks in that acorn. Once he was tall, he thought he was gonna tell me what to do. Him and his short-haired wife. I only met her once. Some barbecue in Lincoln. Which one's your wife? The one over by the charcoal grill, flipping the steaks, electric toothbrush in her mouth. I got my revenge. Let him keep living, to where his teeth fell out, his middle got fat, and his wife left him for a bald-headed man with one eye who's been on government disability for twenty years because he has 'anxiety'.

"My only joy in recent years has been a woman I met over the Internet. Melinda. She manages her own horse farm in Kentucky. We have an email correspondence. Seems to be cooling though. There used to be all these exclamation points in her emails. Now her emails are a lot shorter, and it's all just periods. Promise me something?"

"What's that?"

"If you ever see my ghost in a jar, you'll set me free."

Every Ghoster's worst fear.

Bud said nothing.

Stan nodded. "You have my word. I don't want anyone I know to ever end up in a jar."

"It's one of the few things I worry about."

Stan let a beat pass. "When I asked you my question about having any children, I meant any bottled ghost children."

Jones finished his drink. Set his empty glass down. "I do, but I don't bring them up unless the seller does, because some people are sensitive about buying kid ghosts."

"May I see them, please?"

Bud stared down at his shoes. Like he did each time Stan asked the question.

"If you want to."

The bottled children were in the root cellar.

The three men walked over to the wide wooden door set in the weeds.

"It's unlocked. Just haul the door up."

Stan leaned over. Grasped the rusted latch. Lifted up, the door rising at an angle from the ground, hinges creaking, width wobbling.

Dirt steps leading down. Smell rising of a place that doesn't see enough sunlight.

Bud handed Stan a flashlight.

Jones avoided looking down the steps. "I can probably give you boys a deal on anything you find down there. To be honest, I only bought the jars because it was part of a larger deal. I never wanted them."

Halfway down the steps, Stan turned on the flashlight.

Beam scouting around the dirt-packed walls as he reached the bottom step.

The root cellar was empty except for a wooden bookcase on the left, against the wall.

Four shelves, three bottles on each shelf.

As the flashlight hit the bottles, glittering their dust, the dark interiors tapped into life.

He started at the top row, angling the front of the flashlight down so it only indirectly illuminated the contents, to avoid glare. The first small gray face floated from the back of the jar towards the front. Mouth opening like an anus, big hopeless eyes blinking.

Nope.

Next one.

Nope.

A tear started in his left eye.

Nope.

Next row down. Tiny palms against the inner curve of the bottle, trapped face about the size of his fist.

Nope.

As he usually did, he hummed to himself as he peered within each jar and moved on, because this was not easy.

216

How much is that doggie in the window?

Another small face floating forward, crying, pleading.

"Partner? You doing okay down there?"

"Almost done."

He got down on his knees in the dirt to check the bottom row.

The one with the waggley tail.

When he finished he was disappointed, as he always was.

"You about ready to come up out of there, Stan?"

Who was that American astronaut, the first one to do a spacewalk? When his fellow astronaut asked him to come back inside the space capsule, he refused, saying he wanted to stay out there, floating in space, a little longer. Maybe stay out there forever?

Stan climbed back up the steps, back in the sunlight, squinting like Caesar Rodney.

Bud shot him the kind of look that already knows the answer.

The three of them went back to the farmhouse to negotiate prices.

Stan and Bud talked quietly between themselves for a moment in the living room, then went out to the kitchen where Jones was sitting at the table with another glass of moonshine.

Stan raised himself to full height. Pulled the billfold out of his hip pocket. "Mr. Jones, we want to thank you for taking the time from your day to show us around your collection. We're prepared right now to offer you cash for the prairie woman and the Apache squaw."

"Like I said, one hundred eighty for the prairie woman, eight hundred for the Apache squaw. What's that? Nine hundred and eighty dollars."

"We'll pay you cash right now, for both. Five hundred dollars."

"Well, I don't know."

"And we have an exclusivity contract right here, which I'll fill out and sign, where we'll represent you for six months for Caesar Rodney. Forty-eight thousand dollars, ten percent to us if we sell him."

Bud looked down at the floor. "Not for nothing, but that's a good deal. You get five hundred foldable cash right now, and a chance to get a lot more."

"I was thinking more like eight hundred for the two women."

"If you had all the time in the world, you might eventually be able to get that. But we're on a budget."

"Could you go six-fifty?"

"That would be too high for us." Stan glanced at Bud. "But we could make a final offer of five-fifty."

Toots had lined up some buyers. They'd get three-fifty for the prairie woman, fourteen hundred for the squaw.

Stan and Bud got a hand truck out of the back of their van. Carefully wheeled each strapped-in bottle to the van, loading it with the bottles they had collected elsewhere on this trip, secured them in place.

Jones, watching the operation, waved goodbye to the two bottles. "You don't want the children?"

"Not really our thing."

"You got any children of your own?"

Stan turned around. "No." He secured the back doors of the van. "My wife was pregnant, but the baby was born premature." He shrugged. "Didn't last long." The image he could never get out of his head. His little dead son on the doctor's palm, like something made out of the world's softest leather. Not even large enough to cover the doctor's life line. Swollen eyelids. Tiny limbs going out sideways, like a lizard. Capturing the moment it lost its struggle. "She couldn't get over the death. Guess I couldn't either. Just another divorce in the statistics. She remarried. We don't keep in touch anymore."

They drove back to the motel.

Bud parked the van outside the door to their room. Stan went around its whiteness, pulling up here and there, making sure all the doors were locked.

Over dinner at Jack in the Box, Bud, finishing his seasoned curly fries, looked across the table. "Of course, you may never find him." Not the first time he'd been tactful.

Stan was underwater, looking around at the fish.

Why not just stay down here, until his breath is gone, watching the fish?

Above him, his premature son swam by. Looking down at his dad. Eyes filled with a child's pride. Struggling to swim as best as he could, to get his dad's admiration.

Stan reached up in the cold water, cupping his palms around his little premature baby, all one pound, seven ounces.

Underwater, a phone rang.

He bobbed up onto the surface, limbs going out sideways on his bed.

In the motel room darkness, Bud snoring in the other bed, he snatched up the phone.

Dial tone.

Did he dream it was ringing?

218

He lay on his side, watching the phone, waiting to see if the bulb atop the phone started blinking red.

It didn't.

Only now did he look at his wristwatch.

Just a few notches past three o'clock.

He knew he wasn't going to able to fall back asleep.

Keeping quiet, no reason to spoil Bud's slumber, he got out of bed.

Eased the motel room's door open.

Stepped out into the noisy night.

Lit a cigarette.

Harvest moon, orange and low, like it was just him and that big cold eye.

Will I ever find my baby? Yes? Or no.

Will all my searches over these years ever yield that yolk?

Looked out on the neon and night sky and nearby hills of northern Nebraska.

FLESH GHOST

The hum of the highway, which never stops. Thousands upon thousands of black tires vibrating on black asphalt, at seventy miles an hour. Even louder at night, white and yellow headlights under the dark blue of America's moon.

Most of the patrons in the Golden Eye diner were men sitting alone. Eating by themselves. Not reading. Not talking. Just looking down at the time away from the highway still on their plates.

At the rear of the restaurant, at a table near the twin orange doors of the rest rooms, Stan opened his menu.

What you would expect.

Popular dishes came with photographs. Meatloaf with gravy and mashed potatoes. Roast chicken. 16 ounce porterhouse steak. Fried shrimp. Mommy food mixed with girlfriend food.

Stan flipped to the back cover of the menu. Pictures of pies. Blues, reds, yellows.

Bud, sliding the tip of his right index finger sideways, read the entire menu, including all the breakfast items, the sandwiches, the side orders, as if it were poetry. He looked up, undecided. "Do you think the picture of that 16 ounce porterhouse steak is accurate?"

"I thought you told me once while we were driving through North Dakota or Alabama or Oregon that according to the Internet, most pictures of steaks are photographed in Japan."

"Did I say that?"

Patrick inclined his onion-shaped head. "Can you remember the best steak you ever ate?"

Stan looked around for the waitress. "Sure can't."

"With me, it was a t-bone I had many, many years ago in a shopping mall in Bridgeport, Connecticut. The place called itself a steakhouse, but it was inside a mall, and way back then, you never found a good meal in a mall. But I was waiting for someone, there was a table available at the front of the restaurant, where I could watch the escalator. I forget what the steak came with. So clearly the sides weren't that good. But the t-bone? On that one day from so long, when I was distracted and not expecting anything, I was served the best steak I have ever eaten in my life. The outside was charred black. I cut into the side of it with the cheap knife and fork they supplied, wrapped in

223

a white paper napkin, and the entire inside was a uniform ruby. Not raw. Not at all. Grilled just past rawness, to rare. Each bite was extraordinary. Juicy, beefy, char-broiled flavor, just a touch of heat from ground peppers with each swallow. I've always wondered, and still do, if I had gone back to that restaurant the next day, or the next week, and ordered a t-bone again, if it would be as good. Or if what I got that afternoon was just a fluke."

Bud placed one plump hand atop the other on his closed menu. "Phoenix, Arizona."

Stan lit a cigarette. "I change my answer. This is the one with the wax beans, right?"

"Stan and I bought some bottled ghosts earlier in the day from a couple of ranches, rolled into Phoenix, sold one of them to, ah…"

"Irv Goldstein."

"Former firefighter, did his twenty years, had his pension coming in every month, was still young enough to get another job, as a bank loan officer. Big pot belly. We sold him the bottled ghost of an Indian."

"Navajo."

"Which he had been trying to get for years. In gratitude, he took us out to this Italian steak house. It was nighttime by then, all I remember was it was on a hill, it had a big neon sign, and it was really large inside. Irv knew the owner."

Stan leaned across the table towards Patrick, to keep his voice low. "The thing was, we figured Irv was somehow associated with organized crime. At least on the periphery. Maybe from his years on the fire department, maybe from his new job at the bank, who knows. But he was somewhat connected."

"So he takes us to this steakhouse, and they treat the four of us like royalty."

"He brought along this older, dark-haired woman from the loan department."

"The owner of the steakhouse comes over, doesn't ask us what we want. Tall, blustery guy, curly black hair, with a bunch of corny jokes. We don't even get to see the menu."

"Bud collects menus. He steals them from restaurants."

"Which makes my collection so much sweeter. But I always leave an extra-large tip to cover cost. Anyway, he brings the table an appetizer, I don't remember what it was?"

Stan shook his head.

"We wait a bit longer than you normally would for your main course, then the restaurant owner is back, with two male assistants. He oversees them making this incredible spaghetti tableside, in a chaffing dish. I had no idea at the time what it was, but years later, I found out just by accident that it was spaghetti carbonara."

Patrick politely raised his eyebrows. "That is a good dish."

"After they place on each of our plates a heaping portion of the spaghetti carbonara, using this weird serving spoon with big prongs on each side, a third assistant arrives with this steaming platter of porterhouse steaks. Transfers one to each plate. They smell incredible. Beefy like you wouldn't believe beefy. And I notice, and I can see Stan here noticing, that across the top of each steak is this pattern of wax beans."

"And forgive me, but what are wax beans?"

"They're not beans like pinto beans or Boston baked beans. They're like green string beans, only they're yellow, and the texture is different. Someone in the kitchen had cut the wax beans into two-inch lengths, sliced them in half lengthwise, then carefully placed the wax beans cut side down side by side across the top of each steak. So the top of each steak had a rippled pattern of these beans laid side to side. And having those cut wax beans on top of the steak before they put it under the broiler just gave that steak this incredible second flavor that seeped down into the beef. The best steak I ever had in my life. Absolutely. I've brought this up with all kinds of people over the years, and no one else has ever heard of cooking a steak that way. I even looked on the Internet."

"He spends all his time on the Internet."

"Have you ever gone back?"

"We did. But by then the owner of the restaurant had been murdered, in front of the cash register at a pet shop, and his son didn't know what we were talking about. Apparently it was an off-menu item."

"Could you ask Irv?"

"He's dead too. Massive coronary. Died in the middle of the night on his way to the refrigerator."

Clay, on the other side of the table, tossed his menu on top of his empty plate. "Can we get away from this food talk? What's the deal with the client?"

Tilda lit a fresh cigarette. "He's been seeing creatures he calls demons. Not in the middle of the night. Broad daylight. Everywhere."

"What do they look like?"

"He didn't go into a lot of detail."

"So why did he contact you? Why not go to a psychiatrist, or a neurologist?"

Sitting taller than all the rest of them at the table, she shrugged. "Embarrassment, maybe?"

"How'd he know about you?"

"Actually, he didn't know about me. He knew about you. There was an elderly man in Washington state he apparently knew professionally, and this man told him about his experience with you when you were trying to save his daughter from a Neek?"

"Sure. I remember."

"So when the client started experiencing his own problems, he gave the old guy a call, but the guy was dead by then."

"The elderly father? He's dead?"

"Yeah. Suicide."

Clay shook his head. "Stupid, stupid, stupid."

"Yeah. If people only knew. Anyway, he contacted some other people, and eventually found his way to me."

"But you don't want to do it?"

"It doesn't feel like my kind of job."

Clay reached sideways, rapped his knuckles on the tabletop. "Matt? That's your last drink. Just so you know."

Matt looked down, black face embarrassed.

Patrick stared at the young man a moment. "If you don't mind my observation, you don't appear to be in the best of health, Matt."

Clay chopped his hand in front of him. "He's adjusting. If he doesn't want this life, he can walk away. I told him I'd pay his air fare. But if he's going to continue apprenticing with me, he has to suck it up. There's a little girl in Vermont who's showing a lot of promise, and frankly, I'm getting sick of him crying every night."

Matt took a long pull on his final drink for the evening. "I'm sorry. I'm just having some problems." He ran out of words.

Patrick smiled. "Is it the taste?"

"Well, yeah."

"You told me he looked like a good candidate, Patrick."

"Indeed I did. Although I did say there were issues with him. I told you that. And I still believe he could be a good candidate. He's young, Clay. Keep him around for another job or two. See if he can reach the point where he can swallow it. You can get used to anything in time."

"Stan? You and Bud interested?"

"Really not our bag. Plus, there's a new development in a job we did in Dallas. We have to drive back down there."

"Patrick?"

"Why don't you want the job?"

Clay shook his head. "I doubt he's really seeing demons. Not in broad daylight. Not all over town. It sounds to me like a flesh ghost. I could be wrong."

Patrick turned to Tilda. "How much is he willing to pay?"

"I got him up to twelve thousand. Minus my finder's fee."

"And he's good for it?"

"I'd say so. I did a credit check."

Randall Naughton's office was over on the east side of the city, in a strip mall with four times as many parking spaces as cars. Greek restaurant, nail salon with huge hands in the storefront window, radiology center, employment agency.

Naughton Real Estate Associates.

Lobby about as big as a living room, three soft chairs around a low table. Smell of air conditioning.

On the left wall, a large, black and gray aerial view of Reno.

The right wall held some stylized close-ups of gold bars, hundred dollar bills, stacked silver coins.

The receptionist sat behind a desk, rather than a counter. He could see, through the glass-walled office behind her, a large, dark-haired man on the phone, in agitated conversation, but not so agitated he didn't look up to study who had entered.

"May I help you, Sir?"

Asian. By the squareness of her facial bones probably Korean. Young and pretty.

He gave her his name. "I have an eleven o'clock appointment with Mr. Naughton."

She slid out one of the side drawers of her desk. Pulled from the drawer a thin sheaf of forms kept together with a large pink paperclip. "While you're waiting for Mr. Naughton—"

"It's not that kind of visit. We have a personal matter to discuss."

"Oh!" She looked down. "Okay."

Looked back up, appraising him.

"He doesn't owe me money, or anything like that."

"Oh!" Her natural cheerfulness came back. She raised her thin black eyebrows. "Would you like some coffee?" Right shoulder dipping. "We don't have tea."

Patrick shook his head.

Took a seat at one of the three soft chairs. Set his attaché case on the carpet beside his chair. Didn't bother with any of the architectural magazines. Crossed his right leg over his left.

Watched as the receptionist left a note on Naughton's desk. As Naughton leaned forward in his swivel chair, reading the note while still on the phone. As he eventually ended his call, then busied himself with different papers on his desk.

Fifteen minutes went by.

Patrick, at one point, looking up, caught the receptionist's eye. She smiled at him, apologetic.

When the circular brass of Patrick's wristwatch, surrounded by pale brown hair, showed twenty minutes had gone by, he stood.

The receptionist looked up.

"Tell Mr. Naughton not to contact us again. Kamsahamnida."

That got her up out of her chair, swinging her shoulder-length black hair as she signaled Naughton.

Behind Patrick's shoulders as he opened the front door to leave, he heard Naughton telling the receptionist to bring Patrick into his office.

She touched the muscular back of Patrick's upper arm. "Mianhamnida! He'll see you now."

Big, fleshy man, forearms resting on the arms of his chair. He didn't rise out of his chair to shake hands. Gestured with his jaw for Patrick to take the seat at the front of the desk.

"What?"

Patrick crossed his legs. Smiled. "Are you going to pretend you don't know who I am?"

Naughton's face went harder. "Sell me."

"You're frightened."

Naughton snorted, still glaring at Patrick.

"You're seeing things all around you you've never seen before. Things you're fairly certain no one you know has ever seen before. You want the apparitions to go away, but you don't know how to get rid of them. You made some calls, some more calls, and now here I am, sitting in front of you. How do you prefer to be addressed?"

Naughton looked down at his desktop, as if there were an important paper on it, waiting for his signature. "My friends call me Randall. So you can call me Randy."

"Tell me something about yourself."

"I don't have time for amateur psychology. Every minute I spend with you, I'm losing hundreds of thousands of dollars in deals."

"I won't be able to help you unless you tell me who you are."

Naughton jerked his shoulders around. "What do you want? I'm a big man in this city. In this state. I started as a chiropractor. By the time I was twenty-five, Dr. Woodlawn, who mentored me, said, Randall, you've really made it big. You have the most expensive Porsche they make, your own mansion, with a huge swimming pool. You made it. The guys I went to school with? They're still eating Hamburger Helper to save enough money for their rent. I was jetting all over the world. You know how some people say they've had more ass than a toilet seat? I've had more ass than a whole public bathroom full of toilet seats. Before I turned thirty, I bought an even larger mansion, with an even bigger swimming pool. The seller wanted five million. By the time I finished negotiating with him, I took it off his hands for one point three. And he thanked me. He said, I have to admit, I've never known anyone who can work a deal the way you can. All my friends call me 'Effortless', because I have this effortless ability to make money, and get all the good things in life."

"I thought your friends called you Randall."

"They call me both names. 'Effortless' is an admiring nickname. After that deal, I decided to go into real estate. Where the real money is. I eat lobster and caviar just about every night. I have my own executive chef who prepares it for me. He said to me, Mr. Naughton, I'm glad I work for you, because my other clients, they can barely afford one steak a week. Whereas I'm eating lobster and caviar two or three times a week."

"Are your parents still alive?"

"My mother is. I visit her whenever I can. All the nurses get giddy when I show up. My mother keeps telling me, All the nurses here adore you. They gossip while they're loading their needles about how they'd love it if you asked them out on a date, since you're such a successful businessman."

"So your father's dead?"

"My father went blind in his left eye while I was still really young."

"How'd that happen?"

Naughton's cheeks flushed. "He was putting on his eyeglasses, and one of the ends of the eyeglass handles poked into his eyeball at just the right angle to pierce the eyeball. When he realized what had happened he panicked, and pulled the eyeglasses off his face. Unfortunately, that downwards crook at the end of the handle that would normally fit behind his ear hooked inside his eyeball, so when he pulled forward he pulled the eyeball out of its socket, onto his cheek."

"That must have been horrible."

"Most of my childhood, my dad just had his right eye. That's the image I have of him, growing up. This right eye, rolling everywhere in his face, looking for danger. Year after year as I was growing up. His right eye was his only contact with the outer world."

"Are you married?"

"I get all the beautiful women I want. Why pay for milk when there are cows everywhere?"

"Were you ever?"

Naughton made a dismissive gesture from behind his desk. "She had all kinds of emotional problems. I found this pink box she had under our bed. It was filled with baby clothes. We didn't own a baby! I like women where you do your business, then they get dressed and leave."

"Are you talking about prostitutes?"

"I don't need prostitutes. A prostitute is a female ditch digger. She doesn't have the intelligence or the talent to do anything else. The women I'm with have class. I gave one of them a three hundred thousand dollar wristwatch. She almost fainted. Mr. Naughton, I've never received such an extravagant gift from any of my other dates."

The receptionist rapped lightly against the frame of Naughton's door. "You want me to pick up some lunch?"

"Yeah!" Naughton sat back in his swivel chair.

"It's Two for One Tuesday at Tony's."

"Well. Let me think. Normally, I'd have sea urchin or black truffles for lunch." His fleshy hands reached down, holding his pot belly. "But I had a really rich meal last night, lobster, and sometimes that shit just goes right through me." He winked at the receptionist. "I gotta keep remembering, my mouth is the front of my asshole."

The receptionist dipped her knees.

"Let's see, I could have Porconi's fly in some Kobe steaks for me, but...You know, now that you mentioned it, I could use some Italian. Italian food is what I call 'mommy food'. Let's get two orders of spaghetti."

"Do you want that with meatballs?"

"I'm still full from the Kobe steak I had last night. The special comes with salad, doesn't it?"

She nodded.

"Okay. Let's do that." He pointed his finger at Patrick, showing off to her. "I bought you lunch! You owe me!"

After the receptionist left, Patrick smiled across the desk at Naughton. "Well, I think I know all I need to know about you as a person. Thank you for sharing those details with me, Randy. While your receptionist is out of the office, and it's just the two of us here, no one else in earshot, would this be an opportune time for you to talk about these apparitions you've been seeing?"

Naughton sat back. Dark look on his face. "Yeah, those."

"When did they start appearing?"

His voice was smaller. "Month ago?"

"And what specifically did you see?"

"I was in a property over on the west side. It was a one story with three bedrooms, two and a half baths. I was writing down some notes at the kitchen counter, when I saw someone standing in the downstairs powder room.

"It kinda caught me off guard, 'cause I had been all through the house and didn't see anyone. Sometimes you get homeless people who try to squat in a vacant house, but usually the place is a mess when that happens. Broken glass at a back window where they got inside, food wrappers on the floor, blankets, empty liquor bottles, dirty diapers. But this place was immaculate. What you also get sometimes in a for sale house is people who are driving by, and have to take a leak, or a dump. They see the For Sale sign stuck on the lawn, figure they can sneak inside, do their business, then sneak off.

"I always carry a gun with me, just in case. So I pulled it out, started walking towards the bathroom. Looking through the different doorways on the way to make sure whoever it was I glimpsed didn't have a partner who's gonna jump me.

"I lightly kick the bathroom door open, and there's this guy, standing on top of the toilet. Not in front of it. On top of it." Naughton shivered. "And he's covered in blood. His pajama pants were supposed to be striped, but they were soaked red. I almost shot him right there. Fortunately, I still had my safety on. Fuck.

"So I back out of the bathroom, aiming the gun at him, you know? What the fuck are you doing here? How'd you get in?

"And nothing. He's just standing on the toilet, staring down at me from that height.

"And then I glance in the bathroom mirror, I don't know why I did, but in the reflection I can see the toilet, and the goldfish wallpaper behind him, but he's not in the reflection." For all his bluster earlier, he was now visibly upset. Frightened. "I mean, What the fuck?"

"I'm sure it was terrifying."

"What are those—is it vampires who don't cast a reflection?"

Patrick inclined his head. "Well, in legends. But it wasn't a vampire you were seeing."

"It was broad daylight. They can't come out in daylight, can they?"

"Vampires don't really exist. It wasn't a vampire that you saw."

"Well, what did I see then?"

"Let me ask you some more questions first, before I answer. Is that agreeable to you?"

"Well yeah, sure."

"What was the next apparition you saw?"

"I was at a lawyer's office, it was for a closing on a house. After the keys were turned over, on my way to the elevator, I stopped off at the men's room. Did my business at the urinal, was washing my hands at one of the sinks, when I heard this rattle coming from one of the stalls.

"Honest to God, it was so loud I thought it was a rattlesnake. I didn't have my gun with me, so I just hurriedly turned off the water, didn't even try to dry my hands, just started towards the door, and the front of one of the stalls bangs open, and there's this guy inside the stall, his eyeballs are rolled up into his skull, he's hanging like three feet off the ground, and he's covered in blood."

"When you say he was hanging three feet off the ground, do you mean he was hanging from a rope, like a noose around his neck, or—"

"No! No! He was just suspended in the air. It scared the fuck out of me."

"Did he look like the first apparition you saw?"

"How the fuck do I know? I yanked the door to the restroom open, ran outside, ran down the corridor to the elevator bank. I dropped all my papers on the corridor floor, but I was too afraid to go back and pick them up. So what is it? How do I get rid of it?"

"You've seen it since?"

"Yeah! Like, all the time now. All kinds of apparitions. Old people, young people, children. This is gonna sound weird, okay? But there's one right in this office, standing over there, in the corner by the filing cabinets. It's been here three days now."

Patrick turned around in his chair, looked where Naughton pointed. "Has your receptionist seen it?"

In an awed voice Naughton said, "No. I asked her, the first day it appeared, would you get me something from that filing cabinet, please? And she did, without saying anything about the guy standing right the fuck there, next to the cabinet."

"And he's there now?"

"Yes! Don't you see him?"

"I wouldn't. What's he doing?"

"Well, goddamn it, how are you an expert on these things if you can't see him?"

"That's not the way it works. What's he doing?"

"He's just staring at me. He stares at me all day long. For three days now."

"Does he look angry? Sad?"

"No. Just a blank face. All of them I see, all over the city, street corners, supermarkets, bus stops, they just have blank faces."

The receptionist came back with their orders.

Naughton shut up.

After she delivered the tall white bag, she smiled prettily at Patrick, left the office.

"Shut the door all the way, please."

She backtracked.

Naughton popped the white Styrofoam lid on his container.

A shallow tub of cooked spaghetti noodles, covered in spaghetti sauce.

"All this red. What the fuck was I thinking?"

He pushed the container to one side, popped open the lid for his salad.

They ate in silence.

The spaghetti wasn't that good. Overcooked noodles, too much sauce. Patrick gave up after a few forkfuls.

Naughton only ate half the salad in his container. "So what do I do?"

Patrick lifted his attaché case from the carpet, placing it flat on his side of Naughton's desk. "I'd like to perform a simple experiment with you, if that's okay."

The other man became more alert. Stopped chewing. "Will it hurt?"

"No."

Patrick snapped the front latches of his attaché case. Let the lid rise. Reached in, grabbed what was rolling inside in his two big hands.

"Are those lemons?"

"Yes."

"What are you going to do with them?"

Patrick pulled out a lemon squeezer, a glass. "I'm going to squeeze these lemons into this glass, then I'd like you to drink the lemon juice."

"Why would I do that?"

"It's a test. If it turns out as I believe it will, it'll confirm what I already suspect. But I can't be sure until you've finished drinking the juice."

"Are those regular lemons?"

"They are. I picked them up at a Trader Joe's on my way over here. The glass is from my motel room."

"What's this supposed to prove?"

"It's really best if you drink them first, then I tell you. You can add sugar to the juice before you drink it, if you like."

"If you're fucking with me…"

"I'm not."

Naughton stared at the lemons a moment, then reached for his phone. Pressed a button. Patrick heard a buzz behind his back.

Naughton spoke into the phone. "Susie? Get me a bunch of sugar packets, okay?" He hung up the phone.

The receptionist knocked on the glass door. Entered the office. Walked behind where Naughton was sitting, pulled out a drawer in the credenza behind him.

She lifted out a dozen or so pink and white packets of sugar. Noticed the lemons on the desk. "Is this enough?"

Naughton sat back, chair squeaking. "Yeah. Probably. Thanks."

She placed the packets in front of him, with a slight rustle. Shot a look at Patrick, no longer smiling. Excused herself.

"Shut the door."

She backtracked.

"So, I just squeeze all these lemons into the glass, add the sugar, and drink? Do I have to drink the whole glass?"

Patrick, slanting back in his chair, reached into his front pants pocket, pulled out a penknife. "I'll squeeze them for you." One by one, he sliced the lemons in half, placed each yellow half in the lemon squeezer, cut side down. Held the hand squeezer over the glass. Gripped the two long handles of the squeezer, squeezing until the two handles met, lemon juice dribbling down into the glass.

When he was finished, the glass was half full.

Naughton, chin resting on his chest, looked from the glass to Patrick. "Did Jillie put you up to this? Is this a practical joke?"

"It's no joke."

Naughton tore the tops off six sugar packets. Poured the granulated sugar into the glass. Looked around, then instead picked up a pen. Dipped the pen upside down into the glass, stirring the sugar into the juice, dissolving it.

With his left hand he pinched his nostrils shut, back of his hand resting against his forehead so he could maneuver the curved rim of the glass to his lips.

Had to tilt his head back to pour all the juice inside his mouth, Adam's apple bobbing.

Banged down the empty glass. Made an eye-squinting face.

"Can I drink some water?"

"Not yet. Remember when you go to the doctor, and he asks you to stick out your tongue?"

"You want me to stick out my tongue?"

"Please."

Naughton obediently spilled out his tongue, letting it slope down.

The tongue was completely black.

"What?" Naughton slid the middle drawer of his desk open, rolling his chair back, unintentionally banging it against the credenza. Got out a mirror, brought it up to his face. Stuck his tongue out at himself.

Put the mirror down on the desktop.

He didn't look so good.

Patrick watched as Naughton went into thought. When his head raised, the bluster was gone. "Is it cancer? Something like that?"

Patrick put the motel glass and the lemon squeezer back in his attaché case. "I don't know if you have cancer or not. But, really, that's irrelevant at this point. Let me ask you this: Have you noticed any marks on your body? Cuts, or holes, or anything at all out of the ordinary?"

"No. Fuck no."

"We have to go to your home. I would prefer to tell you what I know there."

Patrick could see the other man was trying to keep his voice from trembling, but couldn't. "You have to tell me now. I can't stand any more of this not knowing."

"Would you be willing to give your receptionist the rest of the day off, so it's just us in the office?"

Naughton once again picked up the phone. Listlessly punched a button. "Yeah. Susie, take the rest of the day off. And switch the sign in the front door to "Closed" on your way out, please." He hung up the phone, having some trouble getting the receiver back on the handset.

Susie came into the office without knocking. Stood by the filing cabinets, where she could keep an eye on Patrick. "Mr. Naughton, is everything okay? You want me to call anyone?" She mouthed, The Police?

He shook his head. "I'm fine. We have something to discuss, in private."

"So, I'll see you tomorrow?"

"Yeah! Bright and early."

She stood her ground. Looked at Patrick. "My phone has a camera. Would you mind if I took a picture of you?"

And Patrick had to admire the courage of that. Naughton probably wasn't an easy boss. She probably even thought sometimes about quitting, complaining about him to her girlfriends at the bar, yet here she was, obviously frightened, not hiding it too well, but being loyal.

"I admire your pluck, but honestly, I don't enjoy having my picture taken. I know the good manners your parents taught you will keep you from taking my picture against my permission."

"But Mr. Naughton will be back in this office bright and early?"

Patrick inclined his onion-shaped head. "I mean him no harm. I'm here to help him. He's the one who called me. I didn't even know he existed until three days ago."

After Susie reluctantly left, Naughton looked across his desk at Patrick. "I'll be back here in my office tomorrow, bright and early?"

Patrick shook his head.

Naughton decided he would prefer to have the rest of the discussion in his home.

They traveled there by separate cars.

Naughton's house, despite his earlier description of its grandness, was actually rather modest.

One-story home cramped by privacy fences on a street where some neighbors hadn't mowed their lawns.

In the kitchen, while Naughton was deactivating the silent alarm, musical beeps rising in the air, Patrick glanced out the rear picture window. Nothing but pale grass and, ordered to one corner, a dying avocado tree.

"Where's your pool?"

"I said I plan on installing a swimming pool. I just haven't got around to it."

Naughton fixed himself a whiskey. Patrick asked for ice water.

They sat on opposite sides of the kitchen table. Naughton gulped down his drink, got up out of his chair, came back with the bottle, poured himself a double.

"So tell me."

"The lemon test established you're what we refer to as a flesh ghost."

"Okay. Whatever."

"A flesh ghost is someone who has died, but doesn't realize he's dead. He continues to go about his daily activities as if he's still alive. But he isn't."

Naughton finished his new drink. Poured another. Bent his face forward, suppressing a burp. "You're saying I'm dead?"

"Yes."

"How can I be dead? I'm still paying my mortgage! I eat food. I go to the bathroom. How could I do all that if I'm dead?"

"A flesh ghost continues to exist in this world, even after he or she has actually died."

Naughton was obviously running through rebuttals in his mind. Ready to bend back his fingers to list his arguments. "I still interact with people. I interact with Susie! How could I, if I were a ghost?"

236

"You're a special type of ghost. The type of ghost who is adamantly unwilling to accept the fact he's died. But just because other people can see you, and interact with you, doesn't mean you're alive. The thing about flesh ghosts is, they ignore anything that contradicts their image of themselves."

"That's not me. I've always been brutally honest with myself."

Patrick made a gentle shrug. "But have you, really? You portrayed yourself to me as someone who's quite wealthy. But you really aren't, are you?"

"Well, maybe I exaggerated."

"Did you really buy a five million dollar home for one point three million?"

"Not actually, but…"

"Do you really eat lobster and caviar all the time?"

Naughton went silent.

"Did you really buy a three hundred thousand dollar wristwatch for one of your prostitutes?"

"She wasn't a prostitute!"

"Did money exchange hands?"

"Yeah, but it wasn't like you're making it out to be. She enjoyed being with me. Maybe she would have refused the money I gave her."

"Did she?"

"No, but…"

"Did you even buy her any kind of wristwatch?"

"I thought about it! I was at a mall, window shopping, and I saw this wristwatch, it had gold plating, and the thought crossed my mind how impressed she would be if I gave her something like that during one of our dates."

"A flesh ghost is a liar. Someone who lies not only to other people, but especially to himself. The thing about a liar is, they're not that smart. If they were smart, they wouldn't need to lie. They could impress people with their real accomplishments. A liar thinks he's smart, because other people don't challenge what he says. But more times than not, the reason someone doesn't call him out as a liar is because that person feels embarrassed for the liar. The liar thinks he's so smart, fooling everyone, but the truth is he's so dumb he can't see how the people he's lying to see right through him."

"Everybody lies."

"You know, to some extent, that's true. But most people lie about minor things. Someone asks, Do I look good in this? You say, Sure. Did you like dinner? Yeah. But those lies are told to make other people feel good. Your lies are told to make yourself feel good. You lie to puff yourself up, to make yourself seem more important than you are. Your lies tear other people down, so you seem better by comparison. Your lies aren't part of the casual social lubrication in which we all swim. Your lies are the closed world in which you exist. Your world is nothing but lies."

Naughton didn't speak.

"The first time you saw an apparition was in your master bathroom?"

They left the kitchen table. Walked through the master bedroom into the master bathroom.

Patrick looked around at the tiled walls, the shower stall. "Why is there so much blood in here?"

"That's not blood."

"What is it?'

"I don't know. Is that relevant?"

Patrick walked further into the master bathroom, to the toilet alcove.

A corpse was lying on the travertine floor of the toilet alcove. Rotting. The corpse had Naughton's face.

"What's this?"

"I don't know."

"It looks like a dead body."

"Maybe. I don't know."

"It looks like your dead body."

Naughton was looking up at the white ceiling.

"I'd like you to remove all your clothes except for your underpants."

"You're kidding me!"

But Naughton did what he was told.

Stood in his master bathroom, holding his hands in front of the crotch of his white underpants.

"What are those two long slashes on the insides of your thighs?"

Naughton didn't look down. "It's a rash. I keep meaning to go to a dermatologist."

"They look like knife wounds."

"No, it's a rash."

"The thing about flesh ghosts?"

Naughton stared at Patrick with hatred. "What?"

"They're all suicides."

"That a fact?"

Patrick nodded.

"So you're saying I committed suicide?"

Patrick nodded.

Naughton snorted, shaking his head. "I am the last person in the world who would commit suicide. I love life!"

Patrick went out into the kitchen. Opened a few drawers. Came back with a Chef's knife.

Naughton saw its gleam in Patrick's hand.

"Are you going to cut me?"

"I'm not going to. You have to. You have to commit suicide a second time. Think of it as a reboot of your death."

"What if I don't die the second time?"

"No flesh ghost has ever survived a second suicide."

The big man started crying. "But I don't want to!"

"You kind of have to. Where did you commit suicide the first time?"

"Sitting on the toilet. With the lid down."

"Sit there again, then."

Naughton sat. Pulled some toilet paper off the roll. Wiped his eyes, blew his nose. The frightened red eyes that looked up at Patrick were a little boy's eyes. "I really don't want to die!"

"You're already dead. You use computers, right? Ever go to delete a file, and a pop-up window asks, Are you sure you want to delete this file? All you're doing is clicking, Yes."

He handed the Chef's knife down to Naughton. "Just lay the knife blade on the scars on your inner thighs. Then saw down deep on both sides. The two wounds are where your femoral arteries lie beneath your skin. You'll bleed out quickly. It won't be like falling asleep, but it will be like passing out on your feet. Like you had too much to drink, and you stood up too quickly."

Naughton positioned the tall, shiny blade against his left inner thigh. In a tiny voice he asked, "Isn't there some way I can be saved? Like a do over?"

Patrick shook his head. "Not once you've committed suicide. There's no way back from a successful suicide."

Naughton said nothing for a long time, feeling the hardness of the blade against his inner thigh. He lowered his face. Burst into tears. "This isn't fair! It's really not. I'm not a bad person." In a high voice he said, "Ever since I've been a little kid, I've been afraid. Everything scares me. Do I have cancer, is someone in a supermarket going to be rude to me and I don't defend myself, is a woman I have feelings for going to make fun of me, is someone going to trick me out of my money, is some little kid going to move in next door and start hitting baseballs through my window, is my house about to require expensive repairs, will I be talking to a group of people younger than myself and after a while I realize they're subtly making fun of me, will I run out of money before I die and be homeless, will I die completely alone with no one to hold me? I've wondered my entire life, Are other people as afraid as I am? Do they just hide it better? Do they?"

Patrick said nothing for a long time. When he spoke, his voice was quiet. "Life is a comedy. Not a drama. That's what God intended. Everything that happened to you in life, that you see as so tragic—You just have to see the humor in each situation. Which you clearly can't."

Naughton's face twisted. "So when an innocent child dies from leukemia at age twelve, that's supposed to be funny?"

"Exactly."

"You're sick!"

"Everything here is filled with joy. You just don't see it. And I can't make you see it. Cut your thigh."

Naughton looked up from his seat on the closed toilet lid. "My father committed suicide." The little kid's face again. "He used to stand at the foot of the stairs, fingers in his pants pocket, playing with all the coins under his handkerchief. He must have had a hundred nickels, pennies and dimes in that pocket. They made the right side of his pants sag. I'd hear him from upstairs in my room, like some big fish at the bottom of the ocean." Fresh tears. "I don't want to leave this world. I realize now I really like it." The high voice again. "I want to put my clothes back on, go out to the kitchen, order some home delivery Chinese food, and see what's on TV."

"You've already left the world. Cut your thigh."

Naughton looked down at his bare thigh. Drew the sharp blade of the Chef's knife across, skin and black hairs sliding with the pull of the blade. Bright red blood leaked out of him, on both sides of the silvery blade.

"Oh, God."

"Now the other thigh."

"Oh, God." He slid the blade deep across the buried blue artery of his right inner thigh. The same bright red blood oozed out of his body, sliding down the flesh of his leg, dripping with an audible pitter-patter onto the hard travertine tiles of the toilet alcove.

"Oh God who is in heaven, please look down at me with pity, please save me, your unworthy servant, from the horror I have done."

Naughton's drowning face looked up at Patrick. "Am I going to hell?"

"There is no hell."

"Is there a heaven?"

Naughton, sitting on the closed lid of the toilet, stopped talking.

His face was nothing but eyebrows and ears.

Blood dripped down rapidly from the insides of his left and right thighs.

Patrick stepped back so the spreading red pool didn't get on his shoes.

Naughton looked back up at Patrick. His face was gray. The light in his eyes were tiny specks.

The lights winked out. Left eye, right eye.

The flow of blood from his thighs slowed.

The large red puddle of blood on the floor inside the toilet alcove, having spread by now across the bottom of the bathroom floor to the base of the bathtub, had a scarlet skin on its surface, like pudding.

After another minute, the body sitting on the toilet seat fell sideways, fell off the toilet seat, sprawling in elbows and knees between the toilet and the alcove wall.

Patrick unzipped his pants.

Pissed on the corpse.

Waited a moment, looking down at the dead body.

It didn't move. It was as dead as a branch no longer attached to a tree, just dry wood ready to be whittled into a whistle.

Walking through the merchandise of Naughton's empty rooms, Patrick let himself out.

Full-Haunted House

There's a freedom to this, a joy, driving the highways of a faraway state late at night, headlights in your rearview, headlights growing towards you, as if you were journeying deep into outer space, silhouettes of mountains just below the black sky, nothing in that midnight but your hands, the curve of the steering wheel, the length of illuminated road in front of you. That cowboy spirit of stopping at a brightly-lit gas station at one o'clock in the morning, with all the other night travelers, no one ever talking to each other from their isolated pumps. Going inside the station to pay for your gas, country music from a radio by the cash register, songs talking to you and you alone, watching a colorfully-wrapped burrito slowly revolve within the humming microwave.

They were in Lafayette, Louisiana when Toots sent an email to Bud's phone.

Stan kept his eyes on the road while Bud read.

"Remember that lady in Dallas? The deaf and dumb one?"

"Sure."

"She wants us back."

"For what?"

"I don't know. But Toots says it's a money is no object deal."

Sylvia Doone seemed like she was waiting right behind the front door for them. The door swung open before the echoes of the doorbell ended inside.

She wasn't as attractive as Stan remembered. Face a little pinched. Like the months since their last visit had not been kind. No shorts this time. Pair of brown slacks. Maybe since this was a money no object assignment, she felt she didn't need to show her legs.

But even so, probably feeling it couldn't hurt, she gave Stan a hug, softness and curves, which caught him completely off guard. More than once in the months since their last visit, on the road, late at night, Bud snoring in the adjacent bed, thoughts of her had sprung up, and he was sure now that was going to happen again, probably exactly what she wanted.

Pulling back from the hug, addressing them both, but mostly Stan, with an extra-bright smile, to make up for the sadness on her face, she started signing.

Both men remembered the routine. Looking at Colin, the slight, graying man standing to her left. Colin lifted his chin. "I am so happy to see both of you again! I told Colin last night, This will be like old times!"

In a situation like this, someone speaking out loud what another is signing, there's a tendency to answer the puppet rather than the puppeteer. But Stan remembered his manners. To her bright brown eyes he said, "How is Brandon?"

She faked a laugh, taking a step back. Hands flying. Colin again: "Cutting to the chase! You guys must be in a hurry."

"It's not that. But I'm assuming there's a problem?" As soon as he put it that way, he realized it came out sounding like he was a plumber. And the leak under her kitchen sink was, once again, dripping.

They sat around the kitchen table at the rear of the house. There was a new cook. A younger woman, slant-eyed and brown-skinned, the type of Mexican beauty who looks Asian.

All four of them were served abalone steaks. Pounded first with a wooden mallet to tenderize, then fried in a skillet. Melted butter glittering in the mallet's march across the lightly-breaded surface.

Bud cut off a slice of abalone, looking at Colin. "Weren't you a vegan?"

"I used to be, yes." He had to put off sliding his first bite of abalone into his mouth when Sylvia, ignoring the meal in front of her, started signing again. Uncertain what to do with the fork in his hand, he laid it back down on his plate. "I want to show you Brandon after lunch. When you first bottled him I would sit his bottle on the table while I ate, so he could be with his mother, but it was clear to me early on that he did not appreciate this!"

Stan swallowed a chunk of abalone. Absolutely delicious. And hard to find. Harvesting wild abalone off the coast of California was illegal now, until the population reached sustainability levels again. Most farmed abalone went directly to the Japanese. "How did he convey that to you?"

She signed enthusiastically. Colin gave up on his meal. Cleared his throat. "Good question! I could tell by his glaring eyes, the sadness of his face, which was even sadder than it normally is. It is so frustrating for me! To not be able to communicate with him anymore other than in the most rudimentary way. If only he could sign! But of course, he has no hands now, how would it be possible?"

"So why are we here?"

Hurt look on Sylvia's face. But at least she was able to chew, lips pressed together, while she signed.

Colin watched the hand wavings, that first bite of abalone still resting, speared, on the end of his fork tines, on his white plate. "You guys are rushing this so much! I'll pay for your motel accommodations no matter how this meeting turns out. And give you a thousand dollars to boot just for hearing me out. So please relax. But if you agree to my proposal, in addition to all this, I will write you a check for fifty thousand dollars."

Stan stopped his fork in mid-lift. Bud stopped chewing.

They glanced at each other across the kitchen table.

Colin watched Sylvia's swinging hands. Looked at Stan, Bud. "Ah ha! Now I have your undivided attentions."

After lunch, they made their way through the back of the large house to Brandon's room. His filing cabinets were still there, against the walls, making the room seem smaller. Filled with almost endless variations of the few photographs he had taken of his fiancé while she was still alive.

Brandon himself was in his large jar, placed on a small table by the side of his former bed.

Sylvia sat down on the edge of Brandon's bed. Brandon, in his jar, slid against the curved glass of his prison, dark eyes growing large.

In that moment it occurred to Stan that Brandon was the only bottled ghost he had known before that person's death. He avoided looking at the movement in the large bottle.

Sylvia pet the glass side. The darkness within swam to the opposite curve.

Colin bent over, watching her hands. "He misses his fiancé. You never did find her."

"Not for lack of trying. Do you remember what my face looked like when we came back from that mall? How do you know he misses her?"

She let her hand fall from the glass side of the bottle. More signings, hands moving low, by her lap. "I told you we can't communicate, but we have."

Bud made a face. "How?"

Since Sylvia hadn't been looking at Bud, Colin had to sign his question to Sylvia.

"I used a Ouija board."

Stan shifted his hips. "That's a really, really bad idea."

Head down, hands moving, low again, above her lap. "I know. But I was desperate!"

"What happened?"

"He spelled out on the board that he won't have anything to do with me until I bring his fiancé to him."

Everyone in the room waited while Stan thought it over.

"How long does it take you and your partner to earn fifty thousand dollars?"

"The last time we went to that mall, the ghosts on the upper two floors were stronger than any ghosts we'd ever seen. We almost didn't get out."

"I will have my accountant work with you, free of charge. If you allow him to see your tax return for this year, I will adjust my payment to you upwards so that my check includes the taxes you would pay on the amount. In other words, you will receive the fifty thousand dollars tax free."

"Bud?"

Bud glanced at his partner. "A lot of money. But..."

"Will you at least consider?"

Stan gave an unhappy shrug. "Let Bud and me talk it over tonight. We know someone in the area I want to consult. See what he says."

Otto Munum lived south of Dallas, across the Trinity River bridge, in Oak Cliff. A neighborhood of older homes and one-story shops still close enough to the metropolitan area the skyline of the city was visible above the treetops. Once a high crime area, it had become a bit safer when gays started moving in, charmed by the older architecture.

Otto's house was set back two hundred feet from the street, the deep front lawn mowed, but all the same looking neglected.

The narrow dirt driveway had weeds, loose stones.

They parked by the screened-in front porch.

Before Stan and Bud could exit their sides of the van, Otto was already out the front door, hustling over.

Round face. White-haired crew cut.

"Mr. Costello? It's an honor, sir."

Stan shook his hand. Expected it to be moist, based on Otto's blushing face. But the hand was dry and strong.

Otto started back towards the house, looking over his shoulder at them. "I prepared a little repast for us to enjoy while we talk."

Inside, rooms filled with cardboard boxes stacked atop each other, on the carpets, the furniture, blocking the windows. Books and magazines spilling out. Otto directed them to a cleared area in the kitchen, an old sofa pushed against one wall, by the window. Every space on the walls was crowded with framed photographs, stapled newspaper articles, complex designs made out of twist ties. As Stan sat down on the lumpy cushions, a large dog with one blind eye loped into the room, jumping its front paws up on Stan's lap.

"Heel, Spirit! Heel!"

The dog stilted its hind legs forward, lolling tongue headed towards Stan's face.

He held out his hand for Spirit to sniff, always a good idea with a new dog. Once the frantic eyes absorbed that information, he scratched behind the dog's ears, to get on its good side, and to stop its advance.

"Heel!"

Stan glanced at Bud.

Otto pulled Spirit's tail. Grinned good-naturedly. "He ignores me. Like everyone else! Should I put him in the bathroom?"

"It's up to you."

Otto tilted his head to one side. Eyes wet. "I hate to restrict him. It's just that..." He lowered his voice to a whisper, glancing at Spirit. "He's dying. The vet thought it was diabetes, but then they took some x-rays, and his insides are just...packed with t,u,m,o,r,s. He doesn't have long. He can't keep his food down. He throws up twenty times a day. The only thing he seems able to digest are raw egg yolks."

Bud, legs crossed away from Spirit's enthusiasm, reached out nonetheless to pet his head. "Fifty percent of dogs over the age of ten develop cancer at some point."

"I had no idea it was that high!"

"There may be support groups on the Internet."

"I should check." Otto gave an embarrassed smile. "I spend a lot of time on the Internet. Me and Spirit."

Stan interrupted Bud and Otto. "I appreciate your willingness to see us on such short notice."

Otto snorted. "For you? You're legends. Shall I get our snacks?"

Refrigerator door opening. From that swing-out, clinking of little bottles stored on the molded white shelves of the inside door. Parallelogram of light projected onto the ceiling.

He bustled back with a wide silver tray of neatly arranged treats. Set it down on the table in front of the sofa, as if it were the aerial view of a perfect land ruled by a loving God.

Pulling a straight-backed chair up to the other side of the table, he sat down, facing Stan and Bud on the sofa. Right index finger pointing to the treasures on the tray. That right index finger sure wanted to impress. "We have a selection of cheeses. Brie, Gorgonzola, Cheddar, Gouda. Plus of course crackers and pumpernickel bread for eating them, and some really nice pickled herring, and Taramousalata! The Greek roe spread? Have you ever had it? And these are half-sour pickles I jarred myself, last weekend. Never been exposed to heat. A cold pickling, which is the best. You can still taste the cucumber in the crunch of every bite. Oh! I am so sorry. Spirit! Heel!"

Full-Haunted House

Bud got up off the sofa, stooping over, helping Otto pick up the different spilled foods from the kitchen floor.

Once Otto came back from the trash can, apologizing all over again, Stan raised his hand. "We're here to ask you about Hoover Manor."

"Absolutely. It was converted to a mall, but you already know that, right?"

"We were in it about half a year ago. At that time, the top two floors were heavily infested with ghosts."

"Well, it's gotten a lot worst since then. The developers originally had retail establishments on the lower two floors, and excursions tourists could take to the top two floors, although really the tours only went to the third floor, but now the entire mall is shut to the public."

"That's kind of what we had heard through the grapevine. But what happened?"

Otto avoided their eyes. "What happened was a Fear Ghost found the mall. It was probably attracted to the site because of the high concentration of ghosts. And ghosts do carry a lot of fear."

Bud nodded. "If you have a lot of fish in one area of the ocean, eventually a great white shark shows up."

Otto raised his white eyebrows to Bud. "I've also heard that because of the Fear Ghost, they're seeing inbreeding ghosts." He glanced from one man to the other. "And prayer ghosts."

Bud looked at Stan. "Doesn't sound like our type of gig. Remember what happened to Claire?"

"I didn't think you guys would be interested. That site right now is probably the most-infested haunting in America. Maybe the world."

Stan kept absent-mindedly petting Spirit's head. "We've never seen prayer ghosts. I've heard about them, but…inbreeding ghosts we saw once—"

"—Florida, down by the Keys."

"—But I don't ever want to see them again. There are some things, some 'things' that are just too much. At any price."

"How much were you offered? If you don't mind me asking."

"Fifty thousand."

"Wow. But I wouldn't do it. Fuck, no."

"Two hundred dollars?" Stan had his checkbook out.

"That's more than generous. I'm glad I could help you guys. Sorry about the hors d'oeuvres."

Bud regarded Otto while Stan wrote out the check. "Seriously, Otto. Go on the Internet and try to find some support groups. If you'll give me your email address, I'll research some links, and send them to you."

Otto, hands hanging between his knees, teared-up. "He's all I have. I'm sorry he knocked over our tray. But he's so hungry all the time, now. Anytime he sniffs food, he goes crazy."

Bud squeezed Otto's knee. "Of course."

"I lost my mom two years ago. She had both her legs amputated because of a car accident. Plus it really messed up her face. The windshield glass, the metal at the front of the car. You live your life, decade after decade, it's boring, occasionally interesting, then one day, out of the blue, the breath from above. I gave her a cane, so she could tap on the wall of her room when she needed something." He blew his nose, face red. "Between her and Spirit, it seems like I'm one of those people who are here to care for others. Spirit puts his front paws on my lap, tongue hanging out, looking up into my face with such pure love, and even as I'm petting him, and cooing to him, and kissing his forehead I'm wondering, Does he know he's dying? Does he understand? I'm not a good person. I try to live a good life, but demons move around inside me, like intestinal gas. It's painful. I can't ever let them out."

Bud put his hand on Otto's shoulder. "We see a lot of people like you. Trying to do the right thing. Struggling. It's a lifelong struggle."

Otto started sobbing. Spirit, his buddy, jumped off Stan, rushing up his master's body, licking the tears. "It's horrible. My whole life. My whole life! I try to connect. A high heel is a weapon. Ask any woman. And it's a very effective weapon. She's got one on her right foot, and then as a backup, one on her left foot. "

Before they left, Otto asked if he could take a picture of the three of them in his kitchen. For bragging rights.

Back at their room, Stan dropped in some ice cubes, poured himself a whiskey. Bud uncapped a Texas beer. Flicked on the TV.

They called Sylvia. Put the motel phone on speaker.

Stan sat on the edge of his bed, Bud on the edge of his bed, facing each other.

Colin, of course, answered.

"Is Sylvia there?"

"Right next to me. Ready to sign. I'll translate what she says."

"Please tell her we've decided not to take the case. It's too dangerous."

"Hold on."

Stan imagined Colin signing to Sylvia.

"Okay. She says, you have to take it."

"We're not going to. We're not equipped to handle the type of ghosts in the mall."

They both waited for the silence on the other end to be broken.

From the speaker phone in their shared motel room: "Sylvia is asking if this is a move by you to increase your fee."

"Absolutely not."

"Hold on. Okay. Sylvia says, there's been a new development."

Stan rolled his eyes at Bud. "What's that?"

Long pause.

"Last night, after the two of you left, Sylvia had another Ouija session with Brandon. Brandon had our fingers spell out the word, "pencil." So I got a pencil. And paper. You try to anticipate. Then Brandon had our hands, holding the pencil, spell out your name, Stan. Underneath your name, our hands drew a sketch of a small baby."

Stan jerked up his head.

"Brandon had us draw a section of a ruler next to the baby, to show just how small the baby was. It was very small, like a fetus."

Bud looked at Stan, shook his head.

"Then Brandon drew wiggly lines all around the little baby. Like the wiggly lines were attacking the baby."

Stan tilted his glass, ice cubes sliding against his teeth.

"Then Brandon had us draw this large, wavy-edged shape above the baby. Wiggly lines going down."

Bud snapped his fingers at Stan. Shook his head. "No. Absolutely not."

"Sylvia wants to know, does that mean anything to you?"

Stan poured a new drink. "We'll call you back." Hung up.

The motel TV on the bureau kept talking in the otherwise quiet room. "Thieves overnight drove their pick-up through the storefront of a liquor shop in Addison, and as captured on this video, had some unexpected trouble getting the store's ATM up into the bed of their truck."

Bud raised his hand into the space between the two beds. "Partner…"

"Shut up. Let me think."

"We can't face off against a Fear Ghost, and every other entity it's pulled into that space. It's a hive. We're not that strong."

Stan twisted his head to one side. "What if it's true? Fear Ghosts find a vulnerable ghost, use that ghost to rally all the other ghosts around. Like a fly at the center of its web. What if that little ghost at the center of this massive haunting is my premature son?"

"Stan, listen. Sylvia is a wealthy woman. It would be easy for her to have you investigated, to find out a weakness she can exploit."

"But what if it is my son?"

"It almost certainly isn't."

The ruin of his face, looking across the space between them. "But what if it is?"

"I'm not going."

Like a slap.

"No? Really?"

"And now here's Samantha, who's going to let us know if we can squeeze in one more backyard barbeque before the cold season starts. Sam? I've got four pounds of spare ribs in my freezer. Do I defrost 'em?"

"Stan…I've always respected the pain you carry."

"You have. And I appreciate that."

"But—" Bud led out a sigh. Handed the box of Kleenex that came with the motel to Stan.

Eventually, Stan raised his head. "We were a little family. Me and Julie. And there was going to be my son, too. You have no idea how happy we were. This tiny, shitty little apartment above a dry cleaner's, where you had to shove against the back door four or five times to get it to lock, but we were the two happiest people in the world. And then that night she woke me up. There were still fifty-eight uncrossed-off days on our calendar, but her water broke. And, you know? You just try not to think. You don't think racing to the hospital, or sitting by yourself in the middle of the night in the emergency room's waiting area. And then being called back to her room, the nurse leading you, not saying anything, you just try really, really hard not to think.

"When Julie and me left the hospital, we were both crying. We were so close! We thought, let's get back home, to our apartment, like two shot animals, and we'll curl up inside like two pearls in an oyster, and lick our wounds. And maybe try again? But something changed in us on that drive home, and we didn't even know it at the time. It just ate away everything between us, while we weren't looking. Soon as I unlocked the front door, I knew, and I could tell by the way the back of her head turned this way, that way, that she knew, that it was gone forever. Home no longer existed. All we had left was an apartment we shared."

The next morning, Stan showed up at Sylvia's front door, by himself. Her mouth dropped open. She signed to Colin. "Where's your partner?"

"He decided to sit this one out."

"So it's just you?"

"I can do this by myself. I need to get my fifty thousand dollar check in advance, and I need you to agree I get to keep the money regardless of whether or not I'm successful."

Sylvia, staring into Stan's eyes, nodded. No signing necessary.

She was in short-shorts again. Low-cut blouse.

Back at her kitchen table, she wrote out the check. Handed it to Stan.

Stan endorsed the back. Put it in a pre-addressed envelope. Handed it to Colin. "If I don't come out, I'm counting on you to mail this to the address on the front."

Colin accepted the envelope. Looked at the front. "You have my word I'll do it."

Sylvia snaked her head sideways, staring down at the envelope in Colin's hand. Signed.

Colin looked at Sylvia's hands, then at Stan. "Who's Julie Liddy?"

"My ex-wife."

More signing. Colin raising his chin. "You are an interesting person, Stan! Maybe, after your success, we can have a drink or two or three together here in my home."

Stan drove the white van to a small municipal airport south of the city. Passenger seat next to him empty. For the first time in fifteen years. Empty bag of Cheetos on the passenger side's floor.

He couldn't blame Bud. There's no way this made sense. But sometimes you have to do something that doesn't make sense.

Held his driver's license out his rolled-down window to the guard at the front gate. Glanced up in his rearview mirror as the wooden barrier across the entrance raised. Doomed eyes looking back at him. Parked the van by the tall front of the third hanger. Single engine planes inside, clang of a wrench hitting metal, repeatedly.

Reached behind his seat to hoist to the front the two bags filled with ghost bottling equipment. Slapped open the wide door to the glove compartment. Took out the Springfield semi-automatic. Checked to make sure its clip was full. Slid it into his right pants pocket.

Standing outside the van, he locked it up. Pulled up on the driver door's latch to be sure, like he always did.

The helicopter Sylvia had agreed to pay for was on its pad. As he approached it, both bags slung over his shoulders, clinking, the overhead blades started slowly revolving. No way was he going into the mall again from the ground floor. And fight his way up three flights? He'd land on the roof. Go down, get out.

He hustled his load around the rear of the helicopter. The overhead blades were revolving faster. Buffeting cold air down on his back.

The door on that side of the copter was already slid open.

Stan lowered the two bags from his back. Placed the first one inside.

A hand reached from the interior, lifted the bag, moved it deeper within the compartment. Same with the second bag.

Stan climbed onboard. Sat in his seat. Strapped in. "How'd you get here?"

"Took a cab."

"Why?"

"Changed my mind."

Stan started to say something. Shut up. Cleared his throat. Eyes blinking. Tear in the left eye. "We're not going to waste a second looking for Brandon's fiancé. This is all about finding Keith. Bottling him, getting the fuck out of there."

"No shit, partner."

Stan ducked his head. "I brought the gun."

Bud opened his mouth. Closed it. Looked out his side window as the concrete outside the helicopter slanted away, both of them lifting into the air, letting the world fall away below them.

As they disembarked, each with one of the bags strapped behind their backs, Stan ran around to the front cab of the helicopter. Shouted above the engine's noise. Hair whipping around his face. "You're going to stay here, right? Until we come back?"

The pilot's grin lifted his black sunglasses. "I'm getting five hundred bucks to fly you here. Five thousand bucks to fly you back. What do you think?"

The flat section of the mall's roof wasn't large. They had to walk stooped over to avoid the blades slowing above them.

Stan had a key to the roof's door. He slid it in the lock, twisting right.

The electricity in the mall had been turned off a month ago. Both men put miners' helmets on their heads. Clicked on the light at the front of each helmet.

Stan pulled the roof's door open.

Metal steps leading down. Tortured screams rising up.

He turned around to face his partner. "Short walk back to the helicopter."

"Do you want to go back to the helicopter?"

Stan considered.

Wails from below getting louder.

"No. No, man. Sorry."

"Then let's do this."

Stan in front, Bud behind, they descended the narrow staircase. Yellow circles from their head lamps bobbing around the tall walls.

At the bottom, Stan opened the door to the mall.

The door took them out into a storage room.

Waxy ghosts gnawing each other's feet, spitting out toes.

From where they stood, they could see a doorway at the far end of the room leading to the mall proper.

With the weight of the bottling supplies on their backs, the fear in their limbs, they walked slowly, as if underwater.

The fourth floor had never been converted to shops, because of the heavy ghost infestation, so they came out on the central hallway of the original mansion, doorways running its length on both sides. Leading to bedrooms and bathrooms.

It's hard to say what they expected to find, stepping out into the hallway, but in fact it was deserted.

Quiet.

They looked at each other, bodies bent forward under the weight of the bags on their shoulders.

Stan reached in his front pants pocket. Retrieved a plastic food storage bag filled with metal shavings. Shook the shavings out onto his palm. Tossed them into the air.

They flew up, were snatched in mid-flight. Whisked down the right side of the hall, curving into the last doorway at the end of the hall.

Stan glanced at Bud. "Could it be any clearer?"

They unpacked their supplies outside the last doorway. Setting all the contents down on the hallway's red and black runner. Took off their head lamps, since there was enough light from the rear windows.

"My baby is probably being held right next to the Fear Ghost. We go into the room, try not to look around too much, except to orient ourselves, locate my child, bottle it, get the hell out."

"I didn't see any ghosts through the doorways we passed."

"Bad sign. I know. The Fear Ghost has gathered all the spirits in its lair. As protection. But if we move fast…"

"Okay."

Stan got down on his knees. Trying to hide his terror.

Bud got down on his knees.

Stan brought his hands together. "Our Father…"

"Who art in Heaven."

"Hallowed be Thy name. Thy Kingdom come, Thy will be done, on Earth as it is in Heaven."

"Forgive us our trespasses."

"As we forgive those that trespass against us."

"Lead us not into temptation."

"But deliver us from evil."

"For Thine is the kingdom, the power and glory, for ever and ever."

Stan bent his face even lower. "Amen."

They got back to their feet.

One last look into each other's eyes.

Stepped into the room.

Wet pink, wrinkled, ringed, like walking into intestines.

Ghosts flying around the room.

Dark brown shapes pulling up from the floor. No eyes, no nose. Just mouths. Ghosts that had stayed on earth too long.

"Don't look at them."

"I know."

At the far end of the room, hard to see because of all the spirits flitting by, like plastic shopping bags, an enormous, brilliant white presence.

The Fear Ghost.

Orbiting in front of it, something small, dark.

"That's my son! It has to be."

Skeletons filled with white and yellow flesh clacked around them. Bumping into each other. Eye sockets fat with noses. Nostrils sniffing the air. Trying to locate them.

The inbreeding ghosts.

Stan and Bud made their way into the room.

Bud turned around.

Inbreeding ghosts filled the doorway, blocking their exit. Nostrils lifted, sniffing, from their eye sockets.

Stan held onto the bottle he would use. Advanced further.

The noise became deafening. Earthquakes. Nails on blackboards.

Halfway into the room, the brilliant white presence at the far wall noticed them.

Bent itself down, forward, to stare.

They both froze.

A flesh ghost bumped into Bud. He closed his eyes. Sweating.

Tall nostrils sniffing up his arm.

Sniffing his ear.

"You got one on you, Bud. Don't move."

"I'm not."

"Wait for it to lose interest."

"I know."

Bud stared straight ahead. Lips moving.

Tall nostrils lowered to his pants. Sniffing his crotch. A second inbreeding ghost, attracted by the attention of the first, jerked over. Sniffing the seat of his pants.

That small dark ball orbiting the brilliant white presence was still about fifteen feet away.

And then the brilliant white presence turned black. Turned cold. So cold, they started shivering.

A gaggle of inbreeding ghosts marched lockstep in front of Stan. Bent forward, vomiting.

Rising out of the vomit, long limbs dripping yellow.

Prayer ghosts.

Sharp elbows and knees and knees rose. Antennae. The front claws, long and fringed. And last, the large triangular heads, green with protruding black eyes.

Skittered rapidly across the floor towards Stan.

"Let's get out of here, Stan!"

But they were already laddering up Stan's back. Sticking to the front of his shirt.

Pulling him down.

Stan reached up. Tried to yank one of the ghosts off the top of his head, but. It crawled down with a slow arrogance, jointed elbows and knees and knees, onto Stan's face.

He shook some of them off his legs. They jumped back up. He staggered around, confused.

Lost his balance. Arms flailing.

Bud let out a whimper.

Stan managed to get back up on his knees, swatting over his head.

Made it to his feet. That doomed look in his blue eyes that Bud knew so well. Reached down, picked up his bottling jar.

The horde crawled up his body. Their weight driving him down, to the carpet. More hopped on top of the struggle. Knees and knees and knees and elbows and elbows.

Stan's features rose out of the frenzy, green joints wrapped around his neck.

"Bud? Help me?" That country-western singer's face.

Sometimes fear is more powerful than love.

"Bud? Please?" Head twisting side to side, eyes lonelier with each swing. "Bud?" His face was pulled down into the whirlpool. The blue stare of those eyes was sucked down.

Bud could no longer see Stan. Just a huge ball of prayer ghosts rolling over, rolling over, across the room's carpet.

Getting bigger every minute.

From within the rolling ball, a loud shot. Flash of light.

The rough green feet must have somehow gotten to Stan's gun. Pulled it away from him.

The ball stopped rolling.

Fell apart, prayer ghosts crawling off. Heads twitching.

On the carpet, on his back. Arms and legs out sideways, frozen, like a lizard.

Part still in his hair, miraculously. But the hair on the right side of the part much shorter now. Singed above the red gap in his skull.

A gaggle of inbreeding ghosts marched lockstep in front of Bud.

Bud ran.

Ran out of the room.

Ran down the hall.

Ran through the storage room.

Vomited on his way up the rear stairs.

Ran across the roof to the copter.

The pilot lifted his sunglasses. "Just you?"

Bud's face crumpled. "Just me."

Back at the motel room, Bud waited for the knock on the door.

Never much of a drinker, but he caught up that first night. Didn't help there was a liquor store on the other side of the parking lot.

He woke up off and on throughout that night. Confused where he was. One of those situations where you wake up, thinking about nothing, glad your teeth don't hurt, then suddenly remember the day before. Spent some time in the bathroom. Under that harsh light bulb illumination you get at three o'clock in the morning. Throwing up into the toilet. Left hand fumbling up the porcelain tank, blind, to locate the lever. Flush.

He turned on the TV around six. Local morning news, syndicated sitcom reruns.

Cried for a long time, fat man sitting up in bed, sheets pulled around him, canned laughter from the TV.

At eight, he took a shower. Brushed his teeth. Gums bleeding. Spat down into the sink, white and red. Combed his hair. Walked over to the restaurant on the other side of the motel. Pushed the glass door open, walked

259

inside, self-conscious, hung-over. Everyone on the stools, in the booths, behind the counter knew each other. The waitress called him 'Hon.' Got a breakfast to go.

Ate it in bed. Scrambled eggs, ham, toast. Pissed at himself for only getting two cups of coffee.

Talked on the phone again, for the fifth or sixth time, to Toots.

The knock on the door came at one.

He pulled the window drapes next to the door aside. To make sure who it was.

Unlocked the door, went over to one of the chairs around the small table that came with the room.

Clay walked through first, followed by Matt. Bud was surprised Matt had decided to stay as Clay's apprentice. His black face was gray, and he didn't look young anymore.

The three of them sat down around the table as if they were about to start a game of poker.

Bud looked at Clay. "Thank you for coming."

"Thank me with cash."

"Fifty thousand. All yours. Like I said on the phone."

"Where's the fifty thousand right now?"

"I have the check right here." Fingers tapping the breast pocket of his shirt. "It's made payable to Stan and me. Either/or. Only requires one signature. You bring Stan back, and I'll endorse it over to you."

"What's the deal with the client?"

"She thinks we're looking for her son's fiancé. If you're able to—"

"Fuck that. I'm only bringing out one. From what you said on the phone, it's a dangerous environment. I don't want to spend one extra minute in it."

"But you can do this?"

Clay's homely face wrinkled. "Of course I can do it. You think these are the first prayer ghosts I've seen?"

"There's a lot of them."

"More the merrier."

"Stan believed his son was also in the room. If it's at all—"

"Fuck that."

"I could pay extra."

"Can you pay another fifty thousand dollars extra?"

"I don't have that kind of money."

"Then fuck that. What do I do with Stan's corpse?"

"I made arrangements with a local funeral home. They'll embalm him."

Clay waited impatiently for Bud to stop crying.

Matt stood up, got the box of Kleenex from the table beside the rumpled bed. Brought it over for Bud.

After wiping his eyes and blowing his nose, and pulling a fresh Kleenex to dry his fingers, Bud handed Clay a slip of paper. "This is the address and phone number for the funeral home. You can drop the body there. I'm making arrangements to have it shipped back home."

A day passed.

And a night.

Bud was watching a singing competition, gorging on food from a nearby Taco Bell. When there was a knock on his motel room's door.

He rolled off the bed, abandoning his food. Touching the sides of his hair with his palms. Drew the drapes beside the door to the right.

Unlocked the door.

Clay walked through.

His stomach was huge. He had trouble getting through the door.

"I dropped the body off at the funeral home. Carl Raunscheinger, or whatever his name is, he said it's going to cost extra if you want an open casket."

Bud stared at Clay. He looked like a different person. Like someone from a sideshow. "How many prayer ghosts did you have to eat?"

"Quite a few."

"Did Raunscheinger say how much extra?"

Clay lowered the bottle to the motel's carpet. "I'm not your mother."

"Where's Matt?"

"Didn't make it."

Bud took the fifty thousand dollar check out of his pajama top pocket. The pajama top was buttoned wrong, left side lower than the right. Didn't want to ask, but did. "He's dead?"

Clay took the check, read it. Put it in his pants pocket. "He wasn't right for this. I had my doubts the first time I met him. Patrick should never have referred him to me."

Bud tried not to be accusatory. "So you just left his body on the fourth floor?"

"Whose body did you want me to come out with, his or Stan's?"

"It's just...he seemed like a good kid."

"Okay. Then why don't you go back up on that fourth floor, and get his body?"

Bud said nothing.

Clay turned to leave. Turned back. "You know, I never saw where you and Stan fitted into the rest of us. He was this boat burning in the middle

261

of the ocean, has been ever since I first met him, and you're some fat fuck who's essentially buying and selling old comic books. Just an observation."

"Thanks, Clay."

He looked Bud up and down. "Everyone reaches their limit. Even if they kid themselves they don't have a limit. When they do reach it? And realize they're a coward? All they can do—the best thing they can do, for themselves—is turn around and walk away."

"What's your limit?"

"Someday, maybe I'll discover that."

It felt like asking Clay out on a date. "Do you want to know when the funeral service is?"

Clay's wide face laughed at him. "Seriously?"

"It must be incredible to wake up each morning, go out your front door, and have a view like this while you're drinking your coffee."

Mr. Fleischer raised his bald head, looking out over the blue of the Pacific. The whites of distant sail boats. "It's all been worth it."

Bud, standing next to him, much shorter, far less muscular, nodded. "How many heads of cattle you have?"

"Varies. I keep mostly Black Angus, but they can be really temperamental. Some of them. I tried mixing it up with some Herefords, they're a lot more docile, but everyone wants Black Angus. Know what Black Baldies are?"

"Sure don't."

"Cross between the two. Not that bad, actually, but again, my buyers really only want the Angus."

"So, of all the ghosts you showed us today, I guess the ones we'd most be interested in would be the civil war soldier, the old farmer, and that teenage girl from the Roaring Twenties."

Fleischer kept squinting at the ocean, grinning at how great his life was. "Well, make an offer then."

"We're thinking, nine-fifty."

Fleischer shot him a sideways snort. "Nine-fifty? For those three?"

"What's your counter offer?"

He took his time. Blue eyes tracking a far-off sea gull. "Maybe two thousand. Maybe."

"Outside our budget."

"I don't have to sell them. They didn't pay off the mortgage on this ranch. Those cows did."

Bud turned around towards the cattle grazing on a green cliff overlooking the ocean. "Do they ever fall in?"

Fleischer's grin turned into a scowl. "Excuse me?"

"Just curious. Do they ever get too close to the edge of the cliff, and fall over into the ocean? It's quite a drop."

"Listen, I only deal with serious buyers. You just wasted two hours of my day. And my two hours are worth a lot more than your two hours."

Bud and Toots drove back to the motel.

Bud parked in front of their side by side room doors. Killed the engine, pulled up the hand brake, but didn't open his driver's side door.

Toots, in the passenger seat, short sleeves showing some of the blue and red tattoos on her arms, smiled at his discouraged profile. "It'll probably take some time."

"Stan had the touch."

"You will too. In time."

"I'm off my game."

"It's only been three months."

"Yeah." Hands on top of the steering wheel, eyes staring through the windshield at families unpacking their SUV's. "You know, I'm nobody. I'm this pathetic little man who eats too much junk food, bores everyone I talk to for more than five minutes, and sometimes I think the best thing for me to do is just jump in one of these motel swimming pools late at night when no one's around, and sit on the bottom of the deep end."

She sat up in her seat. "Knock, knock."

Bud glanced over at her pink hair. "Really?"

"Knock, knock!"

He rolled his eyes. "Who's there?"

"Orange." She smiled at him.

"Aren't you supposed to say, Apple?"

"No! Come on!" Poked his beefy shoulder. "Knock, knock!"

"Who's there?"

"Orange!"

"Okay. Orange who?"

"Knock, knock."

Bud let out a long sigh. "Who's there?"

"Orange!"

"Toots, I really, sincerely believe you're telling the joke backwards."

"Knock, knock!"

"Who's there?"

"Apple."

He threw up his hands in exasperation. "Apple who?"

"Apple you glad I didn't say orange again?" Punched his shoulder, laughing.

"That is so stupid. You got the joke wrong."

"You're smiling!"

"If I'm smiling, it's only because it's so stupid."

They got out of the van.

Bud went around back. Opened the double doors to make sure the bottles were intact.

It was getting dark. The outside lights of the motel's restaurant, next to the office, flickered on.

They hadn't eaten there yet, but after so many, he knew almost exactly what the interior would look like. Who the customers would be. What the staff would look like. But, not a bad thing?

Toots waited on the sidewalk. "Know what you're going to get?"

He looked inside the back of the van. "Chicken-fried steak, mashed potatoes, green beans cooked with onions and bacon, and for dessert, peanut butter pie."

All the bottles looked fine.

Bud reached in, rubbed his knuckles against the cold glass of one of the jars.

Stan's floating ghost stared out at him.

Bud shut the left rear door of the van.

One last glance inside.

Shut the right rear door of the van.

About the Author

Ralph Robert Moore is a novelist, short story writer, and essayist whose fiction has been published in America, Canada, England, Ireland, India and Australia in a wide variety of genre and literary magazines and anthologies, including Black Static, Shadows & Tall Trees, Midnight Street, ChiZine, and others. His previous books include two novels, Father Figure and As Dead As Me, and two short story collections, Remove the Eyes and I Smell Blood. His website SENTENCE at www.ralphrobertmoore.com features a broad sampling of his fiction, essays, and autobiographical writings. Moore lives with his wife Mary in Dallas, Texas.

Made in the USA
Middletown, DE
20 March 2017